PRAISE FOR *ALL THE M*

'A story as gorgeously gothic as its title. This is a novel of blood and bones, of salt and silver, of an absolutely haunting richness. I was compelled from the very beginning and held rapt to the end.'
Kat Howard, author of *An Unkindness of Magicians*

'Like the sea at its heart, Slatter's haunting story is treacherous and lovely in all its dark depths.'
Heather Kassner, author of *The Bone Garden*

'Two uncanny houses, Hob's Hallow and Blackwater, bookend Angela Slatter's new novel like grim sentinels. Whether they are cursed or enchanted, majestic or moldering, refuge or prison, only reading to the end will tell. Meanwhile, the landscape stretching between these gothic structures abounds with corpsewights, kelpies, ghosts, rusalki, werewolves, clockwork mechanicals, and —most alarmingly—actors. And across this treacherous terrain walks Miren O'Malley, scarred, furious, and growing in power. All the Murmuring Bones is brutal and beautiful throughout, with moments of tenderness hard-won and harder-kept, and, pervading all, an atmosphere of inescapable threat like the taste of salt wind and the sound of silver bells ringing in the deep.'
C. S. E. Cooney, World Fantasy Award-winning author of *Bone Swans: Stories*

ALL THE
MURMURING
BONES

A. G. SLATTER

TITAN BOOKS

Print edition ISBN: 9781789094343
E-book edition ISBN: 9781789094350

Published by Titan Books
A division of Titan Publishing Group Ltd
144 Southwark Street, London SE1 0UP
www.titanbooks.com

First edition: March 2021
10 9 8 7 6 5 4

A CIP catalogue record for this title is available from the British Library.

Printed and bound by CPI Group (UK) Ltd, Croydon, CR0 4YY

*To Betty and Peter, my parents and patrons of the arts
− or my art at least.*

1

See this house perched not so far from the granite cliffs of Hob's Head? Not so far from the promontory where once a church was built? It's very fine, the house. It's been here a long time (far longer than the church, both before and after), and it's less a house really than a sort of castle now. Perhaps "fortified mansion" describes it best, an agglomeration of buildings of various vintages: the oldest is a square tower from when the family first made enough money to better their circumstances. Four storeys, an attic and a cellar, in the middle of which is a deep, broad well. You might think it to supply the house in times of siege, but the liquid is salty and partway down, below the water level, you can see (if you squint hard by the light of a lantern) the silver crisscross of a grid to keep things out or in. It's always been off-limits to the children of the house, no matter that its wall is high, far higher than a child could accidentally tip over.

The tower's stone − sometimes grey, sometimes gold, sometimes white, depending on the time of year, time of day and how much sun is about − is covered by ivy of a strangely bright green, winter and summer. To the left and right are wings added later, suites and bedrooms to accommodate the increasingly large family. The birth date of the stables is anyone's guess, but they're a tumbledown affair, their state perhaps a nod to lately decaying fortunes.

Embedded in the walls are swathes of glass both clear and coloured from when the O'Malleys could afford the best of everything. It lets the light in, but cannot keep the cold out, so the hearths throughout are enormous, big enough for a man to stand upright or an ox to roast in. Mostly now, however, the fireplaces remain unlit and the dormitory wings are empty of all but dust and memories; only three suites remain inhabited, and one attic room.

They built close to the cliffs – but not too close, for they were wise, the first O'Malleys; they knew how voracious the sea could be, how it might eat even the rocks if given a chance, so there are broad lawns of green, a wall of middling height almost at the edge to keep all but the most determined, the most stupid, from toppling over. Stand on the stoop of the tower's iron-banded door (shaped and engraved to look like ropes and sailors' knots). Look ahead and you can see straight out to sea; turn to the right but a little and there's Breakwater in the distance, seemingly so tiny from here. There's a path, too, winding back and forth on itself, an easy trail down to a pebbled shingle that stretches in a crescent. At the furthest end, there was once a sea cave (the collapse of which no one can recall), a tidal thing you wouldn't have wanted to be caught in at the wrong time. A place the unwary had gone looking for treasure as rumours abounded that the O'Malleys smuggled, committed piracy, hid their ill-gotten gains there until they could be safely shifted elsewhere and exchanged for gold to line the family's already overflowing coffers.

They've been here a long time, the O'Malleys, and the truth is that no one knows where they were *before*. Equally no one can remember when they weren't around, or at least spoken of. No one says "Before the O'Malleys" for good reason; their history is murky, and that's not a little to do with their very own efforts. Local recounting claims they appeared in the vanguard of some lord or lady's army, or one of those produced by the battle abbeys in the days of the Church's more intense militancy, perhaps one marching to or from the cathedral city of Lodellan when its monarchs fought for land and riches. Perhaps they were soldiers or perhaps they trailed along behind like camp-followers and scavengers, gathering what they could while no one noticed, until they had enough to make a reputation.

What *is* spoken of is that they were unusually tall even in a place where long-legged raiders from across the oceans had liberally scattered their seed. They were dark-haired and dark-eyed, yet with skin so terribly pale that on occasion it was muttered that the O'Malleys didn't go about by day, but that wasn't true.

They took the land by Hob's Head and built their tower, called it Hob's Hallow; they prospered quickly. They took more land, and gained tenants to work it for them. There was always silver, too, in their coffers, the purest and brightest though they'd tell no one from whence it came. Next they built ships and began trading, then built more ships and traded more, roamed further. They grew rich from the seas and everyone heard tell of how the O'Malleys did not lose themselves to the water: their galleons and caravels, their barques and brigs did not sink. Their daughters and sons did not drown (or only those meant to) for they swam like seals, learned to do so from their first breath, first step, first stroke. They kept to themselves, seldom taking wives or husbands who weren't of their extended families. They bred like rabbits, but the core of them remained tightly wound around a limited bloodline; those bearing the O'Malley name proper were prouder than all the rest.

They paid naught but a passing care for the opinion of the Church and its princes, which was more than enough to set them apart from other fine families, and made them an object of unease and rumour. Yet they kept their position and their power for they maintained the impression of worship for the sake of appearances. They were neither stupid nor fearful. They cultivated friends in the highest of high places, sowed favours and reaped the rewards of doing so, and they gathered secrets and lies from the lowest of low places. Oh! such a harvest. The O'Malleys knew the locations of all the inconvenient bodies that had been buried – sometimes purely because they'd put those bodies there themselves. They paid their own debts, made sure they collected what was theirs, and ensured all who dealt with them knew that what was owed would be returned to them one way or another.

They were careful and clever.

Even the greatest of the god-hounds found themselves, at one point or other, beholden to them. Sometimes an ecclesiastic of import required a favour only the O'Malleys could provide and so, hat in hand, he came. Under cover of darkness, of course, in a closed carriage with no regalia that might give him away, on the loneliest roads out of Breakwater to the estate on Hob's Hallow. He'd take a deep breath as he stepped from the conveyance, then another as he looked up at the lofty panes of glass lit from within so it seemed the interior of the tower was on fire. He'd clasp the golden crucifix suspended at his waist for fear that, upon crossing the threshold, he might find himself somewhere more infernal than expected.

More than one such man made visits over many years. Yet men of this sort mislike owing favours to anyone – especially women, and there was a time when females held the O'Malley family reins – and those very same priests offered all manner of excuses, threats and coercions trying to avoid their obligations. None worked, and the brethren found themselves brought to heel each and every time: an archbishop or other lordly cleric was unseated and moved on like some common mendicant, and the smile on the lips of the matriarch was wide and red.

It was the sort of loss – an outrage – that had never been forgotten, not in several hundred years, and it was unlikely to ever be. Indeed, the Church's memory was long and unsleeping, and in each successive generation one of its sons at least had sought a way to make the family pay. No matter that the O'Malleys had given a child to the Church for as long as anyone could recall, that they paid more than their tithes required, and supported several almshouses in the city. They even had a pew with their name on it in Breakwater's cathedral where they sat every Sunday whenever in attendance at the townhouse they maintained in one of the fancier districts. Oh, their boredom during services could barely be contained, but they kept the form.

No, an insult once given to the Church was never forgotten nor forgiven, and generations of godly men had devoted a good deal of their lives to ill-wishing the O'Malleys past, present and future. Much effort and energy were consecrated to the cursing of the name, gossiping about the source of their prosperity and plotting to take it from them. Many was the head shaken in rue that pyres and pokers were not options available as a means of enforcing conformity in this particular instance – the webs woven by the clan were too strong to be evaded or undermined.

It wasn't only the more godly members of Breakwater society at odds with those who lived out on Hob's Head. Those who took O'Malley charity or made good-faith bargains with them often found that the cost was much higher than could have been imagined. Some paid it willingly and were rewarded for their loyalty; those who complained or baulked were justly requited. As time went on, business partners thought twice about joining O'Malley ventures, and the more cynical counted their fingers twice after shaking hands on a deal, just to make sure all digits remained. Those who married in – whether to the extended branches or the main – did so at their peril. More than a few husbands and wives were deemed untrustworthy or simply inconvenient when passion had run its course, and were disposed of quietly.

There was something not quite right with the O'Malleys: they didn't fear like others of their ilk. They, perhaps, put their faith elsewhere. Some said the O'Malleys had too much saltwater in their veins to be good and god-fearing, or good anything else for that matter. But nothing could be proven, not ever.

Their dealings were discreet, but things done ill always leave echoes and stains behind. Because they'd been around for so very long, the O'Malleys' sins built up, year upon year, decade upon decade, century upon century. Life upon life, death upon death.

The family was simply too influential to be easily destroyed but, as it turned out, they brought themselves down with neither aid nor agitation from either Church or peers.

It was their bloodline that faltered first – although no one but they knew – and their fortunes followed soon after. Fewer and fewer children were born to the O'Malleys proper, but for a while they'd not been bothered, or not overly so, for it seemed like nothing more than a brief aberration. Besides, the extended families continued to multiply, and to prosper financially.

Then their ships began to sink or be taken by pirates; then investments, seemingly shrewd, were quickly proven unwise. The great fleet was whittled down to a couple of merchant vessels making desultory journeys across the seas. Almost all their affluence bled away, faster and faster, until within a few generations there was just the grand mess of a home on Hob's Head. There were rumours of jewellery, silver and gems buried beneath the rolling lawns – no one could believe it was all gone – but the O'Malleys had too many debts, too little capital, and their very blood was running thin...

And so the family found itself much diminished in more ways than one. Unable to pay its creditors and investors, unable to give to the sea what it was owed, and with too few of other people's secrets to use as currency, the O'Malleys were, at last, in danger of extinction.

The estate used to be carefully tended by an army of gardeners and groundsmen, but now there's only ancient Malachi – barely breathing, regularly farting dust – to take care of things. All the walled gardens are overrun; to enter them would be to risk having sleeves and skirts torn by thorns and branches with too much length and strength, and their doors are sewn shut with brambles. All but one that is, the one the old woman – the last *true* O'Malley – uses when she seeks fresh air and solitude. In the house, Malachi's sister, Maura – younger by a little and less given to farting – does what she can to keep the gilings and decay at bay, but she's one woman, arthritic and tired and cross; it's a losing battle, though she keeps her hand in with herb magic and rituals to ensure the kitchen garden continues producing vegetables and the orchard fruiting. There are two elderly horses to pull a rickety calash and be gently ridden; three cows, all almost beyond giving milk; several chickens whose lives are likely to be short if they do not begin to take their duties more seriously. Their years of being productive have been extended by Maura's tiny rituals, but there's only so much small magics can do. Once, there was a legion of tenants who could be called upon to work the fields, but now they are few and the land has laid fallow for a very long time indeed. The great house is crumbling and the massive curved iron gates at the entrance have not been closed in a decade for fear any movement will tear them from their rusted hinges.

There's just a single daughter left of the household, whose surname isn't even really O'Malley, her mother having committed the multiple sins of being an only child, a girl, insisting from sheer perversity on taking her husband's name, and then dying without producing further offspring. Worse still: this husband had no O'Malley lineage – not a drop – so the daughter's blood was thinned once again. She's eighteen, this girl, a woman really, raised mostly in isolation, taught to run a house as if this one isn't a ruin waiting to fall, with a dying family (decreased yet again by a recent death), no fortune, and no prospects of which to speak.

There's an old woman, though, with plans and plots of long gestation; and there's the sea, which will have her due, come hell or high water; and there are secrets and lies which never stay buried forever.

2

'He was a terrible husband, you know, Miren,' my grandmother says with a sigh.

We're watching the coffin (a death-bed made at great expense to ensure he stays *beneath*; golden locks and hinges, padded silk interior stuffed with lavender which calms the dead, the joins sealed with eldritch adhesive over which spells have been sung) be carried down, down, a'down into the crypt beneath the chapel floor. The pallbearers have paced across the painted labyrinth of a pilgrim's path that decorates the aisle, and now they're at the great dark void in front of the altar. The flagstones have been pulled up so my grandfather Óisín can be laid to whatever might count as rest for him. Some of the mosaic tiles – merrows and ships and things with wings that might resemble angels in poor light – have been chipped. Someone (Malachi) was careless. I hope Grandmother doesn't notice, but chance would be a fine thing. Someone (Malachi) will hear about it, either today or tomorrow; later, if she's decided to hold fire and use the sin at a time when more of an impact can be made, more of a fuss.

No one bothered to light the candles on the wooden chandelier above our heads – an oversight – but the daylight throws beams of colour through the arched stained-glass windows. Still, it takes a while for the eye to adjust in the gloom, and I keep waiting for someone to trip over something, anything, their own feet most likely. It's cold, but then it always is here, surrounded by rough-hewn stone. I can smell the sea air and mildew beneath the wafts of burning incense. I put an arm around my grandmother's shoulders because she's shivering, but that might just be advanced years – mind you, I can feel the muscles beneath her gown, built by years of daily swimming in the sea. She never misses a morning: swam the day my grandfather died and swam today, the day we're putting him in the ground. She gives me a glance, does Aoife O'Malley, barely tolerating the gesture – we're of a height and age hasn't stooped her at all – but I keep the arm there as much to annoy her as to give myself some skerrick of warmth. Besides, I feel the eyes of all the relatives on us and, as prickly as Aoife might be, I do want to protect her from those who think her weakened by the years, easy prey.

The priest come all unwilling, to send the old man off keeps intoning his prayers but they sound like maundering to me. Once, we'd have warranted a bishop from Breakwater, at the very least – he'd have been no less unwilling, I grant you, but we were worth more at one point, and they'd not have dared to deny us. But now… a low-level god-hound with black half-moons under his nails, smelling of alcohol and earth, a fine fall of dandruff on his shoulders like winter's come early. Mumbling his prayers as if afraid his chosen god might strike him down for attending *here*, for laying Óisín O'Malley into the dirt, like it's a seal of approval. Mind you, there's not much choice of clergymen left in Breakwater anymore, no matter what your standing.

'He was a terrible husband, you know,' repeats Aoife as if wittering, but I know enough to do nothing but nod. She's putting up a front, is my grandmother: harmless old lady, recently bereaved. Bereaved of a terrible husband certainly, but leaving no doubt for those in earshot that she'll still miss him *terribly*, because she was a good wife in spite of him. In the face of marital adversity, she, Aoife O'Malley, did her very best to be a tender, loving, considerate, respectful spouse.

Which is precisely what she was not. But, as I say, I'm not fool enough to contradict her in front of others. Though we might bicker when it's just us, I'm loyal in public, no matter what. All these relatives from various family offshoots are here only to see what they might get out of the old man's death. And they're not proper O'Malleys, not true ones, pedigree all mixed and mingled − like myself − the products of marriages made with men and women not of our line. Their blood thinned. Honestly, though, such breeding had to be done, for all my grandmother laments it. How many times can a line fold back on itself without bringing forth a monster? Gods know, we've had our share, and Malachi's whispered to me that there are strangely made coffins down there in the earthy deep, hiding the secrets no one else would keep.

But Aoife's an O'Malley twice over: born one and then married to one. She's proper, double-blooded, the omega. The rest of us are lesser, children with ichor so thin it barely matters. But I was raised in this house, I'm Aoife's granddaughter; I'm one step above the others.

Yet she is the last here of purest lineage.

The cleric's mutterings bounce back up while the strongest of the cousins follow him, carrying Óisín's mahogany coffin (extra long to accommodate his height, adding to the cost) into the depths. I can see Aidan Fitzpatrick's strong back, shoulders broad beneath his coat, hair so blond and bright even in the darkness as they descend. Finn O'Hara's beside him, and the height disparity makes the going awkward. I think of Óisín tilting inside the box, pressing up against the padded lining, though he'll know nothing of it. Behind them are the Monaghan twins, Daragh and Thomas, then bringing up the rear two cousins so distant that I can't even recall their names. At least they *look* like O'Malleys. The others are blond or ginger, skin freckled or sallow, marking them out. Or once it would have; now those who actually look like proper O'Malleys are in the minority.

Aoife and I are the only ones in the front pew, even though there's naught but standing room at the back of the small chapel. No one dared to sit beside us, or even across the way. I'm unsure if it's that proximity to Aoife is a situation to be avoided, or no one wanted to get too close to Óisín's coffin just in case he popped up again, shouting at them all to go home; possibly some alchemical combination of the two.

Me? I'm nothing to avoid; there's nothing frightening about me.

Mostly, I suspect the crowd has come to make sure Óisín is *truly* gone, and that can be done from a comfortable distance. I know his faults all too well, but I'll miss my grandfather sorely. He taught me everything I know about the sea and its moods, about ships, about business, and all the superstitions that sailors are heir to. I suffer no illusions: if I'd had brothers, if my mother'd had brothers, there'd have been little chance of me getting the education I did. The days of the O'Malley women's power being unquestioned are long gone, and more's the pity. Aoife's a rare creature, a force of nature, elemental, my grandmother, utterly uninterested in others telling her what to do, but even she's had to bow her head and give in now and then.

I think, some days, that Óisín was lonely and he liked my company, in his study here and on the trips into Breakwater, inspecting the vessels and cargo. He liked taking me for lunch in his favourite club, quizzing me about tides and knots and trade routes. Mind you, if I got anything wrong I never heard the end of it, and was left in no doubt as to what a disappointment I was. But I made a point of not getting things wrong, not after the first few times. In my pocket I can feel the weight of the small knife that was his, its handle inlaid with mother-of-pearl, given to me before he took to his bed for the last time.

'A terrible husband,' sighs Aoife yet again, louder for those in the back, just in case anyone missed it. Third time's a charm: she's making it a fact to be carried forward and forth by all those whose ears it touches. Aoife O'Malley's always believed that the truth is what she says it is.

This time I reply, 'Yes, Grandmother,' though I feel a little disloyal, but Aoife's the one I've got to live with now. No buffer any longer, even if that buffer was nothing more than Óisín's desire to gainsay his wife.

The pallbearers seem to be taking an awfully long time down there, and there's no longer even the rhythmic whine of the god-hound's chant. I strain my ears, listening for the sound of boots on steps, or wood on stone as they shift the coffin into one of the niches, perhaps a cough or two in the stale air of a tomb that's not been opened in fifteen years, not since my mother died of fever, following my father by a mere week.

I listen harder still, hear twice as much nothing. I know better, yet the absence makes my heart beat faster. I imagine everyone can hear it, but Aoife doesn't look at me, registers no sign. What's happening down there? Did they go too far? Did the stairs change? Grow in number, descend further? Are my cousins even now being welcomed somewhere unaccountably warm? From habit, I touch the spot just beneath the dip in my throat, feel the thick black fabric of my high-necked dress and the warm lump of metal under it: a silver necklace with the ship's bell pendant engraved with what might be scalloping or fish scales. Aoife also wears one; she says my mother did as well. As all the firstborns did.

Listen, listen, listen...

Aoife's delicate head turns and she stares at me through the thick lace veil. I realise I've been squeezing her shoulders. I loosen my grip and press out a smile from behind my own veil; not as thick as hers, but then I've less to hide.

Footsteps at last! As if all they've been waiting for was the release of my tension. The cousins emerge, two by two – do they look paler than when they went in? Daragh, a little faint? Has Thomas finally let his breath go, gasping as if he'd held it in the whole time he was below? Only Aidan appears indifferent: a duty has been done and he's been seen to do it. Nothing more.

He's got the family height, but that's all. Thinning blond hair, blue eyes, and beneath his costly, well-tailored frockcoat (only the *truest* of O'Malleys have been afflicted with this grinding embarrassment of poverty), he's fighting fat. In his thirties, he'll keep it away only as long as he maintains daily physical activity: the riding, the boxing, the tramping across the hills, bestriding the decks of the ships he owns. He looks at Aoife, but not at

21

me; then again, he seldom bothers to address me beyond 'Hello' and 'Goodbye', as if I'm still a child, the little cousin, safely almost-invisible. I'm used to that, and comfortable with it. They exchange a nod, then he returns to the second-row pew where his sister Brigid – once my friend – with her pale eyes, soft curls and weak chin waits. I imagine I feel the heat of her glare on the nape of my neck, but that could be sheer fancy. The others disperse to the back of the chapel.

The priest intones a final blessing and bids us go in peace. Aoife wastes no time; we progress down the aisle at a sprightly pace she might want to reconsider in her guise as a fragile grieving widow. I squeeze her arm, and she gets the message after a moment. Her speed falls away a little, steps become smaller and slower, no longer those earth-eating strides to put men half her age to shame.

Behind us come the relatives and remnants. I glance over my shoulder and watch them through the black froth of lace as they pour along in our wake like well-trained waves, as if afraid we might escape if not quickly pursued.

'Just this last trial to get through,' murmurs Aoife.

'Yes, Grandmother,' I say, but I'm thinking, *What then? How do we go on? How do we return to embroidery and reading, managing those three tenant families and Maura and Malachi, tending the herb garden and testing their properties, riding those ancient horses, walking the sea brim, making do from one day to the next? How?*

And there is, I must admit, the thought singing at the back of my mind that there is only Aoife now, and when she is gone I might leave Hob's Hallow and all the obligations of this place and the O'Malley name behind me.

'How's our darling Aoife, Miren dear? Is she quite well?' asks Aunt Florence Walsh, who's really just another cousin, yet so old it's easier to call her "aunt". She's short and round, but none of the fat remains in her face, which means she's wrinkled with sunken cheeks. Wrapped in black, she looks like a prune topped with silver hair that appears soft as a cloud. I can tell from experience it's nothing of the sort: as a child I touched it, expecting floss, yet finding something sharp and dry and prickly. I felt for days afterwards that there were shards beneath my skin, and I was slapped for my trouble, which I never forgot.

'She is very well, Aunt. How kind of you to ask.'

It's nothing of the sort. The old carrion bird is younger than Aoife by a few years but looks older. In her head, I think there's a race to see who survives longest; I wonder how many others are taking bets. I know who I'd put money on, if I had any.

'She's very adaptable, our Aoife; I'm sure she'll survive whatever life throws at her.' Aunt Florence reaches towards me, touches the tiny pintucked frills on my sleeve as if to judge their value. This gown is old, greening with age for it's not even mine – my mother's, I think, and worn at her own grandparents' funerals. I suspect it belonged to another O'Malley or three before that. The style is antique, but all that matters is that it's black; Maura took the waist in a little, for I'm more slender than Isolde was. For a moment I consider slapping away the spidery hand with its grasping fingers, a long-delayed revenge, but her bones would probably shatter. It's tempting, though.

'And so resourceful. Look at all this!' She gestures to the spread of food and drink laid out in the long hall once used for balls when we could afford to entertain. Sideboards circle the walls and tables form a line up the middle; all are weighted down with provisions. Everything's (well, in *this* room) been cleaned and polished and tidied by the four maids Aidan Fitzpatrick "loaned" us, an unusual attention to duty for this last office for my grandfather. Both Aoife and I have grown used to a light fall of dust most of the time, with even my grandmother accepting that Maura's getting too old for much beyond rubbing a cloth across easily reachable surfaces in a desultory fashion. Florence's icy blue eyes gleam as she says, '*Most* impressive with such a pinched purse.'

'Grandmother can be *most* persuasive when she wishes, Aunt, as you and Uncle Silas well know.' Florence's husband, long gone, unlamented by most, was rumoured to have been talked out of a good portion of money not long before his death; never paid back either as Aoife had also convinced him that the debt should be forgiven in his will. Even more rumours abound as to how she managed to sway him. Aoife is, as Florrie's observed, resourceful. Ruthlessly so.

Aunt's face convulses; the benign expression she tries so hard to cultivate simply cannot stand against the malignance that lives inside and it pushes up like some great sea creature surfacing. A glimpse, then it's gone. I'm not afraid of her, but for a moment my knees felt shaky, perhaps because in that moment Florence looked rather like Aoife. Not in the features, no, but the ill-intent.

'You've got more than enough of her blood,' she says, and it sounds like a curse. She smiles. 'I'm glad she's well. Take care of yourself, Miren.'

Aunt Florence moves off, slowly, and I watch as she makes her way through the press of black-clad bodies. She stops here and there to say something, touch someone. Some recoil from her; others lean in.

The crowd seems to have thinned, but I doubt it's because anyone's left yet − although those planning to get back to Breakwater before dark will want to go soon. Relatives will be wandering the house, of course, spreading like webs from wing to wing to see what they can see. It's not often they have the chance nowadays to visit; invitations to dine have been thin on the ground for some years. Hopefully they'll not steal anything; not because they need to steal, but because a souvenir is something to crow about in future. They'll be hard-pressed to find anything of value; even the multitude of silver objects – vases, busts, plates, cutlery, door handles, jugs, goblets, what-have-you – have gone, sold to pay bills over the decades. Only Aidan Fitzpatrick's been a regular caller, asking after Aoife and Óisín's health, checking if they need anything but not, I've noticed, actually giving something of consequence. Just enough to stave off the bailiffs, not enough to rescue them.

Us.

Florence disappears from my view and I glance again at the feast. How many more creditors will this bring to our door? How did Aoife coax anyone to extend credit? She knows as well as I do there'll be nothing going spare after Óisín's will is read. We'll be lucky to keep the house, but the last of the ships will need to be sold off to cover what's owing.

Not to mention the death duties.

Once, we'd have known what they might be, what portion,

but there's no longer a council to decide that. It's been thus for almost four years, since a woman arrived in Breakwater and began to make it her own. The gathering of men who'd governed gradually died off, apparently naturally or accidentally, and those who remained were happy to benefit from Bethany Lawrence's new order. She has her finger on the pulse of the city and where she applies pressure, it either speeds up or halts altogether. The tales we hear from the tinkers who travel the length and breadth of the land say she's called the Queen of Thieves behind her back (sensibly), and she gathers taxes and bribes and tithes as surely as both Church and State once did (the archbishop, too, is her lapdog, by all accounts, accepting whatever scraps she throws to him). Mind you, it's said she keeps the municipality clean and well-run. What might she demand from us? Rumour has it that the rich families of Breakwater have found themselves either providing coin or favours when an inheritance is in the offing, sometimes both. It strikes me as the sort of deal an O'Malley might once have made, but she's not one of us. Neither Aoife nor Óisín have had contact with her and she's never approached either in person or via go-between; a sure sign of how insignificant we've become, that predators don't give us even a glance. Or perhaps, just perhaps, some of our reputation remains, some echo that makes even the powerful wary.

Perhaps we'll hear nothing. Perhaps our poverty is too deep, too known, for anyone to bother demanding anything of us. One can but hope.

'Miss, shall I put out more of the salmon?' One of the borrowed maids appears at my elbow.

26

I shake my head. 'No, it will only encourage them to stay.'

The girl bobs her head, gives a curtsey and moves off.

Soon they'll all be gone, these family members here to see what they can see, not to give comfort in a time of need, merely to celebrate that it's not us who've gone *beneath*.

I remember Óisín as I sat by him in the days before the reaper came. There was no pale wailing woman at the window, nor did a storm blow up when he died – that only happens when the women go; no one knows why, or if they do no one's saying. I remember my grandfather becoming a scared child, shrunk into himself on the vast mattress where our matriarchs and patriarchs have bred and slept and died. I remember him weeping that no one would lament his passing, a sudden wish, a need for affection when he'd never given much himself. And I wondered at that, that he'd be yearning not for absolution for his sins, which surely must be numbered in a very large book, but for love.

Yes, soon they'll all be gone and it'll just be Aoife and me, rattling about at Hob's Hallow as it decays around us, Maura and Malachi teetering along the lip of the grave. Yet I cannot see beyond the moment when the door closes behind them all; cannot truly imagine what shape my life might take in the weeks and months to come. It's like enduring a storm, I suppose, though a strangely quiet one: *Just hang on*, Óisín used to say, and I hear his voice now, *hang on to whatever's solid*. A seaman's mantra. What he'd tell me whenever Aoife took me swimming in the sea.

And abruptly I'm aware of the hole in my middle: the old man *will* be missed. I clench my fists, press them against my stomach, and blink hard to keep the tears away as I take the steps, twenty, thirty, to get to the expanse of windows at the other end of the ballroom. If I know anything for certain it's that neither love nor hate is ever simple.

Some cousins try to speak to me, but I move past as if I've not heard and they fall away. At last, I'm standing in front of the bank of diamond-shaped panes, staring out.

The overgrown lawn is the brightest of greens, rolling gently away to the cliffs. Both sky and sea are grey; the optical illusion of it makes it seem as if they've been stitched together, a patchwork quilt with only the subtlest of seams showing. It looks like the horizon is missing; what might happen if that line were gone? That line to which we all head, knowing we'll never catch it, but driven toward it like a seabird following a migration path year after year, life after life.

I imagine the sound of the waves because I can't hear it in here over the murmur of voices, the clink of fine china tea cups, the chewing, the tap of boots across marble floors. But I know it thuds and retreats with the constancy of a heartbeat, the shush and crash as it hits the shingle down below. Just the thought of it helps to calm me, which is funny because when I was very small I was so terribly scared of the noise. *All the waters in the world are joined, Miren,* Aoife used to say — *what use being afraid of them?*

That was neither help nor comfort, of course, when she was teaching me to swim by throwing me into the icy sea. That's how I learned, unwillingly; she kept heaving me in no matter the weather or how I wailed. She would toss me off the rocks that erupted from the water (not so far from the collapsed cave) and I would sink. The first few times she rescued me; then she let me go. Let me plummet for so long that I thought I'd drown and I realised the only way to survive was to save myself with the long strokes and powerful kicks Aoife herself used. I've wondered for years if she'd have let me perish in the end... or if I'd waited just a moment more would she have dived in after me again, pulled her hopes and future from the waves in the form of a sputtering, coughing, terrified three-year old?

Just hang on to whatever's solid, Óisín would say, but it took me a long time to realise he meant I had to rely on myself: I was the only solid thing in that angry sea.

How long I stare is a mystery, but I'm pulled from my reverie when I see two figures striding across the grass. From their direction they've come out from under the postern gate and are heading towards the spot where the church once stood, however briefly. One is in a long black mourning gown, the wind plucking at her veil, which she flings back with irritation so it trails behind her like a wing.

'What're they talking about, do you think?'

I didn't notice Brigid come up beside me. She's short and dumpy, blonde curls, pale grey eyes, but her voice is lovely and she sings when asked. No one asked her for Óisín's sending-off, but then no one sang him away at all.

I glance sideways at my cousin. The colour in her cheeks is high as if she's annoyed or embarrassed or she had to work up the courage to speak to me or she's afraid I won't reply. We're not friends. Not anymore. Once we were. When Óisín still ran the office in Breakwater – before he sold it to Aidan – I would get to visit with Brigid. She would come out to Hob's Hallow too, and we would play. It didn't matter, then, that she wasn't a "proper" O'Malley; I didn't listen to Aoife's contempt for the lesser branches. It went on for years and I thought she was my best friend, but when you're fed crumbs of resentment and pride, when you lose trust in someone…

'I don't know,' I say. Then add, because there's no shame in it, at least not for me, 'Perhaps a loan.'

'This house will fall, you know.' Yet she says it with no trace of spite, just a kind of sadness, like she's speaking of an old pet soon to die.

'I know.' And then we watch the two figures outside in silence.

Aoife's almost as tall as Aidan; she's talking avidly, hands waving. I can see her expression: sly, wary, hungry and smart. And Aidan, listening intently, looks a little like her. When he opens his mouth, the features rearrange into a different creature, the son of a thinned blood, and then both their faces are lost to me as their direction changes and they walk toward the camouflaged horizon, into a wind that carries the breath of a storm.

3

The library has a high ceiling, once painted with scenes of our maritime glory, but largely the art is obscured by cobwebs and smoke grime and has been for as long as I can remember. A face peeks through here and there, a limb, a roiling cloud, a ship's sail, a sea monster's tail, but mostly what's there is up to the imagination. When I was small, I wouldn't look lest I conjure a nightmare of those elements. Back then I thought there couldn't be worse things than bad dreams. Three of the walls are covered by overflowing bookshelves, and the fourth is mostly window, swathed with red curtains, thick with dust, to keep the night and the worst of the cold at bay.

Aoife's in an embroidered housecoat of the deepest maroon, hair piled high, silken silver, no trace of the darkness of her youth; there's a glass of winter-lemon whiskey by her elbow and she's seated in one of the threadbare wingback chairs, staring into the flames of the hearth. Not long ago she gave a deep sigh that I recognised as a letting go, a signal that from *here* we move forward. But to where?

I'm still in my mourning gown; I spent the afternoon farewelling guests, then helping Maura clean up the mess because Aidan took his borrowed maids home with him. Afterwards we packed three baskets with as many leftovers as possible, and I walked to the three tenanted cottages to deliver them. There's more food than we can get through and someone at least should benefit somehow from Óisín's passing. The Kellys and the Byrnes were grateful; the Widow O'Meara accepted what I brought but gave me the same look she always does, and I hurried away just as I always do.

I go to one of the shelves and take a book down from its place nestled between family histories, and tomes of maritime law that my grandfather loved more than anything of flesh and blood. There are many volumes with the golden "M" on their spine that denotes "Murcianus" – *Murcianus' Little-known Lore*, *Murcianus' Mythical Creatures*, *Murcianus' Strange Places*, *Murcianus' Songs of the Night*, *Murcianus' Book of Fables*. There is even a *Murcianus' Magica*, but it is an incomplete version, the true one having been lost centuries ago in the sack of the Citadel at Cwen's Reach, or so it's said.

But the one I take down is different, heavy in my arms, and I hold it almost like a shield as I approach Aoife. My fingers trace the embossing on the cover, no longer easily visible. In the front, I know, there are missing pages, nothing left but the tiny jagged shreds of paper like the edges of butterfly wings. It's always been that way and Aoife claims not to know what was there; that the story, the very first story, was missing when even she was a girl and no memory of it has been kept.

'Will you read to me?' I ask without much hope, for I'm eighteen and Grandmother's not read to me for the longest time. Maura, to whom I'd run for comfort as a child, never read me anything, but used to tell fairy tales. Maura's singsong recountings were of children taken away to hidden places; of women turned into birds and bugs; of soul clocks and dark magic; of boys who sometimes went on two legs, sometimes on four; of girls who changed their faces, grew horns, and danced away from their old lives; of brides stolen by robbers and heroes laid low by a woman's curse. And she told me, too, of places other than here: Lodellan and Bitterwood, Tintern and Bellsholm, and stranger places like Calder in the Dark Lands where the Leech Lords reign.

Aoife, when she was in the mood, would read from the book wherein generations of our kind have written tales that might be lies, might be true. Scribbled in different hands, some harder to decipher than others, but all ones that, as a child, I took as gospel.

Perhaps, too, I remember my own mother reading to me from the black-covered volume, the pages yellowed, discoloured with ink and age, with the fingerprints of the dead and tiny drawings to enliven or mar the margins. Perhaps I remember a voice sweeter than Aoife's, gentler, more like to laugh than not, whose tellings were less frightening, so I did not wake from nightmares, but rather slept cradled in the arms of my ancestral memories. But perhaps I imagine it. Perhaps Isolde is merely a thought I once had and will never be anything else. But perhaps, just perhaps, my mother's voice left a trace in my dreams. There's not even a hint of a memory of my father, Liam; all Aoife's ever said about him was that he was *unsuitable* and a few other words besides, none of them complimentary.

Other families might have stories of curses, cold lads and white ladies, but we have old gods, merfolk and monsters. I never doubted, when I was little, that these stories were true. Now, less a child, I'm not so sure.

But this night, for whatever reason, I need to hear such tales again and, for whatever reason, Grandmother is feeling generous and she nods. I place the book in her lap; the soaring points of her chair look like a throne with the wings of a bat. I curl on the green velvet chaise longue across from her, prop my head on a cushion, feel the warmth of the fire spread through me, knowing it will be too warm by the time the night is done, but not caring. I don't ask for a particular recounting. It's the telling that matters.

For the moment, there is peace.

And Aoife begins, in a voice that sounds only a little like an old woman's, to read something I've not heard for many a year.

Three children there were in the house: the firstborn, a girl to inherit; the middle a boy for the Church; and the last another girl, and a grief it would be to her mother if she fulfilled her purpose. The family had argued it back and forth, but the order must be respected; they did not get to pick and choose, the children's great-grandfather reminded.

There was nothing to be done about it: the tithe had to be paid whether they wished it or not.

And so the children's mother lowered her eyes and bowed her head. She sat in the nursery day and night, held the baby with her red-gold hair as if to take all the moments with her she could. When the rest of the family stopped watching her with suspicion, when she felt herself free of their gaze − for who amongst them would go against the patriarch? When women ruled the O'Malleys there was more give and take, a greater flexibility with rules and boundaries; but the great-grandfather's tenure had seen a tightening of the reins that held his women in check. Now, it seemed he'd never die, and those of his own blood found themselves hoping for his demise. And his granddaughter, the mother of the babe in question, was tired, tired of her bent back and bent knee, of giving way in all matters large and small and, without ever really knowing it when it happened, rebellion flared in her.

And so the day before she was to say goodbye to her littlest, she sent the oldest and middle children to the sea. 'Take the path', she said, 'down to the shingle. Be careful not to slip. There's a cave at the far side of the cove, you'll love to see it, love to play there, perhaps find treasure, my sweets!' She wrapped them up warmly, for the day was grey and cold.

The eldest, Aislin, knew better than to question her mother, yet her excitement was tempered by some instinct. The boy, Connor, was more enthusiastic than his sister, not so wary, and the girl said nothing to dampen his spirits. She knew this excursion was important from the tension in her mother's body, from the way her eyes were so dark and hard, the way her lips pressed so into whiteness. Aislin nodded and took her brother's hand.

'But don't,' their mother said as she adjusted the silver bell necklace around her oldest child's throat, 'let anyone see you. Let's make it a game. How clever can you be? How quiet and sly, my little mice?'

So Gráinne sent those children, she did, down to the pebbled beach. She sent them by the secret ways that all the youngsters of the house knew, but adults tended to forget: the long dark corridors where no one but the servants went and only then rarely. They scampered through galleries inhabited by nothing but gilings, for their home had always been made bigger than it needed to be, extensions created for prestige and to excite envy rather than to house any more bodies. They passed by family portraits whose storm-black eyes watched them go, eyebrows seemingly on the verge of lifting. Past weapons that had gathered dust and rust, not taken from walls in anger for years and years; past silver vases and busts on pedestals, past tapestries heavy and rich, depicting scenes of the family's history, with sights of the sea, always the sea, and ships upon it, the very things that helped make the O'Malley fortunes.

They sneaked past the library door, past the chair where their great-grandfather spent his days dozing when he wasn't making pronouncements about fates; past the office in which their father and his brothers spent their days counting and recounting the gold and silver brought in by the O'Malleys' mercantile empire, planning and plotting and strategising to make more; past the solar where the great-grandmother, grandmother and aunts spent their days in embroidery and schemes, as women will when forced to sit idly by.

It was only when they moved through the great subterranean kitchens that the children's stealth came adrift. A single scullion caught sight of them, a girl thin and curious, and she followed. At a distance, she followed, but follow she did. Through the potager, then the gardens proper, trees and shrubs, flowerbeds, past wells ornamental and true, past the folly built only last year to look like a small ship because the great-grandfather had an obsession with such things. She was cold, for she'd not thought to put on a coat, but she still followed, lips taking on a blueish tinge, fingers turning numb so she had to rub them against each other and bury them in her armpits to keep them from cramping entirely. She followed them as they came to the cliff edge, to the spot where the switchback path began.

O'Malley children had no fear of rain or grey skies, and no fear of the sea either for they learned to swim almost before they could walk. But they were careful on land, found it somehow treacherous the way it sometimes gave way without warning, when it promised such solidity. So the children were wary as they took the path down to the pebble-strewn cove.

But when they reached the beach, their steps were sure once again: closer to the water, they were more certain. Behind them, the maid struggled, trying hard not to trip, to make any sound that might alert her quarry, but by that time they were nearer to their objective and focused utterly on that.

They came at last, did the children, to the sea cave, cut deep into dark layers of basalt. The tide was out, for Gráinne had paid attention to the hour when she sent her children away, but the entrance was still so small, hardly more than a gap in the rock, as if a mighty hand had pulled the stone up in a curve as easily as a drape of fabric. Aislin got down on her knees and, after the smallest hesitation – it wasn't fear, no, you couldn't call it fear, more a considered caution – crawled inside, followed swiftly by her brother, who suffered no such qualms.

And the maid waited, not daring to pursue, and feeling that somehow she'd made an ill choice in giving in to her curiosity.

It was dark, the space they squirmed through, damp and close and smelling of dead things the sea had claimed and wouldn't let go. Just when it seemed they'd crawl forever, when Aislin was sure the darkness would suffocate them, a weak gleam showed up ahead and a voice trickled through to them. A voice so sweet that it drew them on, made Aislin forget she'd ever thought about trying to turn back. Surely, there was treasure here, just as their mother had promised.

When Aislin and Connor could stand once again, they found themselves in a cave most assuredly, although they couldn't say how far they'd gone; Aislin had a sense that the path had begun to slope down at some point. The area into which they stepped was large, large as the formal dining room at the manor twice over, two-thirds filled with black water, the other third a sandy bottom so soft their boots sank. The only source of light was the algae growing on the walls, which glowed a blue-green, made their faces look sickly, and showed the creature that still sang as it lay in the shallows, part-in and part-out of the liquid obsidian.

The woman's bottom half couldn't be seen, but Aislin sensed movement in the water, a shift of the fluid caused by the press of something powerful, teasingly silver just like a hint or a taste of truth. The creature – woman, surely, for it was broad-shouldered, heavy-breasted, with long ropes of sable hair with pearls braided into them. But Aislin couldn't quell the suspicion that the woman – thing – was much bigger than any person she'd ever seen, even amongst her tall family. The mouth was wide and filled with sharp teeth, the nose a little flat, the nostrils a little high, the eyes big and black with no white at all, but she clearly saw the children, for she smiled with that wide mouth and beckoned them closer. It – she – stopped singing and the sweet echoes dropped from a ceiling so high it was lost in shadows, dropped and dripped and trickled down to make ripples in the surface of the pond.

Aislin thought she'd never seen anything stranger or more beautiful, but she stayed where she was, the silver bell of her necklace seeming to vibrate against her skin; Gráinne knew the girl was cautious. Connor – ah, who knew what the boy thought? – took the steps needed to bring him within the creature's reach.

The mer didn't seem to look at the boy, but kept her eyes on Aislin, and the girl saw there, or thought she did, something cold and clever, almost admiring, with a lick of contempt. Admiration, for the girl was smart enough to stay back; contempt, for the girl said nothing to keep her brother safely with her.

The creature's arms were scaled, Aislin noticed that then, and their reach was long as it grasped Connor and drew him in. The nails were more than nails, they were claws, and the thing had no care for keeping the boy calm; the talons dug in further and further, so fast Connor barely thought to scream for a moment. And then he did, and when he did it seemed he'd never stop, and the walls that had rung so recently with a siren's song now echoed with Connor's last noises.

Aislin, unfrozen so fast, dropped to her knees and scuttled to the tunnel, which was wetter as the tide began to come in, steeper than it had seemed going down. As she crawled, rivulets of water poured towards her as she left the strange light of the sea cave behind and wiggled in a panic towards the tiny speck of sunlight left above.

And that's the finish of it. None of the tales in this book end with the words "happily ever after".

'Is it true, Grandmother?'

Aoife smiles and her face transforms, though I don't know

39

whether it's for better or worse, but she's more beautiful, younger, when she smiles, that I must say.

'Is it true, Grandmother, the story? Are any of them?'

She shrugs, does Aoife. 'You know there was an Aislin, once.'

I know where Aislin's portrait is in the main gallery upstairs. Even in her middle years, she looks like me; the silver ship's bell pendant hangs around her neck. Or we all look like her, I suppose. And she in turn looked like all those who went before, with their dark hair, darker eyes and strangely luminous skin, as if the moon lives just a little within us. I know there's no image of her brother Connor there and, though there's a headstone for him set into the south wall of the chapel, I'm willing to bet there are no bones sleeping behind it. But Connor should have lived, and the baby…

There's a painting of her, that younger sister, Róisín: she's eighteen, wearing a nun's habit. No one but an O'Malley knows that she should never have been named for she was meant to belong to the sea – it's harder to lose something once you've called it, owned it – and her birth shouldn't have been recorded because she had another purpose. I also know that there is no portrait of my own mother (I wonder if Aoife burned it) for Isolde had somehow offended her parents before her death; Maura and Malachi have both told me that I look like Isolde, but I wonder.

'What of the maid, Grandmother? The scullion? She disappears from the tale.'

'People disappear all the time; perhaps she went away with the fairies.' Aoife grins more broadly, but her gaze is cold, her tone too. 'Don't be a child, Miren, you should be beyond such things, such stories.'

'Then why do you keep the book, Grandmother?' I ask, and her hands, with their long fingers, the blue tracery of veins, convulse around the cover before she can stop herself.

'Stories are history, whether they're true or not,' she says, and there's that beauty again, and I'm awed at how she once looked; no wonder neither Silas nor half the men in Breakwater could say *no* to her. There's a hint there that beneath her skin she never was very kind. I know that; she raised me. I wonder, as I have always done, whether she was kinder to my mother when Isolde was small.

I do love my grandmother, not simply from duty, but Aoife O'Malley (proper O'Malley, the daughter of first cousins, married to a first cousin) has never been what you'd call kindly. Even as she's grown older, there's been no mellowing, and only the slightest slowing of her movements. She's smart, is Aoife, but not very patient, so the times when she's found me especially challenging, I've paid for it when her temper's snapped.

'What did you discuss with Aidan this afternoon?' I ask at last.

She shrugs dismissively. 'That we'll go and visit him in a few days, when the will is read. Perhaps we'll stay overnight rather than race against the dark to get back here. It will be nice, won't it, to have a sojourn in town?'

Nice perhaps if you've any money to spend on amusements, on a fancy meal or a scandalous show. Perhaps she's hoping Aidan will open the mouth of his purse out of pity. But Aoife's never been a fool or one to believe in fairy promises.

'Go to bed, Miren. It's been a long day.'

In my bedroom with its almost-empty armoires, writing desk, duchess with an age-pocked mirror, canopied bed and tiny bathing corner, I undress. I take off the corset and examine the impressions the whalebone has made on my torso, I dip my fingers into the furrows in the flesh, then move them until they find the scar just above my right hip (there are other scars but I don't touch them, don't seek them out). Raised, still pinkish despite the years. A brand, really, though the finer details have been lost in the healing: a Janus-faced mermaid with two tails. The same figure that adorns the family crest, the same image left only as an embossed impression on the cover of our book of terrible tales since the silver foil is long gone.

And I dream, that night, about mothers who choose between their children, who decide which one is loved less, and send them into the void.

4

It's three days before I can bring myself to go to Óisín's study. I stand on the threshold, wicker basket in hand, surveying. I don't want to be in there but Aoife wants some of the account books to take to Aidan Fitzpatrick for his inspection. Why, I'm not sure, for all they'll do is confirm what everyone already knows: we're impecunious. The room smells like my grandfather and that's a kind of comfort – old paper that's become foxed, and port-wine tobacco from the red-gold meerschaum pipe shaped like a giant squid on the windowsill where he used to tip the ash out. (I'll give it to Malachi, I think; someone should get joy and use of it.) Yet it's cold with no fire having been lit, with the curtains pulled so no sun can get in. The air's not crisp but stuffy.

The desk is black, ebony, but for the inlaid mother-of-pearl on the sides, woodland scenes rather than seascapes: centaurs and maidens, all finely made. As a child I'd sit on the floor and trace the patterns, tell myself stories. I was allowed to play at Óisín's feet if I was quiet.

And quiet I was, so I suppose he decided I was teachable. It began with ships: how to recognise them, which amongst our fleet were fastest (outrunning pirates was a concern, since our own days of brigandry were well behind us), which were best for what sort of cargo and how much might be carried, and what it might be sold for. How to time an arrival so that one of our brigantines or caravels might be anchored off Hob's Head for the evening; how a lifeboat might be sent ashore in the dead of night bearing any particularly valuable items to be secreted in the tower's cellar (because we weren't too fine to stop smuggling). Then the next morning, the ship would moor at the Breakwater docks, close by the Weeping Gate where men and women waited and wept for their loved ones lost to the sea. Then the maritime tax agents would board to take their share of our hard-earned merchandise. My grandfather taught me how to value the exotic items we shipped: the fabrics and gems, the wines and brandies and whiskeys, the wood and metals sought by artisans, the toys and weapons, the animals wanted by the very rich as pets or morsels… and to calculate bribes, to assess what a man might sell his soul for, yet thus far I've found no chance to deploy this skill.

In a better world, I'd have put that knowledge to good use, but even then we were diminishing. So he taught me old things, past things, gave me knowledge for which I would have little service.

The study is a small room, the smallest I think, in this vast place. It's in the central tower on the second floor. There's just the enormous desk and its chair, also an overstuffed wingback on the rug by the fireplace, and the shelves built into the walls; it's sparse, no doubt. There's dust on all the surfaces, testament to Óisín's dislike of anyone coming in here. I can't imagine Maura changing habit now; this room will decay like the rest.

I wonder at how I've avoided where he idled most of his time at home: this room. I think about this too: Óisín spent his early years in the offices by the docks in Breakwater, but when those closed (because who needs such a place of business to manage two meagre ships?) and the townhouse was sold to Aidan (the funds used to eke out an existence at Hob's Hallow a little longer), he retreated to this tiny space. He passed his days here, hunched over account books and those that dealt with the law of the sea, which he'd pilfer from the library and keep until Aoife noticed the holes in the shelves and kicked up a fuss for their return – the library was *her* place. One of their battlefields, one of many.

Sometimes he'd walk the gardens (carefully avoiding the walled one Aoife had claimed as her own), growing more gnarled as the rose bushes and yew trees did, but I don't think he'd taken the switchback path down to the shingle in years. Unlike his wife, he'd stopped swimming. It was too hard for him to come back again, with the arthritis mining through him. He'd take his meals, mostly, with Aoife and I in the small dining room, then retreat to his suite on the third floor of the tower. They shared a room, once, and they must have had some sort of passion, I suppose, for they made a daughter. Or perhaps that bedchamber was simply another battle that Óisín lost or gave up.

I put the wicker basket on the desk, then pull the curtains aside to let in some light and it floods the den. Motes of dust spin through the air like snowflakes. Above the fireplace is a painting of a ship, the *Heron's Bow*, Óisín's first: built at his direction, captained by him for three years, lost to a storm the first year he stayed on land. He passed the helm to a cousin, Aidan's father Fergus; upon hearing of his death, Fergus' wife Oona died on the spot. Water's dripping onto the canvas from somewhere above. A burst pipe; there's a bathroom located on the next floor, I think. I must remember to tell Malachi.

It looks like the ship's in a tempest, that it's drowning. The bookshelves are to the left, and I can see the dark blue spines of the account books. I cross the room in six steps, and lay my hand on the first demanded volume. It sticks to its neighbour and I pull harder, hoping the damp from above hasn't seeped elsewhere. At last it comes with that strange noise of one thing peeling itself from another. Sticky leather, not damp. It's heavy – what book in this house isn't? – and I lay it in the basket. The second is easier, and follows the first. The third is weightier and I almost drop it. The back cover flaps open and a thin sheaf falls to the threadbare rug in front of the hearth.

Carelessly, barely looking, I put the book with its fellows, then hunt up what was dropped. It's actually a bundle of envelopes; I flip through and count. Three. Paper of varying quality. They're tied together with a black velvet ribbon. How long has my grandfather kept them? The handwriting of the address is fluid and elegant, each letter perfectly formed, and I don't recognise it – so not billets-doux from Aoife in a better time. All to Óisín alone, and no sender details to be seen, but the red seals at the back have been broken, some fragments lost so I cannot make out what image might once have been imprinted when the wax was hot and malleable.

Not hidden, or not really. Not in a locked drawer. But then Óisín knew Aoife well enough to realise she'd have gone straight for a locked drawer in the desk. That she'd have had no interest in *these* books because she already knew how parlous our financial situation was – pure chance that she wanted them for Aidan! – so this was the best place to hide them.

I'm about to untie the ribbon, see how old these missives are, see who they're from, when I hear a shuffling step in the hallway. I stuff the things into my pocket, pressing them down deep, hear the paper crunch and crinkle. I hide them because Óisín did. I hide them because I have no secrets in this house. I hide them because I'm not above stealing the ones he left behind. Not too good, me, for second-hand secrets.

Maura appears in the doorway, hazel eyes red-rimmed, long grey hair in a thick braid hanging over one shoulder down past her waist, white apron pristine with a lack of work over an ancient black gown that was, I think, one of Aoife's. She wore it to the funeral and seems set to remain in it as long as possible. She was fond of Óisín, was Maura, and she'll grieve a long while. Had it been Aoife going into the ground, perhaps there'd have been a spring in her step; they're of an age, grew up together, were never friends. Maura and Malachi were children of the estate, back when we had more tenants than we currently do. Their father owed a debt to Aoife's father, one he couldn't pay, so he sent his two oldest children to be servants in the house. They were free, my grandmother told me, to go and visit their parents – the O'Malleys weren't entirely monsters after all – but when a few months had passed Maura and Malachi ceased to bother.

'Herself is calling for you,' says Maura in a voice that's surprisingly sweet. She doesn't sound like an old woman. 'Shouting, in fact.'

Looks like butter wouldn't melt in her mouth, but she's been around Aoife too long to be coy about her.

'I'm doing her bidding,' I say and point to the basket. I keep my other hand away from the pocket, though it feels like the papers therein are slowly smouldering, and surely Maura will notice.

But she doesn't. She just smiles and says, 'Not fast enough. Hurry up. The Fitzpatrick carriage has arrived and she's anxious to be away.' She says it with a tone that tells me what she thinks of this grand gesture. We've got our own conveyance, but it's a dreadful wreck of a thing. Aidan's, however, is fancy, new and well-maintained, his with employees dressed in the Fitzpatrick livery of cream trews, sky-blue frockcoats with silver buttons and smart black stovepipe hats. It has the O'Malley coat-of-arms on its doors, which Aidan's not actually entitled to, but who's to gainsay him if he wants to display a silver Janus-faced, two-tailed mermaid? 'You'll be staying two nights in Breakwater. I've packed you a case, it's at the front door.'

'Enjoy your rest,' I say and grin. I collect the basket and pass her by. She leans over and kisses my forehead and I catch a whiff of her: age and grief and a musty dress. I don't pull away or try to breathe shallow. I just wish she didn't hurt quite so much for a man who wasn't very kind to her; I know Óisín sometimes shared her bed. There are small graves in one of the gardens, where servants' children have been laid to rest over the years (not in the chapel with the O'Malleys, though more than one had a claim to the blood of the house). And Maura tends to more than one of those little graves, visits them every Sunday.

She pushes me away. 'Hurry or Herself will be in a right frame of mind.'

I hurry.

5

The road to Breakwater from Hob's Head is badly rutted yet Aoife, settled into a corner, manages to drop off within a minute of waving Maura and Malachi farewell, a sure sign she's planning a long evening tonight and wants to be bright and alert. There are shadows beneath her eyes, though, and I think her skin looks a little looser, as if it's let its grip go. The corners of her mouth tilt down and she snores softly.

I envy her the ability to nap so easily, and stare out the window at the marshlands as we pass. The road is built up high but still washes away in the worst of the weather that comes sometimes. Not at the moment, though, no dreadful storms for a while yet. The sedges are tall and very green with flashes of purple where the sea lavender blooms, swaying in the breeze like dancers, the only thing to grow here so close to the ocean because of all the salt. It takes something strong and strange to thrive in such an environment. Once upon a time, local women would harvest them and beat them into fibre then fabric, make it into clothing. Once even O'Malleys wore such things, before the money came and silks were easy to come by. Eventually, the family didn't even like their retainers to wear sea-cloth, and gifted everyone on Hob's Head – all the tenants, all the servants

– with clothing of proper cloth; not even our poorest folk would look like peasants. Ah, it was good while it lasted.

Sometimes a bloated figure rises from the swaying grass, greying with dark green veins trailing just beneath the skin to carry dead blood. Not ghosts, no, heavier than that, still bodily things: corpsewights. Those who've found no rest. Normally they reside in graveyards and lay traps for the unwary, Maura said, but these... they drowned; they washed ashore and woke though they shouldn't have. They don't wander, they stay close to where they roused for their minds no longer work as they should – lucky, for what might they do if they could find their way home to terrify the ones who loved them in life? The god-hounds say they've no soul left, but what else might animate them if not that?

I'm not afraid of them. They don't pursue carriages or horses (they've got a dislike for the beasts, and Malachi told me he'd seen a cart horse kick a wight to pieces in his youth), and they'll only attack if you approach them, or walk over them all unawares, if you get within reach. But attack they will, so I know enough not to wander in the marshes. I wonder, sometimes, if any of them were O'Malleys.

They're sad things, really, but the coachman must see them too, for I hear the slap of the reins and a hard-breathed command to the horses and suddenly we're flying. All the grasses blend together, the clouds move so fast the earth might be spinning like a top, and we don't slow down until we reach the forest.

Here, the trees close in, meet each other above the road and form a canopy. There's more to fear here, I think, than the marshes: bandits and robber bridegrooms; wolves on four legs and two; trolls who come out of the dark places; yellow-eyed boys with cows' tails and hollow backs; hind-girls with antlers who dance; bears by day but something else by night; hobgoblins birthed of shadow and spite that will follow you home and steal your sleep for a start. Yet the coachman apparently feels safer *here*; perhaps it's the presence of two heavily armed footmen on the rumble seat, and the hefty youth carrying a cudgel sitting beside him. Or perhaps he simply doesn't know enough to be afraid, not having been raised with all of Maura's tales of the things that might come for you once the sun has fled.

I put my hand in my pocket, thinking of the thin bundle of letters, then remember I left it at home, slid beneath the mattress of my bed. The lack feels like an old wound, but I recognise that as no more than unsatisfied curiosity.

After a while and to my surprise, I fall asleep too.

* * *

'*Five* dresses,' says Aoife in a tone that clearly states no defiance will be brooked. Yet I can't help myself.

'But, Grandmother,' I say, then drop the words beneath my breath so no one else in this very expensive modiste's boutique might hear me, 'the *cost*.'

Cousin Brigid, who is sitting on one of the pretty pink chairs, sipping elderberry tokay, gives me a glance that says I should know better. She didn't even grow up with Aoife and *she* knows better. I think of all the coins − *whole* coins, *entire* gold coins, not even snapped and split into smaller change − that will be left here all for frippery.

Yet Aoife merely raises one elegant eyebrow and pats my hand.

Having no sooner arrived at the five-storey townhouse − which is a narrow building that goes up and back rather than across but is in an excellent neighbourhood – we were out the door again and into the carriage to go shopping, accompanied by Brigid. Our cases were whisked away by an army of servants too large for those meagre possessions, taken up to bedrooms on the third floor or fourth.

Aoife's already pointed to three frocks, those waiting on the carved wooden dressmaker's mannequins for customers who are in a rush; these are mostly made, and can be swiftly fitted and altered by the three quick-fingered apprentices who wait on the modiste's word while one has tea or one's hair done in the establishments nearby. None of these dresses are black, or grey, or even that shade of lilac which might be mistaken for a mourning gown in dim light: emerald green, peacock blue, sunshine yellow. Óisín's not even a week in the ground and she's ordering *these* for me.

'Now,' drawls my grandmother to the modiste, Madame Franziska, who is a tiny woman with red hair teased up to almost half her own height, but attired to perfection in a turquoise shot-silk suit of long skirt and fitted jacket with slashed sleeves. There's a white blouse beneath the jacket on which I can see pintucks and a prim collar trimmed with lace, fastened with a gold coin for a button, the head of a goddess carefully kept upright so she's facing a particular direction, as if it's important for the madame's very existence. The outfit is expensive and beautiful, and even the apprentices are better dressed than I. I should simply shut up and let Aoife order these. I should let her worry about where the money's coming from. I should let her be the adult. I should just be pleased to have something pretty and new and mine for a change, not hand-me-down clothes and second-hand secrets. Mine. '*Now*, something for the playhouse this evening.'

The modiste smiles, clicks her fingers and one of the apprentices scurries away as if she knows preciscly what her mistress wants. Perhaps she does, perhaps they've worked together so long their communication requires no words. Or perhaps this is simply a kind of theatre itself, something agreed upon as standard behaviour whenever someone with too much money and too little sense wanders in off the street.

I throw another glance at Brigid. But Brigid will soon marshal us to cobblers' emporiums, where we will purchase delicate shoes and evening bags to match. Thence to jewel-smiths for new earrings for me, a necklace, bracelet, brooch and rings for Aoife, and whatever else she wants, I imagine. My grandmother has none of my qualms about spending money as if it's air.

But for now: this.

The apprentice scampers back. The three of them are identical and I cannot tell one from the other as their outfits match. Perhaps with time and study I might be able to distinguish that the eyes of one tilt more than those of the other two, that there's a star-shaped freckle on one's cheek, and the third is just that bit plumper than her sisters, but that's not to be. Besides, I'm mesmerised by the gown.

It's red and black, lace and silk, with pearls and jet sewn into flowers; it's slender with a mermaid tail of a skirt, long tight sleeves, high back and a plunging neckline. It's exquisite and scandalous, and I want it and I hate it, but I want it more.

'Grandmother,' I say and it's barely a breath.

'Try it on.' Aoife looks at the modiste sternly. 'We'll need it delivered for this evening.'

The modiste nods, her hair swaying dangerously like it might collapse at any moment. She clicks her fingers again – I notice her nails this time, painted gold and decorated with tiny pearls and shining stones – and all three apprentices are stripping me out of my old black frock. We're the only ones in the store; the doors have been latched, the curtains pulled across: a sure sign that someone more important than anyone else on the street has taken over, and that great amounts of coin are being extracted from their purse.

And the dress fits.

It fits so snug that the lace looks like tattoos on my skin. Once, when I was a child, we drove past the port and I saw the women on the street corners, waiting for custom; one of them had artwork all up her arms and across her chest and throat. Colourful and strange, I'd never seen anything like it, so glorious... so defiant. I think I look like her now, but Aoife merely nods as if that's the desired effect. Brigid's face is rigid, set in lines of distaste. I'm not sure if she's thinking what I am or just bitter that she couldn't fit into a dress like this even if she wanted to: she doesn't have the height and she doesn't go in and out in the right places.

'No...' I start to say, but Aoife talks over me.

'That looks well enough, nothing to adjust. We shall take it with us.' She smiles, and says, 'Send the bill to Mr Fitzpatrick.'

The modiste nods again as if this is only to be expected. And Brigid glares at my grandmother and I think she's a fool if she lets the old woman see what's inside her head and heart.

'Now, come along. We've got more to do, then we must rest before this evening.'

And we're out in the carriage once again and I remember that Aoife had said five dresses, but we've only taken four. I'm about to open my mouth but then I think we've spent so much already and won't Aidan be displeased? I seal my lips.

* * *

Lying on top of my bed in the black and red dress, staring at the ceiling and trying not to vomit. Not that I ate much in the restaurant; the gown wouldn't allow it. My hair is still up in all those carefully constructed curls Brigid's lady's maid created, with strands of jet wound through, and I can feel every single copper pin in it. If I fell into a pond I'd sink straight to the bottom from their sheer weight.

I can feel, too, the finger marks made by Aidan on my right wrist, like a bracelet I didn't ask for yet will never be rid of.

I wonder if all this would have happened if Óisín hadn't died? Would he have kept me safe or was this something that was always planned? Would he have sat me down and explained it the way he did maritime law? Made sense of it, made me want to help the family? Made me consider this all a duty?

The fire in the hearth flickers and flips, throwing shadows around the room, up the walls and across the curtains that hang on this bed, but I'm not really seeing that, I'm seeing the evening over and over in my head.

6

The Paragon Theatre has a restaurant in its basement, no tables out in the open, but closed "cabinets" set around the walls in a circle, each with its own door for privacy. Just enough room inside for a table and chairs for four, and a thin servitor. Bookings are hard to get, expensive, exclusive, the food is cleverly arranged to please the eye although the taste is somewhat lacking – bland rather than awful, which is why they get away with it I suppose.

Aoife and Brigid accompany us: Aoife in a magnificent purple gown with newly acquired amethysts, Brigid looking like a little girl in a pink silk dress that washes her out. I wish Aoife had been kind enough to guide her in dressing; I wish, briefly, that we were still friends and I could have said something without causing offence. But Aoife is not kind unless it gains her an advantage, and she thinks Brigid has nothing to offer. And I remember too well what was done by my cousin.

'Did you like the quilt on the bed?' Brigid asks quietly as we ride in the carriage.

'Oh. Yes. It's lovely.'

'I made it,' she says with a smile.

'Such clever work,' I reply, wondering at this sudden pleasantry.

'It's a gift for you. You must take it home when you return to Hob's Hallow.'

'Yes, thank you. Of course.'

At dinner, I sit beside Aidan (in blue velvet frockcoat, embroidered waistcoat, black silk trousers and highly polished shoes with gold buckles), who speaks mostly to my grandmother, occasionally to his sister, and not at all to me until we've finished our meal and it's time to take our balcony seats for the performance. Then he stands, pulls out my chair and offers his arm with a smile (strange to see such an expression aimed at me). He says, 'Shall we?' as if it's the most agreeable idea in the world.

I hesitate, for he should by rights be escorting Aoife; she's the oldest, the most important, but my grandmother senses my hesitation and gives a curt nod (*Go on, girl, don't be an idiot*), and I know better than to question. So I put my hand on his proffered arm, touch the softness of the fabric beneath my fingers (I wear no gloves for they'd cover the long lacy sleeves and ruin the effect) and the muscle beneath the fabric. I feel too close to him and my breath catches.

And so we leave the restaurant, up the small flight of steps to the foyer, which is a masterful mix of cream and gold paint, statuary and chandeliers, crimson-suited men-staff who check tickets and direct people to the correct doors, and women in low-cut ebony dresses, carrying trays heavy with drinks in crystal glasses. We cross the open space, heading towards the grand staircase.

'Now, Brigid, don't they look fine together?' I hear Aoife say, and glance over my shoulder at her; something's lodged in my throat, a formless panic. Aoife's taken my cousin by the arm and is holding her back so Aidan and I might walk on ahead, across plush red carpet. We garner glances from the other theatregoers: curious, speculative, judgmental. (*Out so soon in public after a funeral! And that dress!*) Some just plain stare. I catch sight of our reflection in the mirrored walls as we ascend, and we *do* look very fine together; tall and well-made, towering over others. I'm caught by my own image: I've never been dressed in such a way before, never had make-up on, but Aoife herself painted my features – cleverly, not overdone, just highlighted what's already there. There are heavy diamond and ruby earrings that brush against my neck, diamond and jet bracelets around each wrist – all bought with Aidan's coin.

I've been told I'm lovely by my grandmother and Óisín, by Maura, the tenants… but growing up alone and mostly isolated there's been nothing and no one to reinforce this, so it's hard to know what it means, really. But here, now, with others watching, all these gazes, male and female, glued to me? I know at last that "lovely" means "visible", no matter how much I might wish not to be. For a panicked moment I want to scrub the paint from my face, scrub myself out of existence, have no more eyes upon me, trying to pierce me, divine me, to know me, to take a piece of me for themselves.

But then I draw a deep breath, lift my chin, push back my shoulders. I'm Aoife O'Malley's granddaughter and that means something, even if it's only that I'm proud and look like I think everyone's beneath me. I'll take what armour I can.

Aidan sees me to my seat, then attends to Aoife and Brigid. Brigid's expression is set: stoic, displeased. If we were friends, perhaps it wouldn't be. Perhaps things would be different. Perhaps I could look to her for help.

But help from what? That her brother has paid me attention for the first time ever? That I'm here in this theatre for the first time ever, and there are eyes upon me like mouths licking the flesh from me? That I can only feel my heart thudding in my chest and I think it might be rattling my ribs? I'm being a fool and I know it.

Another deep breath, and a serving girl steps into our box and offers glasses of champagne with strawberries floating in the liquid. I sip too deeply. This is my second (there was one with dinner), and it goes to my head far too quickly. I'm used to drinking winter-lemon whiskey with Óisín and Aoife, but this stuff is different, strong in another fashion. Aidan sits beside me, doesn't look at me, but I feel myself observed and glance up.

Across from us, in another balcony seat in the rarefied air of the theatre, sits a blonde woman. Delicate features, eyes slanted like a cat's, her dress of green even more scandalously cut than mine, her hair a tremendous confection of curls and gems. In one white-gloved hand is a champagne glass and in the other the mouthpiece of a smoking pipe, one of the exotic sort of coloured glass that bubble and puff out smoke like an intricately shaped small dragon. She's looking at me, at Aidan, a long considering gaze; there's no friendliness in it, only calculation, as if I'm a prize she might sell.

On the other side of me, Brigid's lips barely move as she whispers, 'Bethany Lawrence.'

Our Queen of Thieves. I've never seen her before. She looks younger than I ever thought. Beside her is a tall, handsome young man with thick, ruddy hair; he's beautifully dressed and most solicitous to her. Without knowing his function, I can still guess his position in her entourage. But he doesn't look cheap, doesn't look *hired*. So perhaps he is something else?

Before my mind can pick further at the idea, there's the smell of smoke as candles are snuffed, and the noise from the audience subsides at this signal. The curtains hiding the stage part with a whisper to show a single woman standing on the dusty boards. Her dress is silver as the moon, her hair black as night, lying down her back like a slick of oil. She appears tall from where we sit.

She opens her lips and begins to sing. I don't understand the language, but it's beautiful as it washes over the ears. Her voice is heavenly, and I sit forward in my seat as if to be closer to the notes, as if they might touch me somehow. Maura sang to me when I was a child, but I've not been able to convince her to do so for many a year – lullabies have grown as scarce as bedtime tales from Aoife. I could read for myself, sing for myself, but there's something magical about song and story when they're given, something unique.

I feel this woman's melody is a gift, even though its words are incomprehensible.

I notice, after a while, that she does not shift from her spot. She does turn, however, left to right, hands reaching forth in gestures that are simple and repetitive. There's a stiffness to her; at first I think she stays put because she's in shoes too high to risk steps, but then I notice the joins in her elbows, at her neck and shoulders, wrists. I lean forward further, almost draping myself over the railing, so I can squint at her, harder and harder. It's not elegant, and I'm ruining the effect of all Aoife's make-up, all Brigid's maid's hairdressing, and the dress is growing more and more constricting, but I can't help myself.

There! At the corners of her mouth are lines; they run down to her chin, visible as she opens her lips to let the sound out. The stilted motions, the repetition: she's an automaton! Now I can see the silver patterns running up and down her bare arms are not tattoos but perhaps decoration, perhaps some part of her functioning.

There's a movement beside me, hot breath against my ear, and Aidan is whispering, 'Do you like her?' and there's a strange catch in his voice that I don't understand.

I barely take my eyes from her to answer. 'Oh, yes. I've never seen the like.'

He says no more, but sits back in his seat, a smug smile on his lips, and my attention returns to the mechanism on stage. She continues to sing and I cannot tell if it's a love song, or one of grief, or a call to arms. Perhaps it is all three; perhaps that's the only thing it *can* be.

When she is done, I feel bereft. The curtains close so she can be removed without anyone seeing how she must be carted away like a piece of machinery, as if she's not a work of art. I have a music box at home that belonged to my mother, or so I'm told. I remember it used to play tunes once, but it's a long while since it's produced more than a sad weak chime. The way I felt the first time its tune began to die? That's how I feel now. I lock eyes with Brigid and for a moment it seems we share something wonderful; then her expression changes as she remembers she doesn't like me at all.

The rest of the performance is quite ordinary, or maybe not but merely seems so to me. There are jugglers and dancers, girls who climb ropes into the air which appear to have no anchoring, four small plays, a jester who tells filthy jokes that make Aoife snort.

The automaton does not appear again.

But when the show is done and we leave our balcony box, Aidan does not lead us down the way we came, but rather along a dim passage hidden behind a curtain. We weave our way downstairs, past walls slung with ropes and heavy sacks, chains and hooks, and other things I don't recognise. It's softly lit until at last we come to the back of the stage itself, which is glaringly bright – so many candles! – now that magic is no longer needed to enchant the audience. People scurry to and fro, lifting one thing, dropping another, their thick make-up clownish this close; the costumes that seemed so magnificent from afar are in truth moth-eaten and falling apart. No one says anything to us, they simply glance at Aidan, who in turn acknowledges no one, but leads us to another set of stairs, this one set in a corner and a spiral, tightly wound downwards.

We're beneath the theatre now. I don't look at Aoife and Brigid coming along behind; I don't acknowledge Brigid's muttering. I follow Aidan's broad back, a skip in my step to keep up with his stride, though we're of a height. He's excited, pacing like a hound on a scent. At last we come to a door, which he throws open as if he's got a right to, reaching back to grab my hand and sweep me in with him.

The automaton is in the middle of the small, cramped room – but it's finely outfitted, a dressing room for a leading lady, no doubt: a deep pink chaise longue for lounging about, a mirrored duchess with candles to gently light a face, racks of dresses heavy with sequins and crystals. But *she's* tilted to one side as a small man in a brown suit, half under her skirts, fiddles about like a pervert. He begins to swear, fighting with the voluminous petticoats, flapping at them as if they're an attacking bird around his head. Then he's free and he sees Aidan, and his entire demeanour changes.

'Mr Fitzpatrick, sir! A delight to see you.' But his face, mostly plain, is having difficulty forming the correct expression. He's younger than Aidan, not that much older than I, and has kind eyes. I think his smile might be nice under different circumstances.

'Ellingham, my cousin was fascinated by your automaton. I thought perhaps she would be amused at taking a closer examination.'

'Of course, of course, sir. Nothing's too much trouble for family.' He stands, drops the tool he was using, and wipes his hands. 'Miss Fitzpatrick—'

'Miss O'Malley,' corrects Brigid before I can. Her voice is like an arrow. Strictly speaking I should be Elliott, but Aoife's always insisted I go by O'Malley.

'Ah, my apologies, Miss O'Malley. Come closer, she'll not bite, my Delphine.' He laughs as though it's a joke he's told before.

'Is she… alright?' I ask, indicating her angle, his ministrations.

He grins. 'Skirts caught in her hip joint. Boys need to be more careful when they carry her is all.'

I step up to the automaton, look into her face. There's no animation to the features and from here I can see the places where the painted porcelain of her cheeks and forehead are starting to peel away; her glass eyes are black, but there are not so many lashes left around them, though the brows are dark and definitive. There are tiny chips in the red of her lips; the wig on her head is a little askew from the tilting of her for the purpose of fixing whatever the little man thinks is wrong with her. He doesn't set her aright; she's leaning sadly like a broken thing.

'How does she... work?' I ask, and reach out to touch her gown. The netting is rough, the silver sprayed onto it; it feels like Aunt Florrie's hair, although perhaps not quite so prickly. The beads are cheap and they catch the light with greed. I gently smooth the fabric to cover her, give her some dignity she can't claim for herself.

'A winding mechanism, Miss. There's a spot in her back where I puts the key.'

'Did you make her?' My fingers touch her face, lips, cheeks. The porcelain is cold. She's shaped with large breasts, a tiny waist; part of me wants to look beneath the skirts, but that seems impolite.

'Oh no, Miren!' interjects Aidan, though he's standing well away from us, watching. 'Found her on his travels.'

Ellingham nods, leans towards me. 'She's been with me a long time. There were toymakers in the old days who'd create dolls that had a little bit of soul in 'em. Don't see 'em anymore. I think she might have been something like that, once, or almost.'

'Is there a soul in her?'

He shrugs. 'Not so I've noticed, but who can tell? Who knows what she does at night when I'm asleep?' He grins. 'Sometimes I wake up and think *tonight's the night I'll catch her dancing*! Hasn't happened so far, but maybe one day.' He winks, and I think I might like him a little.

64

'And the language she sings?' I run my fingers down the silver tracery in her arms, take her hand. It's colder than her face.

'Whoever made her gave her that voice, Miss. That language. I don't know where she came from, don't suppose I ever will.' He smiles. 'We travel a lot, Miss, and each new city I wonder if I'll hear the like, and maybe find her story.'

'Not yet though?'

'No, Miss. But our time in Breakwater's almost done and we're off again in a few more days, so...' His smile is kind and genuine.

'Thank you,' I say, and I'm not sure if I'm talking to the automaton or the little man. Her hand, in mine, trembles, shivers, convulses, tightens its grip, then is still so swiftly that I cannot be certain if it happened.

Outside the theatre, Aidan's carriage awaits. He helps his sister and my grandmother in, then offers me his hand. I reach out, but he wraps his long fingers hard around my wrist, like a manacle. 'We do look very fine together. We shall do all manner of things *together*.'

I stare into his eyes, and his grip tightens so I feel my bones grinding. With his other hand he strokes my throat, below the dip in the neck where the silver bell rests, lingering over it. I say nothing. The moment stretches until he changes his hold, assists me up into the conveyance, then climbs in after me. I sit close beside Aoife; I do not meet Aidan's gaze though he's opposite me. Brigid, next to him, stares. Is it because she's never seen me rattled? But I know the blood's drained from my face; suspect that beneath the makeup I look like a ghost.

When we finally arrive at the townhouse, Aidan aids Aoife and Brigid once more. I climb out the other side of the coach rather than go anywhere near him. Struggling in the tight skirt, I must jump to the ground with no one to roll the steps down for me, but I don't care. I can feel his eyes on me as I go towards the front door, ignoring Brigid's questions: *Are you well? You are very pale, Miren. Would you like a tisane to sleep? Is it a headache or your monthly courses or both?*

Aidan does not follow us. He climbs back into the vehicle, heading off for an evening of entertainment most likely fit only for gentlemen.

In my borrowed room, I lock the door. I glare at Brigid's gift then toss it aside, the maiden's quilt with all the dreams and hopes and spells sewn into it. I'd put it in the fire if I dared, if it didn't seem a shame to destroy such a pretty thing. When it's in a heap on the floor, I throw myself on the bed and weep.

7

The docks aren't quite deserted, but almost. It's the sweet hour before the bustle of business begins. Some few women and men – sailors, stevedores, whores – wait, smoking cigarillos; others curl in corners, drape across crates and such uncomfortable things, sleeping off their night's indulgences. Women and men, again, in bedraggled finery amble towards destinations that might be rented rooms, might be the dressmakers from whom they've hired their night clothes – presumably *not* from Madame Franziska's establishment. No one gives me a second glance.

I left the townhouse before dawn broke the sky, wearing my old black dress and a cloak equally black – gods know it took me an age to struggle out of that evening gown, to remove every pin from my hair, to clean the makeup from my skin. I've not slept, or barely. I've been running through my head the events at the theatre, Aidan's sudden attentiveness, the seeming kindness of showing me the automaton like it was a child's distraction, the bruise on my wrist that's now clear to see. Aoife's smiles and comments, her wild spending. Brigid's increased sniping and hostility.

I'm to be sold, a bought bride.

Aoife's going to rebuild our fortunes with my purchase price.

And Aidan... doesn't he think perhaps that linking himself so closely to the O'Malley core, the dying heart of the family, might affect him? His wealth? For though the outer branches have remained safe and prosperous, grown strong, the true O'Malleys have withered on the vine until there's just one scheming old woman left with nothing to offer... nothing but a granddaughter who's the closest thing remaining to a pristine O'Malley.

Aidan.

Aidan wants it all. He wants to rebuild what we once had. He wants the house on Hob's Head, overrun by his servants making it all bright and shiny again. He wants to make the name mean something once more. He'll take the last O'Malley girl to wife; though her father's an Elliott she's been called O'Malley since her parents died, it's the purest blood he's likely to find. He'll get children on me. He'll start the sacrifices once again: a child to inherit, a child for the Church, a child for the sea so she gives her bounty to us once again. Will he take the name O'Malley? Or does he think it's cursed? Will he keep Fitzpatrick and think he can avoid misfortune that way? As if Fate won't recognise him?

For hours I've wandered aimlessly, watching the sky creep from black to grey to the palest dirty blue. I've covered so much of this city on foot, at first thinking myself protected by my cloak and my height – but I honestly suspect now it's that the Queen of Thieves prefers her city to be orderly. She might make her fortune skimming off others' ill-gotten gains, but that doesn't mean Breakwater is chaotic. The streets, mostly, are tidy; houses are well-kept; there are rough men and women but they seem to be waiting patiently for orders. This empire is *organised*. Murder and mayhem and theft may well be her business, but it *is* business to be exported to other cities and towns. Óisín's little knife is in my pocket, but I've had no cause to use it.

I even wandered through the assassins market, located at the crossroads just outside the main gate into the city, which I'd heard of but never seen. Newly sprung up since the arrival of Bethany Lawrence, another source of income and organisation: all manner of commerce did I witness there. Women and men, old and young, sitting, standing, reclining, waiting. And customers approached in droves, some furtive, some quite open in what they did, most business-like. One of the tinkers who'd passed by Hob's Hallow had told how the Queen of Thieves has made it so convenient for people to find the assassin of their dreams in Breakwater that folk come from all around. The port city will present the greatest range of skilled killers for your delectation. Middlemen and guildmasters – leaning against lampposts or sitting in tents – established a client's requirements: What message might be sent in this death, should it be clear to others not to interfere in the manner the victim had, or was the message for that single person alone? Clients would then be put in contact with the murderer most appropriate to their needs. Poisoners, those who favoured the garrotte or fire or water, those with a taste in sharp things or bludgeons, and those whose preference was for ranged weapons and a distant death.

But even I could tell who were wolves and who were sheep. I was raised by Aoife O'Malley, wasn't I?

I marvelled, I confess, at the sheer number of people there, at the idea that this was done out in the open, that there should be no constable or guard here to make arrests. Elsewhere this sort of thing would be done in hidden places: back rooms, sewer tunnels, in the depths of forests, on deserted roads – once upon a time, in the tower rooms of Hob's Hallow. Not in Breakwater. How long before it spilled into the daylight? I watched as a creature was summoned from a cauldron then decanted into a bottle and handed over for a fistful of coin; an imp, tiny and grey-green that coughed fire. I thought, briefly, oh so briefly, about becoming a customer myself. Aidan dead in his sleep; I'd not be fussed how, as long as he was gone from my life.

But then, wouldn't Aoife simply find another suitor for me?

I'd thought… I'd thought I would be free. Not quite yet, but with Óisín's death I was one step closer to being released from my grandparents. Then there would just be Aoife. It's not that I don't love them, though they're hard to love, it's that with them gone… I'd be beyond their rule and regulation. I'd make decisions for myself, although who knows what they'd be. I've never thought of myself anywhere but Hob's Hallow, and I've never thought of myself as marrying anyone – it's never been discussed or brought up in even the vaguest of ways – I just thought…

That they'd be gone one day and I'd be free.

That the big old house would be mine. As if there would be no debts still owing – as if Aoife wouldn't keep running up bills.

Óisín's will is to be read this morning.

So. If not Aidan, then perhaps Aoife. A quiet death, gentle, something to send her off in her sleep. But why would I pay another to do that? And how? *There are the jewels*, a voice in my head said, *the things she bought you with Fitzpatrick money; the earrings, the bracelets*. Hasn't Maura taught me enough about the plants in the gardens? Aren't there enough blooms of

70

nightshade and foxglove, wolfsbane and even daffodils to suit my purposes? Brew a tisane, sprinkle some across her food. Who'd know?

Who'd know but me?

Me.

I would know and though she's never been easy, Aoife deserves better than that, something more honest.

Just like I deserve something better than a marriage not of my choosing.

As I moved through the crowd of killers and customers I sensed myself under scrutiny. It was a slow thing, the realisation, and I couldn't tell when it had begun, only that it was suddenly there though I'd been aware of it for a time. I stopped beside the fountain at the centre of the crossroads market and looked around casually. Too many faces, too many hooded heads, too many bodies moving too quickly. And then the sensation was gone, as if the watcher had departed. I left there soon after witnessing a woman raise a spirit. She did not do so for any purpose beyond showing a potential client she *could*. That someone's death might be so casual and coolly done. Another woman poured water into silver pans filled with gravedust, to make a hulking figure coalesce slowly from that poor material; another murderous monster. Unlike other cities, Breakwater doesn't burn its witches, not when Bethany Lawrence can make money from their talents.

Dawn is approaching and I should return to the townhouse, but I can't quite bear to just yet. I'm drawn by nostalgia to the docks, by the thought of visiting the old offices once again. Where Óisín would teach me.

Though it's a long time since I was here, the map of the streets is tattooed on my heart and mind. Some days Óisín would drop me on a corner and I would have to find my way back to the offices or the townhouse. It didn't take me long to learn the shortcuts. I pass by the house where once a woman set up a brothel staffed entirely by her own daughters. The front stairs are polished to a high shine; the Queen of Thieves is reputed to have set up residence here – the two muscled men either side of the door seem to support that. The façade is a floral mosaic, a parquetry of coloured gems turned into red roses, green vines. Some still whisper it was created by magic. The front door is ebony, carved with mermaids and sirens – it makes me wonder how no O'Malley ever owned this house – and the brass knocker looks like a piece of rope twisted into a circle. I don't go close enough to peer in the windows, I stay resolutely on the opposite side of the street.

Then I pass beneath the Weeping Gate, the sound of my boots loud on the boards in the early morning, until I'm at the end of a pier where no vessel is moored. Behind me is the old building that once housed Óisín's offices, O'Malley Maritime. Rundown now, the windows boarded up, shards of broken glass littering the sills, the door firmly closed; Aidan has his own bureau a few streets over. Neither of the remaining O'Malley ships are in port and who knows when they'll return, or if? Will their bellies be filled with cargo or will they have given it all up to pirates? Do they already sleep on the bottom of the ocean, hulls splintered, mariners drowned, their eyes eaten by fish, their bones become thrones for crabs?

The toes of my boots hang over the edge of the dock; the morning breeze kicks at my skirts and tips the hood half off my head. I pull it back all the way and lift my face to the sun, which is burning away the last of the dawn clouds. The water smells awful, not like the sea off Hob's Head, which is clean and salty. This is contaminated by humanity; a greasy sheen lies across the brownish, brackish liquid.

I could throw myself in. End it all. But what O'Malley can't swim? What O'Malley wouldn't fight the drowning? And after all the effort Aoife went to to teach me and my subsequent fear of the sea... How hard would it be to throw myself in just to give my life up when I'd fought so hard to save it from the waters? I could tie weights to my ankles. But where to find them? And why give up my existence just to avoid Aidan? That voice in my head, the one from the assassins market, pipes up again: *Marry him now, murder him in a month, a year, inherit everything.* But I think that's my grandmother's voice, or at least the part of my blood I got from her.

They cannot make me say the words. They cannot make me agree. I square my shoulders; I can just say no. I'm stubborn, Aoife's rued it all these years. They cannot force me.

I sigh, feel a weight go from me, even if it's only temporary, even if it's a false relief; I'll have to deal with it all again later and it'll be worse then, for Aoife and Aidan will both be at me.

I close my eyes... then the silver ship's bell necklace gives the slightest ting, and that's when something cold and wet grabs at both my ankles and pulls me into the brine.

My lids fly open and I watch as the world tilts and turns, and nothing's on the right angle. The back of my skull grazes the edge of the dock, stunning me, but I remember to gulp air before I go under into the cold, cold water. I drop like a stone and that surprises me, although perhaps it shouldn't. Then I realise I'm not sinking but being dragged; the grip on my ankles is still there and tight and my cloak floats behind me, wet and heavy, as if reluctant to follow and my skirts are fluttering up too, blinding me when the liquid is already so dark. I throw a glance upward: the light is brilliant as a diamond, sharp. Below all is murk. I seem to sense two other bodies beside me, keeping pace: pale and fast, sinuous, hair streaming, no legs but tails.

They never take us!

They wait; they're meant to wait for what they're given!

Then that voice says: *But they've not been given their due in such a while! There have been no spare children, not since before Aoife was born. What do they care that I'm the last of a line? We've not paid our debts in far too long.*

And I don't know whose voice that is but I cannot fault it. The back of my head hurts and the water around it begins to turn a reddish-purple where a cut bleeds. I tear at the clasps of my cloak and it lets go reluctantly, but now without it to add to my resistance, I'm moving faster downward. I begin to kick. Or I try. I'm strong from riding, walking, helping with the small harvests – though I avoid swimming when I can – but when I raise my knees it's like pulling them from sucking mud in the marshlands. I kick again and one of the hands lets go. Another kick; it connects with a head or shoulder perhaps. It can't hurt too much with the water to cushion the blow, but it gets my other leg free.

If only I had the time to remove my boots, but I need to get away from these things. Up, up, up, and I'm being paced by them; I see faces flash in the gloom, mouths open – laughter? Are they laughing at this? – they swim like dolphins, leapfrogging each other, flashing close and away, their skins bright as the moon, their tails whipping around, so lengthy and thick! Above, I can see the hull of a boat, a small craft; I swim harder, curse my boots, my dress, keep going, break the water, hook my hands over the edge and kick and kick and kick myself into that little, little boat. Much to the surprise of the fisherman sitting in it.

As I struggle in, I'm certain I can feel those hands again, scaled and webbed and so, so strong. Were they really there? Did I imagine it? Or were they just playing?

The fisherman stares at me, and I at him. He opens his mouth but whatever he might say is lost as he points over my shoulder. I turn. Half a dozen feet away three heads break the waves. Dark-haired, dark-eyed, moon-skinned, teeth sharp in their laughing mouths, gazes hard; these creatures so seldom seen, so close. Then they duck-dive and are gone.

Yet I cannot get out of my head the mocking sounds I heard beneath the surface, other voices as clear as if they sing in the air above, as if there was no fluid betwixt lips and ears.

When you are gone then we will be free. And it's not lost on me that those words are quite similar to the ones I've thought about my grandparents.

But they could have had me if they'd wished, could have dragged me down, all three of them. What was there to wait for?

8

'What were you thinking?' Aoife's not stopped shouting at me since the fisherman delivered me to the doorstep half an hour ago. As I've only just finished coughing up brine, I've not been able to answer her. Sitting in a tub in the bathroom attached to my bedchamber, red as a lobster in ridiculously hot water, I can't quite feel rid of the cold deep inside. As if my immersion in the harbour by the Weeping Gate lodged it in me, as if the mer's hands transmitted it like a disease.

'I wasn't thinking at all,' I lie − best not to tell her that I was thinking about how to thwart her and Aidan's machinations, at least not until I'm safely back at the house on Hob's Head, with the Hallow's strong walls around me and familiar things to make me feel safe, even from Aoife. 'I wasn't thinking about anything, but...'

'But what? You know the will is to be read this morning, you know we are expected there. Now we'll be late!' she snaps as the maidservant pours another jug of water over my hair and begins yet another scrubbing with orange-scented wash to rid me of the reek of the harbour. I fear it will never be enough, that I'll be cold and dank-smelling forever, even though no one else might notice. The cut on the back of my head stings and the girl's fingers make it worse every time they move over the lump.

'Be careful!' I snap. Then, more quietly, I say to Aoife, 'I didn't... fall.'

'Slipped? Like an idiot child.' She's pacing now, is Aoife, a swift angry motion, and I wonder if it's care for me or fear that her plans could have gone so badly awry because of my clumsiness.

'No,' I say and look meaningfully at the maid.

Aoife raises a brow. 'Girl, get you gone. I'm sure you've better things to do.'

And without a word, the girl drops my hair, rises, bobs a curtsey and departs, wiping her hands on her apron. Aoife takes her place, kneeling with a creaking of knees; her fingers in my hair are far more tender.

'Now, what happened?' She gives a gentle tug on my locks to say *Be quick about it.*

'I was pulled in, Grandmother.'

'Pulled?' Her fingers still, her tone drops.

'By one of *them.*'

'Them?'

'If you repeat everything I say we'll not get very far very fast,' I point out, and she pulls my hair to teach me the value of a civil tongue. I continue, 'Three that I could see. One dragged me in, the others watched and laughed as it towed me a'down.'

'Male or female? The one who...'

'I—' For a moment I'm unsure, then I remember their laughing faces as I huddled in the rowboat. 'All female.'

She clicks her tongue.

I've never witnessed them up close, never had them approach in that way. The mer can sometimes be seen from the beach or

77

the promontory at home, heads bobbing, some days difficult to distinguish from seals. But near enough to touch? Never. The silver bells around our necks are meant to mark us out as the oldest, to keep us safe.

'I heard them sing, beneath the waves: *When you are gone, then we shall be free.*'

Aoife rises. 'No. *No.*'

And then she too departs, leaving me to untangle and wash my own very long tresses, for which I've not nearly enough hands. I stay in the bath until it's so cool it begins to remind me of the harbour, and with that uncomfortable idea I climb out.

My old black dress has disappeared, no doubt disposed of on Aoife's orders. My boots... ah, they'll be gone too. On the bed in the other room is the green brocade from yesterday's shopping trip; it looks too fine for around the house, but there's the reading of the will to attend. And there are tiny embroidered house slippers in golden silk, barely fit for walking in but there's no choice, is there?

Someone has reinstated the maiden's quilt on the bed and I stare at its patterns: bells and flowers, rabbits and doves, bows and horseshoes. I wonder what's been sewn into it? Swans' feathers for fidelity? Tiny silver charms in each corner for hope of a good match, a magnificent wedding? I can't imagine that Brigid would wish me well on that account. Does she know what Aidan's planning?

I think again about throwing it on the fire, sending all those yearnings and wishes up the chimney in smoke. But what might that do? For me – to me, my future – forever? For someone whose only hope has been a quiet life alone I find myself unwilling to lay a curse upon my remaining years, however few or many they might be. No marriage ever perhaps, and would that be such a terrible thing? No Aidan, no one else to please or obey?

Yet I leave the quilt alone for the second time, merely pull it back until it's a scrunched mess at the foot of the bed. I'll remove it entirely before I sleep tonight. I towel-dry my hair then brush out its tangles before twisting it into a simple braided bun. As ready as I'll ever be, I go to leave my room.

The door is locked.

I turn the handle again and again, bend to peer through the keyhole: an empty corridor waits beyond. I swallow down the panic. What is Aoife doing that requires me to be trapped in here?

Breathing deeply, I go to the window and look down: too high to jump down from my third-floor room to the muddy alley between this house and the next. There's no rooftop for me to leap to. Just the long drop below, where I'd break a leg or my neck, which seems a high price to pay.

Nothing to do but wait it out.

I sit by the hearth and fold my hands in my lap; I cross my feet at the ankles. There are no books in this room. I think of that thin sheaf of letters beneath my mattress at home. I wonder who wrote them to Óisín; I wonder why he hid them and if Aoife knows about them or not. I like the idea of having something secret from her. I wonder if I'll ever return to Hob's Hallow to read them. But there's no answer to that and I'll simply drive myself mad with what ifs, so I think instead about the O'Malley book of tales.

I have read them all; even before Aoife said I was too old to have them told to me, I would sneak into the library late at night and pore over them. There are so many, some merely margin notes commenting on another tale, some no more than a paragraph, some take pages and pages and might be a small book all on their own. No blank folios at the back for anyone to add new stories, nothing in there from Aoife or Óisín – or nothing they've admitted to. I love that book, those stories, because they made me feel... real. Without siblings, without parents, I've always felt alone. Perhaps if my grandparents had been different, if Brigid hadn't betrayed me, I'd not have needed those tales so desperately to ground me, to make me feel part of something.

Those tales, I remember them all and so I tell them to myself to pass the time.

A long time ago, the old people say, there were three mer-sisters, each with a dearest wish. But longing is dangerous and one heard tell of a fin-wife – not quite one of the merfolk, but the sort who sometimes walked the earth on two legs – and that fin-wife could grant wishes for a price. The sisters agreed that they would pay whatever cost might be demanded, and they sought out the one who could deliver their hearts' desires.

The fin-wife was ancient and ugly, her life of wickedness laying heavily upon her soul – though it's said sea-kind have no soul, this is a lie that makes it easier for humans to enslave them, to think them lesser as they make them into unwilling wives – yet she had no regrets and no wish to change her ways. She listened to the mer-girls, then gave them their task. The details do not matter, only that they agreed to a cruel thing, an unjust deed, and they carried it out with no compunction.

And upon their return, bearing the bloody trophies of their success, which they laid at the foot of the fin-wife's throne, their wishes were granted.

The lover of the eldest, long-gone, was returned; but, no longer as he had been, no longer a kin creature, he took her life to sate his own hunger.

The middle one was granted legs and lungs so she might join her human beloved on the surface; but, given these things beneath the waves, she drowned.

The youngest, having requested only the return of their dead father's famed weapon to do him honour, cut her finger on its poisoned blade and expired.

The door remains locked and no one has come. The back of my head aches where I hit the dock.

Far away and just as long ago there was a rock in a river where rusalky maidens sat and sang. Their songs seemed beautiful, if one did not listen to the words. If one did then it was likely one would follow the lovely tune off the cliff to either break upon the rock below or drown beside it, much to the maidens' delight. They look, in the daylight, like glorious girls with long locks in every shade, glowing skins and eyes, red lips and white teeth, figures to catch the eye. Luminescent toes dangle in the flowing waters, long fingers comb shining hair. By day, they are wondrous to behold.

But when the sun sets, or when they doze on the rock, they forget themselves and can be seen in their true form, for they did not begin as sprites, but rather as human girls. Murdered maids, those dead by their own hands in grief and despair, those whose own acts haunted them beyond their passing, lose the pleasing form they had when they lived. The rot of life and death can be seen, the skin has a greenish tint, the eyes sunken, the hair straw-like, the marks of fingers and fists visible on throat and face. In winter times, too, they are in a between state, for the light is never quite right to weave their illusions, so they hide then, but for the sunniest of days.

They'll take revenge on those who wronged them if they can, or even just on those who tread too close to their places. But they're business-like in death even if they weren't in life, and they will make bargains. A rusalka's tears are magical things; they can be used for good or ill, or any shade of magic in between (although mostly for ill). There's a story told of a quilter who, crossed in love, badly betrayed, made a wedding quilt for her once true love and his new bride. She sprinkled it with the dust of nightmares and the tears of a river maiden; the bride was turned into a beast with the tail of a fish or perhaps a dragon. No one knows what happened to either.

It's well past lunch.

In olden times when wishing still helped, there was once a church built at Hob's Head.

Sometimes the O'Malleys forgot to whom they owed their fortune. They'd take up with some god-hound or another, and for a while the bishop would hope he might bring the family back to the Holy Mother Church (as if they'd ever been in its bosom before). But then the women of the family would put their feet down, for they remembered (they always remembered) where their allegiance lay.

And as a result, a father, a brother, an uncle, a grandsire, a son would go into the ground a little sooner than expected. It taught the others a valuable lesson.

There is no church on Hob's Head, just the little chapel in the manor house. But that wasn't always the case. An O'Malley patriarch decided to build one, fit for his family's overt worship, and for all the tenants around and any strays who might decide to join them. Perhaps the bishop promised him a god-hound of his very own to say prayers on a Sunday and become a fixture outside of Breakwater.

It was built right on the promontory so the view would be spectacular, the sound of the waves inspiring, and the peal of the bells across the water unparalleled, for they had been specially made. At great expense, they'd been cast at some far-flung foundry and made entirely of O'Malley silver. And on the day that the church was to be consecrated, the Breakwater bishop himself was in attendance, bellringers brought from far and wide to ensure the very first sounding of them would be perfect.

But as the congregation waited outside, preparing to enter the new church, there was a great rumbling, then a crack and a creak, and the structure and the cliff on which it stood fell into the sea. No O'Malley was injured, the only deaths being those of the bishop and the bellringers. So, no O'Malley blood was spilt, not then, but an O'Malley lesson was learned.

The sea-folk hate the sound of holy bells above all things.

The sea-folk love silver above all things.

Some days, they say, you can hear the ringing from beneath the waves.

I fall asleep thinking I hear a dim chime rung at the bottom of the ocean; wondering what it would be like to have sisters; pondering maidens changed by death, bitterness and bile.

* * *

The sky's a plum bruise outside the window when I'm woken by the sound of the door being unlocked. Brigid appears in the doorframe. Her expression is at first surprised, as if she expected to find me *otherwise*, then annoyed. She's got a large silver key attached to the silver chatelaine at her belt, a sure sign of housewifely power.

'Come along,' she says curtly as she folds her little hands at her waist. 'They're waiting for you.'

'Why'd she lock me in?' I ask as I follow. I rub at my neck, which is stiff from sleeping sitting up.

There's a pause before she says, 'To keep you safe, I suppose.'

I'm about to speak but then I figure she knows about the mer, that either Aoife's told her or – more likely – the maidservant listened at the door after she was dismissed, then informed Brigid. Aoife's unlikely to share anything with Brigid; she thinks the girl's a sidenote, a by-blow. The only reason she gives Aidan the time of day is his money. I press my lips together and say no more.

Down the stairs with their green carpet, polished banister and intricately turned balusters. Past the paintings of landscapes and Fitzpatricks with their receding chins and thin blond hair. Along the hallway to the dining room with its blue curtains, sideboards groaning with more dishes than four people can eat

– but honestly, I'm starving after a day without food and could probably devour it all myself – shining silver candlesticks and salvers, vases of crystal and gold. And there at the small table – this is the informal dining room, after all – sit Aoife and Aidan, one at each end so that it might be argued that both are at the head. A single chair on either side for myself and Brigid, though ten could easily be seated for a meal.

The same girl who began washing my hair this morning is there, eyes downcast. Brigid and I take our seats. I do not look directly at Aidan.

'Serve,' says Aoife, and the maid slides a gaze at Aidan. He gives a slight nod, which Aoife notices. Her lips turn into a thin line and I wouldn't want to be that girl for all the pearls in the sea. Soon, we've bowls of soup in front of us; it smells rich and hearty, with beef and potatoes, leeks and carrots, cracked barley. I try to be ladylike, try not to eat too quickly, but I can see from Aoife's expression that I'm failing. I sit back, pause, let the liquid settle. I butter a slice of bread and take dainty bites of that when all I want to do is scoff it down then follow it with another and another.

When all the bowls are empty, the second course is served: rare roast beef, more potatoes (baked this time), a spiced kedgeree with eggs and haddock, roast pork with rice, pheasant pie, lark jelly, a selection of cheeses and more bread, this time in the form of white rolls, each made to look like roses in bloom. Aoife has a lemon-whiskey in front of her, Aidan red wine; Brigid and I have simple water with lemon (good for the complexion, but gods know I'd have preferred something stronger). When we are eating again, Aoife glowers at the servant.

'*You* may go,' she says, and the girl is smart enough to simply drop a curtsey and leave. The door closes behind her and Aoife waits a few moments, her hands stilled above her plate. When the sound of footsteps recedes, my grandmother glances at Aidan, who nods.

'Miren.'

'Yes, Grandmother?' I want to say *I know what you have planned* but I don't.

'You are aware, I know you are, of our parlous financial position.'

I merely nod.

'I met with the solicitor today' – *as if I didn't know, as if I wasn't meant to be there, as if she didn't lock me in my room* – 'and matters are even worse than I feared' – *as if she didn't know* exactly *what our position was* – 'Your grandfather had been hiding things from me. The last of the ships must be sold.'

Yes.

'The sale of the contents of the house *might* just make up the difference and keep creditors from hounding us.'

Yes.

'Your grandfather left you his share of Hob's Hallow, just as I shall. You are our sole heir, Miren.'

Yes – to whom else would you leave that crumbling pile?

'But I wish you to inherit more than a debt. Your cousin Aidan has offered another way.' She speaks as if this is all a foregone conclusion: her words suggest there is a choice, but her tone, oh, her tone! It is all business. *Miren, this is how it shall be, you have no choice in the matter.* She inclines her head towards our saviour.

Aidan pulls a small square box from his pocket. The wood is honey-coloured, the hinges and clasp golden. 'Miren, if you would do me the honour of becoming my wife, it would solve many problems.'

Now there's a proposal any girl would be happy to hear!

He flips open the box and the contents fair bulges out. It takes up all the room that is to be had inside. Against a bed of black velvet sits an enormous baroque pearl. It's creamy silver, shaped almost like a teardrop, and tiny rubies run around its base, set into the ornament itself so they look like drops of blood. All mounted on a thick band of silver engraved with scales, of course. He must have had this made especially.

Aidan rises and grasps my hand. He does not kneel, and I do not resist. He pushes the ring onto my heart finger. It lies heavy and cold. I do not speak and I do not look at him, and he does not wait for me to do so, but returns to his seat. He expects nothing, not even consent.

Across from me Brigid's face is like thunder. Can't she see I want no part of this? There'll be no help from her.

To my left, Aoife looks satisfied.

'There,' she says. 'It is done.'

Still I do not say a word, and they take my silence for acquiescence.

9

The air across the salt marshes is strangely foul, as if all the corpsewights are standing by the roadside to watch as we pass. But I can catch no sight of them. It seems unlikely besides, so something must have died in the reeds or even further out on the beach, an animal washed ashore and rotting.

Aoife and I have barely spoken since we left Breakwater, although periodically she reaches for my hand as I sit beside her and examines the ring with approval. It makes my finger feel like a lump of dead flesh, so heavy and cold it is. It's a tether, a chain. I don't say this to my grandmother. I don't snatch my limb back, for to do so would be to begin a battle I'm not yet sure how to win.

Across from us, on the other seat, on the lap of one of the two new maids, is the wicker basket I used to carry the account books, now replaced by a large parcel Brigid handed me as we climbed into the carriage. It's wrapped in brown paper and tied with a cream silk ribbon. She said, 'A gift to my soon-to-be sister,' and smiled, but her lips couldn't quite hold the shape. I'd left the quilt behind, but she ran down the stairs and pressed it upon me. It seemed I wasn't soon to be rid of it, but I was polite and gave my thanks.

I *will* burn it at home.

We have fresh staff as well: the maids and, above, are two lads to aid Malachi — must be crowded up there with the coachman, his boy and the two footmen (one handsome, the other extraordinarily plain). They are to begin the process of making Hob's Hallow suitable for Aidan and his bride, though the place belongs to the bride already, or at least to her grandmother. But the townhouse isn't a grand enough "seat", and so Aidan and Brigid will move out here.

I think about one of the footmen; he's not one of those who came to collect us a few days ago. He handed me into the carriage (Aidan did not bother to see us off, which was a relief, and Aoife did not care for she'd already got what she wanted) and when I looked at him I thought, yet again, how much I do not want to marry Aidan. The footman is tall, with sleek black hair, green eyes that tilt at the corners, lips cut into a perfect bow, cheekbones so sharp they'd slice your fingers if you stroked his face. He looked into my eyes and smiled, and I — I squeezed his hand.

'Take care on the step, Miss,' he said, and his voice was low as he squeezed back.

Aoife's been very careful to keep me away from any male I'm not related to — indeed, the cousins' visits are so few and far between that I've wondered sometimes if that's intentional too. Raised with only old men around me, but for short-lived tenants' sons, no one's who ever looked so handsome. Or at least not for a long while.

I think of the marks Aidan left on my wrist and wonder how much more pain he'll be wanting to inflict; what if I actually *do* something wrong? I press my lips together as my fingers heat up under another man's touch. The carriage won't return to the port-city immediately, not until the maids establish what needs to be bought and brought from Breakwater, then merchants and tradesfolk will be approached or sent and a new life will begin at Hob's Hallow.

'The wedding in a fortnight, I think.' Aoife's voice breaks me from my reverie.

'What?'

She lifts a brow.

'Pardon?' I say pointedly.

'Your wedding in a fortnight.'

'Oh. At the Hallow?' I speak as if I've got an interest in the event.

'Oh, it will never be ready by then. No, in Breakwater at the cathedral. A reception at… Aidan will know somewhere; someone will owe him a favour that can translate into a grand ballroom.'

'We don't know enough people to fill a grand ballroom, Grandmother.' A lot of those relatives who came for Óisín's funeral will still be on their way home – two weeks won't be enough to send invitations and get them to turn around.

'Aidan knows important people, all the fine society of Breakwater. Never fear, my girl, you'll not have a tiny wedding.' From her tone, she's thinking of her own marriage to Óisín in the chapel at the Hallow. She's thinking of my sixteen-year-old mother Isolde coming back from a wedding gods-know-where, her belly full of me, and my father trembling by her side as she asked they be taken in, all sins forgiven.

I'm not certain how much fine society is left in Breakwater since the advent of the Queen of Thieves, but I can see Aoife's got stars in her eyes; she's dreaming of the old days, or at least the ones she was told about as a child. How rich we were, how *significant*, how folk flocked to our doors to beg favours and be able to do them in return. I don't mention there's no dress for me to wear, and vainly hope this might stop the entire process.

'Imagine the look on Florrie's face!' Aoife fair cackles, but I can't resent that at least. Aunt Florence will indeed be a picture when she hears; it might even keel the old bat over at long last.

'Do you miss him?' I ask all of a sudden. Did they find a kind of love for each other at some point?

'Who?'

'Óisín!'

'*Grief is the black cat rubbing at your ankles, looking for attention,*' Grandma Aoife says, which is beautiful until she follows it with, '*Kick it enough times and it goes away.*'

I look at her for a long moment until she says, 'Mark my words, Miren, the O'Malleys are on the rise.'

We speak as if the maids aren't there, or they're deaf, and belatedly I flick them a glance. It doesn't matter anymore, Aoife's done her crowing. And the girls look as blank as slates.

* * *

'And what am I supposed to do with these?' Maura shouts. But she's eying the peacock-blue frock I'm wearing while she does it. A sure sign of change, a new dress. She's not noticed the ring as yet.

Aoife disappears up the staircase towards her rooms, waving a hand at me: *Deal with it.* The maids are standing in the entry hall, small holdalls at their feet, one hugging the wrapped quilt like it'll protect her from Maura and her grey-haired rage. Both are blonde and tiny, one plump, the other in need of a good feeding; both a little younger than I.

'Maura, Mr Fitzpatrick has sent these girls to work for us.'

Maura's wrinkled face freezes in horror. 'To replace me?'

'Of course not, you silly thing. For you to boss around. Go on. Surely it'll make a nice change from Malachi ignoring you – these two have to listen. Ciara' – the thin one bobs – 'and Yri' – the plump one copies her – 'you will obey Maura in all things, and if I hear that you've not then whatever's left of you after she's had her way, I will deal with. Understood?'

'Yes, Mrs Fitzpatrick.'

'Mrs Fitz…' Maura can't quite get the word out and I can see it's hit her like a blow.

I step close and steady her, say quietly, for I've no doubt the maids will be reporting back to either Brigid or Aidan, 'Not yet, Maura. Never fear.'

She notices the ring then and her eyes go wider still. When her quaking's lessened, I pat her shoulder, turn and take the parcel from the plump one, bundle it into Maura's hands. 'This is for you. Brigid made it.'

She smiles then. Maura's always had a soft spot for Brigid, was always kind when she came to stay. Besides, burning the thing seems a terrible waste when it's so very fine. Someone may as well get use of it and I like the idea of our old servant snuggling beneath all Brigid's hard work.

'Now, Maura, show them where they'll sleep, then set them tasks – probably cleaning their own rooms for a start.' I glance at the two boys, perhaps sixteen the pair of them. 'Where's Malachi?'

'Stables,' she grumbles, as if I should have known – and honestly, I should. Maura tears at the corner of the parcel until she can see the lovely fabric within. Her expression lightens and she smiles, not at me, but at the quilt.

'Right,' I say to the lads as I lead them back to the front door and out onto the stoop. 'That way, to the left, then left again and keep walking until you see a tumbledown building. That's the stables. There'll be an angry old man in it, probably smoking a pipe, and if he's not outside, he'll be in the upper rooms.' I can't recall a time when Malachi didn't sleep above the stables of his own choice. 'Tell him I sent you and he's to put you to good use. I'll check on you later.'

'Yes, Mrs—'

'Miss O'Malley,' I say sharply. 'Still O'Malley.'

'Yes, Miss!'

With the lads suitably terrified and scampering, I turn my attention to the piles of luggage that are being unloaded from the carriage. Having left Hob's Hallow with a single small case, I've returned with a trunk of items there's no one out here to see and appreciate. All the pretty things purchased by Aoife at the cost of my freedom. And Aoife herself has returned with two trunks – she found time after visiting the solicitor to return to Madame Franziska while I was locked in a room.

There are four men staring at me now; well, three men, one boy, though the coachman's not climbed down from his perch. He's not there to do heavy lifting and he wants everyone to know that; he's smoking a pipe, giving me a measuring stare. I say, 'Follow the lads around to the stables and settle in. Then find Maura in the kitchens; she'll show you where to sleep tonight.

Tomorrow she'll have a list of things we need and you can go back to Breakwater then.'

He nods, faces forward, flicks the reins and the black horses start. Next, I glance at the others, standing around with the trunks and a collection of small cases, a large crimson box tied with silver ribbon, the baskets of food Brigid had her kitchen prepare, as if we couldn't feed ourselves. I gesture to the coachman's lad (he's not exempted from this kind of labour, not yet anyway), and the potato-faced footman. 'You take that one between you, then return for the other.' I indicate one of Aoife's trunks, which I know is heavy enough with new dresses and shoes (far more than mine) to require two bodies. Next I point the green-eyed footman to my own trunk, which I know is light enough for one man: 'And you, take that one and follow me.'

I lead them inside the tower's foyer; I can feel eyes on my back and it makes me stand straighter. I'm taller than the lad and the potato-faced man by a head; the other man is a little taller than I. I can't work out if it's pride – well, I *know* it's pride, I'm an O'Malley after all – but pride in this decrepit mansion, the pride expected of the mistress of the house, pride in being a rich man's wife and saving this house from its fall? I don't know. I lift my head a little higher as we take the staircase that splits in two at the top. I point to the right, address the puffing footman and lad, 'That way. Go through the door and to the end of the East Wing. Madame O'Malley's rooms are there. Take all of her cases. Try not to get lost.'

'Yes, Miss,' they reply, smart enough not to venture a name.

I don't say anything to the green-eyed man, just crook my finger at him as the others move off. We head towards the door to the West Wing; only Óisín and Maura have slept in the tower for as long as I can remember. I stop, at last, at the entrance to my own suite, pause, breathe deeply, then lead the green-eyed man inside.

'Over there.' I indicate a spot by the window. Later on, I'll have one of the new girls unpack for me. I could do it myself now, but best not to get them thinking I'll do their job for them. I stand near the door, hand on the knob, watching as he carries the trunk to the designated spot and puts it down carefully.

'Anything else, Miss O'Malley?' he asks in a low voice.

'No.'

'There are other bags.'

'Yes.'

He comes towards me, but instead of leaving he puts his hand on mine and together we close the door. I think of everything Maura ever told me about what happens between men and women, women and women, men and men. All the things Aoife didn't mention, all the things she'd done, such terrible things to avoid me learning (poor Mrs O'Meara and her lovely boy). The idea of Aidan being the first to do *this* to me is unbearable.

My bright blue skirts froth between us, him pushing into me again and again, tongue and cock. And he's staring into my face as if he's never seen anything like me (and before this morning, to be fair, he had not). My back's against the stone of the fireplace and I can feel the fabric of my new dress tearing and won't Aoife be cross (and more than cross if she discovers us)? And *I'm* tearing and I don't care and there's nothing but this flame inside me and what will Aidan think to find he's not the first to plough this particular field? It won't matter. And won't

Aoife be angry to know that despite all her precautions, all her keeping me out here at the Hallow with no company, despite her dreadful sharp eye, I'm just like my mother?

* * *

When he's gone – and it's not long after we've finished, which suits me fine as there's luggage to be lugged and what I wanted has been acquired – and I'm lying languidly on the bed, I remember the letters.

Feeling the heat of him cooling on my skin, I pull the bundle out from beneath the mattress. The ribbon is tied so tightly that I have to use Óisín's mother-of-pearl-handled knife to slice it. I unfold the first; the paper is onion-skin thin and cheap, the ink almost bleeding through to the other side. The letter is brief:

Father, Do not look for us. I know we have stolen from you, but we have left our child as a surety. We have honoured the agreement with Mother in spirit if not entirely in deed. Let Miren be the price between us.

And it is signed *Isolde*.

10

'You must have children, Miren, as soon as you can.'

In the library, Aoife's walking back and forth on the rug in front of the hearth. It's early in the morning but she looks like she's been here for hours, pacing and plotting; her hair's still damp from a morning swim. There's a fire crackling, neatly laid and lit, no doubt the work of either Ciara or Yri. And the shelves have been dusted, too, freed of a decade or more of gilings; the lacy coverings on the backs of the armchairs have been changed, furniture polished so I can see my face in surfaces as I move past. Whatever else I might think of Brigid, she's chosen good domestics. The only thing not cleaned is the ceiling, too high for the girls to reach.

'Three,' Aoife says on the turn. 'Three's a good beginning. Maura will need to start you on a course of herbs, make sure your womb is welcoming.' She pauses mid-stride. 'Whatever else your father was, at least he wasn't an O'Malley. Fresh blood for the line. Myself, your mother, no… but you all new and untouched.'

I almost laugh at that. *Touched rather more than you know, Grandmother.*

'That's got to help.' She says this last almost to herself, then repeats, 'Three.'

I reply as if it's an enchantment to be completed, 'One for the house, one for the Church and one for the sea.' I thought this was over; I thought this way was old and almost past, that it needed only Aoife's death for it, too, to die.

She laughs. 'And more after that besides! As many as you can.' She points to a large crimson box on the desk by the window, the one I noticed on our arrival yesterday. 'That's for you. Open it. Open it!'

She still hasn't looked at me. In my pocket I can feel the letters I read last night, weighing more than they should. My eyes feel gritty and sore; I know they are red from all the weeping I did, and not even Maura's eyebright tincture can fix that. I can feel the burn of anger low in my belly, too, but I try to keep it tamped down for I know if I lose my temper now, I'll never get it back. When you're angry all logic, all reason, flies out the window, and shouting, as Óisín was fond of saying wisely, achieves nothing – which was amusing considering how many of his discussions with Aoife were conducted at spiteful volume. But the less I say, the more Aoife will offer... I learned about silence from her, although she doesn't seem to recall its lessons now, not when she's gloating so.

But I *do* want to shout, gods know I do. I want to shout and scream and throw things at her that will break her brittle old bones. I want to tell her that for all she rages about my mother, Isolde was no better than her; Isolde who used me as currency to pay for her own escape, just as Aoife will use me to pay for her own grand schemes. I want to tell my grandmother what I think of her, that I'll do whatever I can to ruin her plans, that I will never marry Aidan Fitzpatrick let alone bed him. But I don't.

Instead I go to the desk, carefully untie the silver ribbon holding the box closed, slip the lid off.

A spray of swan-white spills out.

The fifth dress.

'Radzimir!' says Aoife with satisfaction as she joins me. 'Hard to find not in black, but here it is. Lightened your cousin's wallet considerably. Take it out! It should fit perfectly – it's the same style as the red and black. Madame Franziska and her minions stayed up all night finishing it!'

Mourning silk for my wedding gown. How appropriate.

She's fair giddy, is Aoife, with all her successes. If she had any less dignity, she'd be dancing. How sad that she's so happy to make me so miserable; that the sale of her only grandchild is such a delight. I don't touch the dress, though it seems pretty; teardrop-shaped crystals sewn onto the bodice catch the light, and I can see feathers – swans', no doubt – and roses have been embroidered across the fabric, all in white silk thread.

'Why did you tell me,' I ask, 'that my parents were dead?'

'Because they are.' She runs a finger along a stitched rose stem. 'They took a fever when you were three, you know this. You were ill too, but you were the only one we could save.'

'No.'

'What's wrong with you, child?'

'Isolde wrote letters to Óisín.' I can almost feel her shake as if hit. 'After they had left me behind. After they had stolen something from you.'

I peer at her. She's looking at me for the first time since I entered the room, *properly* looking. Does she notice the shadows beneath my eyes from the sleepless night, the tautness in my

99

cheeks, the lines on my forehead, the bruised red of my lips where the footman kissed me hard? Can she divine, simply by staring, what he did to me, all at my will? Do I look angry to her or just ruined? And is she simply trying to calculate how she might still win?

'What did she say?'

'Enough.' I'm not a fool, I won't offer her information she can use. Didn't she teach me better than that?

'Your mother... your mother... Isolde...' Aoife sinks into one of the chairs by the fire, all her manic energy fled. I sit across from her. She shakes her head, closes her eyes. 'Your mother...'

I wait.

Then her eyes fly open and they're nothing more than black pits and her lips draw back over teeth longer than they should be, yellowed like a dog's, and silver tendrils of hair appear to come free of the chignon tight-bound at the back of her head. And I know these things do not happen, but they seem to and these are the details I notice, and then she begins to rage.

'Your mother was a disobedient whore! She cared nothing for this family and what we – I – did for her! She ran away and got pregnant, then came crawling back and Óisín forgave her like the weakling he was. Let her and that cullion live in this house as if nothing had happened, and then to show her gratitude she stole from us!'

'What did they take?' It's all I can do to keep my voice steady in the face of her fury. But she's not to be diverted from her course.

'And they left you. And you, Miren, were a price to be paid. You are mine to do with as I wish and you *will* marry Aidan and you *will* save this family and you *will* make good on your mother's debt!'

'He wants to hurt me,' I say, and lift my hand, draw back the cuff of the yellow dress, show her the marks Aidan left.

She tilts her head, hesitates, then says, 'You just need to learn how to manage him, Miren, that's all. Don't be such a child. This isn't about you or your whims, this is about the O'Malleys, about saving the family, building us up again, making us count for something.' Her voice goes quiet and she reaches out as if I might take her hand as a gesture of accord or peace or submission at the very least. I do not, and her tone becomes a winter wind. 'You will marry him, Miren, you will have his children and you will dispose of them as you are *ordered*.'

And she doesn't seem to realise she's just used up her last chance.

'I'll not marry him, Grandmother, make no mistake.' I rise and go to the door.

'You'll do what you're told!' Her voice reaches me as I touch the handle, and it's filled again with all of Aoife's fire and spite. 'You'll do it or so help me I'll throw you in the sea myself!'

'Just like you used to when you taught me to swim, and I survived that.'

I leave the library. Something thuds against the door as I close it behind me and I've no doubt she'll have thrown a book or whatever she could get her hands on. I must flee. I'll need money if nothing else; the ring on my finger will fetch a goodly sum, and the earrings and bracelets, but I doubt I can sell any of them in Breakwater. Someone might recognise them – especially the engagement piece – might report me to Aidan before I can vanish.

I cannot take a ship, for I'd be easy to trace on a passenger list, but I need to get as far away as I can. I remember Aoife locking me in that room in the townhouse; I can't rely on my own grandmother. So I go to the one person who might make me feel safe for a while.

* * *

But I can't find Maura in the kitchen. One of the new girls is there – for a moment I'm still so jumbled from the argument with Aoife that I cannot remember which one she is, then recall that Ciara is thin, Yri plump. Aoife's always said it doesn't matter what you call servants, but Maura and Óisín taught me different: Óisín said it made people think you cared, Maura said it was a kindness and a respect.

'Where's Maura, Ciara?'

She bobs a curtsey, pausing in the middle of preparing a breakfast that I can't imagine eating. 'Still in her bed, Miss. She was asleep, tossing and turning; she didn't seem well, so I made her a posset and left her to slumber.'

'Are you making a list?'

'Yes, Miss.' She points to a sheet of rough paper on the bench, held down by the stub of a pencil and some tidily printed words.

'Excellent.' I turn to leave.

'Are you alright, Miss?'

'Yes, thank you, Ciara.' I smile distractedly at her.

Maura's room is in the attic of the tower (the floor above Óisín's old suite), up where one is meant to store one's servants. It's surprisingly cold there. I'm puffing a little when I reach the landing, pause to catch my breath, thinking how the old woman must feel as she does this climb every eve – I think she must be moved down to one of the ground-floor rooms, whether she wishes it or not, then I realise that I won't be there to oversee it. I walk along the narrow corridor. Two doors are open, displaying neatly made beds with small tapestry bags at their foot. The maids have settled in.

I knock on the last door, Maura's, and get no answer. My hesitation is brief and I push it to, and heat puffs out. It's the largest room here, yet still smaller than my suite by quite some margin. But there's a biggish bed, two chests of drawers, a wardrobe, a small desk, a washstand and a blanket box, and I cannot imagine what Maura would have to store in all those things. Then again, this is a huge house; it's old and so is she: she's been its curator for so long I've no doubt she's squirreled things away that caught her eye. Things no one would notice missing.

And why shouldn't she?

Does that cavalier attitude to theft come from the fact that my mother's a thief?

But Maura.

Maura's never sick.

Not even when anyone else has been sick and she's nursed them. She never catches anything, has never spent a moment longer in her bed than she had to, and even as her ability to take care of the house has faded with her physical deterioration, she's still never stopped doing it. The quality has only lessened in line with the degree that she can no longer reach high shelves or low, can't quite see the dust enough to remove it, and the house is too big, her energy too much on the wane.

But now, here's Maura still abed at eight in the morning.

There's a fire in the hearth and the space is overheated. All I can see from the threshold is the snowy quilt Brigid gave me, but as I get closer I notice there are spots on it, up the top edge nearest her face. Some are the dark red of dried blood, some bright and new; and Maura's gasping, eyes closed, a rattle in her chest, a whistle in her throat. I wonder how much of this was there when Ciara came? It would have been very dark, then, easy to miss, and there is more new blood than old so this is a recent thing. The posset is on the bedside table and I can see the pink spot where blood has been expectorated there and almost disappeared.

'Maura!'

She can only puff at me; her eyes are wide open now, face pale and scared. Her fingers are clenched over the edge of the quilt and it's like she's trying to push it off but hasn't the strength... then I realise that's exactly what she's trying to do.

And I can smell something, too, something cloying. I sniff closely at the quilt and the scent is coming from there. Almost... honeysuckle sweet, jasmine sweet – something I couldn't smell before, something not activated until a slumbering body's warmth was present.

Wild woodbine, if administered incorrectly, will cause paralysis... but she hasn't, I don't believe, taken it orally. Maura knows better. So...

I tear away the quilt, throw it as far from the bed as possible, and the old woman sits straight up like a jack-in-the-box, gasping and heaving and trying to get swear words out and air in.

'That fecking thing! That fecking, fecking thing!'

'Oh, Maura. Maura, are you alright?'

'Do I look alright?' She coughs again, but the tone of it has changed, is nowhere near as rough and wheezy. As dire. 'Why would you give me such a thing?'

'I'm so sorry. It was a gift from…'

Brigid.

Brigid.

Brigid who's so clever with her hands. Brigid who made this fine present. Brigid who most definitely is not happy about me marrying her brother. The time of great magics may well be gone but there is still harm that can be done with no more than intent and a spell by anyone with the mind to do so. No need for a proper witch or the blood of one, just ill-wishing and determination.

'Brigid.' I wipe blood away from Maura's mouth and chin with the corner of a sheet. 'She meant that for me.'

'Little bitch.' The front of Maura's white nightgown is speckled red. 'Mind you, it's well-made.'

I laugh at that.

'I didn't feel anything until I tried to get out of bed. Imagine that, a good night's sleep before you die.'

'How considerate.' I plump pillows and put a few behind her back. There's a jug of water next to the posset and I pour her a glass. 'Did she want to kill me, do you think?'

'I don't know, my girl. But… someone would have come looking for you sooner than you came for me.' She shakes her head. 'Fool I am, to be taken by something so simple.'

And I feel guilty, though that's not her intention, she's merely stating the truth. I fought with Aoife so I came looking for Maura because I needed her. I did things out of my usual routine. Otherwise… otherwise I'd have found her too late.

'Did she just want me ill? Was it a warning? Or just the start?' I hold Maura's hand; it's so light and bony, dotted with age spots and dried blood, though it's hard to tell the difference.

We both look at the quilt, lying on the floor like a snake. It is, I think, something to show Aoife. If that doesn't give her a second thought about this marriage, I don't know what will. I could run. I *should* run. Now. But… if this is what Brigid wanted to do to me, what might she try with Aoife, who's pushing her plans to fruition no matter what the objections? I squeeze Maura's fingers.

'Will you be alright?' I ask.

She nods.

'I'll send up one of the girls to get you washed and comfortable. Stay in bed as long as you want, Maura. I'll see you're looked after.' I rise and pick up the quilt, carefully folding it, then I wrap it in an old blanket that's draped on the chair, probably the one she replaced with it on the bed. There's a chest at the end of the bed and I rummage around in it for another rug to cover her. At the door, I turn, remembering why I came up here. I say, 'Maura, did you know my mother was alive?'

Her shamefaced expression tells me. I don't ask why she didn't let me know. I'm not angry with her, but I feel so hollow you could make a drum of me.

Downstairs, I go into the kitchen garden where I've spent so much time with Maura; I pick cat's claw and rosemary to make a tea that will take down any inflammation in her throat. I send Ciara with it, to care for the old woman.

I seek my grandmother, starting in the breakfast room where Ciara has laid out the meal we should have had. No sign of Aoife, but I find I'm starving. I sit and eat porridge and toast, drink two cups of strong coffee, organising my thoughts, practising what I will say and how. Speaking aloud so that my tone sounds reasonable. But really I'm just putting off the inevitable. Eventually, I push away from the table.

Outside a storm begins to rage and howl, blown up from the sea and wild as can be. I try the library just in case she's remained there fuming since our argument, but it's silent. Next her suite in the East Wing, and then all the vacant rooms in there, for naught. And so back to the tower and its empty spaces, even Óisín's old bedchamber and his study. At last, I try the West Wing. I get tired of carrying the quilt so I leave it in my bedroom. I search the parlours which have been unused for years, the storage rooms and dressing rooms, the bathrooms and privies, the sewing room, the grand hall, the dining rooms both large and small, and the chapel.

I even go down into the cellar, the place that was forbidden for so long – though the silver locks on the door have not ever been engaged as I recall, and I briefly snuck in there once as a child before Aoife discovered me and spanked me until my arse felt on fire. But there's nothing there; the space remains huge and dark and the light of my lantern does not reach into all its corners. When I peer into the well, all I can see is the blackness of water at the bottom, and the rippling silver of the grid beneath it. It smells of dust and old fish and ancient blood and bones.

In the end I go outside.

It's after lunch by the time the storm has passed, though the sky remains grey. I'm not worried – if Aoife doesn't want to be found, she won't be. She's more than capable and childish enough to be stalking along behind me as I search for her. I walk through the freshly washed grounds towards the walled garden

I know she likes, where she often sits and schemes. I will tell her about the quilt, show her when we return to the house. I have other questions and I will ask them. And tonight, no matter what, I will leave this house before she locks me in it until my wedding day.

I come to the heavy iron-banded entrance to Aoife's garden. The door is ajar and I push through. The area is not large, but it is overgrown with winding paths, so there's no straight line of sight and you must follow the moss-covered flags as if walking a labyrinth. I duck beneath low-hanging branches heavy with rain, smell the competing scents of roses and jasmine. Malachi keeps this place for her, not tamed, and certainly not tidy, but merely 'at bay'. A wildness she likes that is managed by another.

At last I come to the corner where there's a wooden bench, worn smooth by the years of her skirts and the elements against it. There's a small table with drawers underneath where she leaves a book and a silver flask of whiskey. For a moment, I think she's asleep, and I call out softly so she isn't startled. But she doesn't rouse and, as I get closer, I realise there's no movement of her chest, no twitching of her nostrils as air goes in and out.

I lean over Aoife and stare into her face, dotted as it is with rain, her dress and hair soaked through.

All the tension of life, everything that kept her still lovely and vibrant is gone, and it's as though the flesh is simply waiting a decent amount of time to fall off her bones. The high neck of her dress looks crinkled, her hair is tumbling down from its careful chignon, but her eyes are closed and I suppose this is what peace looks like. I have no tears, but my heart feels like it's twisted itself into a ball and is clenching tighter, ever tighter.

I pick her up and she's ridiculously light, as if it was only her spirit that weighted her to earth… and I think about that storm, the madness and grief of it, and I realise it was for her death. For the last true O'Malley. I carry her from the garden, across the lawns, back towards the house. She's almost weightless, like twigs wrapped in a blanket. She's dead, taking all my answers with her.

11

We lay Aoife out on her bed and Yri assists me to strip away the wet black mourning gown and underclothes. Ciara is still sitting with Maura and I don't want the old woman told of this just yet for she'll insist on helping when she's too weak. I wipe my grandmother's body down with a damp cloth soaked in lavender, as much to calm her spirit as for the sweet scent. On her right hip is the scar, her brand, the Janus-faced, two-tailed mermaid, the first child's mark. I touch it lightly before I draw up a sheet to cover her and the one on my own hip seems to burn.

Yri is standing limp and useless. I tell her to bring me the big crimson box from the library desk where I left it this morning. She goes with relief. I wonder if she's ever seen death before; so soon to join a household, a fresh start, to be faced with this.

I draw up a chair to sit beside Aoife. I hold her hand and contemplate how I feel, how I *should* feel, how I *do* feel. Grief-stricken, sad, but still so angry – I can't deny that. Angry at Aoife and my mother, at Maura and Malachi and Óisín, who all knew Isolde had left me behind. That she lived still. My grandparents were pillars of my existence. Pillars are strong, if cold and hard; they are at least a support. I had – have – Maura for kindness and affection; Malachi for gruff gentleness. While it would have been nice to find strength and love in my grandmother, at least they weren't entirely missing from my upbringing. I look at her hand lying in my own: long fingers, pale skin, blue veins, only one or two liver spots, neat nails. I remember her holding me as a child; I remember her carrying me to the cliffs and showing me the sea, telling me to listen to its song, that we belong to it, and it to us. Then I remember her taking me to the rocks below and throwing me in. She was willing to sell me to regain a fortune. But I loved her because children always seek something to love, and I'll miss her nonetheless.

Still, I whisper, *I'm free* to her.

I look at her face and it's strange to see her without that avid *want* she always wore, without her eyes bright as they sought opportunities, weaknesses to exploit in no matter whom or which situation. Her lashes are long, like feathers on her cheek. I'll not see those dark eyes opened again.

Then I notice her neck.

The marks that weren't there ten minutes ago when we undressed her are now clear as day beneath the ship's bell necklace she wears that mirrors my own. In and around the delicate dip in her throat I can see oval bruises, as if thumbs were pressed there; around the sides are lines, like fingers applied too hard to gain leverage. And the shape of a bell, too, quite distinct where the pendant was pushed hard against her. They get darker and darker, those marks, as I watch until they're the purple of a blood blister. I'm reaching out to touch them when the hand in mine convulses and grabs at me and Aoife's neat nails dig into my skin.

I throw myself backwards with a shriek, tumble from the

chair and across the floor until I fetch up against the legs of her dressing table. A gasp comes from the door, and there's Yri, clutching the big red box in front of her, mouth and eyes wide.

'Did you see?' I shout, trying to expel all the fear from my chest along with the air in my lungs. 'Did you see her move?'

The girl nods.

I roll onto my hands and knees, then use the table to haul myself up. When I think my legs will bear me, I move towards Aoife and Yri takes tiny steps from the doorway until we meet at the bedside. Even as we watch, the bruises on my grandmother's neck are fading, fading, fading. Her eyes remain closed; the hand that grasped at me is hanging over the side of the mattress with that lack of tension only the dead can achieve.

'Did you see *that*?' I ask, and she nods again, but I must be sure. 'The marks on her throat – them. Did you see them?'

'Yes, Miss,' she replies in a trembling voice. 'Yes, I did. And saw them go too. What does it mean, Miss?'

I shake my head. 'I don't know. I don't know.'

I've heard tell how a murdered corpse will bleed from the eyes, ears and mouth if the killer comes close by, but there's no crimson on Aoife, she might as well be bloodless; I've heard of bodies turning to wights before their funeral and running away lest they be put in the earth; I've heard, even, of those buried when they appeared lifeless, yet sounds were heard from their graves days or weeks later. When at last someone gathered the courage to investigate, to dig them up, they found folk who'd woken from whatever deathly slumber they'd fallen into in a box that couldn't be opened for love nor money nor with any amount of prayer. And they were always dead by the time they were

112

reached, even those rich enough to be buried in an aboveground crypt, for the shock of it was enough to carry them off.

But this?

This thing I – *we* – have just witnessed?

Oh no. I've never heard of its like before.

Yri's shaking so much I can hear the box rattling. I take her arm gently, though it is an effort; instinctively I want to panic, I want to squeeze hard to feel something human, solid, *living*. To wipe away the sense on my palm of having touched something unnatural, something I'll never be able to wash away. It didn't matter when Aoife was just *expired*... but...

'Yri, you cannot tell anyone about this. I don't know what it means, but... you cannot tell anyone. Whatever was done to her... someone thinks they can get away with it. If anyone knows what we saw, neither of us will be safe,' I say. 'Do you understand?'

Her eyes double in size, then I wonder if she thinks I had something to do with Aoife's death. Who heard us arguing this morning? Anyone?

Yri nods slowly. 'Will you tell Mr Fitzpatrick?'

'Of course. Send... no, it's too late in the day, I don't want anyone being caught near the salt marshes in the darkness. As soon as dawn breaks tomorrow, we'll send one of the footmen. But for now... help me with her, Yri.'

She trembles even more as I take the box from her, and shake out the mermaid-tailed wedding dress. It's mean, I know, but there's some small satisfaction in this act. Yri has such tremors in her fingers she's barely any use at all as I dress Aoife in the gown she intended for my sale. A wise woman, perhaps, would not be doing this, not after what she'd already experienced, with the threat of her grandmother becoming a heavy ghost. But if I were wise, I'd have fled when I had the chance. I'd have run away from Breakwater early that morning before the merfolk tried to drown me; I'd not have returned to the townhouse and foolishly believed my grandmother had my best interests at heart. I'd have stuffed my pockets with the shiny new jewellery and I'd have run before anyone thought to look for me. But now… now she's dead and I'm free. The bargain she made with Aidan is broken.

When Aoife is properly attired — the dress is a little tight but it hardly matters, she's not in a position to complain and soon enough there'll be less of her — I brush her hair until it lies like an argent stream over one shoulder, reaching down past her waist.

'Will… will… will…' Yri tries to get the sentence to form.

'I'll stay with her, I won't make you. You've seen enough. But go and get Malachi for me.'

When she's gone, I lean over Aoife, smoothing the bodice, stroking the sleeves, and I whisper meanly, 'It was to be *your* wedding anyway. This suits you best.'

* * *

The grandfather clock in the corner chimes eight, and Malachi sits on the other side of the bed from me, puffing on the red-gold meerschaum pipe that used to be Óisín's.

I thought he'd be nodding by now – we've been sitting for hours – but he's alert, just very still. He blinks every so often, breathing surprisingly quiet. His hair is the same iron-grey as Maura's and you can see her in the cast of his face; there's granite-coloured stubble on his cheeks and chin, but he's clean-shaven every morning. He rises early and is asleep mostly before seven rings at night. He told me, once, that's what happens when you're old: your bones want to sleep but your mind won't have any of it except at the most inconvenient times because it knows you're just pacing out your days unto death.

Malachi was married when he was younger, but Caitlin died in childbirth along with their daughter. Maura says he was never the same (and that's when he moved into the big room above the stables), but that's what people say, I think, when they get tired of another's grief. Maura's been impatient with him for as long as I've known them, and he's been the way he is all my life; I've nothing to compare it to so I cannot tell if she's exaggerating or not.

'Did you know my mother?' I ask, which is a stupid question because of course he did, living his life at Hob's Hallow man and boy. What I mean is *Did you know she was alive?* But that's equally stupid because if Maura knew then so did he.

He gives me a glance and gods know it's one he might have learned from Aoife. 'I know she's not dead.'

'Why didn't anyone tell me?' And to my annoyance, I sound like a wounded child.

'Did you ever go against your grandmother? Not your little defiances. In any way that counted?' His grey brows rise and he looks amused.

I think of the wedding dress Aoife now wears like a dead bride; I think of my refusal to marry Aidan; I think of my stolen secret, the letters beneath my mattress once again; I think of my plans to run, so easily derailed.

'No.'

115

'Aye. *No*. If we'd told you we'd have been turned out of the home we've lived in since before you were born, missy.' He nods. 'She was afraid, I think, that if you knew you'd want to follow them. If you thought there was an escape.'

'Did she know where they went?'

He laughs. 'If she did, do you think she wouldn't have had your mother dragged back here and your father drowned in the nearest body of water? No, she didn't know.'

Isolde wrote to Óisín alone, but she still didn't tell him where she was.

'Your mother… your grandmother had her plans and your mother had hers and they were never going to fit together. Isolde ran away then came back with that pretty boy in tow. He just followed her along like a pup that couldn't believe its luck.'

I think about the last letter from Isolde, three years after she left me, so twelve years ago:

Father,
We are settled, we are established. The silver mine is seeded and working, and she is once again producing. The estate is called Blackwater, north of Bellsholm, more or less, and I think it would make you proud to see it. I wanted you to know that I am safe. I shall not write again.
    Isolde

Óisín knew she yet lived but he told no one. My parents have money – had it *then* – yet she did not offer to send any relief; did not ask after me. Óisín didn't write to beg aid – and how could he? She gives no address – but then it's not as if she didn't

116

know the state of the O'Malleys when she fled. When she stole whatever she did and left me behind in place of a payment. If only she'd sent something, I wouldn't have been sold to Aidan. Aoife would have had her fortune; she'd not have thought to match me with him. Or would she? She always had plans, and if she'd had money, she'd have been in a better position to negotiate with him.

'She'd have done anything, wouldn't she? Aoife?' I ask, and there's a catch in my voice. I don't know why I expected her to have loved me more than she did or at least more than her plots and plans. I touch my necklace, play with the bell, hear the gentle noise of its tongue against the body, dulled by my fingers.

'Ah, missy. Your grandmother... Most people give back to the world the same treatment they received. Aoife was used as a bargaining chip by her parents and she wasn't of a mind to deal with you or Isolde any differently.'

'Her? What happened to her?' I laugh, thinking I know everything about her.

He pauses, hesitates so long I suspect he's fallen back to his usual taciturnity. This is, in fairness, the longest conversation I can ever recall having with Malachi. Even when he taught me to ride horses, how to groom them, he was economical with his speech. Then he says, 'They made her marry her brother.'

'What?' It's like he's slapped me. 'What?!'

'Óisín. He was her own brother. O'Malleys haven't answered to anyone for the longest time, missy. Their parents thought there'd be another child, that there'd be a third and the pact could be honoured again. The mother was pregnant, and they sent Óisín off to a monastery near Lodellan to learn his craft, to be the tithe to the Church. I think they hoped he'd return as a bishop for Breakwater… but Saorla miscarried again and again and by the time Aoife was eighteen there was no longer any hope of another child, so… the parents sent for Óisín. They thought… they thought brother and sister would strengthen the bloodline.'

I stare at Aoife's calm face, willing her to wake, to answer all my questions, to hear an apology that's not mine to make. But she's gone and I know she won't be back; there'll be no more signs or wonders or horrors from my grandmother.

'She was bought and sold. Her parents failed to lift the O'Malleys again, when there'd been so much hope. Any wonder she was obsessed with succeeding when her whole life had been consecrated to it and warped out of true? Who was to gainsay her? And Óisín, gentle boy raised by god-hounds? Who was he to defy such a sister? Some folk make a point of not visiting pain on others when it's been done to them; most people, though, think it's their due to inflict a little of their own agony. Aoife was no better than anyone else.'

I look at him, and he continues.

'Any wonder she was determined you'd be the instrument of salvation? Marry you off, take your children, dispose of them in the old way? Feed the sea its due, get your fortunes back? See the O'Malleys great again? What's the cost of that against your little life, your happiness? Still and all, it's hard to forgive a graceless heart.'

The lads from Breakwater would have told him why they were there. Maura would have told him about the upcoming marriage. And I wonder at the finger marks on Aoife's neck. I wonder that Malachi was the one who kept the garden for her.

That he would have known where she was. And I wonder how much he hated and loved her. I wonder if there's still enough strength in his gnarled old hands to have made those marks and if her final success was the last straw.

Then he leans forward as if he can hear my thoughts, 'I'd never have hurt her, missy. For all she could be hard, when my wife and child died, she was kind. For a long while I drank a lot and wouldn't allow anyone close. When your grandfather grew tired of me, Aoife was the one who intervened, told him that a life blown off course needed as much time as it needed to find its way again, but that I would. And I did.' He sits back. 'She could be awful, as you know, she was as wilful as the storm, but she did have kindness in her and sometimes she let it out. Mostly, though, she was so concerned with rebuilding, saving what was slipping away because that was the burden her parents passed on. It marked her like a map and she couldn't ever see beyond the lines of that landscape.' He draws on the pipe, a cloud of blue smoke encircles his head. 'Very few people are entirely good or bad, missy, but some ignore the calling of one or the other better than the rest of us.'

I'm silent for a long moment. A tear creeps down my cheek, but my voice is steady when I say, 'Thank you, Malachi.'

Then he points the pipe at me; I rise and open one of the windows to let fresh air in. 'There's one more thing you need to know about your mother, missy. Everyone loved her, even Aoife. Loved her a great deal. She was your grandmother's greatest hope.'

'Did Aoife's heart break when Isolde ran?' I think of her rage whenever my mother was mentioned.

He nods. 'Perhaps, but more than anything your grandmother didn't like being defied. I could tell you many things about your mother, but only one is of use to you: she was a witch. A proper one, one with magic running in her blood – nothing like Maura and her little rites; she's not a true witch by any stretch. Proper witches need no props, just their will.'

I sit back in my chair.

'No one knew, not really. Not beyond us, the family. But Maura, damn her, saw it, taught the girl herbcraft and more and Isolde took to it. Maura just makes her tonics and tisanes for health; Isolde experimented. You don't need much more than intent and ingredients to do small spells, but when a woman is born with magic in her veins? Then she can really make things happen. That was your mother. She could call storms, had a talent for making things big or small, and that's hard graft; she could enchant almost anyone she set her mind at – even Aoife wasn't proof against her, although she was the strongest. Charming can be a tricky thing, not everyone succumbs, and even those who do sometimes figure something's not quite right... and they get resentful, suspecting their will's not their own. And Isolde, thank the gods, wasn't mean-spirited, but she'd touch your hand and you'd be the happiest you ever were in your life, you'd swear devotion to her and it took some time for that to wear off. She was mostly sweet, mostly kind, she thought the magic was a plaything. But, missy, your mother was a witch and she could bend others to her will – and that will was as powerful as Aoife's.'

My mother was a witch and she left me behind, like a kitten in a barn; no better a mother than a cat.

12

It's early afternoon when Aidan arrives riding a fine black stallion. I sent the potato-faced footman with a message as soon as the sun rose. Behind him comes a cart containing an ebony wood coffin with gold fittings. A priest — the same one who mumbled over Óisín — sits beside the driver, looking miserable. Poor man: two visits to Hob's Hallow in such quick succession! As if consecrating two O'Malleys will see him damned. Who knows, it just might.

Aidan dismounts, throws the reins to one of the stableboys as if there's no doubt they'll be caught. The lad's nervous and pale, but he manages, then leads the beast away. Aidan comes towards me and takes my hand, says, 'I'm so sorry for your loss, Miren.'

'Yes.'

'So soon to be bereaved again.'

'Yes.'

'Well, I do hope this is fine enough for her.' He gestures to the death-bed, which is very fine indeed, so highly polished I can see my face in it. He's sourced it very quickly, has Aidan, but then again, for a man of his wealth I doubt there's much waiting for anything. I've changed into another made-over hand-me-down mourning gown, so plain that even the jet buttons don't stand out against the black fustian; I had to take it from Aoife's closet. My hair's pulled back in a tight bun and there's no makeup on my face. I don't look like a bride, at least not a joyful one. The ring on my finger still feels like a stone – I don't really know why it remains there, only that somehow it felt like it needed to stay for a while at least, until I'm done with *him* forever.

He lets my fingers go, then, and I can't suppress a shudder, thinking of the night at the theatre, his hand around my wrist, squeezing. He was drinking, his self-control was low, and he showed his true self too readily: that the hurt was for his pleasure and also to punish me for whatever bargain Aoife had driven him to, whatever high price she managed to extract. She'd made him feel like a boy, a powerless boy, I've no doubt, and he was going to get his money's worth of revenge on me in whatever shape he could. Well, without Aoife's will and determination, there is no deal. Soon, this will all be over.

'Come in,' I say and turn around, do not check to see if he follows. As I take the steps I feel the weight of Óisín's penknife in my pocket, tap-tap-tapping against my thigh.

* * *

The funeral is small and quick, and I think how annoyed Aoife would be to have so few witnesses. She'd have wanted us to wait, to recall all the mourners who came to see Óisín off. Yet there's just Aidan and I, Maura and Malachi, Ciara and Yri, the stable lads, the cartman and the potato-faced footman. No one's seen the green-eyed footman since… well, no one can recall, and I confess I'd not looked for him after I'd had my use of him. Aidan, the footman, the biggest of the lads and I carry Aoife a'down, though Malachi protests. I tell him that this is my duty, but truly I don't trust him on the stone stairs in the gloom.

The priest goes ahead of us holding a lit torch and we follow him slowly. The coffin is heavy, but though there's only four of us for this office, Aoife's so light she barely makes it worse. This is my first time here – where I thought my parents rested – and I find I'm holding my breath. There are niches cut into the walls not so far down but there's nothing in them but wooden boxes: well-made to stay intact, to keep the dead beneath.

The flickering flame makes every bit of darkness come alive. The steps stop abruptly, or abruptly for me because I'm looking around like a child, trying to take in every detail. I'm not afraid, but didn't I see my own grandmother rise from her death, however briefly? What could be worse? Again the walls are lined with niches. At the foot of the far wall is another set of steps, leading further down, down where Óisín was laid not so very long ago. In the centre of this first chamber is a bier made of stone with engravings along its sides. If you slid the lid off, there'd be another coffin in there, one of the first O'Malleys. Aidan tries to move forward, to head towards the next set of stairs, but my feet are planted.

'No,' I say, and I don't care if he thinks me hysterical and overcome with grief; my voice has certainly gone higher than its natural wont. I indicate the bier. 'Here.'

Because I don't want her lying beside Óisín. I don't want her forced to lie unwillingly beside him for an eternity, because wasn't a lifetime long enough? Let Aoife rest up here, above the first of us, the last queen the O'Malleys will ever see.

Aidan chooses not to argue with me, not here in the almost-dark, not in front of servants or witnesses. But his expression

123

tells me he's adding this to a list of things to be corrected; that he'll have the crypt reopened when he's here as lord and master and have the old woman moved to her proper place – the one *he's* chosen for her. He nods to the others and we all give a little heave to get the death-bed onto the flat surface, then angle it into place so there's minimal scraping and pushing. The lad struggles but does well and I pat his shoulder then shoo him up the stairs. He goes gladly, followed swiftly by the footman and Aidan.

I take a moment longer, looking around, aware of the priest's gaze on me. I put my hand on the box and think, *Here is the thing I didn't tell you: that I loved you no matter what.*

'She'll burn, you know,' the priest says. He'd not be saying that if Aidan were here, whether Aidan pretends to follow the god-hounds' tenets or not. 'Witch and whore, defiler of the laws of man and Church and God.'

'Interesting, the order of your words,' I say, then lean close so my breath reaches his face, and I hope it feels like a curse. 'So will you, burn. I'll see to it. I won't even have to leave the comfort of my home. I'll send a hex on the wings of a crow or in the belly of the next fish you eat. You're well aware that witchcraft travels in the blood, fool priest.' His face goes pale so it stands out in the dimness of the crypt like the moon against a night sky. I turn and walk up the stairs. His footsteps behind me are rapid, as if he doesn't want to remain below on his own, but not so fast that he will catch up with me.

Up in the air I signal Malachi to begin the closing of the tomb once again. The god-hound scampers out. I send the maids and Maura off to make a meal, and leave the lads and footman to help Malachi. I walk down the aisle with quick long steps. A hand closes around my upper arm and I shake it off before Aidan can get too good a grip.

He must notice something in my expression as I turn because he steps back – and I can see once again that calculating look, the mental jotting of things that must be fixed.

'Miren, I realise you are distressed but I feel we must talk. There are matters to be discussed and settled.'

He saw Aoife's body when we loaded her into the coffin, saw the white dress. Does he know it was meant to be my wedding gown? Perhaps not, but perhaps he guessed. Perhaps Brigid told him. Brigid. I have a matter to settle with her. I nod, slowly, as if considering.

'Yes, Aidan. At dinner, if you please; I would like to rest a little before then. It has been a trying time, cousin.' I'll play the fragile female for a while if I must.

'Of course. It will be pleasant to speak alone.'

No, it will not.

'A suite has been prepared for you in the East Wing,' I say. 'Yri will show you. I shall see you at dinner.'

The ring on my finger burns cold.

* * *

In my own room, I take Brigid's quilt from where I hid it in a cupboard.

I've borrowed Maura's fabric shears, the big ones, and I slice away a large corner. I wear a pair of thin leather gloves, though it makes the going slow; having cut into the thing, its magic will likely spill or be easily rubbed off and I don't want Brigid's spite on my bare hands. I pull the stuffing from between the two halves, then slice the fabric again into the coarse likeness of a doll. I stitch it together roughly − Aoife would frown at my laxity − and soon there's a flat thing. I gather the stuffing up and push it into the figure so it looks like a small dumpling of a girl. It doesn't need clothes or features, just my intent and the materials to hand. I snip at another corner and pull it apart to find what I'm after: a lock of blonde hair. Brigid made this, it would have been enough to simply use the materials she's touched, but this curl, so personal, so intimate? She used it to strengthen the spell; I'll use it now to do the same as I stuff it inside the head. Neither of us needs the blood of a witch in our veins to do this, merely intent. I'm careful not to prick my own finger while I make the thing for it'll do no good to risk an infection, but I'm equally careful to make sure I use the bits of the quilt with the most of Maura's expectorated ichor on it; her fear and anger will be embedded there. I take the tiny blue vial Maura gave me earlier and upend it: a glittering grey fall tips into the doll's head. When I was little and having nightmares, Maura taught me to put a full glass under my bed: in the morning, the water would be black, having absorbed the bad dreams. Maura then made the *aqua nocturna* into this, dust of dreams. Finally, I sew the last gap closed.

I hold the mean little thing and a tear drips onto it. I'd not realised I was crying. How did we come to this, my cousin and I? When we were twelve, there was a boy. Rian, the son of one of the tenants, the Widow O'Meara's only child, and so handsome. Charming, too, and he liked me. And although nothing ever happened between us, it was sweet and exciting and secret − a secret of my own. Nothing but that one single kiss down on the shingle just that one day. Who would I share such a secret with but my cousin Brigid… and who but Brigid would run and tell my grandmother? There are marks on my skin that have never gone away. Unlike Rian O'Meara, who disappeared one morning, never to be found, soon after the night Aoife beat bloody furrows into my back.

I blink to clear the tears and assess my work. It's an ugly little thing, lumpen and imprecise in its shape, but the magic is there and it will work. I carefully remove a glove, then take out Óisín's pocketknife to prick the tip of my thumb. I press hard against it with my pointer finger so three droplets weep out and drip onto the doll's head; I whisper an ill-wish for Brigid, then carefully bandage the cut on my finger. I wrap the dolly in a shawl and hide it in the blanket box at the foot of my bed.

Then I get ready to go down to dinner.

* * *

Aidan is already seated in the small dining room when I arrive. At the head of the table, as though it's his right. He smiles when I enter the room, but as I've not bothered to change into one of the pretty dresses Aoife bought and make myself presentable, the expression is hard for him to maintain. He gestures to the place laid opposite him. It's a small table, this one, only meant for four, so the distance between us isn't really enough for my liking. Yri serves our first course, but doesn't meet my eye. She leaves as soon as she can.

'We will need to get you a new wedding dress,' is how Aidan begins, as if we're taking up a conversation only recently interrupted. 'I know it is soon after so much bereavement, but your grandmother would have wanted us to go ahead. It will be a small wedding in Breakwater; the archbishop has agreed to preside as a personal favour.'

'Aidan, our engagement was purely to please Aoife. She is gone.'

'But you will want to marry. You will want position and money. You will want the house restored.' He gestures to the faded curtains, the air of decay that still hangs in spite of Yri and Ciara's cleaning efforts.

And I shake my head. I love this house but it's not worth the cost of my freedom. It's not worth the cost of marrying Aidan Fitzpatrick. Whatever soul I might have, O'Malley though I might be, it is mine and I'll not sell it at any price.

'Aidan, thank you for your kind offer, but I will remain here with Malachi and Maura. The house devolves to me as per my grandparents' wills. I will live out my days at Hob's Hallow and when the time comes, the O'Malleys will be gone.'

'You are very anxious to throw your young life away, Miren,' he says evenly. 'Upon what do you propose to live? There will be no funds to cover your expenses even after the ships are sold – if they ever return to port. And you cannot fail to remember how much I have done for you. How much I have *spent* on you and your grandmother.'

I pull the giant pearl ring off my heart finger, where it never belonged, and I slide the thing across the shiny dining-room table so it hits Aidan's dinner plate with a *ting*.

He stares at it as if it had addressed him in perfectly formed sentences. Aidan reaches out and picks up the hefty thing, weighs it in the palm of his hand as if he doesn't very well know its value.

'Yri,' he says, then clears his throat. 'Yri told me what happened when you were watching Aoife.'

I freeze, think that I should simply have murdered the girl to stop her mouth rather than trusting her. She's not here to work for me. She'll answer to Aidan, who pays her way. Still, it smarts to have been so stupidly trusting. Aoife's in my head, smugly smiling.

Aidan continues, 'She told me about the marks on your grandmother's throat and that you and Aoife had argued in the morning, rather violently.'

I swallow.

'I would hate to think that I needed to report these matters to either the Church or the authorities. Not when you stand to inherit everything now Aoife is gone.'

There are no authorities anymore, I think, but I say, 'There have been strangers in this house, Aidan. All the new staff. One of the footmen is missing...'

The thought is there suddenly like a dagger.

He raises an eyebrow curiously. 'There was only ever one footman, Miren. Ugly chap, looks like a potato.'

I stare. I cannot tell if he's lying or not. But then, who else would send the green-eyed man here? Why else would he have disappeared so thoroughly? Unless he too is dead, lying in some as yet undiscovered location around the estate, at the foot of the cliffs, in another garden, or in the well in the cellar? But why would he have gone down there?

I open my mouth to say, 'But Maura and Malachi saw him,' then I stop. If Aidan's behind this, I won't put their necks in nooses. I swallow again, hard, but before I can answer he says, 'I think, Miren, you will find your life more pleasant if you continue along the path your grandmother laid out for you. The

O'Malleys will be saved. We will have children, they will serve their purpose. The sea will be paid its due and we will rule the oceans as this family once did.'

In his eyes is the same look Aoife used to get, all ambition untempered by sanity. All want untempered by sense. I look down at my plate, at the meal I've not touched. Roast chicken, mashed potatoes, withered greens. There's a basket of fresh bread in the centre of the table, curls of butter beside it. I take up the cutlery and slice the meat. I eat. I eat because I haven't eaten all day. I eat because I'm going to need my strength. I eat because it will make Aidan think me submissive and accepting of my fate.

'I was thinking that, after we marry, we shall spend the first month in Breakwater while Hob's Hallow is renovated.'

'What will you have done here?' I ask, as if I am interested. Already I can feel my heart separating from the only home I've known. But still, the idea of him changing this place, putting his stamp on it and bending it to his will makes my skin crawl. Perhaps the whole house will fall into the sea with him in it. The thought makes me smile and he thinks it's for him. It is only bricks and mortar; it is glass and plaster and stone. It is no longer safe.

'Óisín's study is very small. I will have men knock through into the next room, and perhaps the one after that to make a much bigger space.'

'There is damp in one wall,' I say conversationally. 'The workers will need to be careful the whole next floor doesn't come down on them.' He grunts acknowledgement. I go on, 'And I would like to move out of the West Wing.'

He nods. 'Yes. New suites for both of us. I've thought of that.'

And he goes on to tell me how he will design the rooms himself: one large bedchamber for us to share, with individual sitting rooms on either side for privacy. I nod. I smile. I notice there is neither wine nor whiskey at the table and I'm grateful for that. He's still trying to hide himself, if only for a little while, even if he's blackmailed me into marriage, even if he's made me suspect he had my grandmother murdered. For what reason? She was giving him what he wanted just as he was giving her her heart's desire. I want to scream and shout. I want to demand he tell me the truth.

But how much truth will he bear me knowing? How much can I learn before he decides I can be got rid of? After children, obviously. I pass the title of Hob's Hallow to him, I pass the O'Malley name, I give him heirs to do what must be done. And then? I'm as unnecessary as any girl who refuses to obey her husband; like those in one of Maura's stories, who took the key he gave them and looked into the rooms he forbade them from entering.

'This is pleasant, isn't it? Isn't it, Miren?'

'Yes, Aidan. It is pleasant.' And I smile like a doll, like a moppet, like a toy he might play with any way he wants.

When Yri brings in the dessert – a simple trifle – I smile at her too. *No hard feelings*. I thank her kindly for all her help with Aoife. I tell her that I cannot imagine being able to run the house without her even after such a short time. She blushes with pleasure and I think about jamming my dessert spoon into her left eye. Instead, I finish the last mouthful.

'Aidan, if you will forgive me, I would like to retire now. It has been, as you know, a very difficult few days and I am exhausted.'

'Of course.' He comes to my end of the table to pull my chair out. I rise and he stands close to me and my heart feels like it's trying to leave me through my throat. He touches my hair. 'We will be happy, Miren, I believe this.'

I smile and he leans to kiss me. He doesn't taste like the green-eyed man; he doesn't feel like him either. When he's hard against me I gently push him away.

'Our wedding will be soon enough, Aidan.' I lower my lashes. 'It's best if we wait.'

He's still and awkward but he steps back. He grabs my hand, though, and pushes the ring on my finger once again; forceful and clumsy. I don't grimace, but touch his face as if in tenderness. 'It's not so long to be patient, is it?'

Aidan manages a smile. He will drink on our wedding night. And I'll wake bruised the next morning in more places than I knew I had. I kiss him once more, quickly. 'Good night, Aidan.'

Up in my room, I sit on my bed and wait. It doesn't take long. I think, from the lightness of the footsteps, it's either Yri or Ciara who comes. And I hear the door lock with a finality Aidan would surely find satisfying.

13

I kick away my shoes with the pretty little heels, then strip off my dress, making sure not to leave the pocketknife behind. From the wardrobe I drag a pair of dark trews, a shirt, a knitted sweater and an old navy pea coat; they all used to belong to Óisín. I've worn the outfit before, when my grandfather used to take me out in a little rowboat to fish, but it's not frequent attire – I actually do like dresses and skirts as long as they've got pockets. I dress quickly, but set the coat aside: it's too bulky for what I'm about to do. I fold it tightly and tie it with a leather strap that can act as a spare belt should I need it.

I grab a pair of solid boots from the bottom of the cupboard, then stuff them and a pair of socks into the duffel bag Óisín used to take to sea with him. They go on top of a change of clothes, a loaf of black bread, a pouch of tea leaves, a flask of winter-lemon whiskey and some dried meat that Maura packed earlier today, plus a largish bag of salt for 'dealing with things'. She means all the things she told me stories about when I was a child. Right at the bottom are Isolde's letters. The little poppet is still in the blanket box; I retrieve her, wrapped in the shawl, and push it into a space down the side of the bag.

There's a small velvet purse on the bedside table, containing the ten gold coins from Aoife's reticule, all scored with lines for where to break them to make change. Not to mention the jewellery, hers and mine; I pull the engagement ring from my finger and add it to the glittering pile. It'll be the first thing I get rid of, I promise myself. When the strings are tightly tied, the purse goes into the duffel too.

I tie my hair up tightly, fix it with copper pins so it won't come loose, then open the window.

Unlike the Breakwater townhouse, the path from my bedroom window on the second floor is not impassable. Admittedly, I've not climbed out this way for a year or two, but needs must. I toss the bundle of my coat out first, careful to make sure it lands as far from the house as possible, then I sling the duffel across my back and take a deep breath. The roof is not too sharply sloped and I've a good handhold on the slates; my feet grip exceedingly well. I only almost slip twice and when my heartbeat comes back under control – *Hush,* I say, *even falling to your death is better than having Aidan to husband* – I finally get my hands around a drainpipe and shinny down to the ground. I pull on my socks and boots, grab the coat and push it into the newly freed space in the bag, then pick my way through the front gardens.

I don't go to the stables, for the lads have been sleeping in a back room beneath Malachi's quarters, but to the ruined gates that mark the boundary of Hob's Hallow. Malachi is waiting there with Aidan's black horse all saddled and ready – our old nags would never get me far enough or fast enough away. We did not know I would need to flee this night, but it's never hurt to be prepared. Gods know I'd hoped my intended would simply accept my refusal, but I know my family too well; I spoke with both Malachi and Maura before Aidan arrived this morning. Had I not needed it, the food would have simply been returned to the kitchen, the horse to the stable. Malachi shouldn't have been out here waiting; I'd told him to tether the horse then go to bed.

'He's dangerous,' I say. 'Aidan. He's dangerous. I hate to leave you—'

'Don't fear for us, missy.' Malachi nods. 'We've been dying a long time, maybe he'll do us a favour and make the waiting shorter.'

'But—'

'If we come now, we'll just slow you down and you're sure to be caught. Ah, missy, we'd die rather here now.' He takes off his flat cap and puts it on my head. 'Cover that face.' He grins. 'When you find your mother, give her our best.'

I hug him hard and after a moment he hugs me back; I think of Maura's arms around me this morning, imagine her standing at the window of her attic room, staring into the darkness, imagining me here. Malachi smells like porter, pipe smoke, winter-lemon whiskey and dust. Then he pushes me away, his tolerance for affection spent, and helps me into the saddle. The beast is well-trained, obedient, for Aidan likes his things broken.

Malachi clears his throat, lips quivering. 'Be on your way, missy,' he says sternly. Then: 'Run, Miren, and don't look back.'

* * *

It wasn't even close to midnight when I left Hob's Hallow, and I estimate I've been on the road for almost two hours now. The sensible thing would have been to take Óisín's pocket watch, but Aoife gave it to Malachi after my grandfather's death and it felt wrong to ask for it back. I'll buy another somewhere along the way, perhaps trade one of the earrings in the bag for a timepiece to set my life by. The night's cool as it can be by the sea, but not cold. There's little light to see by as the sky is clouded, which is all the better for a night-time flit, but it also means I don't give the stallion his head. What's the point in escaping if I'm found the next morning with my neck broken beside a horse whose leg's been snapped in a ditch or fox hole?

I do urge him up to a trot, I must admit, as soon as we're far enough away that the sound won't carry back to the mansion and alert, well, anyone. I think, briefly, of going to Breakwater and reporting what's happened to someone… who? The archbishop who'll do Aidan a grand favour by marrying us? Or the Queen of Thieves who does nothing without a pound of flesh in payment? The last remaining former councilman who kept his skin intact by poisoning two of his former colleagues to please Bethany Lawrence?

There is no one who would see justice done for Aoife's death and there's no one I can rely on not to return me to the tender mercies of my betrothed. The moment he put the engagement ring on my finger was the moment, apparently, when he took over the reins of my fate. One day, perhaps, I'll be able to send for Maura and Malachi. Perhaps they'll be safe. I feel sick with guilt and fear. I could turn back, sneak into the house through the kitchen. No one would ever know. But I think of Aidan's expression at the theatre and my wrist aches where the bruises are still blue. No. Flight is my only option.

In the distance, I see the lights of Breakwater, or some of them at any rate: some cantons are pure darkness where the good citizens are abed, others ablaze where denizens carry on their existence in the gloom: the assassins market, the courtesans quarter, the inns and dancehalls where entertainment of a particular sort might be found. But I'm not going to those areas, no. I know precisely where I'm headed, if only for the shortest of times. An hour, perhaps, before I'm there, and I need to figure out how to do what must be done.

There's a noise in the seagrass to my left and the horse snorts with fear and rears. I smell a foul odour over the scent of the salt water, something rotting. The moon breaks through the clouds as I try to calm the animal and I can see what's caused this whole ruckus: a corpsewight close.

All but hunched at the shoulders as if so very cold, clothes tattered and still dripping from the sea where surely it met its end. Blond hair in draggled ripples around its face, and that face grey-green in the strange moonlight. Mouth agape and only holes where eyes once were, eaten away by fishes or perhaps birds; it's blind, poor thing, poor monster.

It's so near to the road, I think – then I realise *we've* strayed from the path. At a glance I can see where we've come adrift, where the road actually is, not so far away and clear in the sudden moonlight.

A dreadful moan issues from the corpsewight, and though I feel sorry for it, lost as it is, unable to rest, I'm even more terrified of it. I dig my heels into the stallion's sides and urge it back towards safety. We race towards the city lights, unheeding of holes or hazards, just desperate to get away.

* * *

I dismount some way outside the walls, tie the horse to a clump of bushes and thank him. If I take him into the city it will be clear where I've gone and that's not what I want; besides, I can't know who might recognise Aidan Fitzpatrick's favourite steed. Leaving him here, at a crossroads where travellers converge and meet, join caravans for safer passage, that will confuse anyone in pursuit of me. No one keeps track of those cavalcades, no passenger lists, so I might be anywhere.

I wander towards the gates and wait for a gaggle of night-revellers to push their way out from the city, those going to homes outside the walls, small farms and the like, those heading off to do mischief elsewhere. I pull Malachi's cap down over my forehead so my face is shadowed, square my shoulders and push into the group, pressing against the flow. I'm taller than most of them; I make a point to walk like a man, lay claim to all beneath my feet as if it's my right; other men step aside and soon I'm inside Breakwater proper.

I take a moment to get my bearings, then continue on through the avenues, doing my best to stay away from lamplights and overly lit windows, keeping my face turned away, my head tilted just so. No one speaks to me. The crowds dissipate the further I get into the expensive neighbourhoods, and at last I'm in front of my goal.

I check to make sure no one's around then sneak down the thin alley between one townhouse and the next. The room I was in was too high to climb from, but Brigid's is on the first floor and a drainpipe runs right by her window (where I can see pink lace curtains). The sash is up to allow in the fresh air at night.

I take off my boots and socks again, secure them to my duffel, swing it behind me and begin my ascent. I'll admit I'm puffing a little when I tumble over the sill – I do a fair amount of physical activity, but it doesn't generally involve climbing the sides of houses. I sit on the floor for a few moments, back against the wall. I vow no more windows this night if I can help it. I watch my slumbering cousin, curled on her side, mouth open like a child's and a slight whistle as she breathes, in and out, in and out, different tones for each. I wonder if everyone looks innocent when they sleep, even though you know what they've done in their waking hours?

When I've caught my breath, I open the duffel and pull out the shawl. I crawl over to Brigid's bed and unwrap the cloth, which I then use to keep between the poppet and my hand. Gingerly I lift the mattress from its base and push the wicked little doll into the gap, as far as I can. It's only as I'm withdrawing my arm that Brigid stirs.

She rolls onto her back and begins snoring in earnest, the little whistle still there but accompanied by a stentorian bellow of a thing. What a delightful surprise for the husband to whom she will no doubt one day be sold in order to further Aidan's schemes of empire. I wait a moment or two, then press my palm firmly over her mouth.

My cousin's eyes fly open and I hiss, 'Hello, Brigid.'

14

There's just darkness and close air, the creak and rattle of wheels on the road, the peculiar rhythmic shake of the cart, the occasional snort of the horses pulling us along. The driver and his companion speak only a little, and then in tones so low I cannot make out the words. Beside me is a hard form, cold despite the heat, uncaring of my presence but no less disconcerting for all that. The hot, quiet dark, the unmoving form; I have Brigid to thank for all this.

* * *

I pressed my hand down harder, felt the teeth grind behind her lips, thought about pressing harder still until there was blood, blood like she made come from poor Maura's mouth, but I didn't. It took her a moment to recognise me with my cap and male attire, my hair hidden. I could see in her gaze, though, in the lambent glow from the last of the hearth fire, that she was wondering not just why I was there, but why I was hale and hearty and not coughing my lungs out. I put a finger to my lips, and when she nodded, I removed my hand. She managed to stop herself from asking, 'Where's the quilt and why didn't it work?'

Instead she said, 'What are you doing here?'

'I, cousin dear, am running away.' I sat on the edge of the bed and she scootched herself up against the pillows, staring big-eyed as I continued, 'And you are going to help me.'

'Why would I do that?'

'Because, Brigid, you don't want me to marry Aidan any more than I want to marry Aidan.' I folded my arms. 'And this is easier than trying to kill me, don't you think?'

'I didn't want to kill you...'

'I gave the quilt to Maura.'

A tremor travelled through her features and I thought she might cry. She has no reason to hate Maura, who was always kind to her. Maura would give Brigid the pick of the fresh biscuits in the kitchen – when I complained later she told me that I lived at the Hallow and always had the first of treats, but Brigid wasn't there all the time. Couldn't I share, just a while? I could. Look where it got me.

'I found her in time. She's well enough.' Well enough until Aidan decides to ask her where I was.

'It wouldn't have killed you,' she said defensively.

'Maybe not, but I'm young. Maura?' I shook my head. I wondered how much Brigid knew of Aidan's plans, and decided it was just enough to make trouble for him. 'Trust me, Brigid, you don't want any death on your conscience. And I swear I will come back and haunt you.'

'Well, if anyone was going to... I... I just wanted to make you sick, hurt. Just a little to teach you a lesson,' she said, then asked, 'Does Aoife know?'

I stared at her. Or perhaps she knew even less of Aidan's plans.

'Aoife is dead, Brigid. She... she died the morning after we returned to Hob's Hallow.' And she stared at me in return, shocked. Her brother came out to the Hallow without telling her why. I tossed up whether or not to tell her how Aoife died; decided *no*. 'But Aidan still thinks to marry me.'

'Of course he does.' She shook herself.

'Help me get away now and I'm out of your hair forever.'

'That's too good an offer to refuse,' she sniped, and I was suddenly pierced. In these last few days I'd lost my grandfather, buried my murdered grandmother, discovered my dead parents were actually alive and left me behind to pay a debt, abandoned Maura and Malachi to an uncertain fate, and been promised to a husband I knew wanted to hurt me. Brigid's casual snark slipped between my ribs when I'd thought myself armoured against her.

'Why?' I cried out, too loudly, then bit down on my sobs. 'Why do you hate me so?'

'Because you hate me! We were so close, then one day... one day Mother said I wasn't allowed to come and visit, and that you didn't want to see me again.' She hissed at me, arms wrapped around her curled-up knees, fists clenched. Her face turned red with anger, but tears gathered in her eyes.

I rose and turned my back to her, then swiftly pulled up my sweater and shirt so she could see the mess Aoife had made of me. Once a year, perhaps, I arranged two mirrors in my bedroom and examined the landscape of my own flesh to see if it had changed. Brigid gave a sharp intake of breath. What she saw was a relief map of scars, turned that strange white of mounds of skin raised over deep wounds when they heal.

'Do you remember Rian O'Meara? Do you remember he kissed me? I was so excited and I told you... and you told Aoife...' I paused, licked my lips. 'You told Aoife and she did this to me because she thought I was going to be a whore like my mother.'

'No—' Brigid sounded strangled.

'That's what she yelled at me as she beat me. That I was no better than a slut, letting a common cur touch me.' I felt my cousin's fingers on my skin, so light as if they couldn't believe what was beneath them. I pulled my clothes into place and faced her again. 'And she made sure that I knew you had told her.'

Brigid's face was stricken, her lips moving like a fish gasping to be put back into a pond. 'Rian disappeared not long after. His body was never found. And his mother always looks at me in the same way, as if it was all my fault.'

Tears made dark marks on Brigid's nightgown and the white bedlinen. 'She... Aoife asked me... she told me how important you were to the family, that you had to be protected from anyone who might harm you, because that would harm the family.' She was in full flow now, tears and snot and sobs, the words being pushed out over the top. 'And you talked, when you told me, of running away with him.'

And I remembered then all the stupid girlish things I'd said. Things that meant everything to me in that moment, and nothing in the ones since. Because I could see years later that the words that had come from my mouth then had been a child's infatuation, no more, no less. But I didn't know it then, and nor did Brigid. And she'd feared so she'd told.

And Aoife... my grandmother had had the best use of her little spy and didn't think she'd need her again. Perhaps she was jealous, herself, of my closeness with Brigid when she'd not had anyone like her. Perhaps – and I thought this might well have been the most likely – she was just so enraged that I might be like Isolde, that I might so easily derail her plans by opening my legs too soon, that she visited a revenge on me that she hadn't been able to deliver to my mother. Because Isolde had a baby inside her and the O'Malleys' salvation depended entirely on new blood and that could not be risked.

'I didn't know,' continued Brigid, 'that she'd done this. I... I only knew that you didn't love me anymore and it hurt.'

I sat on the edge of the bed and ceased trying to contain my own weeping. We held hands and sobbed. We cried until there were no more tears, and it felt – for me at least – as if poison had been drawn from a wound.

'Where will you go?' she asked at last.

I shook my head. 'I don't know, but it's best if you have no idea. If Aidan thinks you know, do you think he'll stop at anything to get the information out of you?'

'No. You're right.' She put the fingers of one hand around the wrist of the other as if soothing bruises.

'But I need to get away from here, by a means he can't easily trace.'

'I... I can get you to someone who can help. He can take you elsewhere, then...'

'I can make my way from wherever to wherever.'

'Yes.'

'Thank you, Brigid.'

'Will you... will you perhaps write to me? One day?'

'One day. When I'm safe.' I almost said *One day I will send for you*, but refrained. Who knows what might happen to either of us? I would not make promises I might not be able to keep.

While she dressed in dark clothes, I surreptitiously took the little doll from beneath her mattress and threw it onto the flames in the hearth. It went up terribly quickly, with a snap and a pop like bones breaking.

'What was that?' she called from the dressing room.

'Something in the fire,' I said, then under my breath, 'bad dreams and ill wishes.'

* * *

In the little courtyard at the back of the Paragon Theatre, the troupe was moving to and fro, packing their carts and wagons, seven in all, when we arrived. I waited in the shadows while Brigid approached. It seemed strange that they'd be preparing to leave so very late – or rather, so very early, for it was almost 3 a.m. – but my cousin had said Ellingham liked to get a head-start on their travel. They always departed after the final performance so they weren't trying to exit a city in the morning at the same time as every other merchant or caravan.

'Mr Ellingham,' she called, and the little man's head popped up immediately from the group of men hefting a shiny box the shape of a coffin but twice as wide onto a covered cart.

'Miss Fitzpatrick!' His face lit up with genuine pleasure as he approached her and I noticed Brigid's mien took on a similar glow. 'I did not expect to see you here again, not so late. Have you changed your mind?'

His tone was so limned with hope that my heart hurt a little. *Why, cousin, how sly!* Aidan clearly did not know. Were all the women in Aidan Fitzpatrick's life destined to defy him in one way or another? Then she shook her head regretfully and his joy disappeared.

145

She drew him away from the light, from his fellows, to where I waited in the shadows. Her hand on his arm, the movement of her lips and the way his eyes followed her very breath were all so clear to me – how could Aidan *not* know? Because he does not look, does not care to, has no concern for what anyone else wants or needs. Ellingham's expression as Brigid speaks gradually changes and he searches for me. I step forward into a patch of lesser darkness.

'Miss O'Malley,' he says haltingly. 'Brigid tells me you are in need of aid.'

'In need of a swift and clandestine way out of Breakwater, Mr Ellingham. Can you assist?'

He pauses as if considering, then nods. 'We make for Lodellan, but you may leave us anywhere along the way, as you choose.'

'Thank you, Mr Ellingham.'

'It will not be comfortable, at least not for a while, if you wish to depart covertly.'

'I'll make no complaint.'

'Then come with me, we'll not let my people know for the moment. A secret seldom survives being shared.' The troupe had dispersed, back inside the theatre to gather final possessions. Brigid and I stared at each other, lost; finally, we exchanged a few words, and a tight hug. Then Ellingham escorted me smartly across the courtyard to one of the covered carts.

And that is how I came to be lying in the dark beside the automaton, Delphine.

I don't know how long I've been here; I napped, I think, soon after Mr Ellingham closed the lid on me. So tired, I barely had time to feel afraid of the inert thing beside me, of the blackness that closed in with the falling lid, and the *snick* of the latch. I remember hearing the city guards call as we rolled out beneath the gates and Ellingham answered cheerily that they would return next year in the same season with a new show, new performers, but always his beautiful Delphine. The soldiers cheered; apparently anyone could be thus affected by the glorious singer and her strange arias.

A few minutes later, drained of all adrenaline, my head resting on my duffel, all memory ceased.

When I woke there was still the roll and rumble of the cart, the mutter of voices, and the walls of the box began to close in. I didn't know where we were, how far from Breakwater, whether or not Aidan might have found me missing from Hob's Hallow, whether he had returned suddenly to the city to seek me out, whether Brigid had betrayed me or he'd pulled the information from her by some unpleasant means, so I kept my mouth shut, bit down on the desire to kick and hammer and scream to be released. I thought briefly of my cousin's farewell, of asking her why she did not go with Mr Ellingham, and her reply: 'Aidan would hunt me down and he would kill Orin. He'll hunt you too, you know. Hide yourself well, Miren.'

I shift position for I've grown sore and cramped. I put a hand out to steady myself against the automaton and feel something give in her chest. I start guiltily, praying I've not broken anything, and when there's nothing further to suggest I've destroyed Mr Ellingham's pride and joy, I begin to whisper to the automaton, one of my favourites from childhood.

I was sixteen when he plucked me from the sea.

Caught in his fisherman's net, I thought I would drown until he lifted me into the too-small boat and began to hack at the rough fibres to release me. I should have known then how soft his heart was, to see him ruining a net so, but I was terrified. In his haste he cut me, split the skin down by my tail a good eight inches and saw the two fine-boned ankles lying within. He sat back, astonished, and I fought my way free of the pelt until I was naked and shivering in my human skin, huddled at the bottom of that little, little boat.

His family told him to throw me back, to return my other skin and send me home. He refused.

I learned his language and gave him children, two boys and three girls, all in the space of ten years. We were happy for a long time, in our cottage on the tiny island inhabited by no more than ten families. They were all related, his cousins at one remove or other. And they were dark, some of them, so I knew they had selkie blood for all they thought themselves better than me. It made me laugh to see his mother come a-visiting, mouth all twisted like she'd sucked on something bitter, she with her black-as-the-sea-depths hair and eyes so pitchy you couldn't tell the pupil from the iris. She'd look at my children, her grandbabies, and something in her face would soften as she watched them frolic on the seashore like pups. Sometimes she'd look out to sea and she'd wear a longing expression that her mind didn't know, but her blood did.

We were happy until my man began to drink. I'd made him prosperous, for the shoals gather where selkie wives bide. His nets were never empty and the purse was always heavy from the sales at the mainland markets. The money, it was, that led him astray. He would come home drunk, barely able to row across the short span of water separating us from the town, throw himself onto the bed and snore fit to bring the roof down.

148

When I begged him to stop he turned on me, called me fish and beat me for daring to question him. He was no longer the man who had saved me from a net.

I could simply have gone to the beach, knelt down and spoken to the waters, told the fish to go away. I could have pulled my old pelt down from the top of the cupboard where he'd hidden it all those years ago (as if I wouldn't sniff out the scent of my own skin). I could have taken to the water once more and left them all behind, but my children held my heart. My pride yearned though, for revenge, and I called up a storm just as my mother and aunts had taught me long ago; called it up one eve as he rowed home, worse for liquor and new-found temper.

They say there had never been such a storm and there's never been one since. I found him the next morning, when my anger burned low and regret took its place. He lay across the rocks, his clothes torn, his limbs broken. There was a skerrick of breath left in him.

I made my way to the cottage, ran back down to the rocks.

He was already very cold, limp, and for a while the selkie skin would not take hold. When I began to despair it took a grip at last, adhering to his shoulders, down his back, across his chest and limbs, and finally up his neck and over his face. He coughed; it sounded like a seal's bark. Wriggling, he heaved himself out of my arms and flopped down the rocks to slip into the cold sea.

He comes often, not only when I sing. Our children swim as well as their seal blood allows and they play together; somehow they know it is their father, although I have not told them, and they seem not to grieve. Some nights, I simply sit there with him

damp and warm beside me, and we speak of things beneath the
sea, things I will never again see.

There's no knowing who first wrote that one down in the big book, if it's truth or a pretty lie. But there's love and loss, revenge and redemption. I wonder what happened in her ever-after: how long she lived as a human, how long her children stayed with her, what happened after she died. Did she turn back to a seal then? Or become nothing more than sea foam, nothing more than dreams?

I think of the little poppet so briefly beneath Brigid's mattress. It wouldn't have done her any greater harm than nightmares, but I find I don't carry that hatred for her anymore. She was used by Aoife, shifted about like a pawn under the guise of keeping the family safe. Perhaps I should have put the doll under Aidan's bed, let him suffer, but it wouldn't have worked quite the same, for I made it specifically with Brigid in mind. It might have caused him some discomfort, however there's no point in me handing him another thing to use against me: if I prove too much trouble, he could accuse me not only of my grandmother's murder, but of witchcraft too. They keep telling us, all these god-hounds, that magic great and small has gone, yet that's just wishful thinking on their part. They cannot burn every single woman, tempting though it might be.

I find I'm exhausted again by the skittering and scampering of thoughts, and I settle down to sleep once again.

15

I'm sitting up beside the little man on the driver's seat of the covered cart. Behind us the automaton's box quietly rattles with our movement. A few hours out of Breakwater, the caravan came to a halt and Mr Orin Ellingham set me free, much to the interest and amusement of the troupe, who peppered their leader with questions. A lad, Ben I think his name is, asked 'Are we recruiting like this now?' and laughed at his own joke.

'You could probably do with a break, Miss,' Ellingham said and pointed me to the woods off the side of the road. Dignity be damned, I fair ran to relieve myself after hours in captivity. When I returned, a grinning woman with red-white hair offered me brown bread with cheese and jam and a mug of hot tea, all of which I scoffed. I could smell my own sweat and the musky scent of the automaton's clothing, which surely hasn't been washed in a long time, and I wondered when I'd next have the chance to bathe; it didn't bother me enough to ask or try to find a stream.

By then he'd told his people that I was in trouble and needed their help, that I'd cause no difficulty (we both hoped). *Call her Molly,* he said – which wasn't the same as telling them my name – and I could see from the grins and lifted eyebrows that they knew this too. There were nods and tips of caps, but no more questions were asked and I wondered how often it happened, that they smuggled people from bad places. Part of me wanted to relax then, but I couldn't help but feel Aidan was mere seconds from arriving; the back of my neck burned as if his breath was too close.

I hoped the feeling would lessen and a few hours later, it seems to have settled into no more than a low hum in a corner of my mind. Two roan horses plod ahead, drawing us along; behind come the prettily painted wagons and carts bearing the remaining twelve souls of the troupe. Actors, actresses, singers, jugglers and clowns all have at least two other roles – driver, cook, props master, wardrobe mistress, scene painter, general dogsbody. The road is not so well-maintained as those closer to cities and towns and villages. We're winding through a forest of oak and yew, a lot of scrubby underbrush ranging off into the distance to be lost in shadow. There's just birdsong and the occasional fox cry, some snuffling of things that might be badgerish but diurnal.

To the left, between the trees, I spot a house, or what's left of one. As we continue on, there are more buildings, all ruins. Most are overgrown with vines, tall grasses creeping across their steps and porches and up walls, but the timbers that can still be seen are as black as ash. Ellingham notices me looking.

'Southarp,' he says. 'They say an abbot put it to the torch after the townsfolk burned his lover as a witch.'

I shiver. 'And no one ever rebuilt it?'

'Abandoned. They say he made a bargain that no one would escape. They say the ghosts remained for long years until one day they were gone. Never seen one there myself, though, in all the time I've travelled these roads.' He grins. 'Perhaps they hide when we come past.'

'Do you ever camp here?' I keep my eyes on the ruins. Did I see the swift blur of a white mist darting behind a tree? Or is it my imagination?

'Oh no. Even if I were willing, this lot?' He jerks a thumb over his shoulder to indicate the troupe. 'Gareth would never allow it. Yellow as piss, he is.'

The man driving the wagon behind shouts something rude; he can't hear us but I'm guessing this is simply a repeated action. He knows when Ellingham points thusly an insult is attached.

He nods. 'First came by here with my da – he brought this lot together after Mam died and he couldn't bear to stay in one place anymore. I guess I caught that from him.'

'Do you ever consider settling down?' I think about Brigid.

He shakes his head. 'Not really. Who'd keep them in check?' Again, the thumb; again, the profanity.

'Miss Molly, Miss Molly!' A voice from beside me, half manly, half boyish. I look down into blue eyes; the lad, Ben, running along by us. His eyebrows join in the middle. He's holding out a wildflower, vibrant purple. I take it with a grin. 'Thank you.'

He hares away, his cheeks burning, back to one of the other wagons.

Ellingham snorts with laughter. 'Won a heart, you have.'

'Speaking of which, how long have you loved my cousin?'

He startles and I touch his arm gently to calm him.

He sighs. 'You noticed, did you?'

'Only because I was looking, I suppose.'

153

'I met her four years ago, the first trip to Breakwater without my da. I was a bit older than Ben then but not much.' He frowns again. 'I'd known Aidan a while before that, when he was different – he was a friend to my father too. He brought Brigid to the theatre one night and I thought I'd never seen anyone so pretty.'

I say nothing, cannot remember a time when Aidan behaved differently, but then I suppose men do not behave the same with each other as they do with women.

'We didn't say much, then, but I made a point of running into her the next morning.' He lowers his voice. 'I delayed our departure by five days, ruined the schedule, but it was worth it.'

'Aidan can't possibly know?'

'Oh no. Even when he was a friend, even then he'd not have approved of me courting his sister.' He shakes his head ruefully. 'You remember? When he wasn't as he is now?'

'No, I don't,' I say honestly. 'My family... the O'Malleys are the source, the core, and all those offshoots like the Fitzpatricks... aren't *proper* O'Malleys, do you understand?' The look he gives me says not. 'They're *lesser* for all they've got more money than us. It's the name, you see, the name that carries value and no one's ever thought twice about making the non-O'Malleys feel bad about their lack.' I shake my head. 'It's stupid, I know, and it's caused a lot of resentment. What I'm trying to say is that we're not close.'

'But didn't you see him and Brigid growing up?'

I shake my head again. 'Very little. Or rather Brigid for a while but... my grandmother didn't like that.' I purse my lips, think about Aoife destroying my only friendship. 'My grandparents kept me very isolated. Tried to make sure I was... untainted.'

'And how did that work?'

I think of the green-eyed footman. 'Rather less well than expected.'

He laughs and I continue, 'Aidan never paid me any mind until my grandfather died... after that Aidan and my grandmother made a deal. Oh.' It strikes me for the first time that perhaps Óisín's death was all they were waiting for. Perhaps that was what he and Aoife argued about in his last days, when I could hear the shouting falling down the tower like water, but couldn't make out the words. Perhaps he wouldn't have been telling me that the marriage was for everyone's good because he was the one preventing it from happening... 'Oh.'

Ellingham doesn't notice my distraction, talks on. 'Aidan was always ambitious but for a long while he was fun, and a good man to have on your side. He didn't walk over everyone and anyone to get what he wanted.'

'Then what happened?' The idea of an Aidan who could gain friendship, let alone loyalty, without paying for it strikes me as ludicrous. But as I've just told Ellingham, I didn't know Aidan much at all before all of this, so I should listen and learn.

'The first time I noticed the change was a couple of years ago when we returned to Breakwater to perform. He came to the theatre as he always did, but he wasn't so friendly. It wasn't like being greeted by an old comrade, but like he thought he was better than me. He spoke sharply to his sister and I could see she didn't like it either, wasn't used to it. When I asked Brigid later what had happened, she said he'd made a large investment and it wasn't doing well. He was stressed, she said.'

'Then?'

'The next year we returned, and Brigid was no happier. She said his financial crisis had passed, but only because he'd taken a loan and as far as she could tell it was costing him more than he could afford. Brigid had asked to go away, to a finishing school somewhere like Lodellan.' He licks his lips. 'He told her she wasn't going anywhere beyond his reach. She was as much a currency as anyone else in this world, and she'd be married off when he could make best advantage of it.'

'Did he take the loan from Bethany Lawrence?' I think of the blonde woman at the theatre, the way she looked across at me. At Aidan.

'Brigid didn't know for sure, but that was her guess. That the woman offered him a bargain and he's been beholden to her ever since.' He shrugs. 'It changed Brigid's life, not for the better, and she says she lost her brother though he still walks the house, eats meals with her, speaks with her.'

'I wonder what the deal was?' I look at him curiously.

He laughs. 'How would I know? You're his family. I only remember that he no longer wanted to meet for a drink at the taverns when I arrived. Brigid and I got much sneakier then, for neither of us wanted to consider what he might do if he found us together, friendship and family be damned.'

'And she won't run away with you?'

'No, whether because she can't bear the idea of the life of a lowly travelling player or because Aidan would surely hunt her down, I cannot say.' He pauses. 'I don't think I want to find out.'

'It's because he'd hunt *you* down, Mr Ellingham, trust me.' It's important to me that he know the truth, that he doesn't think the worst of Brigid. I'm unaccountably sad for both of them. Ellingham's not finished, though.

'All I know is that since Bethany Lawrence took over Breakwater, Aidan's coffers are overflowing. Woman's got her knife at the throat of the city; no commerce comes in or goes out that she doesn't get a cut of... and she sends her minions into the world to make sure she gets a cut of whatever dark business goes on there too.'

'Who is she?'

'Ah, you know what happens when no one owns the truth: rumour swirls up like poisonous fog. Some say she's from Lodellan, the cathedral city. That her family was a good one, but there was some scandal with her sister. They say the woman burned to death on a prison hulk in Roseberry Bay. A family destroyed, a fortune lost, a reputation in tatters. Yet here comes Mistress Lawrence to Breakwater, two nephews and a niece in tow, and no shortage of funds to buy property and pay others to do her deeds.'

'If she's caring for the children...'

'Ah, but there's only the oldest lad still left; and she's got a little one of her own. The other two disappeared early in the piece and no one the wiser as to their whereabouts.' He shrugs again. 'Perhaps she's had nothing to do with any of it. Perhaps they're a most unfortunate family. But if not? If her closest blood can be treated like that? Why would she care for anyone else in the world? She only preserves those of use to her and I hope Aidan keeps that in mind in his dealings.'

There's a long pause while I feel the threat of my cousin and that ruthless woman hanging above me. Then I shake myself:

what value could I possibly have to the Queen of Thieves, me with no more than a crumbling mansion and two lost ships to my name? Aidan just wants a trophy to bring him Hob's Hallow, the O'Malley name of which he's been deprived. Anything more is just my imagination, stirred by Ellingham's rumours.

I clear my throat and say, 'Where did you find her?' and tap on the top of the casket behind us. I ask because I don't want to hear any more about how Aidan Fitzpatrick was once a likeable man; he may well have been likeable to a *man*, yet have always been anathema to a woman.

Ellingham smiles fondly. 'She saved me, my little singing angel, just at a time when I thought I'd have to sell up, send this lot off to make their fortune elsewhere. But I found her and there's nothing like her in all the world as far as I can establish.'

He gives me a sideways glance, as if deciding whether or not to trust me, then realises I already know more than enough to get him into trouble, all because Brigid asked him to help me. 'We went off the beaten path, took a wrong turn, and came to a deserted house, tumbling down, no roof to speak of. It had been a mansion, once, but no longer. I found a trapdoor in the floor of a great hall. Down there she was, on a chair, covered in mould and with vines wound about her, sitting there like she had been waiting for someone for so very long. I touched her and suddenly this voice came out, such a beautiful thing. I took her with me.'

'I'm glad,' I say, and I am. I hate the idea of her alone in the darkness forever. Bad enough she's in a box all day. Then Ellingham darts back to our earlier topic.

'I take it you weren't interested in marrying Aidan?'

'That's an understatement, Mr Ellingham. My grandmother wanted it; she thought it would save the family fortunes.'

'They say the O'Malleys have funny ways.'

That makes me laugh. 'Oh yes.'

You have no idea. I finger the spot on my hip where the mermaid scar is. I think of the third child, the one for the sea. It had not been done in so long I thought it was finished. I thought it was something from the old times when the O'Malleys could get away with anything. I didn't think it would ever be something I would be expected to do. Didn't think I'd ever be Gráinne making a terrible choice, giving birth with the intent of throwing a child away. Myself, Isolde, we only survived because we were sole children; and Aoife, forced to marry her own brother in the hope of more pure O'Malley offspring.

'So, you've journeyed a lot, seen many places big and small?' I hesitate but sooner or later I'm going to have to ask someone.

'Aye, same route, every year and about.'

'Have you ever heard, Mr Ellingham, of an estate called Blackwater?'

'Blackwater?' Ellingham's brow furrows as he thinks, but eventually he shakes his head. 'Don't believe so.'

I could tell him that Isolde's last letter mentioned the name of the house she and my father had built, of the estate that had spawned a village: *north of Bellsholm, more or less*, she wrote. From Óisín's lessons, I know Bellsholm as a small port town on the Bell River, nothing so large or busy as Breakwater, but of Blackwater I'd never heard. No real surprise, for my mother *made* it. But if I tell him *north of Bellsholm, more or less* then he might tell anyone else who comes looking for me. So I simply say, 'Oh.'

159

'The others might know, I'll ask them tonight.' He smiles at me. 'Subtle like.' I grin. 'Someone will know, Miss O'Malley, don't fear.'

He's a kind man and I'm sad to think Brigid cannot be with him.

16

It's six days before we reach Bellsholm. We arrive late at night and camp on a flat grassy patch of land on the outskirts of the town. On our route there are many small villages and hamlets, nowhere big enough to justify taking the automaton from her box. Ellingham is very aware that one day she'll stop working. He doesn't know how old she is, or much at all about her inner workings because he's never been brave enough to take her apart for fear he won't be able to put her back together again; he does remove the front panel from her chest and dusts regularly, however. Instead, the inhabitants of those tiny locales have had to be content with songs and jokes in whatever passes for a tavern, and some small skits that the actors seem to know like the backs of their hands. There have been no complaints because anything is better than nothing in places where you have to make your own fun most of the time. People who appear with the express purpose of entertaining you? Now, that's something special. The troupe has been paid in eggs and homemade breads, lengths of fabric and balls of wool, in rapid shoe repairs and vials of perfume and medicine. Anything but coin, but no less valuable.

We're not far from the harbour, where I can see the lanterns which illuminate the docks, their reflections in the water moving constantly. Viviane, the woman with red and white hair (costume mistress and cook), sits with me by the fire and tells me about the town. She was born here though it's so long since she left, she no longer has family or a house to visit here.

'It's smaller than Breakwater, but it sprawls lazy as a big port,' she says as she mends one of the costumes. 'See those lights?' She points away to our right. 'Houses crawling up into the foothills; farms too and a foundry, tannery, carriage maker, carpenters and joiners; a hostelry too for those who can't be bothered to come into town. To the north is the Singing Rock.'

'What's that?'

'Ah, now don't go wandering there, that's where the rusalky gather.'

I sift through my memories and come up with one of Maura's warnings: rusalky aren't creatures who begin in the water, but end there. Maidens murdered and those who take their own lives, all ill-fated in love. Some can't pass on and remain in their watery grave, transmuted into something else, creatures with a malign will. Their only goal is to bring others to drown. I say, 'Ah,' and Viviane sees that I understand.

It's better organised here than Breakwater, she boasts: the wharves are overseen by a strict harbour master, the streets leading away from the water and winding their way to form a grid. The only strangeness is the Vines District, a created island in the middle of the town where the richest have their grand mansions. It's surrounded by a diverted channel of the river, and accessed by only six tidy bridges, each one guarded by an armsman day and night to ensure the wrong sort don't cause mischief for their betters.

162

Ellingham has taken Ben, who's given me a wildflower every day, has hairy palms and index fingers longer than his middle ones, to see the owner of the Aoide Theatre, where they will soon settle in for an eight-week season. It's not *quite* in the Vines District, but located a stone's throw from one of the bridges, making it one of those places the rich and poor may mingle, should they so choose. Ellingham told me he's training Ben to become the manager for the day – far distant – when Orin himself decides he's had enough. Ben's a good lad, always quick with a joke and a helping hand. Thus, everyone else has departed to find their own peculiar brand of amusement, for as of tomorrow everything will be about the performances to earn their keep. So, tonight is for their rest and my last night with them.

I could have gone with them and enjoyed a meal in a tavern and the company of others. I could have patronised one of the finer brothels for women on the far side of Bellsholm – where the men are handsome and do as they're told (Viviane had said this wistfully). But I chose instead to remain with Viviane, who knows much and is good company, and who has trusted me with the least onerous of the mending so I might do something useful. Ellingham won't accept anything from me, no matter how I insist.

'What will you do tomorrow?' asks Viviane. 'When will you leave, *Miss Molly*?'

'I'll visit the jewel-smith Ellingham recommended,' I say. Bellsholm is a better spot to dispose of some of the pieces; let them be taken apart and made unrecognisable. I'd love to be rid of the engagement ring, but it's too unique and too difficult to get the right price for here. I need a bigger city, perhaps Lodellan itself, though I've no plans to go that way, so the thing must remain with me a while longer. 'I'll buy a horse, food. Choose a road.'

'Looking for Blackwater,' she states. Not a question. I know Ellingham's asked his people as if it's his own enquiry, but no one's come up with anything. And everyone's looked at me once or twice, as if to ask how can we think them so stupid as to not connect my sudden presence with Ellingham's sudden queries?

There's not much point denying it. I nod.

Viviane says, 'Best to ask any tinkers you meet on the road. We tend to travel the same route, year in, year out. We seldom go off the beaten path because we don't need to. We stay where's safest, although I'm not saying sometimes we haven't gone out of our way from desperation and met with trouble in the form of robbers and the like.'

'What's happened?' I ask.

She laughs. 'Orin Ellingham can talk almost anyone around. Instead of stealing from us, all three times we've been fed and performed for them.'

'Even blackguards need amusement, I suppose.'

'Do you have a knife? Some kind of weapon?'

I pull out the pearl-handled pocketknife and she laughs again.

'I know it's not much,' I say, 'but it's hidden and unexpected.'

'True. That's your backup, though. You need something bigger, something that might act as a deterrent.' Her hand moves swiftly to the boot peeking out from beneath her skirts, then there's something silver and sharp in her fingers. 'There's a weaponsmith next door to the jewel-smith in the Vines. Tell him I sent you.' A swift flick and the knife disappears again.

We settle into silence for a while, both of us drawing thread through fabric with her brass needles; the firelight's not ideal but this isn't fine work. Then she says, 'Who are you running from?'

'A man,' I answer, then, not wanting to continue that line of conversation, ask, 'Why did *you* leave Bellsholm?'

'A man.'

We snort.

'A man I didn't want to marry,' I admit.

'A man I did want to marry,' she answers.

'Did you?' I ask. 'Marry him?'

'Yes,' she says. 'And it was a bad decision. When I left him and our house in Briarton I joined this lot.' She nods. 'Now *that* was a good decision. I hope yours is too.'

I think about Aidan's fingers around my wrist, about his insistence that he knows best. I think about what he'd do if he knew what I'd done with the green-eyed man, and that makes me smile, until I remember what I suspect the green-eyed man did to Aoife. Then I think again that he freed me, at least in part, from my grandmother. It's hard, still, to feel grateful for that.

'I do believe so.'

* * *

I was out of Bellsholm before midday, heading north, according to the signpost by the hostelry on the outskirts. My freshly acquired grey horse would excite no envy; I carried a bedroll, a tinderbox and charcloth for the starting of fires, a pocket watch, three knives (one at my belt, one in my boot, one slid into a concealed compartment on the saddle), and my duffel was filled with a plentiful supply of bread and dried meat, and a full waterskin. I'd exchanged an emerald necklace of Aoife's for more than enough money to buy my new possessions, and for the leftover to jingle fatly in my purse. Viviane sewed most of the rest of the pieces into the hem of my coat where they'll be harder to find should someone try pickpocketing me, or anything more violent. Before I left, I took one of the earrings I'd worn to the theatre that night with Aidan and wrapped it in a piece of silk. I hid it beneath the pillow of the cupboard bed in Viviane's wagon; it will help when times are hard.

That was six hours ago and, apart from one event, it's been without incident. I've found a clearing off the road where I might make a small fire without attracting unwanted attention. The final floral tribute from Ben has wilted, but instead of throwing it away, I put it into a pocket. I can't bear to get rid of it; such small, beautiful, simple gifts made me happy for a time.

I'm sadder now than I was at my farewells, for tonight Delphine will be brought out of her casket and set up on the stage. Viviane has made a new dress for her, orange silk and gold lace, with an underskirt of deepest purple. The automaton's hair has been brushed and reset into a high style rather like the one I wore to the Paragon Theatre that single night, and I wonder if it was done on purpose or unconsciously. I'll miss hearing her sing. I think, sometimes, of those hours in the box beside her, of the sliver of soul inside her. How much awareness went with that little piece of spirit? How must she feel to be sealed in there? Would she weep or scream if she could?

I shake my head as if the thoughts will be dealt with so easily, and for a while, they are, purely because I replace them with something worse. The road I chose, heading towards the mountains, Ellingham said. It goes north (*north of Bellsholm, more or less*); one would like to think my destination will be easy to find. It also passed by the Singing Rock where Viviane warned the rusalky spent their days. I might not have gone so close, but then again I might, curious to see another sort of water creature. Perhaps because they were once human, girls like myself, who'd met a terrible end, I somehow thought they'd be less dangerous.

Perhaps it was simply that I heard them singing and wanted to hear better, for the sound was divine. Mostly, Maura had said, they can talk a person into the water, wishing to visit a little rage on anyone who'd not passed on as they had. But I'm an O'Malley, there's salt and who knows what else in my veins, so their airs did no more than delight me. I tied my horse to a tree and found a rocky outcropping to perch upon as I watched them sing.

Their skins were all colours, as was their hair; I seemed to discern that not all were beautiful in life but their deaths had conferred some sort of loveliness, a strange vibrancy. Yet there were moments when I could see through them, see the scars their lives and demises left upon them; I could see the rot beneath the ripeness.

They saw me too, but I didn't seem to bother them, although one or two appeared put out that I was not ensorcelled, that I did not leap into the water – and a lucky thing that was, too, for after a while three heads bobbed to the surface, nothing like the rusalky, or perhaps their foreignness struck me because I did not expect to see them, not again.

The mer from Breakwater, I believe the same who'd pulled me in, drifting and showing me their teeth. Then the rusalky noticed them and the commotion began. The dead girls climbed up their rocks in the middle of the river much like ladies threatened by scampering mice, yet they hissed like cats as they prepared to launch themselves at the mer. They'd not left the river out of fear but merely to get a better purchase for a leap. They transcribed a perfect arc, each one.

Their illusions were lost and all I could see for the longest time were creatures of green and black putrescence, shaped roughly like humans, and a stench rose from them that was enough to make me gag. I scrambled from my roost and ran to my horse. I didn't need to know who won.

It was hours before I allowed my poor mount a respite; it seemed hours before I stopped shaking. And I was careful when choosing this camping spot to make sure there were no lakes, ponds or streams nearby. That might well keep me safe for a while, but how can one run away when all the waters in the world are joined?

17

On the afternoon of the third day out of Bellsholm, I reach a crossroads, a major one with a signpost at its centre bristling with so many wooden arrows that it looks like an elongated hedgehog. There are the four compass points at the apex, place names cascade down beneath. I examine each board with its neat black writing – Cwen's Reach, Bitterwood, Tally's Tarn, Silverton, Gevern's Mount, St Allard's Way, Heloise's Grove, Foxfire Ridge, St Sinwin's Harbour, Lodellan, Seaton St Mary, Able's Croft, even Breakwater – yet not a one says "Blackwater". I chew my lip, trying to decide: *North of Bellsholm*. But what if I make my way northwards, more or less, and find myself lost and none the wiser? I might head towards Lodellan, the cathedral city, and perhaps improve my chances of finding someone who has heard of my destination. More taverns, more coffee shops and tea houses where folk of all manner gather and talk, exchange information and stories. Somewhere I might find a hint of what I need? Perhaps it would throw Aidan off the trail, should he somehow divine my direction.

While I'm hesitating, staring at the black lines until they cease to make sense, the horse shifts nervously beneath me and whinnies. I glance around: the sky has become grey and is getting darker as clouds scud above us and the wind picks up. Not just a sun shower then. Casting about for shelter, I spot what looks like a cottage atop the slight hill before me. I urge my steed towards it, and as we get closer it becomes clear that there's another structure nearby.

A gallows, occupied.

Three bodies, all dancing energetically in the breath of the oncoming storm. The horse is reluctant to get any closer to the gibbet, stamping even when I tell him to stand still. I don't know how long they've been dead, these gallowscrows; not so long, I think. I've seen corpses before, not just my grandparents, but tenants and those washed ashore by Hob's Hallow, so they hold no fear for me. One's barely a youth, with the merest hint of a beard on his cheeks, thirteen, no more, wearing green and red plaid trews. The flesh hasn't started to melt from their bones yet, but the birds have begun to have their way: eyes are gone, and mouths hang open to show only the stubs of tongues; sweet meat and a treat for the ravens and smaller birds. And there are flies buzzing loudly where other scavengers have made tender entry. One raven sits on the head of the man I take to be the oldest, and pecks to open a wound on the cheek, then tears a long strip that comes away easily. The man's black leather waistcoat is open and flaps in the breeze, and the one in the middle twirls on his noose, bright blue jacket too vivid given his circumstances.

Maura used to tell me that every brigand worth her or his salt sent a prayer to Galagatyr either before a job or on the scaffold. Never before a trial, for that would be a waste of breath: if you've been fool enough to get caught, the Gallows God won't listen to you. But perhaps when you're awaiting the long drop and the short stop you might squeeze a little pity from the hanging deity's cold, cold heart. Looking at these three, something tells me they weren't the praying sort.

Beneath the scaffold are lush and glossy gallowberries. They are a rich purple and look enticing, but Maura always said they're not to be eaten. Required for the darkest of magics, you shouldn't even pick them unless you're prepared to use them; what good might come of a plant that grows in a place of death? I'm not in the least bit tempted.

A drop of water, hard and slick, hits me on the forehead. At first I think it's blood from the raven's meal, but then realise the storm is breaking. The droplets come down harder now and the horse is unhappy. He moves swiftly away from the dead men and towards the cottage.

I dismount and hammer at the door. No answer. The place has an air of neglect, but it never hurts to be polite. I lead the horse to the left side where there's a small lean-to, closed in enough for shelter but not so much that the beastie will feel hemmed in. I steer him into the space and, to my surprise, see there's a bale of hay waiting there as if left especially for us. I remove his saddle and blanket, find a bucket in a corner and fill it from the well in the garden, all while getting pelted with hard rain. I give him one last pat on his velvety nose, then scurry to the front (only) door of the building.

The handle turns and the wind almost pushes me inside as I call, 'Hello?' Again, no answer. The interior's dark and I use my tinderbox to scratch up a quick flame on a piece of charcloth. In the flare of light, I see a lantern on a table just in front of me; there's the swirl of fuel in its reservoir as I shake it. It sputters for a moment when I touch the cloth to the wick, catches and floods the cottage. It's just one room: a hearth against one wall, three narrow beds, a table and four rough wooden chairs, all but one broken. There is a little kindling in the fireplace, which I use. I feed the small blaze with the fragments of furniture.

There are two windows, the glass cracked but still in situ. Through them I can see the storm clouds growing ever darker, the droplets thudding against the panes, hitting the ground and churning the dirt into mud. The sound of the rain on the roof is dulled by the thatch, and there's a leak in one corner that drips down onto one of the narrow beds. There's dust on the table and floor.

I hang my coat to dry on a hook set into the wall by the fire; my trousers follow suit and I remain in just my shirt, which is mostly dry. I untwist the bun my hair's been in for days, feel the tension release in my scalp as I massage it with my fingers. There's a rough scab over the cut from the Breakwater dock, and it itches rather than aches. Soon it will be gone entirely.

I clean off the tabletop and make a meal of bread and dried meat, sitting in the sole solid chair. It feels strangely civilised after all the days on the road, eating by campfires first with the troupe, then on my own. How quickly that became normal that this should feel so alternate now. There's a tin cup, overturned but clean, and a small cauldron beside the hearth. I put it outside the door until it fills with rainwater, and brew a strong black tea with the leaves Maura packed.

I've not touched the winter-lemon whiskey, though I've yearned to, but keeping my wits about me is paramount.

When I'm done, I wonder if I'll ever bear eating bread and dried meat again, once I've found "home". I take my mother's three letters from the front of the duffel and read them once more – as if their contents might have changed – while I wait for the tea to steep. The first offers me as a price. The second merely tells how after a shaky start they are doing well, that she hopes he cares enough to hear this, that she misses him. She does not ask after her child. And in her last is the name of their new home and the promise to write no more.

No other mention of me but that I am part of a bargain. It's as if I ceased to exist once she gave me up. I read all the letters again to see if there's something I missed. I hold them to the light of the lantern, thinking perchance something might be seen in the smoke, but no.

North of Bellsholm, more or less. Perhaps it was all a lie. Perhaps these letters are nothing but untruths to lull Óisín into a false sense of security, to stop him from hunting for them, or perhaps merely a torment for the life he'd given her.

Perhaps, perhaps, perhaps.

And I feel a rage erupt inside me, a fire shooting through my veins. In a fury that would have made Aoife proud, I stand then raise the only intact chair and smash it against the stones of the chimney breast. Tears and inarticulate shouts are all I can muster, but it simply boils down to *why*?

And *how*? How could my parents leave me behind so easily? It wasn't as if I was newborn – I was three, a small person, not a damp, dribbling, shitting lump. Was I so unlovable? Did they dislike me so much? Was I nothing more, from conception, than a part of a plan, a toll to be paid?

When my tantrum runs its course I'm so very tired – so tired that I almost don't take precautions. I don't like the smell of

173

the beds, the two that aren't wet from the leak, so I pull out my bedroll and spread it in front of the fireplace. I take the sack of rock salt Maura insisted I carry – it's getting light now, but I purchased another in Bellsholm – and I make a rough circle around the bedding, with enough space that I can roll over in my sleep without fear of breaking the boundary. I also make a line of it in front of the door and across the windowsills. I put the pocket watch beside me where it can be easily seen and I slide my knives beneath the bedroll. I lie down and am asleep in a trice, every ounce of spare energy seared away.

* * *

Three raps on the door come less than an hour before dawn, or so my pocket watch tells me. My exhaustion was total and I've slept entirely through the night. I think perhaps the owner has returned. But who knocks on their very own door? The fire is still burning, brighter and longer than it should, and I can see clearly around the room. Three raps once more and I say nothing. Then again, three raps and I think perhaps that will be all, for three is a magical number, isn't it? A number of secrets and messages and gods. Then a voice, a lad's: 'Please, Miss, we beg your aid. Please, Miss, we'll not hurt you, but we need your help.'

As I check the circle of salt around me is intact, I slip my knives up my sleeves. I say, 'Come in,' and immediately regret it.

The three men from the gallows shamble over the threshold. That's when I notice that the rain has run under the door and melted away the line of salt there. It's taken so long otherwise I suspect they'd have been in here much earlier. Still, they didn't need to knock, so perhaps they're being polite for some other reason.

The marks of death have been erased. They're not quite solid, yet they lumber beneath their own weight as if all they remember is being men and alive, and are still anchored by that. I can see through them to the remaining night and rain beyond the open doorway. It's not a clear view, not a perfectly clean window, but like a fog shifted in a breeze, a fog that thickens and thins, thickens and thins. Their faces are as they were before the birds took their tithe, but the young men don't look any better for it: their expressions are avid, malign, and I'm grateful to Maura for her tales and the sack of salt, and especially glad I didn't neglect to lay it out this night.

'Evening, Miss,' says the tallest, the oldest, the one wearing the leather vest.

'Evening, Miss,' says the middlest, his jacket brightest blue.

'Evening, Miss,' says the youngest in his red and green pants. His grin is worst of all.

'Good evening,' I say, for it's best to be polite in these situations. The knives won't help me here and only the salt and my wits will keep me safe until the morning light burns these spectres away. Still, it's not going to be comfortable. 'How may I help you fine gentlemen? It's rather late – or early – to come a'calling.'

'And we apologise for that, Miss, but we don't get around much in the sunlight nowadays.' The oldest smiles, and it might once have been charming. 'As you can see, we're not the men we used to be – perhaps you'll offer assistance with that.'

'How?'

'Well, Miss, a great injustice was done to us, our lives torn away,' the middlest speaks and he's got a lovely voice; I wonder if he sang when breath still filled his lungs.

The youngest says, 'We'll tell you our stories and if you can decide which is guilty and which is innocent, then we might walk freely into the light.'

'And if I cannot tell who is guilty from who is innocent?'

'Ah, there's the rub, Miss. Then we get you, and that circle of salt won't help you one bit.' The oldest grins wider and there's something wolfish in it.

'I've hardly agreed to anything.'

'Ah, but here you are, sitting in our fine cottage and all. Looks like implied consent to me.'

I don't know how he thinks he'll get past the circle, and it's probably a lie to make me nervous. But I'm not sure I have much choice for I can't get past the circle either, not unless I want to be pickings for ghosts. I nod. 'Then tell me your tales, and I'll make my decision.'

18

'My name is Fox, and these are my brothers.' The oldest takes
the floor as if it's a stage. The others lean up against the wall
opposite, but they're not solid, so their top halves pass through it
and disappear. When they come back in, there's no rain on their
skin or dark hair. I focus on Fox.

He's got blue eyes and brown locks; he buttons up his
waistcoat carefully as he speaks. I notice the ring on his right
hand, a blue sapphire surrounded by diamonds; an engagement
ring, a feminine thing, or something passed mother to daughter.
'I followed my father into the family business, commerce, and
made a success of it. Enough to present my suit to a rich man and
ask for his oldest daughter in marriage. They were delighted to
join our houses – she brought a fat dowry – and a grand wedding
was celebrated. We were happy for a time and when I asked
my wife to help me with the acquiring and selling of goods,
she readily agreed. But soon enough there were complaints: the
goods were 'hard'. She'd bewitched rocks and stones and fallen
branches to look like bread and cakes, sheep and goats. She was
ruining my business, not to mention being a witch. What else
could I do? I had my family to think about, my reputation. I set
her alight and watched her burn. I saved the world and those I

love from a sorceress, yet for this the authorities hanged me.'

'Thank you for your tale, Fox.'

'And? Do you judge me true or false?' he demands.

'Oh, how I can tell when I've nothing to compare it to? I will listen to all your stories before I render judgement. It's the only way to be certain.' I say this politely but firmly and he glares at me but backs away nonetheless.

The middle brother steps forth, while Fox hovers above the narrow bed where water drips. The moisture bothers him not at all. I squint at the next raconteur: in his hair are prickly-looking lumps. Large burrs.

'My name is Jacob and I too joined our father's business. I also married a rich man's daughter, and we were happy for a time. She loved to ride, did my wife, and I bought her the finest steeds. We would gallop over hill and dale; but she distracted me so much from my duties that my part of the enterprise began to fail. I had to sell all but one of her horses to keep food on the table, and she became angry with me. The day came when I was obliged to sell her last, her favourite. But she spoke harshly to me and mounted the beast, it reared up, unsettled by her ire and noise, and she was thrown. Her neck broken, and I a widower so soon. But her father did not believe my tale and came for me with his men. And they hung me beside my brother.'

'Thank you for your story, Jacob,' I say.

'Well?'

'As I said, I will hear all before I give judgement and I have one last recounting to consider.' I nod towards the youngest, who takes his brother's place. Jacob goes and leans against the wall once again, careful not to pass through it this time.

The lad smiles, holds up a finger – there's a green stain on the tip – and begins. 'My name is Joseph and there was a rich man's daughter I would have married, but her father judged us too young for such things, though I had such potential to be just like my brothers. We made our plans to elope, she and I, but her father found us out and locked his daughter in her room. Seven days I waited to hear from her, for her to escape and return to me, but in the end only a letter came. Her father was right, she wrote, and we were too young. I wept. I wept but I sent her a gift to show there were no hard feelings: a dress of the brightest green, a blameless gift. But she died soon after and her father ensured I was hung beside my brothers.'

All three move to stand at the edge of the salt circle, peering down at me. 'And so?' says the oldest. 'Who is the innocent party?'

I clear my throat. 'Well, Fox, you are clearly lying because why would a rich man's daughter who brought a fat dowry need or choose to cheat customers with hard goods? That ring,' I say, and nod at it. 'It was hers, and I can see there's blood around its edge where you cut off her finger to take it. I doubt she was even your wife, but some poor girl kidnapped on the highway. You were justly requited.'

The other two laugh. Fox steps back, hangs his head.

'Jacob, why would you become poor when you joined the family business, which you are all at pains to tell me was so prosperous? And I can see burrs in your hair. You put them under your bride's saddle, so that when she mounted the barbs bit into the horse and he reared, throwing her. It was happy, though predictable, chance that she broke her neck. The mark of your sin is upon you and you were justly requited.'

Fox and Joseph snigger. Like his brother, Jacob steps back, hangs his head.

The lad fixes me with eyes as blue as a summer's day and smiles.

'And you, Joseph, you learned your brothers' craft well, yearned to do as they did much sooner than you should, and gave a woman the only value you deemed she should have. You sent your love a poisoned dress, did you not? I can see the marks on your fingers where you touched the thing; it made you ill. Perhaps it would have carried you off before long, but you were found out and they strung you up alongside your brothers. You too were justly requited.'

Joseph falls away to stand beside his siblings. I look at the three of them. 'You were all rightly hung.'

'Too clever by half. Not that it will matter to you, Miss,' says Fox, and points to the floor. A trickle of water has run from the bed beneath the leaking ceiling along a runnel in the dirt floor and is about to reach the circle of salt. There's no salvation for them to have and none for me. Despite judging their cases, they think they'll get me anyway. I can see their rage burning up inside them, anticipation making them heavier, more solid. But I know something they don't: that outside the sun is breaking through the clouds and the rain stopped some while ago.

The beams of light pierce the brothers' bodies and they all scream, though one would hardly think it would hurt them. And then they are gone and I am alone, just as the trickle of water breaches the salt barrier.

Before I ride away − the horse appears happy, well-rested, contented − I make a point of visiting the gallows. I kindle a fire from the sticks of the chair I broke in my temper, then use a flaming brand to set the corpses alight as they hang there – they go up like tinder despite being wet from the storm. I wait only long enough to make sure that bodies and gibbet all are certain to burn.

19

Another two days and I encounter no one on the road, which is partially luck and partially intent. Whenever I hear the sound of carriage wheels, of horses' hooves, I duck off into the trees and hide. The horse, whom I've not named, keeps quiet too. Perhaps in hope of gaining a name through good behaviour. The last time I spoke to someone was just after leaving the gallows hut; a woman at a farmhouse gave me bread in exchange for some coin bits. I asked if she'd heard of Blackwater, but she squinted and asked if it was some new kind of plague. I'm still afraid of being noticed and remembered – would Aidan bother to hunt me this far?

The thing about avoiding other people is that you spend a lot of time with your own thoughts and mine are neither pleasant nor useful for I have no answers, merely speculations and more questions. At Hob's Hallow, there was plenty of solitude if I wanted it, but there were also people to talk to when I sought company. I think back to all the times they annoyed me and offer a silent apology. Aoife and Óisín gone, Maura and Malachi equally lost to me – and I hope they're safe.

I hope Aidan hasn't sought to punish them for my escape. I hope he thinks I achieved it all on my own; it's not too far a stretch to believe, after all. He sees me as an untamed thing requiring a firm hand so I'm sure he's utterly certain it was my own mad scheme. What will he do? He can't inherit Hob's Hallow without me, at least not yet – as I recall he must wait ten years before he can have me declared dead and put in a claim on the estate. But then, so might any of the other distant relatives with a mind to do so. Let them fight over that crumbling pile, let them waste their remaining years doing so.

Perhaps he'll bide his time then apply for the estate to be transferred to his own name, his own family... but to whom? There're no longer any judges in Breakwater, no one to make such decisions. Perhaps the Queen of Thieves will be his judge; perhaps they'll make some mutually beneficial new deal. Or perhaps she'll take it away from him. Perhaps he'll marry some prim miss from one of Breakwater's last good families, if any of them choose to remain in a city of thieves. Perhaps a rich girl from elsewhere just to be sure there's new blood in the mix – if he can't have his cousin to wife, then let us thin the line once again, but strengthen the chins! Will he search for me? And if yes, for how long? Or will he not bother, reluctant to throw resources after an unwilling bride?

I've passed perhaps ten small towns and large, but always keeping at a safe distance; no one can talk to me nor get close enough to see my face isn't that of a boy, no matter that I tuck my hair away. Stopping at the remote farms for food is a means of trying to hide, to not be noticed – perhaps it's not so clever, but I rather hope that they're so remote that no one else will find them. Late one afternoon I come to a deserted-looking village – not quite twenty ruined cottages. I wonder what happened here?

Then I notice that it's beside a wide river where the bridge is gone – taken by a flood by the looks of it. I wonder what else the flood washed away.

I urge the horse partway down the bank, but again not too close. The beastie isn't happy and I'm learning to pay attention to him – gods know I should have ridden on no matter the storm back at the gallows house. Getting soaked would have been a small price to avoid the murderous brothers.

The river appears shallow in parts; there are rocks and sandbanks one might use to ford, but only so far, and there are also spots where the water has the darkness that only comes with terrible depth. I put my hand to my throat, feel the silver ship's bell beneath the collar of my shirt, wonder if I dare risk the crossing here. I wonder if the mer would have, could have, come this far; how could they know which way to go, which tributary to follow? Who knows when the bridge might be rebuilt? Perhaps never, by the look of the decayed village, and certainly it won't be soon enough for my needs. Shall I let fear of the mer paralyse me? Sit here until Aidan or his agents find me and drag me back to Breakwater, recaptured because I feared to get my feet wet? Wouldn't that make Aoife rage? Of course, she'd probably want me caught.

Well, no, more than fear of wet feet: more serious. Dragged a'down by creatures who want me gone. There are plenty left with thinned O'Malley blood, but none with the name. Granddaughter of Aoife and Óisín, who were siblings, and daughter of their daughter Isolde. Until I find my mother, I'm the last of my kind. Once it was Aoife, now it's me.

I hobble the horse so he can't go too far, remove his tack, then sit beneath a tree. Reposing here for a bit (at a safe remove from the river's edge, of course) while I eat the apple I stole from an orchard on the way and ponder my options seems like a good choice. The horse can graze and we can both have a rest, he his legs, me my arse. I feel I'll have calluses sooner rather than later.

Soon I'm lying on the grass and staring at the sky through the branches and leaves above me. It's so blue, not a cloud to be seen, and I try to make my mind as featureless, as blank. Too many thoughts, fears, uncertainties cartwheeling there. And that ever-simmering anger at my parents. As much as I'm fleeing Aidan, I'm also rushing towards Isolde to demand an explanation. Part of me... part of me is still a child hoping to find a home, parents who'll tell me it was all a mistake, and they've been waiting for me for so very long to find them. That I *had* to find them, it was quest, my burden, *my price*. That, at the end of this road, all will be well.

I don't know when I stopped staring and my eyes closed, but at some point I must have, for I wake with a start a while later. I sit up and look around. The light has changed and my mount is gone.

The saddle and bridle and blanket remain beside me, but of the grey horse there is no sign.

I rise and wander the riverbank. There: the hoofprints stop and become drag marks where the horse dug his hooves in, tried to stop whatever he'd acquiesced to at the beginning. They become trenches the closer they get to the edge of the water, but it's clear my poor old beastie lost his battle. And him, dying without a name because I was too parsimonious and untrusting to give him one, lest his loss cause me hurt. Well, it hurts no less, I can say that for sure. I look out onto the rapidly rushing river and there is no sign. Whatever happened, it happened whilst I slept and I did not wake.

Anyone too lazy to follow the trail to the river might have simply believed the creature stolen by bandits and counted themselves lucky to escape with their own skin intact. I look back over my shoulder to where the saddle and so on lay. Swallowing, I make a decision.

I yell at the river, 'Come out!'

At first nothing. I'm worried it will be the mer, I half-expect them, but ultimately: no. There's a great bubbling and spurt of white foam out in the middle, in one of those deep dark patches, and abruptly something surfaces.

Neither mer nor combative rusalky, but something different entirely.

Its head is that of a horse.

Black as night, with a broad chest, it presses forward and climbs from the river to stand before me on the bank, but maintains a good six feet between us. The creature clearly doesn't feel entirely confident about coming any closer; or perhaps it's politeness. Water cascades off it and steams and boils. Its mane flows almost to its hooves, of which there are two instead of four, and point backwards. The forelegs are muscular arms, ending in enormous hands tipped with dexterous fingers and thumbs – sometimes they shift into hooves as well, then back again to hands.

A kelpie, a water horse, a nuggle, a tangie; so many names for the same thing. I recognise it only from Maura's stories for you don't see them in the sea or ocean; they don't like salt water, but I'm far from that now. Lakes and rivers, ponds and streams… fresh water, fresh danger…

The kelpie has eyes that look like whirlpools – Maura said they were always pits of fire but it's probably hard to keep flames alight underwater. Impractical. They are the same deep shade as the river, not quite blue, not quite black, but a little of both with some green thrown in for good measure, with white swirling around the outer edges. He – for it's definitely male – smiles and all his teeth show in a wide splitting of lips. The kelpie bows too, which is nice, but the dead men called me 'Miss' very nicely and they meant me ill. This monster, if I'm not mistaken, has eaten my poor horse. Anyone can have good manners but appalling appetites. Around his neck are the remains of a bridle, the leather and silver bits wound round with straggling river weed. The halter is ragged but clearly cannot be removed by the kelpie's own hands.

'Good morning,' I say, wary. Maura said they ate children. Maura said they offered to carry travellers across rivers and drowned them for dinner. Maura said they sometimes steal brides to live beneath the water in dank caves and give birth to horrors that are neither one thing nor the other, but all rage and damned by more than one god. Maura said a lot of things, things that scared me as a child, and which make me nervous now. But I'm also annoyed.

'You are wishing to cross?' he asks, and the voice is a strange thing, like water rushing across my ears. It's not unpleasant.

'Yes,' I reply. 'Which you've made extremely difficult.'

'My apologies. I was hungry.' There's that smile again, and the strangeness of the voice; it makes me feel a little faint and I think how easy it must be for him to convince people to ride with him.

187

'But you didn't eat me, even though I slept.'

'You would not... agree with my digestion, salt daughter.'

'Why do you call me that?' My hand goes to the silver bell beneath the collar at my throat.

He cannot see it, but the creature nods towards my fingers as if he knows what they seek. 'Not entirely human, are you? I can sense it in your veins.'

'Of course I'm human!' It was foolish to speak so loudly; now he knows I'm suddenly uncertain. 'What do you know of my blood?'

'Only its composition, salt daughter.' He bows again.

'What... what am I? What's in me?'

'I only sense the salt. My apologies, I cannot say more.'

I notice the careful phrasing he uses. Perhaps he knows more but will not say. Perhaps he knows nothing.

'You're wishing to cross?' he asks again.

I nod.

'I'll not offer to carry you—'

'Then why did you come when called?'

'—in my usual fashion, but rather I propose a bargain.'

'Indeed.'

'So non-committal.' He laughs and it's a splashing, booming thing. 'I would beg your assistance and in return I promise to do you no harm, and will grant you a boon.'

'What would you ask of me, sir?'

He gestures to the bridle twisted around his face and neck. 'Remove this vile thing.'

'Who placed it there?'

'A man, long dead.'

188

'By your... hand?'

He shakes his great head. 'I wish. He tricked me into thrall. Had me build a castle for him' – he gestures towards something I'd not noticed before, a broken tower peeking through the canopy of the forest on a mountain side – 'then he forced me to plough fields like some common nag. He and his heirs are gone but this shackle remains and so must I. I would be free of this place.'

'I thought your kind did not shift from your home?'

He shrugs and droplets scatter from his skin. 'Not in the usual way of things, but when we are caught... why stay where your shame has been displayed? Do you know how many folk would come and watch as I worked? The villagers brought picnics and sat with their children while I sweated in the sun and hauled stones, and could do nothing to retaliate.'

'From that village? The ruin?'

He nods, grins again.

'Did you have something to do with its destruction?'

He puts a hoof-hand against his chest. 'I swear not. When the flood came – and I do not know from where or why or how – and washed out the bridge, it also covered the fields, swept away most of the villagers, and those who survived the deluge did not stay here. There were bodies, too, come down from wherever the flood began, men and women, their throats cut, bloodless all.' The creature shakes his head as if he, eater of men, had never thought to see such a thing. 'I wonder if anyone looked for them.'

'But if I release you, you'll eat travellers wherever you make a new home.'

'It is my nature,' he says truthfully.

'And if I don't help?'

'Then I shall remain trapped.'

Yet I can't quite bear the thought of him chained here.

'Promise me you'll only eat the wicked.'

He pouts. 'How can I tell such a thing?'

'If you can sense salt in my veins, surely you can sense a darkness in someone's soul.'

He grins and laughs and bows again, all those teeth. He nods. 'That does not diminish my food supply unduly, salt daughter. I agree to your terms.'

I hold up a finger. 'Yet here's the thing: you've left me without the means to finish my journey.'

He looks at me like a sulky child. 'What do you propose?'

'In addition to the boon you owe me from freeing you, you will pay off your debt to me by taking me where I wish to go.'

'And how long might that last?'

'How long have you waited here for someone to rescue you from your binding? Your time with me will be but the blink of an eye,' I lie blithely for I don't know when or if I shall ever find Blackwater. I pull the long knife from my belt, wait until the kelpie nods his assent.

He stands still, trusting. He's a full head taller even than me and must bend down so I can better reach. I slip the blade between his hide and the bridle and slice at the leather. It's soaked and hard to cut, so I must saw with all my strength but be careful not to slip and cut his flesh.

At last it's done, and the kelpie stamps his hooves, pulls away sharply and begins to dance, tossing his head and moving sinuous as a seal in the water. I keep hold of the bridle, which feels disgusting and stinks.

'None of that when I'm on your back,' I say, and the kelpie's caper comes to an end.

The wide, wide smile, the teeth, so bright and so numerous, catch the afternoon sun. He paces towards me, and suddenly the sound of his steps is terribly loud, or so it seems. He stops just in front of me; I will not run nor turn my back. He's only promised not to eat me, not to not kill me. I change my grip on the knife, spread my feet so I'm standing solidly. He throws one hand out to the side, then the other, and sweeps into the most elaborate bow yet, with flourishes, and a dancing of his hooves.

'My gratitude, salt daughter. I swore you no harm and my word is my bond.' He rises. 'I promised you a boon, also.'

'Yes, you did.'

'Would you have something now? Or later?'

'How will I get it later?'

He nods towards the bridle in my hand. 'Keep that. Take it to a stream or river, wherever you are, and shake it beneath the surface. I will hear you and I will come.'

'Do you know anything of a place called Blackwater?'

He tilts his enormous head, considering. 'I have not heard of it, I swear. Neither from my meals nor from any whisper in the water.'

I feel unaccountably disappointed. 'Then I will take this' – I hold up the bridle and it jingles wetly – 'and I shall call you when I have need.'

'And I shall come, salt daughter. For the moment, let us get well away from this place; I've tarried here far too long. Follow the road. There is a town called Lelant's Bridge where you will find – unsurprisingly – a bridge to cross this river.'

'This? Now?' I hold up my poor horse's bridle for I know there's often an order to such things, to how they work, whether they bind or make slaves.

'One moment.'

The kelpie steps back a little, shakes, shudders and shivers. His outline goes soft as water, then he's solid and four-legged, as emphatically black as my nameless mount was nondescript grey. He paws the ground, rolls his eyes, prances foolishly and makes me laugh. He's much larger and handsomer than Aidan's stallion and I'm childishly pleased about this.

I slip the bridle over his huge head; soon the blanket and saddle are in place. Resting my forehead against his and stroking his velvety nose I whisper, 'I swear I shall release you as soon as I am able.'

20

We travel an hour past dusk – the kelpie seems to have boundless energy, but whether that's a standard state of affairs or merely because of his enthusiasm for escaping I'm unsure. When it's simply too dark to see, we make camp. Or rather, I make camp while he grazes. I ask if he'll retake his shape, but he shakes his head at me and continues to chew on the grass; presumably in his shifted form he's quite happy with this sort of sustenance. I eat the last of my food, but am not too worried; Lelant's Bridge is on my horizon. I'll restock, perhaps ask questions. Perhaps I'm far enough from Aidan's reach – if he's even bothering to pursue me, perhaps I'm not as important as I think I am – and it doesn't matter at all. No one will care what I ask or report it to anyone else.

Perhaps I'm free and do not know it.

How will I ever know?

I can still smell the wet reek of the kelpie's bridle on my hands, though the thing itself is in the bottom of my duffel and I washed my hands in the river (so cautiously that the kelpie eyed me curiously). What I wouldn't give for a proper bath: hot water, a lot of soap and suds and glorious floral-scented oils for my skin. I fall asleep soon after my meal.

When I wake, it's to the sensation of a rough, wet tongue on my cheek and forehead, and breath that smells almost as bad as a corpsewight three days in the sun. I protest and push at a furry snout. I sit and focus: there's a wolf with blue eyes and the broadest grin sitting across from me, behind the veil of the smouldering fire. It's still dark. The beast looks young but there's no sense of menace about it, tongue hanging out, panting, friendly as a dog and looking quite pleased with itself. Then it picks at its teeth with a paw that is now a hand, now a paw. The kelpie-horse is nearby, eyes the wolf with boredom then wanders a little further off. I'd like to think that if there was any danger he'd leap to my defence, but who really knows? I notice on the ground in front of me three wildflowers, pink and red and white.

Though magic's being repressed in most places, it doesn't stop things like mer, kelpies, rusalky, trolls and nixies, corpsewights and ghosts from existing. They just hide deeper in the forests and mountains, in lakes and tarns, cellars and mirrors. It's harder for witches, though, to cover what they are as the Church gets more and more militant about things that don't conform. Hard to know, too, how many burn who are genuinely those who can hex, and how many are merely inconvenient women. Once, simple cunning women like Maura were taken for granted – they kept folk and livestock and plants healthy, but gradually it was decided they did not *fit*. They would not obey the whims and will of the Church and its princes. They had no place in the world.

The beast continues to stare at me, tongue lolling. There's a collar around its neck, with a small leather pouch suspended from it.

'Are you cursed?' I ask quietly, thinking of tales Maura told me of women and men who sprouted fur, sometimes on the full moon, sometimes only every seventh year, depending on the rules of their affliction. Hexes inflicted by witches or god-hounds who use the same magic as the females they'd prefer to burn. Other times some chose to become like this, especially women, when it meant freedom from responsibilities and life in general.

'Cursed? A little inconvenienced, perhaps, having gone out of my way to find you,' says the wolf, then the outline shivers and the boy from the troupe is in its place. Ben. Or at least, his top half is boy, the bottom remains covered in fur. He gestures. 'No pants.'

'I appreciate the consideration, Ben.' I should have known from the flowers! 'I'm sorry, I've no food to offer…'

'Not to worry, rabbits are plentiful and slower than me. I've eaten quite well.'

My pocket watch tells me it's only 1 a.m., so I throw some wood on the fire and build it up until it's blazing once more. Then I toss my coat at the boy for him to wrap around his bare torso. I huddle back into my bedroll.

'We found it,' he says.

'What?'

'Your place. Blackwater.' He grins hugely. 'Viviane and Ellingham have been asking, subtle like, around the streets and traps, ships' crews and tavern folk, anyone as they can find.'

I swallow – grateful but wondering what kind of trails they might be leaving for me, for themselves. And yet what's my choice? Just keep wandering north until I hit the sea once again? The ice? Find a hole in the world into which I might disappear? 'And?'

'There was an old bloke in one of the back-alley stores, a silversmith. Not all there if you ask me – lot of rambling, talking to people who weren't there, but Ellingham's known him a while. Asked him if he'd heard of the place.' Ben shakes his head. 'His face, like he were a kid with a secret. But his son, who's looking after him, making sure he doesn't short-change anyone, especially not the shop, interrupts the moment he hears "Blackwater". Tells us it's time to go, his father needs a rest. And he hustles us out like we're no better than panhandlers!' Ben's expression is one of umbrage, then he smiles slowly.

'But it's not like we're easily fooled – we're players, aren't we? That's our game, fooling folk. So we don't make a fuss, just act like nothing's gone on, and we're off down the road neat as you like.'

'But?'

'Well, we wait, don't we?' The boy says it like it's obvious and I'm a bit of an idiot. 'When the son goes out half an hour later, we nip back into the shop. The old bloke's on his own, but we can hear some bustle out back – daughter-in-law, I suppose – so we talk soft like. And he's happy as a pig in mud, seeing his mates again. Puts his finger up like this, waggled it so we'd come closer.' Ben does the same thing, and I lean forward in spite of myself. 'Said he'd never worked silver so pure as what came out of Blackwater.'

I close my eyes, offer a prayer to whoever will take it; I'm not fussy.

'*But* he said he'd not had any shipments from there for a while.'

'What's a while when it's at home?'

'He couldn't be sure.' Ben taps his forehead. 'Ellingham asked him where the place could be found and he did this little caper and giggled. Said no one would ever find it on a map, coz no one was supposed to know where it was.'

'Aaaah. Then how can I know he was speaking truly and not just spouting fantasies?' I drop my head into my hands. Clearly I should have been fussier with my prayers.

'Well,' Ben says, brow raised, 'I suppose you can't. But he did draw this.' The boy reaches for the little sack on the collar around his neck, fumbles it open and pulls out a tight roll of parchment. He unfolds it, then hands it over, very careful reaching across the fire. I squint at the thick paper in the flickering yellow light. The drawing is very fine indeed, and it shows a map. I can see Bellsholm and a lot of the places I've passed by recently. There's the gallows crossroads with the word "ghosts" writ neatly beside it and I think how useful this would have been some days ago. I wonder how long those men have been dead, how long their bodies had lasted in the elements before I burned them. I wonder whose magic kept them there so very long. There's the village that was drowned, and there's the bridge still intact on the map. I warn Ben about that; should the troupe ever go that way they'll need to find another spot to ford.

The important thing is that I'm heading in the right direction. According to the kelpie, we'll cross at Lelant's Bridge tomorrow, then the trail leads up, into mountains. On the map, a grand house drawn small by a body of water, the name *Blackwater* printed beside in the neatest of hands. Around the outside, marking off a boundary, what looks like a hedge – has he bothered to draw individual leaves? Yes, he has. And a tree on the other side, a face (sex indeterminate) etched into its trunk.

'Thank you, Ben. Thank you so much!' I take one last look at the map, then slide it into the pocket of my trousers, before fishing about in my duffel for the small pouch that contains the few pieces of jewellery not sewn into my coat's hem. The earring that is the pair for the one I left on Viviane's pillow glimmers in the firelight as I throw it to the boy. Ben catches it, holds it up to watch the flames reflected in the facets.

'Don't think Ellingham's delighted about the one you left with Vivi, either.' He laughs. 'But everyone else is. We're happy to have something laid by against the hard times, even if the old man's too proud. He thinks it's bad luck to set things aside, as if you're going to call ill fortune onto yourself.'

'Hide it until you need it.'

He puts it into the pouch around his neck, makes sure everything's secure. He pats it. 'Safe as houses.'

We smile at each other, then he looks sly and says, 'There was something strange, though.'

'What?'

'Well, Ellingham was asking around just like I told you, but that day he was looking for a clockworker or a watchmaker, for Delphine.'

A frost settles at the pit of my stomach, and my throat feels like it's closing over. I think of lying in the box with her, pressing some button or other and feeling that click beneath my palm. Not admitting to it, just hoping I'd not broken anything... I open my lips to offer an explanation, an apology, but his expression of glee stops me. If I'd broken the automaton, he'd not look so, would he?

So instead I say, 'Why?'

'The night after you left, we bring her out on stage just like we always do. She's all in her new finery that Vivi made, and she looks exquisite if I do say so. Our Delphine sings her song just as she always does, but after the applause dies down and we're preparing to take her away, just like we always do, she begins to *speak*. The timing was impeccable, might I add, as if she'd just waited for them all to think her done. But she starts telling this tale, only it's not in her voice, is it? "I was sixteen when he plucked me from the sea…"'

'Oh, gods. Is Ellingham angry?'

'Angry? He couldn't be happier for her to have something new. That's sort of how he found your old silversmith; he was in that street looking for a clockworker to see if they might figure how she might add something *else* to her repertoire.'

I laugh with relief. 'When I was in the box with her, I pressed her chest by accident… I told myself the story to stay calm. I hope Ellingham doesn't break her in his ambition.'

'No worries about that. Clockmaker wouldn't touch her, said she was too precious and she couldn't promise she'd get Delphine back together.' He shrugs. 'Ellingham's happy enough with your tale. The audience loved it, your voice holds the attention.'

'Will you come with me?' I ask. 'Just for a while?'

But Ben says, 'No,' with a reluctance that makes me feel not quite so bad. 'No, Miss Molly, I've been gone too long following you. What will Ellingham do without me?'

What indeed? 'But sleep here tonight, get some rest.'

'Oh, yes.'

Soon enough both our lids are growing heavy. I've been

riding, but Ben's been loping, running to catch up with me. He needs to slumber.

'Goodnight, Ben, sleep well.'

'Night, Miss Molly.'

* * *

In the morning he's gone.

My coat is draped over me, and the fire has been extinguished properly. I've slept over-long despite the bright morning light, but the weight of the past days, and the burden of hope brought by the map, have worn me out. I'm slow to rise, slow to get on the road. But I pat the kelpie-horse and tell him his journey – *our* journey – now has an end in sight. He whickers.

It's early afternoon when we come to Lelant's Bridge, a decent-sized place. There's a weir beneath that aforementioned bridge where the water rushes white and onwards, back to where I met the kelpie. I ask a woman at a baker's stall in the markets which is the best inn for a woman travelling alone, and she directs me to the Maiden's Revenge. It is smaller than most of the hostelries I pass, but the advantage is fewer guests, bigger rooms and private bathrooms; and for some extra gold bits I can have my laundry done. I leave the kelpie-horse in the hands of the inn's stableboy. Before I leave, I whisper and remind my mount that he's honour-bound not to eat anyone here. He tosses his head as if he thinks I'm rude.

The white-haired, quick-fingered landlady named Beck is polite enough to only give me one raised eyebrow – men's attire, fairly filthy by now, and I cannot smell good – then she pockets my coin at speed and happily shows me upstairs. The room is bright, with a patchwork quilt on the high bed, a chair by the window of coloured leadlight glass, a small fireplace, a table should I wish to eat in (there's a dining room downstairs for those who like company) and an enormous bathtub. She turns on the taps without asking me, is generous with the fragrant oils on the little shelf above the tub – at which I do my best not to take offence – promises a meal will be brought up soon, then leaves me to my own devices. I'm still soaking half an hour later when there's a knock. A nervous pretty girl carries in a tray, then takes away my dirty laundry. I stay in the tub a long time, washing my hair, topping up the hot water as and when I wish, and picking at the food on the tray (cheeses, fruit, meat).

When I finally feel clean – bearing a striking resemblance to a prune – I go to bed in the middle of the afternoon, luxuriating in the sensation of crisp cotton sheets, a proper mattress and pillows that aren't my rolled-up coat. I sleep until the sun is gone and then a different girl – friendly and round – arrives with more food (baked ham, mashed parsnips and a custard tart). I shouldn't want to eat more but I do – anything that's not bread, dried meat and pilfered apples. Thoroughly stuffed, I put on the clean clothes from my duffel bag (although part of me yearns for a dress, if only for a little while, and by my own choice), and I braid my still-damp hair and let it hang down my back, then I go out into the streets.

There are night markets, people hawking everything from pots and pans to food, alcohol to knives, hats and shoes and dolls and perfumes. Nothing like Breakwater, though. I shake my head to clear the thought. I walk past a fountain that has leaping wolves around its edge, and I take in every sight I can. There are jugglers and fire-eaters in the main square, singers and musicians to accompany them. I throw silver bits into the hats they've placed on the ground. I feel a smile on my face and a lightness inside that is quite foreign and I know won't last, but I resolve to enjoy it while I can.

It takes a while but eventually I begin to feel uncomfortable. I realise it's the creep of another's eyes over me – I'm being watched. It's all I can do not to swing around, looking for the culprit and letting them know they're sensed. Making my way back through the crowds that still bustle in the square and nearby streets despite the late hour, I duck into alleyways, sprint from one desperately discovered hiding place to the next, wait in shadows, but no one seems to follow me. By the time I make it back to the inn I still haven't shaken the sensation of being observed, and I can't help but recall that I last felt this way in those cold dark hours in Breakwater's assassins market.

The nervous girl is folding washing in a side room off the reception and I enquire if anyone's been asking about me. She looks surprised but isn't rude enough to say, 'Who'd ask about *you*?' She simply says, 'No, Miss,' and hands me my newly cleaned shirt and trousers. I thank her then go up to my room, unlock the door and slip in, quickly latching the thing behind me. I lean, forehead first, against the wood and breathe deeply for a few moments.

The voice comes and almost stops my heart.

'Good evening, Miss O'Malley.'

I spin about, searching. The leadlight window is ajar, its colours dead against the night sky. On the bed is my duffel, open and emptied. And there's a dark form in the shadows beside the lit hearth. It steps forward, into the light, and I see the face of the footman, the green-eyed man whose acquaintance I made so briefly and who, if I'm not badly mistaken, murdered Aoife.

21

As I turn back to the door, scrabbling with the lock, he laughs. 'Oh, Miss O'Malley. I'll be on you before you know it.'

I force myself to stand still, lips tightly pressed together, to avoid the indignity of having him hold me captive. I'm as afraid as I am annoyed; I thought I'd gone far enough, been clever enough. Deep breath, pivot, face him.

He's wearing black, all black: trousers, shirt, weapons belt, vest, cloak. There's just the eyes, a light green, to stand out in his swarthy face. He'd pass through shadows unnoticed. He holds up the silver knife from my bag, wiggles it to grab my attention. 'Now, be so kind as to toss those lovely new weapons at my feet. The one I can see at your belt and t'other from wherever you've secreted it.'

'How can you know that?'

'I'm very good at my job, Miss O'Malley.' When I hesitate, he sighs. 'I would hate to bruise you, Miss O'Malley, as I'm under strict orders to return you intact to your betrothed.' He examines the nails of his right hand, nonchalant. 'Damaged goods would affect my payment. Now, come: your daggers.'

'As my betrothed is your employer, I'd say you have already damaged the goods,' I say, hoping my tone doesn't betray my nerves. I take out my blades and toss them at his feet; no point trying to throw them, I've no skill at that.

He grins. 'And a pleasure it was too, but I think for both our sakes it's best if your cousin never hears of that. It would hardly reflect well on either of us.'

'You really don't understand anything about me if you think I'm worried about what Aidan Fitzpatrick thinks.' I tilt my head. 'In fact, I'm more likely to tell him if it will make him angry.'

He tilts his head the other way, gazes at me with all the intensity of a hawk looking at a mouse. 'But surely you'd like to remain alive a while yet? Your intended doesn't strike me as a... tolerant man.'

'No, but you can't, at least as far as I'm aware, get children on a dead woman.' This man doesn't need to know *why* Aidan needs my children. I ask a question I probably already know the answer to: 'How long have you been working for him?'

He gestures with both hands, indicating an indefinite period of time. 'Not so long, a few months. Jobs here and there, other cities, places where his business interests could be progressed by the removal of a rival or three. I'm new to Breakwater, you see—'

'I don't care. We are not acquaintances meeting at a social gathering. You are not asking me to dance.'

'Indeed not. As I recall we skipped that part.' He smiles again and I want to dig my thumbs in his eyes and gouge.

'Did you murder my grandmother?' I ask, my voice low, the words almost painful as they push up from my throat and out my mouth. He inclines his head and there's something regal about the admission; a prince amongst assassins. 'And Aidan paid you to do that too?'

205

Again, the nod, this time with a shade of pity.

'Why?' I ask and it comes out as a child's cry. It hurts even though Aoife sold me, even though she was seldom kind. She was *there*. She was there all my life. She was my family, my blood, my pillar, and it is hard to let go of that no matter what, impossible for it to be so quickly dissolved and washed away in a tide of hatred. Love is a barbed hook and family the line to which it is tied. It digs deep and sometimes trying to remove it entirely does more damage than simply leaving the obstruction beneath the skin for a scar to grow over.

He shrugs and it enrages me, that Aoife O'Malley is so easily dismissed. 'I don't ask the reasons — one can't afford to have a conscience in this business or one would never eat — I just take my fee.'

I shake my head. 'He'd already made his bargain with Aoife! She'd agreed to everything. What could he possibly have to gain from murdering her?'

He shrugs again and I can see a red tide rising in front of my eyes. I bite the inside of my cheek to keep from screaming. I put my face in my hands as he speaks, 'Mr Fitzpatrick is an impatient man. He works with a variety of folk who are equally if not more impatient. I often find that when people do more than one deal, sometimes the demands of one agreement overcome another.'

'Meaning?' I ask through my fingers, but I think of Ellingham's comments about Bethany Lawrence, about the changes in Aidan when he began having truck with her.

'Meaning bigger fish eat little fish.' He pulls up the chair from beneath the window and sits with a sigh, as if he's a housewife who's had a trying day tramping around the markets. He gestures I should do the same, and I perch on the edge of the bed.

'How did you track me? From Breakwater?' If he'll tell me I might learn something to avoid in future; oh, there's no doubt I'll run again.

He cocks an eyebrow and grins. 'Afraid Mr Fitzpatrick might learn who helped you?'

'Yes,' I admit. 'My friends don't deserve hurt for rendering aid.'

He waves a hand. 'Never fear. I don't reveal my sources; no point in giving away the tricks of the trade. That's not what clients pay me for anyway. Your Mr Ellingham and his people are safe... and Miss Brigid.'

'Gods, please don't tell him about Brigid.' Somehow I'm not sure she'd survive. *My, Miren O'Malley,* I think, *how your heart has turned.*

'On my honour. But I would point out that more than one person saw you and her that night, wandering Breakwater's inky streets.'

I try to breathe evenly. If the assassin brings me back, there will be no reason for Aidan to find out. Of course, he will ask questions, he will want to know who my allies were so I can be stripped of them. How much can I withstand before I beg him to stop hurting me? Another thought hits.

'What about...'

'The old people at the Hallow?' His expression grows grave. 'Ah, now that's another story.' Suddenly he seems hesitant to talk. 'They chose their own end, Miss O'Malley. That should give you some comfort, although I'm not sure how much.'

'What...' I swallow but there's not enough saliva left in my mouth, my whole body. An entire lake couldn't water my parched throat at this moment.

'They took poison. The maids found them the morning after your departure, I'm told.'

'No...' I think of Aidan, that he somehow orchestrated matters, but the green-eyed man must see this in my expression.

'Mr Fitzpatrick told me about them when he sent me after you. He was quite enraged he didn't get the chance to interrogate them for your whereabouts. I'm a good judge of men, Miss O'Malley, I know when one's lying. Your cousin's fury was his truth.'

I think of Maura and those potions she kept in the pantry, the tinctures and tisanes we brewed together. The lessons she taught me, planting and picking the kitchen garden, harvesting the other things that grew best wild along the sea brim, or just below the surface of waters salty or fresh. I think about the herbs that could burn the cold from you, relieve a headache, make you sleep for weeks, give you dreams for joy, or ensure all your days were those of forgetting. I think of Maura making her own choice about how she departed Hob's Hallow, and that she'd have let no one take that from her. I think of Malachi who'd never have gone, not when his wife and babe were buried there, not when he'd lived more of his life there than anywhere else. And he'd have not left his sister, as much as they grumped and grumbled at each other, much as they annoyed one another. He'd not have deserted her anymore than she would him. One last drink together, one final winter-lemon whiskey to chase away the chill, and then to slumber forever.

'For what it's worth from one such as I, I am sorry.' The green-eyed man breaks into my thoughts. 'And now, Miss O'Malley. I feel strongly that we should depart before daybreak. The sunlight gives too much power to witnesses and who knows what you might do if you think you can enlist the sympathies of some bold passer-by?' He gestures to the coil of rope on the floor by his chair; I'd missed that. 'Do I need to restrain you? Or will you be biddable?'

'I shall be biddable.' I wonder if he's as stupid as Aidan was, taking my apparent defeat to be true. 'What choice do I have?'

He gestures to the bed on which I sit, smirks. 'Well, we might pass the night here, with the room already paid for. It wasn't entirely unpleasant the last time, was it?' There's a tiny hint of need in his query; he seems to jest, but in his tone there is a limning of uncertainty.

'Not entirely, no.' I blush and smile. I laugh. 'And to cuckold Aidan once again has its own appeal.'

'I saw you, you know,' he says it almost hesitantly.

'Where?'

'In Breakwater when you wandered through the assassins market, wide-eyed, taking it all in, all the potential for the deaths of others. You looked... luminous.'

I want to deny it, but there was a certain fascination in what I observed that night.

'I watched you a while, followed a little, then you left and I had an assignation to keep.' He smiles. 'Imagine how I felt to see you again at Mr Fitzpatrick's townhouse, to go with you to Hob's Hallow...'

To find you wet and willing and whorish, I think. I slide the coat from my shoulders, then unbutton my shirt until I can slip that off too.

He rises, comes to me.

Why do they all think me harmless?

He might be a good judge of men, but he's an appalling one of women. He knows about my purchased knives, yes, but not about Óisín's pearl-handled knife, hidden deep within my pockets, and it's an awful surprise to him that I slip it across his throat as he's kissing me. He makes a terrible noise; I swiftly wrap my shirt around his neck to keep the blood from spurting too much, but not enough to staunch the flow and accidentally save him. I watch the crimson soaking into the white fabric, wonder if all that red might fill the hole inside of me where Maura and Malachi used to be… the knowledge of what they did to keep me safe… a gift, a weight, a grief I'll never be able to repay, shift or forget.

His eyes are wide and so very green. And angry and afraid and bewildered. The prince of assassins felled so low by a woman and a tiny knife.

'Life,' I tell him as I sit on the bed to watch him die, 'is full of surprises.'

* * *

As I'm going through his pockets I realise I didn't ever know his name, but it causes me no great sadness. He served a purpose. He did me an ill turn and a good one. He is gone. There's a full coin purse – I take two-thirds of the contents – and a golden necklace, which I do not. Coins cannot be claimed by anyone but a unique piece of jewellery? Might as well give yourself up to the local constable or armsman.

When I'm done, I drag him to the window – he's heavy, but I'm an O'Malley, we're tall and strong, and I've spent my life doing physical work around Hob's Hallow when we couldn't afford the hired help. I haul him up and, carefully checking that the muddy alley is empty, tip him over the sill, pushing him away from the building so he doesn't leave any bloodstains on the walls to suggest where he came from. I make sure the sill itself is clean, and wipe the wooden floor with a towel – easy enough to explain away as my monthly courses. Then I sit for a moment. I could stay here. I could stay for the night, wake and eat and leave at my leisure. *But* if someone finds the green-eyed man, decides to question the inhabitants of the inn? *But* if I leave now and someone decides to ask at the inn what guests were here and where are they now? Who departed precipitously? Well, that would look suspicious.

I run a bath once again, and bathe to ensure there's not a trace on me of the dead man. I hide my bloodied clothing at the bottom of my duffel bag – it'll be too hard to rinse here without lye – and check for spatters the clean outfit the housemaid returned to me.

Stay or go? Go or stay? I waver a while longer.

I think of the times Aoife instructed me in how to lie, how to brazen things out. How to appear innocent when I'm guilty. How I got good enough to deceive even her. Keep your lies closest to the truth; do not shout your innocence, only look wounded that anyone should question it; throw suspicion on someone else in an offhanded manner so as not to appear too eager to turn eyes elsewhere.

Mentally, I flip a coin.

I'll stay.

I'll stay until dawn. I offer prayers, again to any who'll listen, that I be allowed to continue on my way. This, after all, was not murder but justice. The green-eyed man had Aoife's blood on his hands; he strangled her, did not even give her the gentle grace of a sharp swift knife or the kindness of poison.

I've done what I should.

I repack everything the assassin had spread out on the quilt, then I crawl into bed and weep at the thought of Malachi and Maura cold and lifeless in the earth of Hob's Hallow.

22

I don't sleep, or at least not for long – in spurts perhaps, like blood from a throat –

before waking hollow-eyed and hearted. The four who raised me are gone, all gone. The hole that opened inside my body last night feels no smaller. The murder – no, the retribution – gave me no pleasure (but perhaps some satisfaction); it had to be done. Revenge, self-preservation, justice. A little of each. Yet it hasn't touched the sides of the abyss, not even as it tumbled down into the well of me, not even an echo as it fell.

Yet the body still demands to be fed and to deprive it would be foolish. I eat an early breakfast in the common dining room of the inn because I can't quite bear to remain in my room any longer: warm buttered porridge, toast and hot coffee flavoured with vanilla and cinnamon. The inn-mistress, Beck, organises the restocking of my provisions for a few extra silver bits. She tells me, too, as she pours more coffee, of the mysterious body in the alleyway beside the inn. I widen my eyes and ask questions she cannot know I know the answer to, as if I'm equally ignorant.

'Man or woman?' I ask, thinking Aoife would be proud of the quick-witted lie.

'Man. Handsome too, before he had his throat cut.' She straightens, put her free hand on a hip like she's settling in for a good chat.

'Who was he?'

'No one knows. He wasn't a guest here and thus far no one's admitted to either meeting him or renting a room. It seems he just appeared where he died – as if by magic.' She laughs cynically.

'No witches around here, surely?' I say, and we exchange a glance. *Witches everywhere*, she answers without words, *but let's keep them secret and unburned*.

'His throat slit!' I say. 'Was it robbery?'

'No, for his gold jewellery was intact, and there remained some coin in his purse. Which is not to say,' she confides, 'that there aren't criminal elements in Lelant's Bridge, but to kill a man and not steal his valuables? Well, that seems more personal than anything.'

I raise an eyebrow and say, 'And that suggests that at least one person in town knew him. Unless…'

She waits for me to continue; the excitement of such a crime is clearly a bright spot in her day; rumour and gossip can have that effect.

'…unless there's a madman about. Who knows what might happen?'

She puts a hand to her chest, shudders. 'Gods forfend!'

'How terrible to meet one's end in such a fashion,' I reflect, 'unknown by those who find you, and perhaps leaving behind others who will never know your fate.'

The landlady nods and pats my shoulder. A group of guests

clomp down the stairs and enter the dining room and, after confirming I'm almost done, she turns her attention to them.

I finish my breakfast in peace. No one troubles me, although the party of six men do throw me glances. I'm clearly a lady for all I'm dressed in trousers, with my hair pinned up primly. When I woke I carefully studied the map Ben brought with him and memorised the turns and twists of it, while I thought about the old silversmith insisting that no one was meant to know about Blackwater. That might explain the lack of road signs, of notations on other maps, of a place in people's memories. Of Isolde not giving her father an address to write back to. An entire estate kept secret…

This morning I'll cross the bridge on the kelpie-horse and head into the unfamiliar. Well, in all honesty I've been doing that for weeks now, but I have a certainty from hereon in that I am advancing towards something old and new: my parents.

Unremembered, thought dead for so long. Isolde and Liam Elliott. Mother and Father. Yet all I can think of is my mother. In truth, I've always wondered about *her*, but my father was simply… an irrelevance? I look like Aoife and Isolde, I look like all the proper O'Malleys… but what does my father look like? Is there anything of him in my face? 'Pretty boy,' Malachi had said, but that tells me nothing. Were his eyes blue or brown, yellow or grey? Or perhaps a light green that seemed to see inside you?

They left me behind.

I can't help but recall *that*. Left me like an extra coin, something they didn't want. Left me behind like a limb chewed off in a trap.

Will they welcome me? Will they like me? Will *Isolde* love me?

* * *

The bridge is wooden and its planks make a hollow sound under my mount's hooves. I feel it echo in my chest. Looking over the rails I scan the river below; it rushes down the weir frothing and fast. I see no sign of heads or tails, no mer, rusalky, morgens or nixies – only the kelpie-horse beneath me – just the liquid untroubled by anything more spiteful than fish. Perhaps I've gone beyond them. Perhaps the mer won't or can't go into water so fresh, with no salt in its makeup. Perhaps they grow sickly and weak when deprived of that chemical. Or perhaps they've simply given up on me.

So, northward I continue. For how many days? Who knows, the map has no scale. But there's that tree to look for, the strange tree with a face in its trunk so neatly drawn by the silversmith.

One tree in a forest, I think.

What, though, if all this is wrong? What if it's all a lie? What if the silversmith was simply mad and I'm following a road laid out by demented fantasies? Where to go then? Where to hide? Will Aidan send someone else after me? Will he assume his assassin could not find me? Chose to flee with me? Was killed by me? Who knows? I cannot write to Brigid and ask. I cannot know if Brigid will be handed her own letters or if Yri or Ciara or whoever will give them to Aidan first.

The sound of my passage changes as the beastie's hooves leave the bridge, touch the packed earth of the road. The rhythm remains, but dulled, now a thudding, deadened, and the echoes in my chest cease. A calm settles over me.

Blackwater. Blackwater is my destination, at least at first. Answers await me there. My parents. Secrets. Secrets that are *mine*, not second-hand ones I've stumbled upon and stolen. I touch the silver ship's bell at my throat; the raised scar on my hip tingles as if it's burning. Then the sensation is gone.

Forwards, then; it is the only way.

* * *

The road rises steadily day by day, and the temperatures drop at night, although the days remain warm. The forest gets thicker the higher we go, the branches meeting above the road to create a canopy. Occasionally a squirrel or fox will dart across our path and the kelpie-horse eyes it speculatively. I've asked more than once if he wants to return to his proper shape and go hunting for things more meaty than grassy, but he's shaken his head. I suspect he's of the mindset that he might as well continue with this unpleasantness until we reach my goal, rather than flipping in and out of different forms.

On the morning of the fourth day I wake, shivering, to find the fire's gone out too soon and the kelpie-horse giving me a reproachful glance; clearly he's regretting his bargain. He hasn't moved from the spot he was in last night beneath the tree. I eat in the saddle, aiming us at the road, which is growing narrower and less well-tended; the undergrowth twines and weaves together, fallen logs are covered in a green carpet of moss, and there are bright red and purple berries growing thickly I know well enough not to eat.

The further we go on and the more neglected the thoroughfare becomes, the more I become convinced that very few take this trail. There cannot be carts going to and from Blackwater bringing supplies in and taking silver away, at least not this way. Perhaps they send it elsewhere.

Only then does it occur to me that I do not know what comes after Blackwater. The map is a simple thing, with no sign of what lies on the far boundary of the estate, the northernmost. What is there? What roads lead down the other side of this mountain range?

Perhaps, a voice in my head says, *Blackwater does not truly exist.*

I've also seen no one else for four days, and unlike the earlier part of my trip, it isn't because I've been avoiding people. There just haven't been any other travellers. This road, I must accept, is the one less travelled by. There's been no sign of a hedge boundary, nor sign of that tree with a face in its bole. I've been carefully looking for that.

My nerves, which have held so well until now – burying Óisín and Aoife, escaping Aidan, the deaths of Maura and Malachi, murdering a man – now begin to sing. No, more like harp strings being plucked by cruelly subtle fingers. It is only now that my goal is so close – or is it? – a new life, so many answers to so many questions, that I suppose I have relaxed enough for the fears and yearnings to break out of the box I put them in. Around me there are no sounds, not even the trills of birds or the calls of badgers and foxes to their mates and young. There is no ocean here and, risk of mer notwithstanding, I do miss it terribly. I miss the daily salt breath of it, the crash and roll that was a constant my whole life – it doesn't matter that I learned to fear it, hated to swim in it. I have been so consumed with flight that this missing, this absence, has been suppressed.

But the kelpie's naming of me as "salt daughter". The assassin's tales reminding me of what I left behind at Hob's Hallow: my grandparents in their cold tomb, and Maura and Malachi too. All these things crash in on me now like a wave, an entire storm.

To distract myself, to make some noise, I dredge up a tale from memory and begin to tell it aloud. The kelpie-horse's ears prick up at the sound of my voice.

A long time ago, the old people say, there lived a mari-morgan, in a lake that was not too big and not too small... indeed, some argued it was neither big enough to be one, nor small enough to be the other. And yet it was just right for the mari-morgan, who suffered not much more than boredom in her long life.

Maidens would come to her pool and beg for boons: beauty, marriage, wealth. And sometimes she granted it and sometimes she did not. They would bring her gifts, these girls, offerings. But only one came who could provide the sole thing the mari-morgan truly desired.

This girl wanted a good husband – oh, she already had one, a husband that is, but he was neither good nor kind. In fact, he was an entirely undesirable sort of husband, yet he was the one she had. He'd displayed none of his worst characteristics, of course, before their wedding, for he wasn't completely stupid. But as time wore on, so his true nature grew stronger and his façade grew thinner until the cruelty entirely broke through and he took a knife to his wife's face so no man would ever look at her again.

Thus the girl, the woman, the wife came to beg the mari-morgan. She said, 'Make him kind. Make him love me. Make him a good husband. Make my life better.'

The mari-morgan knew she could do only one of those things, so she asked what the girl would give in return. The girl replied, 'Whatever you demand.' And what the mari-morgan demanded was a dress.

A dress that did not lose its beauty when submerged, did not become sodden and weighty, that did not drag on the mari-morgan as she swam and dove, danced and darted and looped. A dream of a dress that did not die when deprived of light and air. The creature thought she'd asked too much, that the bargain would remain unfulfilled and she was content with that.

But the girl knew of a book. It wasn't hers but she could get it. She knew that within were all manner of spells, and one of them might well do the trick. So she got the book – the how of it is another tale entirely – and gathered the things she needed, then went to the mari-morgan's pool under the bright blood moon. There, she cut the parts of a gown from the fabric of water and moonlight, and stitched it together according to the spellbook. She decorated it with waterweed and stardust, and the mari-morgan saw it was perfect, and knew she'd do whatever she must to have the pretty, pretty thing. The creature said, 'Bring him here this eve and I shall make your life better.'

And so, the girl, the woman, the wife did. She brought her husband to the water's edge, by means of cajoling and wheedling. And he leaned out over the shimmering surface, looking for the treasure his wife had sworn he would find there. The mari-morgan appeared beneath him, and he thought how beautiful she was and how much she'd be worth if captured, but before he could reach down for her, she reached up for him.

The mari-morgan pulled him under and dragged him a'down, a'down, a'down until the bubbles stopped coming from his mouth.

And his widow screamed and wept and wailed, for a while at least. But the girl hadn't listened carefully enough – and it's terribly important to listen carefully when monsters speak, whether they be two-legged men, or women who live in pools. Yes, she screamed and wept and wailed, but eventually she realised she'd got her part of the bargain: her life had been made better.

Perhaps that one was ill-chosen, but it's what came to mind. Still, all change is painful, cutting and cauterising yourself for something *better*. It makes me think of the great tome I left behind.

Should I have taken the book of tales when I fled? But it was so large, so heavy, and too easy to identify me if I was found with it in my possession. Yet now, without it, I feel it as another loss. A sensible decision, but a hole in my chest, beside all the other holes where Aoife and Óisín, Maura and Malachi once were.

I resolve that when I am settled I will begin a new book. I'll write down all I can remember so at least some version of them remains. They will be changed, there will be things my memory lets go, but they will still *be*. And a trace of a tale is all that's needed to find your way in the world.

I'm about to dig for another when we round the bend and there it is: a high hedge of thickly entwined thorns the height of, well, an O'Malley, with clusters of bramble berries hanging like gems in the sunlight. How long have we been riding parallel to it, unaware of its existence just beyond the dark line of the forest?

It's too regular, too cared for to simply be a work of nature. It's been shaped and sculpted, kept neat and straight and tall.

'Oh,' I say, and rub the kelpie-horse's neck. 'Keep an eye out for that tree, then.'

23

The tree itself takes another couple of hours to find but, once seen, it's not something to be easily missed. To my right, it stands out amongst the rest of the forest. The entry through the hedge-fence (to the left of the roadway) is another thing altogether, with no clear break in the weave of the green barrier. I dismount and approach the tree first. The face is far more detailed – although the work is rough – than the map gave hint of: a woman's face, with antlers carved on the forehead. Maura's stories told of hind-girls who chose their own fate, growing horns as a sign of being untamed and unchained and answering to no one. I suspect this idea would appeal to my mother. I stare at the wooden woman for a long moment, then glance behind me, trying to figure the line of her sight, to where she's staring.

Pinpointing the spot, I pace towards the impenetrable wall of brambles. Indistinguishable, really, this patch from all the other patches that I've ridden past, that I would ride past were I to continue on. Reaching out, careful to avoid the thorns, I wrap my pointer fingers around two branches and shake them for all I'm worth – to no avail. One of Maura's old tales creeps to mind: a girl faced with an impediment such as this pricked her finger on one of the barbs and her blood ate away at the briars, enabling her to pass through.

Tentatively, I snag one fingertip.

It hurts, blood wells, and nothing happens.

A stream of curses, days and days of frustration, comes from my mouth. Loud and wild and angry.

And it's answered by an equally profane litany from somewhere on the other side of the barrier. I jump back from the movement in front of me. A thick panel of the hedge shifts aside, and there's a man shouting, 'Mrs Elliott, you're – oh.' And his tone is one of terrible disappointment. He squints, tilts his head, says, 'You're not… but you look like…'

And I reply, 'I'm Miren Elliott,' laying a claim to a name I've never used before. The words taste strange on my tongue; in the pit of my stomach there's a tightness, for it feels like a betrayal; I've been an O'Malley for so long. But who would know that name here?

The man's scowling now, short iron hair, yellow-green eyes slitted beneath thick brows – not joined in the middle though, so I don't take him for one of Ben's shape-shifting brethren. A greying beard obscures his chin, but it's kept neat and trim, and though his clothes are knock-about, they are clean. He hesitates, staring as if he might be able to see a lie on my face… finally stepping aside. 'Well, you'd best come in then.'

I lead the kelpie-horse through what turns out to be a series of panels in the fence, the man shuffling them back into place as I pass through. The entrance is perhaps six feet deep, and when we step out it's to find a small gatehouse of grey-red stone, with clean sash windows, a well in the garden and smoke puffing from the chimney. Ahead, a narrow path winds off into more trees. I wait while the man finishes his task; wait until he turns to me, his scowl still in place.

'Is this Blackwater?' I ask belatedly.

He says, 'What do you want?'

'I'm looking for my parents, Isolde and Liam Elliott.'

He crosses his arms and stares at me once more. 'You sound like her – that's why I… when I heard you swearing. You've the look of *her*, not so much of him. Well. What do you want?'

'I want to see my parents.' As soon as I say it I think what a fool I am. He'll turn me out again. But he just keeps staring, eyes narrowing, widening, narrowing, widening, as if his process of consideration requires this physical display.

He laughs at last, says just under his breath, 'Won't you put a cat among the pigeons?' And he laughs again, hesitates one more moment and tells me, 'Off you go, missy, I'm sure your uncle will be pleased to see you.'

Uncle?

But I don't ask him any more, don't want him curious as to how little I know about my family – although surely he's wondering already. If he thinks any longer, perhaps he'll start to question why he's never heard of *me*. Or has he? Again, it's a not a question to ask quite yet. I put a foot into the stirrup and swing up into the saddle.

The man points to the path. 'Follow that for a quarter of a mile and it'll split into four. Take the one second from the left to get to the big house. The farthest right goes to the smelter; the one farthest left to the village. The second right is the mine. Off you go, you can't miss the house.'

'Who are *you*?' I ask and can't help but put a little bit of Aoife's imperiousness into my tone.

'Lazarus Gannel. You'll see me again.' He laughs like it's a favourite joke.

I thank him. If I can be polite to the ghosts of gallowscrows, to wolves that walk sometimes on four legs others on two, to man-eating kelpies, even to Aidan Fitzpatrick when required, then I can be polite to the gatekeeper. Indeed, it seems more than wise.

* * *

From "gate" to mansion it's not more than half an hour. I take my time so I can look at the surroundings, drink them in. Also, to give myself some time to think.

As soon as the gatehouse is out of sight, we enter orchards that seem to go on forever. I tell the apple trees from the cherry trees, the apricot from the peach – all look healthy enough but are bereft of fruit. Perhaps there's just been a harvest, yet it seems a little early. There are trellises for grapes, too, quite a lot; a large private concern or a small commercial vineyard, I cannot quite tell – but again, the vines though hale are bare. Further over are fields where wheat and barley should be waving; they're empty. I might think them lying fallow, but it's not the time. I pass on, and soon find where the trail divides and I take the way Lazarus advised.

More trees – oak and yew and ash – more fields empty of crops. Then almost suddenly a vista of groomed grounds opens up before us – although I can see patches where there's neglect and things grow more wildly than they should – like Hob's Hallow once had when an army of gardeners could be

226

marshalled into action. An enormous house is set in the middle like an ornament. There are pruned topiaries and hedges, garden beds that are shaped like flowers themselves, trees trained into archways with rosebushes climbing them. As we draw closer to the mansion, I can see some blossoms, random riots of colour, as if *here*: the house is the heart. Birdfeeders hang from branches but I notice there are no birds to peck at the small mounds of seed. There's a contrast between the lack I've seen elsewhere and the seeming fertility near this home. Yet the place is not entirely pristine; there's an air of neglect, I can sense it, see it even from this distance. It seems as if all should be humming, growing, buzzing, yet there is only this weight of... waiting, of suspension. It is... strange.

There are no labourers in the garden, no one rushing from the sturdy grey stone and wood stables to take my horse. There are no sounds to be heard. There's not even a breath of wind to cool the sweat the sun's broken on my brow. I stroke the kelpie-horse's neck and he shivers beneath my touch.

Blackwater.

When we mount a small rise, I can see the rolling gardens give way to an expanse of green lawn, which is then swallowed by a lake, long and wide and dark. The black water of the place's name. No great originality there, but perhaps the sound of it reminded Isolde of "Breakwater". The surface is still as glass, like polished obsidian; no birds glide across it, neither swans, nor common ducks or even commoner grebes. Are there fish in there? Or is it too inert for any life to be supported therein?

The mansion is bigger than Hob's Hallow, and its component parts constructed at the same time. Not for this abode the wings tacked onto the ancient tower, like an ill-made bird. The stone is the same grey-red stone as the gatehouse, the white-painted front door and window frames appear a little grubby. Four storeys to the main building (including an attic and a semi-basement); a two-storey wing to each side. Those wings continue on the same line for a while, then turn at right-angles to reach out toward any approaching guest; both have a parapet and I imagine walking along them in the evening. A turning circle covered with yellow gravel splits the lawn, then between that drive and the home are eight wooden and metal benches for sitting, enormous red pots beside them, overflowing with lavender flowers. Again, I wonder at the lack of blossoming elsewhere that I've seen since my arrival, yet the clear explosion of plants closest to the house.

I halt the kelpie-horse and stare.

All of this.

My parents have all of this – *made all of this* – and there is no sign of a lack of money. No deprivation, neither paucity nor poverty. No expense spared. Yet I have spent my life in made-over gowns, eating soup and porridge thin as water, my grandparents turning a coin around seven times before they spent it, dodging debt collectors, begging the likes of Aidan Fitzpatrick for the smallest of aid.

And my parents have this.

They did not send anything to help.

My mother did not send assistance though she could not have avoided knowledge of the state of the family – she too grew up in Hob's Hallow.

She did not send for *me*.

I feel as if rage will choke me. I've come so far and here I'll die on the threshold because I cannot swallow down this fury that's closing my throat. And yet: longing. Yearning. I'd give everything if only they'll love me. Explain everything away. Tell me it was all a mistake.

And I know this is infantile – that my heart is still that of a hurt child – so I clench my hands around the reins, feel my nails sharp against my palms. It pulls me back to *here*. The bile subsides. The kelpie-horse moves impatiently beneath me and I've no doubt he's eager to have his service done. Gently, I dig my heels into his flanks; he makes a mild noise of protest at the indignity and we move on.

When we are perhaps five yards away from the semi-circular steps that lead upwards, the white front door with its silver knocker – is that a two-faced, two-tailed mermaid? – flies open and a woman appears in the breach.

My heart stops for the shortest of moments until I realise this cannot be my mother. Cannot be Isolde. This woman is short and very blonde, nearly platinum. She's buxom but almost to the point of turning stout: her apron and waistband are straining against her. There are traces of a little too much fat in her round cheeks and beneath her chin, and her skin shows traces of coarsening. She's pretty but how long that will last is anyone's guess – it's like she's poised on a moment between. Even if she had been tall and slender and dark like an O'Malley, the apron with its stains would have given me pause. Even on the worst days when Aoife had to help in the kitchen because Maura was overwhelmed, she would never be seen in a grubby smock, never be seen looking like a scullion or slattern. She drilled that into me and I can think of no good reason why it wouldn't have been imprinted onto my mother's mind as well.

Then I focus on the dress beneath: sky blue with silver flowers embroidered. Even at a quick glimpse, it's of better quality than one usually associates with a servant. However it doesn't seem made for her; a hand-me-down. I think of my mother giving away her fine dresses to a servant when she couldn't be bothered to help her own family. I shake the thought away.

A housekeeper then, or a maid, and by her expression an unhappy one at that.

'How did you get in? Who are you?' Her tone is barely below that of a shriek. Her hands are on her hips, clenched into fists as if that's the only way she can keep herself from hitting me. She narrows her dark eyes.

'My name is Miren Elliott and I'm here to see my parents,' I say, answering the last question first, and her colour soars from pink to angry red. 'Lazarus Gannel let me in.'

Her face goes slack with shock, all that red choler drains, and she reels away from the doorframe, back inside the shadowy depths of the great house.

Do I stay here? Do I follow her?

While I'm deliberating, there's a disturbance somewhere in the dimness of the entry hall. All I can see is a stirring in the gloom. There are shouts and cries, a slap, and then the noises hush to bare whispers that I imagine moving dust across the air.

Another figure appears on the threshold: a tall man, with light brown hair shot with silver, blue eyes, high cheekbones, a square jaw clean-shaven; emerald trews, a white linen shirt with a loosely tied red cravat, and a waistcoat of violet silk with a border along the bottom of harlequin diamonds in green and purple and yellow. His brown boots are highly polished; they look as if they've never been worn outside. The colours of a peacock. There's a slight smile on his lips, which are full, but as he gets closer I can see a scar mars the right curve of the cupid's bow. He hangs in the doorframe for a moment, then steps out, arms opening.

Is this my father? Malachi said he was a pretty boy. Older now, age has taken the edge off the prettiness, so he's handsome more than anything. But is *this* my father?

'Miren. My darling girl. Miren. Welcome home.'

24

I almost fall in my haste to dismount, then my knees are weak when I touch the ground and it's only my father's arms that hold me up for the longest while. I'm crying and I don't want to, but I cannot stop myself. And the tall man is patting my back and kissing my forehead, and whispering, 'There, there, my darling girl.'

At last, I am done, empty. As the sadness ebbs, my strength returns, creeping in a little ashamed. I push away, still holding his forearms for the comfort of contact, and look straight into his eyes. I'm about to speak when he says, 'Your parents will be so pleased to see you when they return.'

Your parents. And I remember Lazarus Gannel saying, 'Off you go, missy, I'm sure your uncle will be pleased to see you,' and me not asking questions because I didn't want to appear any more ignorant than I already had. The need and hope and want for a parent welled up and crashed over me so that no sort of reason could have made itself known. Seeing this man, I had simply assumed...

And I feel as though I've been punched in the stomach. That everything I thought I had finally gained in those brief seconds has been wrenched from my hands and heart. As if everything I had laid claim to when I used the name "Elliott" is gone, showing the lie of who I am, who I might be. I feel the tears threaten again, although a different kind, those that come on the verge of a howling storm. The noise you make as you crumple to the ground and cease to care who sees you, cease to care if you continue to exist or not. The type of thing that might now unmake me.

We clasp at each other's forearms. His voice is gentle when he says, 'I am your uncle, Miren. Edward Elliott. Liam is my brother. You are with family again. Do not despair.'

He pulls me to him again, kisses my forehead. 'Come inside. Come inside and we shall make you at home. You must tell me everything, all of your adventures. I can tell your journey has been hard, but you are *home* now. Come inside, come inside. You need to rest, my dear girl, I can see that.'

My uncle − Edward − keeps his arms around my shoulders and helps me to the steps leading up to the entrance. I want nothing so much as to sleep. Even more than answers to my questions, I want the oblivion of slumber.

'Never fear, Miren, you are *home*.'

* * *

I wake at some point in the dark hours, not knowing where I am. Moonlight pours in through the panes of glass. I sit up, shaking my head, trying to remember. A pretty sitting room, a pot of tea, some sweet biscuits, some chatter − mine mostly hysterical, I think, my flight from Breakwater, my long search − but not long before I felt irresistibly tired. I have a vague memory of my uncle half-carrying me up the stairs, but nothing more. I'm still in shirt and trousers but my shoes, socks and coat are gone.

As I look around I don't take in much detail of the room, but I do recall that I've not fulfilled a promise. Rising, I stumble over to the bank of tall windows and peer out.

Down there, by the shore, the kelpie-horse waits, a deeper darkness against the lawn, but still not so black as the lake. Did no one stable him after my arrival? I feel... more than weary, I feel sluggish... drugged? Did they slip something into my tea to calm me? I desperately want to lie back down and sleep, but I gave the kelpie my word and it's best if I do what must be done while no one is about to witness it.

I step into a very long corridor, find my way to a staircase, to that marble-floored foyer, that enormous front door that takes me forever to unlock – my hands clumsy, now too large, now too small – then out onto the portico, into the night. The moonlight is so very bright and I'm lost, blinded and blinking. And the mountain air is cold, so cold through my shirt.

I rub my eyes until I see stars behind my lids, and somehow it's better when I open them. Then I hear the gentle whicker of the beastie. There he is, waiting so patiently. When I'm by his side, I put my clumsy fingers to work, undo the bridle and slip it away. He shifts with the fluidity of water back to his proper shape, shakes his head and snorts with irritation.

'I'm sorry,' I say. 'Sorry I forgot you.'

He bows, head so low it almost touches the ground. 'But I'm free, salt daughter, and you've kept your word as I shall keep mine.'

I think of his filthy old tether coiled in the bottom of my duffel, a means to call him back, and point to the lake. 'Can you go this way?'

He nods. 'A simple matter when *all the waters in the world are joined.*'

234

And he's gone almost too fast for me to see; strange to hear Aoife's words from his mouth. I don't stare after him, but turn to the house, feeling sleep creep back through my limbs. I want to return to my chamber before it overtakes me.

* * *

The room is pretty and filled with daylight. The bed has no canopy, but is large and has a silver frame, shaped to look like vines and leaves. The quilt is a deep green and the wallpaper is green too, with fields of flowers sweeping across it. There is an enormous silk rug over the polished wooden floorboards and curtains of gold drape the tall windows. Awake now, I can make sense of the space: there are two doors, one closed, one ajar. The first leads to the corridor; the second to a small bathroom. There are only the slightest remains of a fire in the hearth, which was, I suspect, dying even before I woke last night.

I'm lying beneath the covers and I can feel the grit on my sheets from where I went outside barefoot. My hair is still in its tight bun and my scalp itches. In daylight I can see my coat is draped over a yellow armchair in one corner, my boots peeking out from beneath. A small octagonal table waits beside it, upon which sits an unlit lantern, an exquisite thing of engraved silver and iridescent glass. I rise and poke about.

There is a dressing table in another corner, but there's nothing on top of it, nothing but a silver-backed brush and a hand mirror. No makeup or jewellery; this is a guest bedroom, kept for any visitors who might pass by. There are signs of it being hastily (badly) dusted.

Against one wall is a wardrobe in rose mahogany. When I open it there's not much there: three long skirts, one black, one ochre, one blue, and three white blouses, simple unadorned damask things; two pairs of delicate silk slippers embroidered and embellished with beads also wait. I can only imagine the blonde woman put them here as I slept; they must be scrounged from my mother's wardrobe. In the bottom of the robe is a drawer containing a range of underthings, about my size, in red silk. I've never seen anything like this; I'm astonished Aoife hadn't thought to purchase such items for my wedding night.

The thought of my grandmother, of what I've left behind, sobers me. Then comes the idea that perhaps someone rummaged about in my duffel while I slept. Perhaps they found the bloody clothing. I stop breathing for a moment as I cast around for the bag. But there it is, lying on a blanket box at the foot of the bed.

I open it up: everything is as I left it, nothing out of place. I draw things out until I reach the shirt and trousers stained with the green-eyed man's blood. Things I could have dealt with on the road, but for all my satisfaction at his death I haven't been ready to look at them until now. At the hearth, I crouch down, take the tinder box and charcloth and kindle a new fire. When the blaze is hearty and crackling, I feed it the collar of the shirt, bit by bit, until it's properly ablaze before I put it into the fireplace. The fabric smoulders a little but is gradually consumed. Next the trousers; they take longer, yet eventually they too are gone. I stare at the flames for a while longer, thinking that in them is an end. An end to everything I left behind. I can but hope.

In the bathroom, I run a bath. I add oils and salts, find shampoo. I stay in there a long time. And when I am at last clean,

I brush out my hair and then dry it as best I can with a towel. Finally, I choose the blue skirt and one of the blouses, and make my way downstairs.

* * *

'Miren!'

Locating the small lilac-painted breakfast parlour where my new uncle is just finishing his repast was easy. The path I took last night in darkness and half-sleep has embedded itself in my mind. This place has none of the twists and turns of Hob's Hallow, where a stranger might wander for hours without a guide. But Blackwater is well-lit, carefully laid out; it makes sense.

'How lovely you look! Nelly chose well from your mother's wardrobe.' *Nelly*. The blonde woman. 'Miren, my dear. I would have had a tray taken up, but we weren't sure when you would wake.' Edward looks pleased to see me as he rises from his seat at the head of the table, then enfolds me in a hug. 'Won't you join me? I was about to start the business of the estate, but that can wait. Absolutely!'

'Breakfast would be wonderful, thank you.' I take the chair he pulls out for me, so I am at his right hand. The porcelain clock over the mantle says it's almost ten – late for breakfast, I think. He pours me coffee then rings a bell, sits beside me. 'Uncle, I do not wish to appear rude, but might I ask where my parents have gone?'

He smiles and laughs. 'Not rude at all. A natural question. They have travelled to Calder.'

The very name makes my heart jump. Calder in the Dark Lands where the Leech Lords hold sway; Maura would tell me tales of such vampires when I was being particularly brattish.

Edward continues. 'Not an ideal destination, no, but we have been having problems with production – those Lords are experts on the extraction of silver. Calder has its own mines and your parents – after much deliberation – decided to make an entreaty to the ruler there, to see if they might have some solutions to our… barrenness.'

'How long has this situation been going on?' I ask. My mind goes back to Calder, to what a desperate move that is, to beseech the Leech Lords for aid. Few journey willingly or otherwise to the Dark Lands, and fewer still return. The borders and gateways are guarded, warded so the vampires cannot cross over.

'It's just over three months since they left. Your father, my brother, asked me to come and assist during their absence. Help keep the estate ticking over, and ensure that Ena is well looked after.'

'Ena?'

'Your little sister, Miren,' he explains.

'I – I have a sister?' That hits me like cold water. They left me behind, replaced me with a new child. Isolde is… well, she was sixteen when she had me, now she's what? Thirty-four, thirty-five? Not too old to have another baby. No others in between us – perhaps this one's an accident too?

My uncle's expression clouds with concern. 'Have you not heard much from your parents over the years? Surely they—'

'I have heard nothing,' I say and my voice breaks a little. 'My grandparents… my grandparents told me Isolde and Liam were dead. It is only in the last month that I learned otherwise.'

His lips move but no sound comes out. He's horrified. Then he manages, 'My poor girl.'

238

I cannot bear to tell him that I was left behind. Cannot bear for him to know that I was so easy to abandon. So unwanted. And for a moment, I like the pity. I crave the pity. I *am* a poor girl. But then Aoife's training kicks in and I push away the desire for sympathy. It's a weakening thing; it makes you blind to what's happening around you, it makes you rely on others. 'My sister. I have a sister. How old is she?'

He smiles fondly. 'Not yet a year, almost six months.' His face clouds. 'You mustn't think them terrible for leaving her behind, Miren.'

'They left me behind,' I say, and I cannot help but sound bitter. There is no reason for me to doubt my parents would do the same to my sibling. It makes me hate the child less. Oh, I must admit to that surge of loathing when I heard of her existence, but now... now, I understand Ena's like me.

'They had their reasons, my dear, and your mother especially will want to reveal them to you herself, so I shall say nothing more but to beg you to think kindly of them until they come back home. All will be explained.' He touches my hand. 'You must understand, Miren, this house, this estate, its running affects more than simply your parents and me. The mine, the smelter, the orchards – there is a village that depends on this place. On every aspect of it working properly. So far we have managed to keep going on the stores and stocks set aside from earlier harvests and minings, but those resources are running down. And the crops, the orchards have stopped producing – I cannot divine why. So, we must pray that your parents return with a solution.'

There is a brisk knock on the door, which is opened before Edward says anything. Nelly enters. She's wearing a pink dress, again with embroidered flowers, this time in gold thread; again, it looks tight, as if it's not made for her, and the skirt's a little too long. I look more closely and think there's evidence of rough hemming. So: taken up once and badly. Her lips are pressed tightly together, and she bobs a curtsey to Edward but her heart's clearly not in it.

'Sir?'

'Ah, Nelly. Would you be so kind as to bring my niece some porridge and toast?' He looks to me for confirmation and I nod.

The woman's lips tighten further and I think they might twist themselves into her mouth and down her throat like a corkscrew of irritation.

'Thank you, Nelly,' I say, but that seems to irritate her further; her eyes flare. She doesn't answer, but flounces out, the door closing behind her with something that is barely not a slam.

'You must forgive her shortness. Her nerves haven't quite been the same since the fire.'

I raise an eyebrow.

'I forget you've only just arrived!' He laughs. 'Some months ago, there was a fire. It's done terrible structural damage so that wing is kept locked. Nelly and your parents barely escaped with their lives. Your father is determined to have it repaired as soon as he can.' He smiles sadly. 'So, while I encourage you to explore the house to your heart's content, I must insist you give the East Wing a wide berth for your own safety.'

Then Uncle Edward says, 'And poor Nelly's sleep has been broken while she's been sitting up with Ena. She'll come round the moment she has a good night's slumber. So, you shall break your fast, then we'll take a turn around the estate?

I shall answer your questions and you shall tell me, if it is not too painful, of your life before this and how you came to find us. Perhaps later you will be happy to meet your sister?'

25

'And you said the orchards had stopped producing?' I ask as we ride past the naked trees. I'm on a roan mare, he on a bay stallion from the stables – we saddled them ourselves as there were no lads to do so. Uncle Edward apologised for not having stabled my "horse" which has disappeared; he's sure it will be found wandering the estate at some point. I agree, which is better than explaining I'd entered into a deal with a kelpie – I cannot yet know how my uncle feels about such creatures so best to remain silent. The sun is out and I'm sweating a little beneath the damask blouse, glad of the broad-brimmed straw hat I took from the stand by the front door.

'A blight of some description,' he says. 'No one can identify it. It's not a mould or fungus, not a rot. Yet there's been nothing for almost three months. The fields lie empty and there's not been the birth of a lamb, goat or cow since.' Edward shakes his head. 'They look otherwise healthy, the trees, do they not? Frankly I'm at a loss as to what to do. Do we simply burn them all then replant?'

'It seems a terrible waste,' I say as I think of Hob's Hallow, fruiting no matter the season; of how Maura showed me what to do when I was very small so I could help her with the ritual every year. I urge my horse off the road and over to one of the apple trees. I dismount, smoothing my skirts down – they're voluminous enough that I can take the hem of the back and pull it up between my legs to tuck into the waistband: instant riding trousers.

I crouch, eyes searching the base of the trunk for... aha! There it is. The same tiny sigil Maura demonstrated how to fashion, like an 's' with a diagonal line through it: marks of the craft. It didn't need Malachi telling me my mother was a witch to figure that if Maura had taught me the correct forms, there was no reason she'd not have instructed Isolde before me.

The orchards have been bewitched. They *should* be blooming all year round. But without Isolde here to keep up the tiny red tithes required to pay for the benefits of the magic, the spell has diminished. They are in stasis, they sleep – it's too much for the trees to bear fruit even at their proper time. It won't take much to fix. But not now. Not in front of my new uncle, who clearly doesn't realise what Isolde was doing. Like so many men, he takes good fortune for granted and only questions it when it is gone.

I don't know this man at all. He seems kind and courteous, but so is Aidan Fitzpatrick when he chooses. I'll not give Edward Elliott reason to mistrust me.

'Miren? What is it?'

'Oh, nothing, Uncle Edward.' I rise, turn and smile at him from beneath the brim of my sunhat. One of my mother's I assume. 'I thought perhaps I might recognise it – something similar once happened at Hob's Hallow' – a lie, for Maura's clever works kept such things at bay – 'but I do not know this thing. How mysterious that they remain so healthy!'

'Nature is a mystery unto herself.'

'And you also say the mine is no longer producing?'

'There are some viable seams,' he says in a way that's both grand and dismissive, and rings false to my ear; I wonder how much or how little he knows about mining. 'But a negligible amount is coming out. There are new places where we might dig deeper, but the rock is unfeasibly hard. We might only get through them by blasting, yet the chief engineer is fearful that it will bring down tunnels and perhaps even weaken the floor of the lake.'

'The lake?'

'It runs deep and wide underground – as large as it is above the surface, it is even larger beneath.' He shrugs. 'My brother told me there was an accident some years ago and it took a terrible toll. There are still widows and orphans who mourn to this day. Tunnels had to be sealed off, others pumped dry; twenty miners died and none of the bodies were found – perhaps they still float in the deeper hollows beneath.'

I think about how long this mine has been operating, how long it's been fruitful, producing riches for my parents; riches that never made it back to Hob's Hallow. My hands shake and I clench them so he doesn't notice. With a deep breath I swing back into the saddle.

He sighs. 'Come along, Miren. The village next.'

The temperature drops slightly as the path takes us into a wooded area. Beneath the canopy of trees the light is dim and its warmth filtered out. Just as on the road up the mountain to my new home, there are no sounds of birdsong or badger, fox or wolf. I wonder at it: is it related to the same dearth of magics to affect the orchards? Or is it perhaps that the animals are simply hiding?

One day soon I will explore on my own. It's not that I don't trust my uncle, or no more than is wise, but it is much easier to examine a new place without the company of folk who are used to taking the everyday things of their home for granted.

I notice after a while, however, that there *is* a sound. The trickle of water. Soon a stream is running beside us, and it's nothing to cause fear. A mer with its great tail would be marooned in such a shallow rill. It must flow underground from the lake. There are sparkles of silver in the rocky bed that are pretty but I see no fish there, neither big nor small. 'Does anyone fish in the lake?'

He seems startled that I've asked. 'What an odd question!'

I laugh. 'Not really – I come from the sea, Uncle Edward, a body of water is always a source of food to such a one.'

'Ah! The answer is no, my dear. No one fishes there. There is nothing to take bait, or so I'm told.' He sighs. 'Miren, may I ask how you found us?'

So I tell him a little Again, my trust is a thing so badly battered and so recently, I'll not give it away easily. I tell him of the loss of Óisín and Aoife, but I do not mention how Aoife died. I tell him of Aidan and Aoife's matchmaking, but I do not mention Aidan's cruel hands, nor his hired assassin, nor how the blade in my hand felt biting into the green-eyed man's throat. I mention finding Isolde's letters in Óisín's study, but I only say there was one – and his interest is piqued.

'What did Isolde say in her missive?'

'Very little, I'm afraid. Merely that she and my father had settled here, that it was north of Bellsholm and where it might be found.' I tell such small lies, no one will know. I will not mention the old silversmith, giving away secrets in his senility. This place was hidden for a reason – I think of the concealed entrance in the hedge that I used only yesterday. My parents have gone to great lengths to keep Blackwater's location *undisclosed*. And I consider Aoife and her rages when she spoke of Isolde. I ponder if that was enough to hide away like this? So she would not find them?

'Nothing more? No details of the new home and family?'

'No, Uncle,' I say and lean towards him as if to share a secret. 'You must know that my mother parted from her parents on terrible terms?' He nods. 'My grandmother Aoife never forgave her.' And still I cannot bear to tell him that I was left behind to pay a debt of some sort.

'Oh, my dear girl. And to come here and find them gone again, albeit temporarily! What a blow. I'm sorry I could not soften it for you.'

'You have been so kind, Uncle! I will never forget that.' I smile and reach out to touch his arm.

'Isolde confided some things to me,' he says. 'Troubled, the O'Malleys, but every family has their problems, I think. The Elliotts were certainly not immune! You fled your suitor, you say? Your father left a bride-to-be behind when he met your mother. Poor girl. It seems it runs in the blood. But sometimes what the heart wants cannot be denied.' He smiles fondly.

'Aidan did not want a wife with a mind of her own,' I say stiffly. 'And he would never have approved of me seeking my parents. I would not have made a satisfactory wife, nor he a decent husband.'

'Perhaps he might have come around? A wife can convince a husband of many things, is my observation.'

'Uncle,' I say slowly, 'I believe Aidan has made a bargain with the woman who rules Breakwater like a robber queen. I do not believe he is a good man.'

I wonder at myself, telling so many half-truths to this man who is family. Did I ever lie this much before? Or was it simply a habit embedded in me, one that is now coming to the fore as I'm forced to survive on my own? Is this the best skill Aoife ever gave me? Dishonesty? Uncle Edward has shown me nothing but kindness, made me welcome, yet there is a whisper in my head that says, *It is early days, Miren, be patient.*

'I believe you made the right decision, my dear, to leave.'

'Enough about my trials, Uncle, won't you tell me of the Elliotts?'

* * *

Fifteen minutes of family tales before we reach the village: The Elliott home in Able's Croft. Great-Grandmother Eleanor who hollowed out her wooden leg and filled it with plum brandy to make church services bearable. Uncle Tobias who failed to inform his fourth wife that the first three were still alive and well. Cousin Vella whose fondness for her wolfhounds meant she had each and every one taxidermied after their deaths and placed around her home in their favourite spots, then deposited in her tomb at her own demise. Grandfather Edgar who locked himself in his library one evening and refused to come out, only collecting the meals left for him in the corridor when the deliverer had gone, and continuing thus until one day three days of meals had piled up uneaten and his sons broke down the door to find him dead over a copy of *Murcianus' Magical Rites*, a look of horror frozen to his face. 'We never found out if he managed to summon anything – the house always was filled with strange noises anyway, so another haunting would hardly draw attention.'

We follow the stream all the way to the village, where it splashes over a lip of land and down into a fountain pool at the edge of a square. In the centre of the pool rears the statue of a mermaid. I stare at the thing. It's an idealised version to be sure, pretty and sweet, nothing like the creatures who pulled me into Breakwater Harbour, with their teeth and talons, sharp fins on lashing tails, gashes of gills and scaly skin. This lovely thing was sculpted by someone who's never actually seen the truth of a mer.

There are perhaps forty small, neat houses (some older, some newer built as families expand, I imagine) clustered around the square, straight white fences protecting tiny flowerless gardens. There are people milling about, children playing games and singing rhymes I recognise from childhood. Some folks draw water from the fountain, some produce items – fruit and vegetables which must have been purchased elsewhere, or is it really the last of their stores? There are some livestock in pens, cows and sheep, but there are no newborns to be seen, just as Edward said.

I watch as folk begin to notice us. A red-haired woman with an equally red-haired child of perhaps four (too old to be held so) on her hip sees us – or more particularly my uncle – and her lips thin. Then she sees me and loses all expression, goes blank; her jaw drops. The man beside her follows the direction of her gaze; other heads turn, the phenomenon spreads like flames leaping from one roof to another.

Soon, the press of bodies stops moving altogether and they just stare. I look askance at my uncle, who murmurs with a smile, 'Ah, I see Miriam Dymond's spotted you. You are *very* like your mother.'

As if his words have broken a spell, the villagers begin to shift again, like breath has been restored to them. A stout pink-faced man bustles forward, his yellow coat neatly pressed and his black trews tidier than a working man's should be.

'Mr Elliott,' he says, and there's nothing friendly in his tone, but I can tell the hostility is tamped down hard.

'Oliver. How go matters?'

'If you mean the matter of the crops, then they are as they have been with no change. If you mean the matter of the mine and the smelter, then that goes the same as well.' The meaning is clear: *you have done nothing, there has been no change.* But then his tone varies, becomes hopeful as he asks, 'Any word from Mistress Isolde?'

'Not as yet, but I have hopes. This,' says my uncle and gestures towards me, 'is her daughter, Miss Miren. I put my faith in signs and I believe her coming means that we shall soon see her parents once again. Miren, Oliver is our estate manager.'

Oliver's expression tells me precisely what he thinks of this bit of logic. I smile, lean from the saddle and offer my hand. He hesitates, then takes it. He seems relieved to have done so, as if he expected one thing and found another. I think about what Malachi said, about Isolde being a charmer; I wonder if she worked her magic on these villagers, if that's partially why they stay here in spite of the coming lack of food, the inevitable winter, the obvious dislike of my uncle. Internally, I shudder at the idea of anyone being held against their will. Then again, people are stubborn and hard to shift; they don't like change at the best of times even when it's in their own interests. Perhaps this isn't my mother's fault at all.

'Come up to the house tomorrow, Oliver, that we might discuss the next supply run to St Sinwin's.'

'Yes, Mr Elliott. Good day, Miss Miren.'

'Good day, Oliver.'

We proceed through the square and I notice how, while we've been talking to Oliver, many people have disappeared, that there are doors closing with quiet whispers along our path. Those who remain either throw unfriendly glares at us – at Uncle Edward? – or make a point of looking away. I glance over my shoulder, back the way we've come, and see the red-haired woman spit in the wake of our horses and make a gesture Maura told me is meant to ward off the unwanted: the sign of the horns.

'May we visit the mine today, Uncle? I confess myself most curious to see it.'

Edward Elliott shakes his head. 'Not today, my dear. I have other tasks to attend to and I rather hoped you might spend a while with Ena this afternoon, perhaps give Nelly a little time to herself. It would be a kindness.' He smiles. 'There is no hurry, Miren, the mine will be here tomorrow and the day after that.'

'Of course, Uncle.' I smile. We are almost through the village now, and I notice one last house, painted white and green, with a bench seat in the tiny front garden, beneath a rose bush with no roses on it. The spot reminds me of finding Aoife in her garden, dead as a doornail, and I swallow, blink hard. Then I notice man standing in the doorway, eating an apple noisily, staring at us both. A handsome hard-faced man with thick dark curls, and pale green eyes that remind me of the assassin's, and I swallow again, though I know it's not *him*. His clothes are covered in dirt and grass, his hair is pushed back from his forehead and there is the damp crown of sweat on his brow. A scar, white and tight, runs from the corner of his left eye to disappear into the hair above his ear.

Uncle Edward is making a point of not looking at him, then the man says, 'Afternoon, Mr Elliott,' and there's contempt there and amusement.

My uncle's mouth twists in distaste. 'Jedadiah.'

The man nods to me and says, in a tone not much different, 'Miss.'

I merely nod and we pass him by, then we are out of the village. Part of me wants to look back, see if he's still watching; it's a great effort of will to not do so. There is a small graveyard not far off but we don't go that way.

I can tell from the twist of Edward's lips that if I ask anything now I'll get no answer, so I file it away for later in the box where I keep all those niggling queries to which I am determined to one day have the answer.

26

The crops are fast and easy to do, requiring only a visit to the four corners of each field. A drop of blood from my thumb, a drop of water from the canteen, stalks of wheat or rye or oats blown across my palm by whispered words. A difference should be seen in a few days, perhaps less if my mother is half the witch Malachi said she is. If any trace of her magic remains in the soil. A true witch would get a bigger result more easily, would need fewer accoutrements, not much more than her will and blood. I'm not a witch, but that's not necessary, just knowledge of the forms, the tools, the intent.

The orchards are more laborious, although the ritual is similar: blood and water and air at each corner, but then every single tree must be seen to, spoken to, the tiny sigil re-carved with my pocketknife so the sap flows freely. There are four orchards and about fifty trees in each. It takes me a long while to finish and my eyes are gritty, my throat is sore and my knees and lower back ache by the time I'm done. It's still dark when I rise – the timepiece tells me it's barely three in the morning – so I will easily make it back to the house and my bed. No one will seek me, so I'll sleep as long as I wish.

The moon is full, thankfully, so I did not need to bring a shuttered lantern with me, and it's the perfect time for such workings. It was easy enough to slip out when the lights had been extinguished and the footfalls of Nelly – the only servant to live in the house, which seems strange for such a large place – had faded to nothing as she paced towards Ena's room, far down the hall from mine.

I sat with the child in question all afternoon, yet it gained me no credit with the housekeeper. Ena is a tiny thing with a thatch of dark hair and deep-set brown eyes. She's not as pale as I am, lacking that strange sheen to her skin, but we're enough alike that a family resemblance might be noted. She was fractious and unhappy when Nelly led me into the room, and the same might have been said of the housekeeper herself. She fussed over the child, seeming reluctant to leave, but I could see from the blue circles under her eyes how much she longed for sleep, and the way her brow creased that the child's howling was playing on her last nerve. I laid my hand on the woman's arm and said, 'She'll be well with me.' I've sat by the cradles of tenants' children when they've been ill, the occasional distant cousin too when they've been brought to Maura for her tisanes and tinctures.

The housekeeper recoiled and left the room.

I picked up the child and examined her mouth: the gums were red and inflamed-looking. She howled louder at the touch of my fingertips, but Nelly didn't return. I took Ena with me down to the kitchen garden; the sheer number of medicinal herbs there made it impossible that it had been planted by anyone but my mother. It was curious, to say the least, that those plants continued to flourish despite her absence. I found pellitory-of-the-wall and winter-rocket, plucked them and took them into the kitchen.

There was a highchair by the table and I put Ena in there while I sought a mortar and pestle. I found nothing suitable in an otherwise well-equipped kitchen, so I began to open doors: three pantries containing far more food than the inhabitants of this house could eat, a small room for washing and folding linen and, finally, a proper workroom that any apothecary would have been proud to call their own. Shelves stocked with bottles of dried herbs and tinctures, all neatly labelled in a hand I recognised from the letters my mother had sent to Óisín. There were crucibles and a small fireplace, cauldrons and copper bowls, tubes and pipettes, three quite large boxes made of glass with silver locks on them – and a range of mortars and pestles.

The remains of a shattered jar had been swept into a corner and there was a dried-up brown stain on the floor not far from it – badly cleaned up. It appeared my mother had left in a hurry and had forgotten to tidy up after herself. At the very back there was a trapdoor and I would have continued to poke about curiously but cries from an unhappy Ena reminded me of my purpose. I located arrowroot powder amongst the small bottles and took it and a mortar and pestle back to the kitchen proper.

I ground the herbs, found a bottle of port, mixed some of it in along with the arrowroot, then rubbed it on her gums.

At first she appeared outraged and opened her mouth wide, all the better to get the screams out, but the paste was fast-acting and before she could wail, her expression changed. She smacked her lips as the pain began to lift, and she looked at me in wonderment. Soon she was smiling and giggling, an impressive transformation from the small vile demon with whom I'd originally been presented.

She is well looked after, plump and clean, her hair is thick and shiny and her eyes bright. Clearly, however, the housekeeper has no knowledge of home remedies. Perhaps I will tell her. Perhaps I will not. Any road, the child will sleep much better for it tonight and so will Nelly.

After that I took her for a walk around the grounds. I told her the names of all the trees and flowers, of their properties and what good and ill she might do with them. I asked her questions about our parents that she's too young to answer. Ena just laughed up at me, touched my face and pulled my hair. When we strolled by the lake I watched her gaze turn towards the dark, still water and I thought for a mad moment about taking her for a swim (no waves, no throwing, no fierce Aoife shouting from the shore), but as we got closer I saw there was no sign of any shallows, any bank where we might do something so harmless. I thought of the mer, then, and though I could not imagine how they might get here, I backed away and returned with the child to the house.

In the kitchen I filled a bottle with milk and then in the nursery fed her as I read aloud from *Murcianus' Book of Fables* − my mother has clearly collected the same books as at Hob's Hallow − something about foxes and crows and cheese and stones. Her eyes glazed over − as did mine for that matter – and she became fractious so when I finished the fable, I conjured up something from the O'Malley book of tales, thinking to give her something of our family, though I cannot know what Isolde has shared.

I told her of twins, pearls of the same shell, mer-sisters. Of how they were born of an ill-made bargain between their mother, a mer-queen and a sea-witch. How, as children, they shared everything; but when their mother died and the sea-witch called for them to pay the remaining tithe, all things went astray.

The sisters agreed they would share the burden: the elder (by but a minute) would rule first in their mother's stead, while the younger took her place as slave to the witch; at the end of six months they would swap. But at the end of the slave sister's servitude, the other sister did not return to take her place. She hoped for the longest time, did that younger sister, to see her sibling come through the greeny-black depths, but that day never arrived. With time, the slave sister learned all the sea-witch had to teach her, and the sea-witch, having no more knowledge to impart, departed from this life, and the apprentice-slave ascended the throne of bones beneath the waves. And year upon year, decade upon decade, century upon century, that sister received supplications from new maidens who wanted to beg a favour, who wanted to make the sorts of bargains her mother had with the old sea-witch. And every time, the sister-witch granted a wish, and took in return something precious to the maiden: a tail, a tongue, a fall of hair, bright eyes, a voice. And every time, she knew that her sister-queen had sent those girls as tribute, as a bribe, to ensure the sister-witch did not make her way to the old kingdom and take what was owed her. But one day, one day, they both knew, there would be a reckoning.

Then having told her a story of our family, I wondered if this was perhaps the sort of story that sisters should not tell each other.

By the time the housekeeper returned − looking more rested but no more friendly − Ena was sleeping peacefully. I told Nelly the child had been a perfect little angel, but I did not tell her why. Before dinner with my uncle this evening, I slipped back into Ena's room and reapplied the paste to ensure a fine sleep for all.

Now, as I stand here in the darkness, I feel in these acts − caring for my small sister, reawakening the fields and the orchards − that I am making a place for myself here, at Blackwater. A home.

Though the house is established, it is new in a way I can't truly imagine Hob's Hallow being. That place is so old that its weight sat on me my entire life − the weight of the O'Malleys and their history, the children they had and gave away, their taste for the sea. Though I've always hated to swim in it, I miss the stinging smell of the saltwater every day; it runs in my veins and will ever do so. Where I am, it is. Here, however, I am becoming a different thing: an Elliott with all the potential that offers, leaving behind the O'Malleys and their burdens − or at least until my mother returns.

I can help the livestock as well, but it will be a little trickier to visit every home and slip something into their feed.

Now, beneath this moon, I'm aware once again of the strange silence of the place − and startle when a footstep sounds behind me, clear as a bell. I spin around, seeking shapes in the shadows. For a moment there's a pause, as if a decision is being made. Then there's a rough grunt, almost badgerish, and someone steps from between the trees into the moonlight.

Jedadiah, the hard-faced man from the village. He tilts his head towards the base of the tree nearest me, to where the newly cut sigil bleeds its sap into the world.

'Will it work, do you think?' he asks, and that's not what I was expecting. I don't answer and he goes on. 'She used to do it, too. Your ma.' He grins. 'Used to take me with her for a while too, when I was younger.'

'Why did she stop?'

'She said it weren't proper for a married lady to keep taking a handsome lad from his bed at full-moon.' He laughs. 'Truth was I had no talent for it. Whatever I touched didn't die but it didn't flourish either. She was too kind to say, though.' He laughs again and the sound is loud in the clear cold air.

I put a finger to my lips, but he just shakes his head.

'No one about but me. Them in the big house don't set foot out in the darkness. Might see something they don't like.'

I bristle at his tone. 'What do you know about them?'

'More'n you do, Miss Miren Elliott.'

I slip the pocketknife away lest I be tempted to use it. I have to walk past him to reach the road back to the house − I won't give him the satisfaction of a wide berth, won't appear afraid. As I pass him, however, he touches my shoulder. Doesn't grab me and try to pin me in place, doesn't even keep his hand on me for more than a second. But I stop and look him in the eye.

'Do things seem right to you? In that house? Does it seem right that your mother's been gone so long? Your father, now he's feckless, he might well desert us when things get hard, but your mother?'

'I don't know my mother,' I say truthfully, painfully. 'She left me when I was a young child and I've no memory of her.' I swallow. 'So if you've got a certainty that she'd never leave you then you're far more fortunate than I.' My voice breaks, just a little.

He looks at me with pity then and I think that might be the worst thing in the world. I continue on and just before I'm out of sight, I hear him say softly, 'When you're ready, come and ask me all the questions you want, Miss Miren. I'm Jedadiah Gannel.'

Gannel. Lazarus' son. His tone's so gentle it makes me want to turn around and go back to him. To ask everything. But not enough. So I don't. I'm tired and sad, and stiff-necked as an O'Malley. I feel weak and vulnerable and I don't like that at all. I've had quite enough of that and he's made me doubt, so very quickly and with so very little reason, my uncle and his kindness.

27

'This'll be for *you*.'

Nelly hands me a folded square of fabric with ill-grace, barely waiting for me to grasp the thing before she lets it fall. I get hold of a corner; the rest slips away like water or a wing, showing a bright, tight woollen weave. A shawl in greens and blues and golds, the pattern exactly like that on a peacock's tail. We are at the bottom of the sweeping staircase in the foyer, I on my way to breakfast, she on her way to the kitchen, bearing other offerings.

It's a fortnight since my night-time agricultural ministrations, and for the past week things have been appearing on our doorstep each morning. Loaves of fresh bread, pies packed with apple and apricots and cherries and peaches from laden trees. Bottles of fruit cordial. Jars of preserves. Uncle Edward, though surprised by the influx of gifts, is nevertheless pleased. When my parents return, perhaps they'll be pleased too – perhaps my mother will be delighted at how well I've looked after her people, how I've saved them from *lack*.

'My dear, whatever you have done,' he said in measured tones on the third day of largesse, 'it is very effective.'

'I've done nothing special, Uncle,' I protested, but he gave me a knowing glance as if we were conspirators. I know, having seen how the villagers regard him, that none of them would tell him – although clearly Jedadiah saw fit to let his neighbours know I was in some way responsible.

The fields are a waving sea of crops that will be ready for harvest in another week; the trees in the orchards are heavy with ripe fruit the folk of Blackwater can hardly pick fast enough. And the livestock are showing signs of reproducing. In the end I simply offered the remedy openly to the villagers, along with the advice that it is something that worked at Hob's Hallow. It wasn't a lie, after all: Maura did use little magics to keep the flocks fertile, the animals healthy. And so, the gifts.

And now this shawl, which is beautiful and soft and warm.

'Thank you,' I say.

Nelly mutters something under her breath. Despite the afternoon hours I regularly spend with Ena to give the housekeeper a rest there's no change in her attitude towards me. Indeed, it seems worse. The child has flourished, her teeth have begun to come through, relieving the pain, and she's sleeping all night – which means Nelly is sleeping too. The woman remains unwilling to give up the time my care of the child gains her, yet she seems resentful that the little girl likes me. Would she rather Ena be miserable? Yet she is tender with the babe, I will give her that; she fusses over her as well as any mother.

'What did you say?' I ask. I've kept a civil tongue these weeks, waiting for her to get used to me. But I'm at the end of my tether. She keeps walking towards the kitchen and I follow, glaring at her back, the curls that escape the bun at the base of her neck, and notice again how fine is her dress, yet still ill-fitting; a very well-kept housekeeper indeed. For some reason this enrages me. I raise my voice as I repeat, 'What did you say?'

Still she doesn't respond, and I reach out and grab her left arm, pull and she swings about. The rage in her face melts my own away; I am merely angry, but she positively loathes me. She wants to do me harm. There is something feral in her expression that makes me think of a wild beast.

'Nelly!' my uncle barks from the open door of the library, and Nelly shrinks away like a dog yelled at by its master. I half expect to see her drop to all fours on the marble tiles, tail between her legs. He hisses, 'Apologise.'

It takes a long moment but she does it, forcing the word out between gritted teeth: 'Sorry.'

'Sorry what?' Uncle Edward thunders. His face is red with anger.

'Sorry, Miss Elliott.' She turns away, the glance she throws at him is searing, then heads towards the kitchen once more. We both watch her until she pushes through the door at the end of the corridor and it thuds angrily behind her. Edward shakes his head, the tension draining from his face, and he gestures for me to join him.

There are two seats beneath a tall, arched window. He has been using one, I can tell from where the pipe is smoking in a heavy silver ashtray beside a glass filled with a more than generous measure of brandy. We've not yet had breakfast. I don't say anything. I take the chair opposite. He has been reading one of the Murcianus books – *Mythical Creatures* – the illustrations are beautifully coloured.

My uncle sits, and sighs, gives me a weary smile. 'Please forgive Nelly. She is—'

'She is tired. She is on the edge of her nerves. She will be in better humour soon,' I snap. 'Frankly, Uncle, I am at a loss as to why you keep making excuses for her.' I am surprised that I'm speaking so bluntly to him; much as I like him, I've always kept a distance between the truth of myself and my thoughts, and what I show him.

He looks taken aback, then something dark swims in his eyes, like a shadowy shape beneath the sea.

I take a deep breath, then puff it out. 'I am sorry, Uncle. I am not used to such hostility from servants.' Which is true, but then Maura and Malachi were more like family than they ever were servants. 'I cannot try any more than I already have. It matters not what I do, she gets angrier and angrier with me for whatever reason she has.'

'Miren, it is… concern. She is worried for your parents. She worked a long time for them and they have been gone for so long… I am beginning to worry myself. Nelly is one whose fears bubble to the surface in a way she cannot help. Now you and I are far calmer beings, more controlled.' He smiles lazily. 'But Nelly is all passion, bless her.' He holds up a hand. 'But I will speak to her. Again.'

'Your patience is admirable, Uncle.'

He smiles. 'Have you been to the village again?'

'Yesterday afternoon, Uncle Edward. I treated Oliver's sheep. The last herd requiring my attention.' In the end it was easier to simply call it "husbandry" and feed the animals of each house – cattle, sheep, goats, pigs, horses – a mix of herbs in a suspension of sour milk with a little of my blood mixed in, brewed in my mother's workroom off the kitchen. It looks normal enough (as long as no one knows about the blood), and the beasties lap it up with delight. 'And to check on the Brune child, Nectan. He'd come down with croup.'

'And?'

'And now he is well.'

'You and your home remedies. What a teacher you must have had in that Maura! Your mother was a dab hand too.' He blinks, laughs, corrects himself. 'When she was here. I assume she still is – and I rather hope she's on her way back to us and not ministering to every tinker in ill health she meets upon the road!'

I laugh with him. 'Maura taught her too. I'm not doing anything different to what she would. That's our duty to the people in our care, to make their lives less burdensome when they labour for us.'

It took a while for me to realise Edward Elliott does not like it when I go out on my own. Oh, the gardens are fine, the orchards and fields too, but not the village. A natural concern, I suspect, given how hostile the villagers are towards him, but that hostility no longer seems to extend to me. There are matters they clam up about, but mostly they are happy to have me around, the Coppers and the Cornishes, the Lambournes and the Danes, the Perrys, the Kanes, the Woodfoxes and all the others who now smile and wave when they see me coming. But my uncle's presence would put pay to that.

'And Jedadiah Gannel. Do you speak with him?' This has become a regular question, but I can answer it mostly honestly.

'No, Uncle. I do not speak with *him*.' And in truth, I do not – not since that night in the orchard. But I have seen him. He watches me and I have found that I look for him. But I do not speak to him.

It is not Edward Elliott's fault that they miss my mother so much – he can't compete with her *charm*. I fear no matter who had been left in charge of Blackwater during her absence they would have met with this unfriendliness. People do not like change – even for three months, which seems such a short time – and it was not his fault that, without Isolde to care for the land, the land ceased to care for its folk. I have noticed, however, that no one mentions missing my father or his ways. There seems to be no hostility towards him, just indifference. I think of Jedadiah calling him "feckless", just as Aoife did. I wonder that he made so little impression on the world. Yet my mother loves him, surely she does.

I pluck at the shawl in my lap and make a point of not looking at the glass of brandy in Edward's hand. He spends a goodly portion of his day in the library, reading and drinking and smoking a pipe. I do not mention that I've noticed he does not ride the boundaries, nor check on the crops or the flocks, nor go into the village any more than he must, nor go to the mine or the smelter (both locations which he continues to tell me I'm not ready to visit).

Uncle Edward has grown used to me; he has realised I am doing the work he has been neglecting. I think it is a relief to him, but he still feels he must appear to be in charge, so the lack of his efficacy will not be so apparent, so glaring. And I in turn make sure to discuss the business of the estate with him as if I, not Oliver Redman, am a manager employed to do such things. I couch it in terms of asking his advice, rather than telling; I begin sentences with 'As you know, Uncle Edward', and finish them with 'Don't you think?' Mostly, he agrees with me, although sometimes, just to be contrary, he will contradict me, order an action to which I nod consideration, then ignore completely. I'm polite and respectful of his feelings because he has been so kind to me. And he's my father's brother; it would do no good to upset him, to have him complaining about me when my parents come home. Óisín and Aoife taught me how to manage an estate even though there wasn't much of a one left at Hob's Hallow. And it's becoming clearer and clearer to me that my uncle knows very little about managing anything but the level in a wine bottle.

I wonder why Isolde and Liam left him in charge here; perhaps Liam was blind to his sibling's faults, perhaps he shared them. But Isolde? Surely Isolde knew better. Then again, perhaps she could refuse her pretty husband nothing.

'Uncle,' I say, a reckless urge surfacing, 'might it be possible to visit the mine today? Or the smelter?'

He shakes his head just as I suspected he would. 'Not today, Miren, although definitely next week. I would not want you there without me and as you can see I am swamped.' He gestures at the nothing by which he is swamped. 'No one will look out for you like family, and I would not trust your safety to anyone else.'

'You are too kind to me, Uncle Edward.' I smile though my teeth grind against each other. Next week there will be fresh reasons not to visit the mine and smelter. I keep my mouth shut for I am content to playact while building this new life, a new family. He still tells me stories about the Elliotts, but they are often repeated and the details frequently vary from one recounting to the next. He cannot know how, growing up with tales from Aoife and Maura, a tiny deviation from the course of a once-heard story can set my head ringing. His shifts and missteps are, I think, the result of the alcohol. It will steal the memory from man or woman as surely as a hex.

But I find I forgive him much because I am happy. The continued lack of my parents is an ache, yes. The life I left behind at Hob's Hallow, for all its recent travails, also hurts me to recall. Maura and Malachi, Óisín and even Aoife, the pain carved in my heart for each one. And I cannot deny that the resentment against Isolde and Liam has in no way diminished. But there is much here to love and rejoice in. There is Oliver in the village who discusses the running of the estate with me openly and honestly, and Lazarus Gannel, who always passes the time of day. There is Lucy Forsyte who always has tea and biscuits when I pass by her gate and has made me new dresses so I don't have to wear my mother's hand-me-downs, and there is her sister Ada, whose handiwork I recognise in that beautiful shawl though there's no note. There are the children of the village who run beside my horse when I ride in, and braid flowers into my hair when I let them (it makes me think of Ben and the troupe, and I hope they are well and safe). There is this house, and there is no trace of Aidan Fitzpatrick, and if the green-eyed man sometimes appears in my dreams, grinning at me from two mouths, then it is a very seldom thing indeed. There is Ena, who is sweet. And I will always remember my uncle's kindness; he will always be twinned with the happiness I am building here. And when my parents return then we shall have an accord.

'Bear with me, my dear.'

'Of course. I do have one suggestion, however?'

He raises a curious brow but says nothing.

'Paley Jethan mentioned that there is an annual harvest fete. It will be late this year, but I don't believe that should stop us. We'll fit it in well before the winter weather.' His expression is dubious so I hurry on. 'Think of the good will, Uncle. Think of how grateful folk are that there is grain to harvest, fruit to preserve, animals swelling the herds, so soon after the fear of want was upon Blackwater. Just a small celebration, Uncle; the memory of it would help keep spirits high when the dark months hit.'

I hold my breath while he makes his decision.

At last he nods. 'But you are in charge of it! And nothing must be done to add to Nelly's burdens, or I fear even I might not be able to calm her!'

28

I'm standing in front of the door to my parents' rooms in the closed-off wing. I've not come here before, not only because of Uncle's warnings about the fire damage. I thought I had my bitterness towards my parents under control, that it would wait until their return, that it would be dealt with quickly once we could speak, lance the boil of my anger. But tonight…

Tonight, the waiting has become too long

Tonight, my patience has grown too weak.

Tonight, I woke from a dream of drowning.

My ankles still ached from where the phantom fingers held so cruelly. My lungs were burning from the effort of keeping my breath in. My hair was soaked to the roots, there were patches of damp on my nightgown, and I was shaking entirely.

There was barely any moonlight coming in, and the fire had died in the hearth; only a few embers glowed there. I *knew* nothing hid in the dark corners. I knew nothing from the *sea* was concealed there. But what is rational does not rule in the dark hours.

I cannot even remember the substance of the dream. Just flashes: teeth and talons and tails like whips. And a song that travels through the waters though it should not, a sound like a mourning bell ringing out my doom for all to hear. And the gleeful words *When you are gone then we will be free.*

And I could taste salt in my mouth; still can.

I rose and padded to the fireplace, pushed a twist of paper into the embers until it flared, then applied it to the wick of the beautiful silver lantern. Once lit, the thing threw a circle of glorious iridescent colour around the room. Then I raised it high to illuminate the far reaches of my chamber: nothing. No one.

The idea of returning to sleep was utterly unappealing – in truth I felt I would never slumber again. I could have reset the fire and sat by it to read. Or I could have done what I've done several times since my arrival: explore the main house and its West Wing. The attics are mostly empty, just some pieces of furniture that have been stored up there for lack of a better place. No chests or boxes, nothing to go through in search of secrets or answers. Downstairs, I have been through the kitchen, parlours, guest rooms, sitting rooms, bathrooms, the study my father apparently used, and the library (more than once). In all the rooms there is so much dust that Nelly cannot possibly be doing her job. I have not been into the chambers of either my uncle or Nelly, nor have I been into the cellar (which can be reached via the trapdoor in my mother's workroom) for its door is locked securely with three big silver padlocks just like those at Hob's Hallow.

Nor have I been to my parents' suite, located in the *ruined* East Wing, yet this evening I feel more rebellious than usual. Some nights ago, when equally sleepless, I wandered the darkened halls and into the library. I rifled the desk drawers and in the bottom right-hand one I found, jammed at the back, a ring heavy with twelve keys (not, mind you, one to the locks on the cellar door). Nelly wears hers on a silver chatelaine around her waist − again, very fine for a housekeeper − and my uncle's hangs on his belt. These, therefore, are spares, or at least, judging by their covering of dust, no one's looking for them. Thus they have been lying deep in the hollow I made in my mattress when I sliced its corner open; lying beside the jewellery pouch, and the one with most of the gold I stole from the assassin.

But now I am *here*, having travelled through corridors in the wing that is supposedly ruined by fire and dangerous; it's occurred to me only lately that there is no sign of damage on the outside of the house. I found evidence of the blaze in one of the bedrooms on the second floor, where the walls are painted like a garden with bunnies and foxes and flowers and fairies peeking out from behind tree trunks, but there's barely a stick of furniture, bar an old rocking chair and a broken, soot-stained crib with a burnt blanket twisted at its foot. All I could smell in there was old smoke and something else I couldn't quite identify, something so faint I might have imagined it. The fire had clearly been contained, the curtains and carpet merely singed. I think that it must have been Ena's room − I recall Edward saying that Nelly and my parents had barely escaped with their lives, but this seems an exaggeration, just as the degree of "ruination" is also. Ena must have been with Nelly or Isolde, although how the conflagration started in there I cannot imagine. Perhaps a lantern knocked over, or a candle?

The rest of the wing, however, was perfectly fine. So, my uncle lied or at least distorted the truth. I feel far better about disobeying him. It makes me wonder what other lies he has been telling me. And why.

271

My parents' suite is on the next floor down. The key in the lock moves a little stiffly with disuse, then I push the door open, hold my lantern high.

The room is decorated in shades of silvery blue and stormy green: curtains, bed draperies, quilts, couches and chairs, rugs, the walls. The dressing table is covered with powders and perfumes, face paints, loose jewellery, brushes and carefully created hair flowers and adornments. And dust, still so much dust.

There are two dressing rooms, one to each side of the enormous bed. One contains men's clothing and footwear. The other women's dresses. I can see in both spots where items are missing – absences as if dresses and shirts and jackets and trousers have been picked over, taken as a bowerbird steals shiny objects. Natural, perhaps; my parents would have chosen their travelling attire – except for the fact that in each dressing room there's a high shelf running around the walls, and upon each shelf perch cases and trunks; two full sets, my mother's engraved in gold with "I.E." and my father's with "L.E.".

A small door leads into a bathroom with an enormous clawfoot tub and shelves groaning beneath the weight of bottles of creams and hair washes. Nothing appears to have been taken from here, but I could not swear to it.

Back in the bedchamber, there's a huge hearth and above it hangs a painting: a handsome dark-haired couple, so very well dressed; the man looks slightly younger than the woman – childbearing will add years to a female face. My father is indeed pretty, and he and Edward do bear a passing resemblance to one another. Around my mother's neck is a silver chain and on that silver chain is a pendant in the shape of a ship's bell. I step as close as I can, raising the lantern: I can just make out where the artist has gone to the trouble of detailing the scalloped marks that look like scales. My hand shakes and the shadows dance: this is the first time I've seen my parents.

There is a desk, too, delicate and not overly large, rather a feminine piece of furniture that surprises me. Then again, I know my mother not at all. I assume it is hers, however, because of the large book that rests on its surface. Black leather, scalloped silver shells as a border front and back and the shape of the two-tailed, two-faced mermaid picked out in silver foil. There's an intricately engraved pen in red onyx beside it and a bottle of ink that appears mostly dried out. I open the cover of the volume.

In a fine hand, a hand I recognise from Isolde's letters to Óisín, are written tales, O'Malley tales.

Once upon a time, so long ago, nobody but the storytellers remember...

In a land that never was in a time that could never be...

In olden times when wishing still helped...

Once on the far side of yesterday...

My mother has done what I had planned to do. I wonder how far she has got, if her recall is fresh? I wonder if she will mind if I begin to add to the tome? Will it be a pleasant surprise for when she comes home? I gather it into my arms like a child.

As I'm about to leave, I look up. There are shadows and shapes that catch my interest. I locate more candles and light them, then place them so as to best illuminate the space.

There is a mural painted on the ceiling, a duplicate, or as close as Isolde's memory could get, to the one in the library at Hob's Hallow. Or I assume so: I recognise some elements, those that were still visible beneath the cobwebs and soot at home. In Isolde's era, things would have been not so obscured – perhaps with time, Yri or Ciara would have mounted ladders and spring-cleaned to reveal all. Faces here and there, limbs, roiling clouds, a ship's sail, a sea monster's tail... only the sea monster isn't a monster anymore. Or perhaps any less. It's been turned into a mer or perhaps it always was one.

An enormous sea-queen sprawled across painted rocks, staring down at my parents night after night. Black hair, pit-dark eyes, bare breasts but skin all scaled, and the tail... the tail is split in two, just like the brand on my hip. The brand seems to burn anew, though I have no memory of its original application.

I blow out all the candles, then leave – book under one arm, lantern in my hand – being careful to leave no signs of my passing.

Back in my own wing, I walk on tiptoes along the corridor. My uncle's suite is on the floor above. I'm struck how, just like Hob's Hallow, there are so many empty chambers, but at least once upon a time there were people to fill the spaces *there*. Blackwater, this place built by my parents, feels big just for the sake of it, empty for the sake of it. So much space and they did not send for me. No accommodation for Miren O'Malley. Miren Elliott.

But perhaps they had plans to fill it with more offspring. Ena – the child worth keeping – was a start. How many more might my mother birth? She's not so old... And away from the sea, away from Hob's Hallow, new children might be safe, no nameless ones needed to feed to the waters...

As I approach Nelly's room (beside Ena's), which I must pass to get to my own door, I hear noises: sighing, heavy breathing, gasps and tiny moans. The door is not quite hitched, it's fallen ajar too, which it wasn't when I passed by before, and in the breach I can see Nelly's bed. And Nelly straddling someone, moving back and forth, bucking. And from her partner comes my uncle's voice whispering profanities and threats, grunts. I almost stop mid-step, am almost grasped by an awful reckless fascination, but I keep going, press forward oh-so-silently until I can ease open my own door and hide myself. Then I let go of my hard-held breath.

I huddle beneath the covers, thinking of the book of tales I've hidden away in the bottom of the blanket box beneath quilts and shawls and fresh linen. I wonder, then, why my parents appear to have gone on a long journey without travel bags nor any of the cosmetics to which my mother was clearly very partial. Not even her hairbrush.

* * *

The next day I tell my uncle I am going to the village to make arrangements for the harvest celebration. He yawns and nods, clearly worn out by his night's labours. I ride away in the right direction but as soon as I'm out of sight of the house, I change my course.

The smelter is closer than the mine. I can fit in a quick trip and be less likely to be missed just in case anyone were to ask about the times of my comings and goings I can go to the smelter, then head cross-county to the village, with Uncle Edward none the wiser.

I dismount and leave my horse in a copse, then approach the gathering of four rough wood and tin buildings that stand on a circle of earth. No grass grows within the bounds of the compound. And it appears that there is nothing special to see. I don't step from the tree line myself because there are some few men still working there and I don't wish anyone to note my presence. A few puffs of grey smoke come from the tall chimney stack on the largest structure; inside I imagine there will be a furnace, someone shovelling the silver into it, then the boiling liquid poured into ingot moulds. I wonder how it gets shipped out, where it goes, who from the village takes it or is there a regular pickup by someone? I think perhaps I shall speak with Oliver Redman about such matters; I believe he'll keep any conversations between us.

As I'm about to leave, a man wanders out of the sliding door of the main building. Jedadiah Gannel, shirtless, covered in coal dust and sweat from feeding the forge. He stares at where I am hidden by shadow and low-hanging branches as if he can see me. I hold my breath and stay still until he shrugs, grins, and turns away to head into one of the smaller outbuildings.

29

The day of the fete dawns fair but a little colder than it has been, as if winter is sending her breath on ahead: *Don't forget me, for I've not forgotten you.* But soon enough the sun warms everything, and the warning is forgotten. My loose long green dress cinched in only with a sash (beautifully made by Lucy Forsyte) is perfect for the bright day.

The front lawn is busy, busy, busy: trestle tables laden with food, others entirely with ales and mead, finer wines and rougher whiskeys. Almost two hundred women, men and children scattered across the sward of green, everyone's done something to contribute to this celebration. A group of fellows are gathered around a newly dug fire pit – which I'm certain will make Uncle Edward pale when he sees it, but he and Nelly have not seen fit to join the festivities, and I gave permission for its creation. Soon perhaps we might see a point where Uncle and I part ways on matters of the estate's management, but that day has not yet come... yet every time I make a bold decision, I know I push a little closer. A pig and a steer are both spitted above the flames, and the men, stout chaps all, take turns with the handle to keep the meat rotating. Potatoes and pumpkins in clay pots have been buried in the coals and are cooking there. Fat sizzles down the sides of the meat, and the scent of roasting flesh fills the air. My mouth waters as I walk through the crowd, chatting, ensuring everyone is happy and relaxed, rewarded for their work on the estate, for that seems to have been lacking since my parents went away.

'Miss Miren,' Oliver calls. He's standing by a trestle table and the lot of barrels I found in a small storeroom off the kitchen. No one could have brewed soon enough for today's event, and there's no point in hoarding for three people in the big house. This was my contribution.

'Hello, Mr Redman.' I call him "mister" precisely because my uncle does not. 'All is well?'

'More than well, Miss Miren, and it's all due to you.' He smiles, his cheeks red from the contents of the barrel.

Abel Woodfox stands beside him; the blacksmith is an enormous man, almost seven feet tall, muscled as a bull. Even I have to strain my neck to look up at him as he says, 'You've put the heart back into Blackwater, back into us.'

'You're too kind, gentlemen. This is no more than you all deserve for your hard work. It is appreciated.' I touch Abel's arm, then Oliver's, and smile. Neither of them flinch anymore when I do this, having realised that whatever Isolde did to them I do not (cannot) do. That they'll not be charmed against their will.

'It's nice to have it shown, Miss, is all,' mutters Oliver. The longer I am here, the more time I spend in the village, the more open becomes their dislike of Edward Elliott. Still, I feel obliged to defend him.

'I know my uncle can seem heedless,' I say. 'I fear he is not a man used to managing. And he is concerned, I know, about my

278

parents' long absence. I fear it makes him... neglectful of the feelings of others. Never doubt that you are valued.'

'We'd been talking about leaving, you know,' Abel says, and Oliver tries to hush him. Abel forges ahead, nods to where his sons, Jago and Treeve, are arm wrestling on the stump of a large tree. 'We've been a'feared of starving this winter – the road to St Sinwin's gets impassable in the snow so supply runs can't happen then, and your uncle's unwilling to buy in as much as we need to tide us over.' I try not to press my lips together in annoyance. 'I was worried for my boys.' He grins, more than a little drunk. 'But you've put paid to that, haven't you?' I smile but say nothing. 'It's you, girly, the moment you came back, the land gave once more. We can never thank you enough for that, though we'll do our best.' To my great surprise, Abel goes down on one knee and grasps my hand; Oliver follows him and takes the other. 'We pledge to you, Miss Miren, we will stand by you no matter what.'

'Oh.' I'm at a loss, and try to get them to rise before anyone sees it; before my uncle or Nelly look out of the windows. 'My dear gentlemen, that is so kind, but people will talk! And I do not want either of your wives coming after me with an axe!'

They both laugh and blush, and rise. I pat their shoulders in turn and reassure them lest they feel embarrassed by an act fuelled with alcohol and relief. 'Thank you, Mr Redman, Mr Woodfox, I am more grateful than you know. I will always do my best for Blackwater. I hope you will always feel free to come to me with problems. If I can help I shall.'

I loved Hob's Hallow without a doubt but – and this is the first time I have admitted it to myself – I think it was a dead place.

If I had stayed there, I'd have been entombed. By the house, by marriage to Aidan, by remaining with Aoife in the cocoon she'd created for herself, smothered by the dream she had of reviving the O'Malley fortunes. It would never have been a *life*, but a kind of embalming in wealth and position and expectations. No true existence at all.

But here... here there is something to create and grow and nurture. Here, I feel as if I have a purpose rather than a series of activities done simply to survive, to hold back dust and dirt and eventual death.

'Thank you both,' I say. I look up to see who might have noticed this fealty ceremony, and find myself caught in a green gaze. Jedadiah Gannel is staring, an eyebrow raised, the corner of his mouth quirked in amusement. I want nothing so much as to poke my tongue out at him, but I resist the urge. Instead, I look away, look around, move off from the blacksmith and estate manager.

Children are playing chasey, skipping, hoop and stick, Blind Man's Bluff, tumbling and handstands; a group of girls toy with carved knucklebones to read each other's fortunes, giving rise to great shrieks; several boys are weaving chains of flowers, perhaps for the girls. I keep an eye on the ones who are running and jumping, as do their mothers, to make sure they are not too near the edge of the lake. I can almost imagine that the water eats everything, except there are reflections on its surface, clear and true, of whatever occurs above.

Women sit on blankets, passing out "pick food", things to nibble on before the main meal is ready. Four old dames have settled by a trestle table laden with cakes and breads and other pastries. By the looks of pride, the way they sneer at the younger women's offerings, I can tell these are their own works. Aged matrons with no fear of death or censure, who've spent their whole lives keeping their mouths shut in the interests of protecting the sensibilities of others – *no* resemblance to Aoife there – but now they don't care. They've got sharp eyes, tongues like whips, and remarks to sting the same way salt does when rubbed into a wound.

One of them, Keziah Eddy, lifts a hand to summon me. I kneel beside her chair and greet her, her sister-in-law Keren-happuch Lambourne, and their cousins Zara Stark and Elena Yarrow. Widows all, they live in the same cottage – if they'd stayed living with their families they'd have spent all their time looking after grandchildren. This arrangement pleases them best. I asked them, quietly, when they first invited me for tea soon after my arrival at Blackwater, why they'd not tried the small magics I did to revive the land. They answered that they were reluctant to interfere with whatever my mother had done; that one woman's spell might not work on top of another's, or it might be catastrophic, especially where a witch like Isolde was concerned. Her workings, they said, were grand and powerful; none of them are blood-witches. *You're her daughter*, they said, *that's different, though you're no more witch than we*. But, Keziah had admitted, with things heading towards the grim, they had been discussing something desperate; however, they would not tell me what it was. By their tones and sideways looks, I suspected they'd considered a sacrifice, the blood of a young man to water the ground. I doubt it would have had much effect, not when Isolde had made this earth so very much her own.

'How are you, my dames?' I ask. They smile wickedly; they're out in the sun, they're showing up their own daughters and daughters-in-law, who take the insult well, for a decent sweet roll is worth the price of your pride; everyone returns for second and third helpings, and they're getting a chance to chide and snipe. There's no great malice in them, or no greater than any woman accumulates in a life not designed for herself, and they are very clever; we've swapped recipes for potions more than once since I've been here.

'Well enough, lovely, well enough. How are you?'

'Well enough,' I say with a grin. 'Well enough.'

'No sign of your uncle then? He'll not be joining us?' asks Zara slyly.

'Nor that Nelly Daniels neither?' Elena passes me a pastry filled with apricots and thick cream. I bite into it, shake my head.

'My uncle is going over the accounts,' I tell them what he told me. 'Nelly is tending to Ena.' I would have liked my little sister to be around other children, but Nelly insisted she remain inside, that she was coming down with something; a litany of reasons why Ena should not be exposed to the village brats.

'She is devoted to that child,' agrees Elena, her eyes flicking a glance towards the big house.

'I'm sure it helps her after her own loss,' Keren-happuch agrees.

'What happened?' I ask around a buttery mouthful; there's a lot of cinnamon, but not too much; it's perfectly judged.

'She was pregnant when she and your uncle arrived here, gave birth soon after.'

I am surprised: I'd assumed Nelly had come from the village. 'They came together?'

Keziah shakes her head. 'I believe they met upon the road. Your parents had hired Nelly to be a wet nurse to Ena, sent for your uncle to come and caretake, or so we're told. She used to talk to us, then. She gave birth the week before your mother. Those two little girls, sleeping in the same crib.' She smiles sadly.

'What happened?' I repeat, and she seems to understand I'm asking more than one question. Uncle Edward has only ever called Nelly the housekeeper, no mention of a wet nurse for my sister. And Ena's been bottle-fed the whole time I've been here – or at least by me. What might Nelly do in her own room?

'The accident,' says Keziah.

'Terrible thing to happen to a woman, especially a woman on her own,' mutters Keren-happuch, and the others nod.

'Poor Meraud.'

I think of the burned cradle in the locked wing of the house. Not just Ena's then. I've asked Nelly nothing about herself because I assume she'll tell me nothing. But mostly because I don't like her; it's rendered her of no interest to me. But she lost a child and that must hurt and it's not something I'd wish on anyone. I wonder if my uncle has not mentioned her tragedy out of kindness and sensitivity. Before I can ask any more I'm distracted by childish shrieking.

A group running madly by the lake. A little girl with bright auburn-rose hair is being pursued by boys and girls, all screaming in delight. But they lose track of where they're going, as children are wont to do, and their parents have grown inattentive with sun and food and drink. They go too near the edge.

I'm watching even as it happens; it seems so slow, it seems as if the moment in which it could be prevented is long and it is an amazement to me that no one does anything. The little girl is there, then she is gone; her pursuers stop, a good distance from the water, mouths agape.

The child has disappeared completely, swallowed by the black liquid. Her mother, Miriam Dymond, alert to the danger only too late, is now running back and forth on the shore – no one is going to the rescue. There are those trying to stop her in her tracks, stop her running about like a headless chicken. These are mountain folk, inland folk, there's not a seafarer amongst them. No one is taught to swim from birth, no one but me's an O'Malley here. As afraid as I am of the lake, I'm more afraid of letting a child be taken.

I kick away my delicate slippers, loosen the sash and pull off my dress, dropping it beside the crones, and run toward the lake in only my thin cotton shift. I feel the bell pendant against my throat thud up and down, hear it tinkling with every step.

Behind me someone shouts, 'No, Miren!' but I ignore them.

My right foot hits the spot where land and water meet, and I launch myself forward. It's a good leap, I've long legs, and it seems like an age before I break the surface.

But when I do, it feels like a shock, as if I've been struck by lightning and my heart will explode. I begin to sink like the proverbial stone.

30

You'd think, really, that I'd only sink a few yards, that I'd hit a shelf of rock or some such, but no. Perhaps six feet out into the lake and I keep going down, down, a'down. And the fluid is cold, cold, cold, even colder than Breakwater Harbour.

As the liquid closes over my head, I think I might just drown and make no effort to save myself. My limbs feel so heavy, so sluggish, and it takes every bit of willpower I've got to gather my wits before I die then and there. I tread water, halt my descent to get my bearings, and stare into the depths below me, my shift billowing as if in a strong wind. I'm half-looking for the child, half-looking for mer.

The liquid is a strange green from here, turgid, barely seeming to move despite my thrashing, but at last I see something below me, a pale blur, struggling weakly, increasingly weakly. I duck-dive, kick, and press further into the icy dark.

The child seems to plummet, heavier than she should be, or perhaps pulled, but I can see nothing that grips her. At last, I get a grip on her fingers, her palm, her chubby wrist. My lungs are burning. The girl's eyes are glazing over, the lids beginning to drop. Her hair's like red smoke around her white moon of a face. I pull her hard toward me and clasp her to my chest. She's too far gone to hold onto me, so I have to swim single-handed, kicking like a frog. I want to look behind, I want to make sure nothing is following us, but I don't. *Concentrate, Miren, on up.* I can still feel a shudder through the water, like it's shivering from its own frigidity.

Then I break the surface and the air is ridiculously warm. I strike out for the shore, which seems further away than it should be. There's no gradation, no shallows; my feet scrabble against the steep vertical wall of the lake. Someone takes the girl from my arms, then someone pulls me up too. My legs are like jelly as I'm dragged away from the edge, well away, following the woman who carries her daughter some distance before *her* legs give way. I break free of whoever pulled me to safety and follow Miriam Dymond. She collapses, howling, with the child draped across her lap. The little one remains breathless.

I grab at the girl, lie her flat on the ground. I press at the chest, then breathe into her mouth; I repeat these actions until she spits up so very much fluid it seems a small pond, then coughs and wails. I fall away. Miriam gathers her daughter, rocks back and forth.

I'm hauled to my feet once more, so exhausted I could cry and all I want is sleep, to let the lethargy that hit me with the lake's touch take me down. I look up into Jedadiah's face; the heat of him seems strange but I am frozen through. For a moment I'm confused as he stares at me, then I realise that his expression is one of dread. Not something I expected to see – and he's not staring at me, but past me.

I try to turn, but he presses my face firmly into his chest. I kick his shin in a temper and he lets me go in surprise. I gaze out to the lake.

Three heads, large; pale skin with a greenish tinge; gills that I can see in the necks even from this distance; and tails that flip and splash and slap.

The mer, grinning at me and hissing. No song this time. No need. They stare for a little while, then they are gone with more splashing. Jedadiah has his arms around me again, apparently undeterred by the kick. He's shaking as much as I am, but how much is from the cold of my skin and how much from fear is anyone's guess.

What I realise now that my mind has slowed, my terror has ebbed a little, is that the lake was salty. Not fresh. It makes me wonder how can anyone escape such creatures when all the waters in the world are joined? Idly, I wonder how the kelpie liked this saltiness.

'Did you see them?' he asks, and there's a rough edge to his voice. He knows my answer, that's why.

'They followed me from Breakwater,' I confess. 'They want no one but me.'

He grabs my shoulders and says urgently, 'We must talk, Miren Elliott, but not here. There's more for you to know.'

Any reply I might have given is lost as my name is shouted from the house. Uncle Edward is striding towards us. Nelly hangs in the doorway, appearing somewhat disappointed to see me still extant. Any sympathy I might have had for her is leached away.

'Tonight at the mine. Midnight,' says Jedadiah in a low voice. I neither nod nor shake my head, for my uncle has reached us and wrenched me from Jedadiah's grip as if he were the cause of my ills, not the person who saved me.

'Miren, you're soaked through! What happened?' He's looking at Jedadiah, as if I'm not an adult to speak for myself.

'The Dymond girl fell into the lake, Uncle, nothing more. We are both safe,' I say coolly and point to the child now sobbing heartily in her mother's lap. He barely glances at her and I'm aware that the disposition of the gathering has changed.

Oh, it was already different when I came out of the water, but there was an air of relief; and as far as I'm aware only Jedadiah and I saw the mer. So: the fear had dissipated quickly, replaced by that special lighter-than-air fizz that bubbles up when a tragedy is averted. The celebration might well have gone on, people drinking faster and more, laughing more loudly, better inclined towards their fellows, all because of the failure of fate to take something from their lives.

But now, here is my uncle, and the mood is blackening faster than overripe fruit in high summer. People are packing their baskets, scooping food into them, folding blankets, shepherding children and old folk. They all file past the spit where Woodfox and Oliver slice slabs from the carcasses and dump them onto platters, which the villagers carry away with them. The desertion is a swift process. My uncle has brought the curtain down.

'Uncle,' I say. 'Uncle Edward, be calm.'

'Come inside, Miren. I don't want you catching your death. Let Nelly tend to you.' And he grasps both my wrists and all I can think about is Aidan Fitzpatrick bruising my skin. There's the stink of alcohol on his breath; I pull away violently, feeling like a petulant child.

Edward Elliott locks eyes with me and glares. This is the first time we've been at odds; the first time I've not simply gentled him into an agreement. The first spark of a rebellion in his mind, no doubt.

Then he backs off, hold up his palms. 'I'm sorry, my dear, I should not have grabbed at you. I... Worry makes for fear and fear makes one rash. I do apologise.'

I lower my eyes, shutter my rage, but I can still feel the anger that enabled me to draw a knife across the assassin's throat. I don't want my uncle to see that. Instead I turn to Jedadiah.

'Thank you for your aid, Mr Gannel. I'll not keep you further.' I say nothing else but hope he'll take my meaning as it's intended.

When I feel the heat's gone out of my expression I look back to Edward Elliott.

'Thank you, Uncle. I am rather chilled.' I reach for his arm, then let him lead me into the house.

* * *

I refuse dinner, saying I am exhausted by the afternoon's dramas. I refuse Nelly's assistance, tell her I'm more than capable of bathing myself. I say I need to sleep but will be well in the morning. I know it's childish and ungracious, but I feel... so many things.

Afraid. The mer have followed me. But the more I think about it, the more I wonder. They could have taken me, once again, but they did not. They did not sing any threats. The child went in accidentally. The water of the lake, salty. So salty and so far from the sea. I think of a tale Maura told me once, about how the sea got its briny taste, wherein an enchanted quern fell into the ocean before anyone thought to command it to stop grinding salt, but that's no help at all.

Suspicious. My uncle and Nelly. My parents' room with all their possessions (but those missing clothes) still there, even the cases, even the hairbrushes. My uncle keeping me from the locked wing, the burned cradle; keeping me from the mine and the smelter. Lying about Nelly's position. Never mentioning the dead child.

Robbed. And this I recognise as the most selfish thing: that the celebration was cut short. That the people of Blackwater were happy and enjoying themselves and it was all due to my efforts. They have accepted me, look to me in a way that never truly happened at Hob's Hallow, in part because Aoife was the chatelaine, and in part because we had so few dependents there at the end. I know it's childish, but I can't help feeling deprived not by the mer, but by Uncle Edward.

I wait until I hear Nelly's footsteps going past my door, then I wait a little longer and I am glad for it. There's a light knock and no waiting for any answer. I am beneath the covers in my nightgown. I've left a small vial of sleeping tincture and a cup on the bedside table so anyone will think I've taken it to sleep. I believe they drugged me the first night I arrived with what was ostensibly a tea to calm me. I'm experienced at faking sleep, having practised so many years when Aoife would check on me; when she had gone, I'd sneak to the library and read the book of tales by the light of a single candle. My breathing is even and deep, my lids held still by sheer willpower. Again, I wonder if all Aoife taught me was deceit.

I can sense the flicker of candlelight as someone approaches the bed. The tread is not Nelly's nor is the hand that touches my hair, caresses my face. I smell alcohol and know it's my uncle – but then, who else would it be? It's all I can do to stay immobile.

He seems to remain forever, until I give a deep sigh and roll over, away from his hand. I don't like putting my back to him, but it has the desired effect. I open my eyes a slit and see the candlelight dancing away as he retreats, no doubt to go to Nelly's room.

I wait a little longer, then rise and dress warmly.

* * *

'We found it weeks ago – just before you arrived,' Jedadiah says.

'Two days before you arrived,' adds Lazarus. Father and son are both kitted with stout lanterns, hung around with ropes and grappling hooks, and I wonder how far we are going to dig into the earth. I have a silver knife at my belt, one in my right boot, the other in my left, and the pocketknife in my jacket pocket. Should I be more wary of these men? I barely know them, and yet my instinct tells me I'm safer with them in the dead hours than I am in a house with Edward Elliott.

We stepped into the black mouth of the mine almost an hour ago, following the metal tracks that small carts are pushed along to carry the ore. Thick rough-hewn beams support the rock ceiling, seem to keep the basalt walls from bulging inwards to crush us. I can feel the weight of it all as we go deeper and I'm sweating profusely. In some places small niches have been carved and candles are set therein. Lazarus lights them as we go so we leave illumination in our wake as we tread into darkness. Other spots, there are hooks dug into the beams, and lanterns hang there pushing the blackness back. Lazarus lights them too.

'Who found *it* precisely?' They will not tell me *what*; they say I must see it.

'Vera Penhalligon. She was scavenging, wasn't supposed to be here. You know your uncle closed the mine?'

I shake my head. 'He told me it was simply not producing much but he had people looking for new seams, that the chief engineer was considering how best to get through to other tunnels?'

'Chief engineer? Who's that then? Closest we had was Timon Bleaker,' snorts Lazarus. He's gruff still, but less so than the first time I met him.

'Timon died in the collapse five years ago,' says Jedadiah.

'Never replaced. Your father didn't deem it necessary.' Lazarus's lips thin.

'We're here.' Jedadiah hangs his lantern on a nail in a wooden beam, then begins to uncoil the rope from his shoulder. He threads it through a metal circle lower down on a sturdy-looking post, and goes to tie it around my waist. I step back. He looks surprised, then grins. 'Think I'm going to drop you into a hole and leave you there?'

'Well, it would be the ideal time.'

'It would hardly have been worth dragging you out of the lake, would it?' But he nods. 'I'll go first. Da, you send the miss down after me.'

'Can you trust me?' scoffs Lazarus, then laughs. 'That better for you, Miss Miren?'

'It'll do.' I've got my knives and a willingness to use them if required. But these men don't need to know that. Best if they don't, in fact.

Jedadiah wraps the rope around his own waist and disappears over the lip into the shaft. It doesn't take long before I hear his boots hit bottom. He shouts for the rope to be pulled up.

The trip seems longer than it should, trying not to bar against the rough-hewn walls. I see a light below: Jedadiah has lit a torch. He unties me when I reach the bottom. 'Alright?'

I nod, a lump of uncertainty in my throat.

'This way. And I'm sorry, for what it's worth.'

The tunnel is short and the torchlight dances up ahead of us. A boot is the first thing I see, then a bright blue trouser-covered leg, then the hem of an amethyst jacket, a very fine waistcoat in emerald silk. Peacock hues; just such clothes as my uncle has worn every day since I arrived and, no doubt, quite some days before. But these are stained and darkened with decay. The light licks up, picks out the silver chain of a fob, then a neck and face, skin discoloured and sloughing off rotting flesh. Empty sockets, thick dark hair still attached to a scalp that's beginning to slide to one side. The smell is… I don't know what it is – the death I've been around has always been *fresh*.

'Who… who is it?'

'This, Miss Miren, is Liam Elliott. That waistcoat, that coat, that fob-chain: all his. And his hair, too, very fine that it was in life.' He sighs. 'I'm afraid this is your father.'

I kneel beside the body and carefully pull on the fob-chain. The thing comes reluctantly, dragging the weight of a round watch. I hold that silver circle in the palm of my hand, feeling its coldness almost sear the skin. On the top is an engraving, the double-tailed, Janus-faced mermaid, the O'Malley seal – a gift from my mother, no doubt – worn down, the details blurred as if the owner habitually rubbed it with his thumb, as surely as water will wear away stone.

31

I'm sitting at the white pine table in Lazarus Gannel's small kitchen, nursing a mug of whiskey and milk. I've not said much since they led me out of the mine, except to answer when Lazarus asked if I wanted my father brought along too.

'No,' I said. 'For the moment, leave him here. We'll bury him properly when this is all finished.'

They asked no more and were silent in the almost hour it took us to walk back to the gatehouse. The last ten minutes they've been speaking over the top of my head while Lazarus prepares drinks. Jedadiah is sitting beside me, his hand on mine, and all I can feel is the heat of him when I'm so very, very cold. Cold as if I'd gone back into the black waters of the lake and drifted down with no thought of coming back up again. When the silver mug is put in front of me, I take a deep draught, not caring that it makes me light-headed, not recalling until now that I've eaten no dinner. I ask for and am given a slice of bread and cheese. At last, I feel a single thought pushing to the forefront of my mind, a single question overtaking the whirlpool in my head.

'Why didn't you tell me? When I arrived? You knew he was dead then, why not say something?' I hear my own voice but cannot divine my tone; I cannot tell how I must sound to them.

Again, it's like drowning with only that strange dullness the water brings to the ear. 'I might have entered that house and been killed immediately.'

Jedadiah has the grace to look ashamed or something like it; Lazarus looks me in the eye and says, 'That would have been some greeting, wouldn't it? Miss Miren, I didn't know you from a bar of soap. You've the look of your mother, yes, but who could know what you knew or did not know? What if you went straight to your uncle and told him? And here's us trying to keep the fact we know something's not right from him. Who knew what you'd do?' He shakes his head and grins like a challenge. 'Besides, if you'd been killed so easily, what sort of girl would you be? Certainly not the sort of girl I took you for.'

'Miren, this has been our home for over thirteen years. We all made agreements with your parents – your mother. She brought us here and the big house was already built, and our houses, just as she promised. We've taken those oaths seriously. We've been hoping she would return.' Jedadiah shakes his head. 'And you arrived, and you've done more than right by us, but those first weeks? All we could see was you getting closer to your uncle, you making excuses for him. And how he looks at you—'

'How does he look at me?' I ask sharply.

He lifts a brow as if wondering how stupid I might prove to be. 'The way neither uncle nor father nor brother should look at a niece, daughter or sister, Miren.'

And I notice he calls me by my name without "miss" in front, but I also think about how Edward Elliott came into my room, touched my hair. I think about Nelly's behaviour and how it makes so much more sense if there's jealousy and fear in her soul. She must know. She must know about my father. And if my father is lying in the silver mine, in a disused pit, an oubliette of a thing, then where is my mother? Where is Isolde?

'Eight months they have been here, my uncle and Nelly Daniels,' I say, speaking to myself but aloud to make sense of it – sometimes you only know whether an idea's stupid or not if you hear it. 'Five months without my parents. They met on the road, or so Nelly told the old dames. Nelly was pregnant when she came here, she was meant to be a wet nurse to Ena, not a housekeeper... Who was the housekeeper before?' Things I had not thought to ask – why would I? One sees a structure, a system, one assumes it has been in place a long while... but appearances can be deceiving, assumptions can be dangerous. Nelly keeps the dust at bay, but only just, and only in the areas we use. There are no stable lads, the gardens are tended once a week by the Woodfox boys, and are slowly growing wild with insufficient attention.

'Miriam Dymond.' *Ah.* 'And the Toop girls used to be the maids. Paley Jethan's boys took care of the stables.' Jedadiah leans forward. 'But they were told not to come back to the big house by your uncle. At first they were sent to work in the fields or the mine or the smelter... then the mine began to run dry, the fields and orchards ceased to produce... No one but you has seen the inside of that house in months. Your uncle only ever talks to Oliver Redmond on the front stoop.'

I feel pieces of knowledge that have been scattered in my memory click into place, gravitate to other fragments as if a form of magnetic attraction is at last in play. 'Did... did my parents tell anyone that my uncle was coming? That he'd been sent for?'

Their gazes tell me *no*.

'Did my parents tell anyone that they were leaving?' I ask, trying to untangle the skeins in my mind.

Lazarus shakes his head. 'Ours is not to question our betters, Miss.'

'Did you see them go? Did they offer farewell to anyone?'

Lazarus looks embarrassed. 'I heard them go. It was just before dawn and I heard the horses. I looked out the window, saw the hedge open and them riding out. The day after the fire.'

The day after Nelly Daniels lost her child? It seems heartless that they would have gone then, but they left me behind, didn't they? Their own flesh and blood? Ena, too. What care would my parents have for anyone else?

'Did you see their faces? Any baggage?'

He shakes his head. 'No. I've thought on it time and again since we found your father, and I did not see their faces. I recognised their clothes, your mother's green cloak, your father's overcoat with the silver animals embroidered along the cuffs. But he wore a hat and she had the hood of her cloak over her face and I... But they carried no luggage.'

'You didn't go down to check on them?'

He looks ashamed now. 'I... since your uncle arrived, your father had been... even less solicitous than before.'

Jedadiah says, 'You must understand, Miren, that as loved as your mother was, your father was loved by no one but *her*.' He hesitates, swallows. 'Five years ago he ignored warnings that parts of the mine were unsafe. There was a cave-in and a flood. We never found the bodies, gods only know where they got to... my wife was one of them...'

I slide my hand away from his; I cannot eat his grief at the moment, not when my own is such a filling meal. Then I think of the kelpie telling me of bodies washed down in a flood some years back, their throats cut… but that won't help anyone, that knowledge of the dead being so far from home, out of reach and already reduced to their component parts. It might be nothing more than coincidence; the corpses might not have come from Blackwater. I don't mention it.

I look at Lazarus. 'So by the time they ostensibly left, you didn't care enough to check or to question?'

He shakes his head, takes a gulp of his drink. 'And I'll regret it forever.'

I say, 'You might not have survived either.'

Jedadiah says, 'The next day your uncle came to the village, spoke to Oliver, told him that your parents had gone on a buying trip to Breakwater.'

'He told me Calder. Calder to speak to the Leech Lords about the failing silver mine…' And I'm amazed that Edward Elliott would tell such contrary tales… but I recall telling him when I first arrived that I'd come from Breakwater; it explains why he was unhappy for me to be in the village on my own, why he only tolerated it when it was clear my presence was making Blackwater productive once again, that it might stave off any rebellion from its people for a while longer, any difficult questions… 'When did the mine stop producing?'

'A month after your parents left.'

Did my mother's magic have some effect on the mining as well? 'But Isolde and Liam *knew* Edward Elliott, yes?'

Jedadiah nods. 'He and your father seemed great friends.

They looked alike too, so when Nelly told people they wer brothers…'

'You did not think to question.' My father would have felt no need to tell his workers anything about the newly arrived "friend". Only Nelly would have spoken to the village women, trying to make herself seem bigger and better than she was. Now here is the rub: this man. This uncle. *Not?* I feel sick. I cover my eyes, drop my head onto the table, think how I have been living with a murderer for almost two months, all unawares. And feeling bad for those moments when I have been untrue or deceptive. And I wonder why I have survived, but I can guess: I made the estate work again. And Edward Elliott, whoever he is, has an unhealthy interest in me.

'Was there a storm?' I ask as another thought hits me. The strangeness of it is clear from their expressions. 'The night before my parents supposedly left. Was there a wild storm?'

Lazarus nods. 'I thought… I thought I could hear voices in it. We're used to strong weather up here, but it was… unusual.' He reddens. 'It was another reason I didn't go out. It was still raining.'

Even away from the sea, Isolde was an O'Malley, there was salt in her veins just as there is in mine. The sea mourns when we die, we female O'Malleys, for whatever reason. Perhaps because we produce the children, the tithe we feed to the waters. Perhaps that's why we are a loss. And all the waters in the world are joined. Blackwater lake is salty – salty! – and surely they speak to each other, in those places where fresh meets salt; siblings. Somehow, no matter where we are, the sea knows and it sends a tempest to weep for us.

And I know for certain that my mother is as dead as I've always been told she was. I don't know where she rests or why they separated her from Liam. But she's no longer breathing above the earth or below it. She was dead before I left Hob's Hallow. If I'd only found the letters sooner... then again, she's no more dead now than I thought she was my entire life. Yet still it hurts sharp as a knife.

'Is there... is there another way into Blackwater?'

Lazarus looks as if I might be mad with all these random questions, but there's a method to my madness. He nods. 'A track leads from the smelter through the woods, through the back part of the estate, to the road to St Sinwin's Harbour. Ten days' journey, but that's where the dealers are and where the silver ships from. We live here in secret, Miss Miren, that was part of our agreement with your mother. Most of us, we don't venture out beyond the hedge, only Oliver Redman sends the Cornish brothers with deliveries.'

'And you didn't go down to open the hedge-gate for them that dawn?'

'Your father knew well enough how to do that. I didn't watch.' And Liam would have told his new best friend, wouldn't he? All the things about this place, or almost. This man he'd invited into his life.

'So, whoever was dressed in my parents' clothes might have simply gone along the road until they found that junction and re-entered from there. Their horses, I suppose, were left to wander away.'

Jedadiah and Lazarus sit back in their chairs, neither look stunned. They know – have known – that if Liam Elliott is lying discarded deep in the earth, then he could not have ridden a horse out the gate five months ago. They knew since just before I arrived, and did nothing. What could they do? Now, they look at me, holding their breath, and when I remain silent Jedadiah almost bursts as he asks, 'What do we do now?'

* * *

Jedadiah escorts me back to the big house around four in the morning. We barely speak, but walk close beside one another. When we almost reach the front lawn, we keep to the trees just in case (although no one wakes early in this house), and go around the side, into the shadows of the kitchen garden. I push open the door, then take his hand and pull him in behind me. I cannot confront my uncle, not yet. I want to know what happened. I want Ena safely out of Nelly's hands. I want to be in a position where I can prove all my accusations. I want to know where my mother's buried. So much I want to know, but I must play this game to its end.

But this... this is something I can do, a means of marking my rebellion.

He doesn't pull away, doesn't ask stupid questions, simply follows along behind, careful to keep his footfall light as we go. I lock the door to my chamber... the first time I have done so here, the first time I have felt my sleep might not be peaceful or safe.

In my room... in my room it is much as it was with the green-eyed assassin, but for longer. Also, there is tenderness this night, whereas the other was all heat and hunger. He strokes my back, traces the marks my grandmother left, but does not mention them. Jedadiah asks me what I want, then gives it to me.

He also asks, in a quiet moment, about the mer.

'I don't know why, exactly, but they followed me from Breakwater. They tried to drown me once.' *But*, I think, *did they?* 'My family made their fortune from the sea, but there's not many of us left. Just me, now, of the direct line. Many cousins with thinned blood, but I'm the last O'Malley. I thought there was my mother too, but…' I swallow. 'I don't know what they want.'

I don't tell him of their song, that when I'm gone, they will be free, because trust is something that needs to be earned and I will only give so much.

And after he leaves in the strange greying light just before dawn, I touch the place where he lay until I can no longer feel the heat of him. I lie there and pull my thoughts away from his broad shoulders and deep chest, from the scars on his torso that perhaps I will ask him about one day, and perhaps he will explain. I think about what I need to do, and I ponder how to do it. At some point I go to sleep but it's not many hours later that I wake, sweating, having dreamed myself in the hole in the earth beside my father who turns empty eyes to me and whispers, *I don't know you.*

32

'Good morning, Nelly.'

I enter the kitchen without warning, surprising the woman hunched over the pot of what smells like stew on the hearth. The steam has reddened her face, made her blonde curls limp. I've slept well past breakfast. Ena is sitting in a highchair by the large wooden table, chewing on a rusk, and she's wearing a spattering of it and spittle across her pink skin and down the front of her bib. The little girl smiles to see me and bangs the wooden tray top. Nelly's expression darkens.

I go straight to the child, picking up a damp cloth from the carved stone sink. I wipe Ena down to make her presentable, and she giggles, then I fill a bottle and feed her a decent breakfast. She's biddable and quiet, happy for the having of an attendant Nelly throws me an irritable look. Knowing what I know of her – that she was hired only to be a wet nurse – I cannot imagine she is happy being lumped with housekeeper duties and all the menial domestic work as well as being the cook. Obviously the decision was not hers; I wonder how long my uncle's presence in her bed will keep her biddable?

Then I wonder how long they're planning to stay on here. I wonder how much forethought went into all of this scheme, how long they've known each other? Was Edward the father of poor Meraud, burned to a cinder that night? I wonder if, even as I fortuitously arrived, had they already been preparing to move on? What would they have done with Ena? Having lost her own babe, how attached is Nelly to my little sister? Is she already thinking of the child as her own? A replacement for what was lost? Would they take Ena with them? Or would they leave her behind, with one of the villagers or alone here in this big empty house for someone to find or no one?

'Can I do anything to help, Nelly?' I ask pleasantly. 'I feel that I have not been pulling my weight. I'm sorry for that. How can I make things easier for you?'

She just looks at me, stunned, eyes narrowed.

'Perhaps we could have some of the village girls come up once a week to assist with the cleaning? It seems a ridiculous amount of work for one woman to be expected to undertake. All those rooms, all that dust.'

'I manage,' she says and sounds defensive.

'I'm not saying otherwise, dear Nelly, I simply want to ensure you are happy and rested. I know caring for my sister takes much of your energy and you cannot be expected to do that and keep the house in order.' I frown. 'Are your nights still interrupted? Are you ridden by nightmares? Some other disturbance?'

'I sleep well enough,' she says, then asks, 'Who says I don't?'

Nelly is not the sharpest nail in the jar. My uncle is a charming and convincing liar, light on his feet, always with a ready answer upon his lips; no wonder Nelly is so easily dominated. Too convenient for them to have simply met on the road on their way here.

304

'Where were you working before, Nelly?' She stares at and I take a chance, thinking that my father would have travelled regularly to one place. 'Was it St Sinwin's Harbour? I hear it's an interesting place. Was your position there a good one? I hope my parents offered you a fine living to come here. Blackwater is so isolated, so very quiet, rather lacking in diversions.'

'I'm not the sort who needs *diversions*.' She almost spits the words at me. 'Do I look like some port whore?'

Yes, I think, *and not one of the expensive ones.*

'Oh, Nelly. I didn't mean to imply anything of the sort. We... we just seem to have got off on the wrong foot and, as we have to continue to live together, perhaps we should try to be civil with each other?' It's too late to try to make friends or even pretend – and I don't believe it was ever an option, with whatever Nelly is carrying about in her mind – but in appearing to make an effort I am fairly sure I can begin to destabilise her. Didn't Aoife O'Malley teach me how to deal with enemies? I think of Aunt Florrie and her husband, both of whom spilled spite about Aoife for so many years until my grandmother set her charm on Uncle Silas, managing to seduce him out of a sizable portion of his fortune (a mere drop in the ocean of our debts). With one fell swoop she humiliated Florrie and made a fool of Silas. Divide and conquer, play upon frailties. Nelly's the weak link, she's the one who reacts with anger; Edward Elliott merely smiles and thinks quickly. Nelly has the answers and they can be plucked from her and in those answers lies the secret to my purported uncle's downfall.

Seeking a wet nurse, would my father have known what to look for? At Hob's Hallow, Maura looked after me; here, Ena ould have been the first child for whom he had to take some responsibility. How was Nelly presented to him and by whom? "Uncle" Edward, might he have been the conduit? Might he have met my father in a drinking establishment? Edward is very charming – did my light-minded father find him so?

Why are you here in St Sinwin's?

Business, my dear fellow, and I must find a wet nurse for my infant daughter.

Why, my good man, I have just the woman, of fine character and sound moral virtue!

I imagine them laughing over their shared last name (if that isn't another lie from Edward – *Oh, what a fine coincidence to encounter another Elliott!* – lying to make a connection), and Liam with no friends, with only my mother. How lonely might he have been? How ready to be charmed and befriended? My father paying the bills, making no secret of the weight of his purse. Being taken to meet Nelly Daniels, who clearly managed to put up a better front then and there than here and now. But perhaps she wasn't under the same stresses. Perhaps Liam Elliott's offer represented a new opportunity, a means to get away from another unpleasant situation or to simply find a life more favourable.

But Nelly, ah Nelly. I give her a smile. I note she doesn't deny St Sinwin's at all. I rise, and release Ena from her harness and the highchair. Nelly eyes me, moves as if to take the child.

'I'll keep Ena with me today, Nelly, thank you. It will give you time to attend to more things than you can usually get done in a day. Oh, and do consider my proposal. I'm sure Uncle Edward would be amenable; he is very attentive to *my* requests.'

She says nothing though I can feel she wants to; very restrained of her.

I take Ena to her room and clean her up. I dress her in a pretty frock and sunbonnet, tie the ribbons of her knitted booties, then settle her in the pushchair and take her walking to the village – keeping a good distance from the lake, though there is no sign of any mer today. I greet everyone by name; the sad end to the harvest fete seems to not have left a mark on anyone's attitude, and people are happy to see me. They comment on how Ena's grown, how well she looks, how she's flourishing for a child who's been without her own mother for so long so soon in her young life. I don't tell them that many people survive such a thing.

I don't hurry, I don't proceed in an obvious fashion towards my goal; I am careful that no one watching would think me intent upon anything. When I see the door I want, I walk up at a leisurely pace and knock without urgency.

When Miriam Dymond answers she looks surprised, but steps aside without question and I enter the cottage, pushing the stroller in front of me.

'I didn't thank you,' she says. 'For saving my girl.'

'Everything was rather... disrupted yesterday,' I say, then smile. Ena's dozing by this time, giving little whimpers, her feet kicking out as if she's chasing after rabbits. 'Thank me by answering some questions and we'll call ourselves even.'

Miriam tilts her head and gives me a frank look as if assessing how much trouble my seemingly simple request might get her into. Then she nods briskly. 'Let's talk while it's quiet – my lot are at their grandmother's.'

I follow her through to the small sunny kitchen, painted in a bright yellow. A barely begun beverage is steaming on the table and she asks if I'd like one. I say 'yes' because Aoife taught me that the little signs of hospitality are a way of putting people at their ease. I sit in one of the chairs, keep pushing Ena's stroller, back and forth, back and forth to keep her sleeping.

As Miriam pours a strong peppermint brew into another thick-bottomed mug (no pretty porcelain cups here), she says, 'Well? What do you want to know, Miss Miren?'

'Is your daughter well? No ill effects?'

'Adie is no worse for her dip. And again, thank you for her life.'

It's my turn to shrug. 'Ah, she'd have floated.'

But we both know she wouldn't. Not in that strange water.

'I understand you used to be the housekeeper up at the big house?'

Her lips tighten. 'And cook, with the Toop girls to help.'

I nod. 'And I also understand Edward Elliott changed that?'

Her turn to nod. 'I'm assuming you're not asking this out of idle curiosity or to make me relive a painful experience?'

'Not at all.' I smile. 'Tell me about Nelly Daniels. Keziah Eddy said she used to talk to the folk in the village, once upon a time.'

Miriam slides the mug across to me, sits down and sips at her own. 'I didn't like her before she took my job, but I couldn't have put my finger on why. You get a feeling. She boasted how she'd come from a fancy job in St Sinwin's and wasn't she special to be chosen to come to Blackwater? How

308

Mr Liam had wooed her away with a bigger salary and no *domestic duties*, nothing beyond wet nursing the little miss.' She nods at Ena, drooling and snoring softly. 'And she had her own daughter, Meraud – Merry – same age; they even looked alike. Very different temperaments, though.'

'How so?' I ask, glancing down at Ena.

'This one,' she nods at my little sister, 'used to be a foul little brat. Crying and wailing, pulling at your mother's last nerve. No one in the village would look after her to give Nelly a break. I've had five children and mine can be mean as rats, but I've never seen anything like this one. Only your mother could calm her with that touch of hers, but Mrs Elliott couldn't spend all her time seeing to the child.' Miriam shakes her head. 'But look at her now, she seems to have become a happier creature.'

'How long since you saw Ena?' I ask.

'Five months – five months since your uncle turned me out. Seen you walking around with her, of course, but not up close until today.'

And I think how Isolde hadn't done much mothering – she left me so young, and Maura cared for me even before my parents left – she had no experience when Ena came along. 'Was Isolde not able to feed Ena herself?'

Miriam shakes her head. 'Your mother had no milk... and she was impatient with the child. Loved her, but... You need to understand that my mother used to work for your parents, then when Mam got too old, I took over. She's kind, your mother, everyone loves her, and when she touches your hand you feel as happy as you ever have.' She shakes her head. 'But I wouldn't say we were ever friends.' Then she hesitates.

'Miriam, nothing you can say will offend me. I did not know my parents; they left me with my grandparents when I was a small child, they're strangers to me.' I swallow. 'But I am trying to find the truth about them.'

She nods. 'Your father didn't care for anyone on this estate. He was pretty and arrogant and high-handed, thought himself better than everyone. He was devoted to your mother, but that's all I can say was his saving grace. He never consulted, only gave orders, never took advice, didn't share any information unless he had to. He was a bad manager, and only your mother's hand kept people here.'

I already know Uncle Edward is no great estate manager; my father neither apparently. 'Miriam, who told you that Edward Elliott was my father's brother?'

'Nelly. She said, back when she bothered to say anything, that they'd met on the road, a chance encounter.'

'And they were all in the house together for three months?'

She nods. 'Then one night there was the fire and Meraud died, and the next day your parents left for Breakwater, and that same afternoon your uncle told all the house staff they were no longer needed.'

'What happened when Nelly's daughter died?'

'Your uncle told Mr Redman there had been an accident. That the wing would be closed off, there'd been a fire.' She nods at Ena. 'This is the closest I've seen Miss Ena in several months.'

Told. Told, but no one to gainsay or speak the truth and the only people who knew otherwise were Nelly Daniels and Edward Elliott. I look down at Ena, sleeping there. A thought creeps over me. Two girl children, enough alike to pass as sisters; one happy, one miserable. And this little sister at my feet who's not been seen by anyone but Nelly Daniels for months and who's nature has so miraculously "settled" since then?

I swallow hard. Ena was not my mother's first baby; she would not have been branded the way I was, the way Isolde was, the way Aoife was, nor any of the firstborn O'Malleys.

Edward Elliott emptied the house of witnesses. My parents are dead. What if Edward lied about when the fire occurred? When Meraud died? What if all this was sparked by a tiny murder?

'How was Nelly's temper with my sister? Ena was a difficult child.'

The way Miriam's lips press together tells me all I need to know.

33

When I return to the house, I hand Ena over to Nelly who, I suspect, is the child's true mother. I go to my room and lock the door. From the bottom of the blanket box I pull out the book of O'Malley tales Isolde had begun to remake, the first chance I've had to truly look at it.

There are ten pages at the beginning that are blank and this strikes me as strange. I think of the old version back at Hob's Hallow, of the pages sliced from its front. I carefully go through the tome, examining every sheet, making sure that none are stuck together. I look at the bare folios: I flick water on them, hold them up to the afternoon sun at the window, light a candle to see if smoke will show any secrets hiding there; I nick a finger and try the same with blood, all to no avail. And then, at last, I reach the end. Stuck to the back cover, in no way hidden, is a small fold of parchment to make a pouch. And in the pouch, sheaves covered with tightly written jagged script – in a hand I cannot recall seeing before – on the same sort of paper from the old book of tales, their edge neatly sheared by a knife, perhaps one with a pearl handle.

I put the volume onto the floor beside my chair, smooth the pages in my lap and I begin to read.

There was a woman, once, who sang.

She wasn't beautiful, or at least not noticeably so, not like other women about whom bards crooned or poets wrote, but she was tall and dark-haired, dark-eyed, she moved with a grace that could render her invisible if she chose, or the centre of attention if, again, she so chose.

But she sang.

And she played a harp made not of wood, yet carved in the same shape as might be expected. The strings were knotted from hair as black as ebony and enchanted to make the right notes. The instrument was made of bone, which anyone who got close enough to examine it would realise, though it had been varnished to a high shine. The strings were held in place by finger-bones, yet the sounds that issued from a thing made of death were nothing short of bewitching. And none knew whose bones had been used in the creation of the thing, and none ever would.

And the woman, she sang.

She sang with a voice that might have called souls from bodies, caused hearts to turn from their dearest beloveds, and minds to lose their grip upon any sort of rationality. She sang thus, and thus she made her way in the world.

She might have settled in any number of cities, become a favourite of a prince or kingling, become wife to a rich man, lover to a rich woman, or a creature of means all of her own. But she was never content. Nothing was enough. She made fortunes, then lost them, over and again, not through carelessness or stupidity but boredom. She had made them before, she wanted to see if she could make them again. And she did.

She did.

Without anchor, she wandered. From city to city, town to town, village to village, wasteland to wasteland. She even entered the Dark Lands for a time and left them once more, intact, untouched by the Leech Lords for her voice affected even those with neither soul nor conscience nor regard for life beyond that it might be taken as sustenance. And perhaps there she learned things too about getting one's own way, although the gods knew well enough that she was already well versed in such means.

Still she wandered, through cities great and small, through ruins and wreckages. Until at last she came to a tiny village by the sea where the waves broke over a reef. And she wandered further still, to an even tinier place, where only a few shacks and cottages stood. She walked to the edge of the promontory and stared out. She watched forms duck and dive in the waters below, and after some time watching, she took the switchback path down to the pebbled shingle at the base of the cliffs.

She found a rock and sat, kicked off her boots and dipped her feet into the salt water, and sighed. The sounds of the sea, of the waves and their shifting and plaint, summoned in her a sense of peace such as she had never known. Then she took the harp of bone from her back and began to play. She played and she sang and soon the very waves were dancing to her tune, as if in turn for their enchanting her, she had bewitched them in return. And in those waves were forms, the forms she'd seen from the promontory.

Merfolk, male and female, came to listen; not delicate tiny things, not frail gems, but great muscular beings, proud and arrogant, with shining skin, flowing locks and eyes dark as the bottom of the ocean. After a time, when she was sure she'd gotten their attention, she ceased to play. Then, when all but one had drifted away she began to play once more, for one was all she needed.

The male, for male it was, was pale as if the moon lived a little beneath his skin, his long hair the brown-green of seaweed, his eyes the green-black of a storm. The woman could see the tears of gills in his muscular throat, the light patina of scales across his flesh, the green-scaled armour of his long thick tail almost an entity on its own as it flicked behind him. At last he beached himself and lay sprawled in the shallows, untroubled by the cold of the winds, watching her intently.

After a little more time, she set aside the harp and went to sit by his side. She sat and they spoke, and they spoke and she sat, until at last he told her of a sea cave at the other end of the shingle, not so far away, somewhere they could be alone and not beneath the eyes of his brethren. And she went in through the split in the rock that looked as though the hands of a god had pulled the stone up like a drapery; and he swam up from the depths, into the pool that took up half the cavern, lit as it was with blue-green algae. And there they met and there they mated.

They met there day after day, and she did not need to sing him to her, not after that first time. He was enthralled and she was fond of him in her own way.

He was no prince of the sea, but a commoner (and only a commoner could have avoided his duties for long), yet he knew the secrets of his kind. He knew how the bounty of the oceans might be harvested. He told her all these things in the sanctity of the lovers' confessional; he told her for lovers think that in sharing what is secret they tie the beloved to them. Yet the

315

untruth of this is only ever uncovered in the aftermath, and thus are covenants broken and hearts soon after.

He did not think she would find a use for the knowledge.

Yet he did not know her, he could not know how she hungered, how it had driven her across continents. He could not know how vaunting her ambition, how all-consuming. He could not know that even though she had found a place she loved, the promontory, the sea, that it was not entirely enough.

A place, she thought, to stay and to build. And a challenge, she believed, would be enough for her, were she to achieve it.

The village of Breakwater was so small, so far away, no one had laid claim to the land on the promontory, so she took it for her own. She employed men to make her a tower home, a square thing of no great magnificence, but it kept the elements at bay, gave her a place to lay her head those days and nights when she did not choose a sandy pillow. And she had them dig a well, a strange deep thing, a strange wide thing, in the middle of the tower's cellar, so deep that it went down into the waters below the rock, to where all the waters in the world are joined, and she had a master craftsman fashion a hinged gate whose bars were engraved with spells of entrapment, which could be hidden in the walls of the well, then sprung shut like jaws when the time was right. And a fine strong net hung beneath and a chute there was too, a mechanism that would catch anything that fell from above, then scoop it into a channel that could be accessed by a small vertical tunnel beside the well itself. A means to harvest.

Her lover had told her of the ones who ruled the oceans, the sea-queens; how few there were, how powerful, how shoals came at their command, how the waters disgorged their treasure, how their tails were scaled with the truest silver, purer than anything dug of the earth. He told her how they might be called and caught, of the words and songs that might summon them to the singer. And she had listened.

And every day she asked him to tell her more and she scribbled those tales onto parchments; some she made into songs, some she burned as offerings. And at last she grew gravid and her belly swelled; she worried, a little, what this child might be, more father or mother, but she shrugged and waited to see. And one day, at last, the tower and the well were ready. And one day, at last, she took her harp and a candle, and she went down into the cellar and she sat.

She played and sang and the sounds rang out in the great space, echoed from the walls and the vaulted ceiling, hit the water in the well and travelled through it because the words her lover had given to her had the power to do so. And after a time, at last, there was a splashing and a muttering more liquid than the woman was used to.

And she set aside her harp and walked slowly to the edge of the well and held her candle high. And below, in the well, was a sea-queen. The woman nodded in satisfaction and pulled a lever. The cage beneath the creature closed, with its strong metal net and all its spells carved and sung into its very substance, and the sea-queen, realising herself captured, began to shriek.

The woman picked up her harp and began to play once more, until the sea-queen had calmed. And the woman told the creature how her life would be lived: her scales would be harvested, the children of the woman would be safe on the seas, and in return the sea-queen would be fed. And she made the queen agree to a bargain: that the merfolk would never harm a firstborn of the O'Malleys.

The mer said, 'Yet one of your children in each generation' – for this is how such things are done – 'will be my meat.'

And the woman, after only the slightest hesitation, agreed: a tithe for the prosperity she had brought with her double dealing.

And she would walk the promontory each and every evening as gravity took a greater hold on her. She felt bound to the earth with this child inside her, even though it was the offspring of a creature from the waters of salt and sand. She would look out to the horizon, she would look for him, even though she knew he would not return – she had seen his corpse herself, seen what the others of his kind had done to him for his betrayal. Still she would look.

But who can keep secrets from the waters when they are all joined?

And the place came to be called Hob's Hallow, for those who believed in such things were certain she'd dealt with creatures of darkness, that she'd made her bargains holy by paying her tithes in small lives. And those who believed knew that holiness is neither black nor white, but the red of blood.

34

I walk out into the deepening afternoon; soon the sky will bruise into darkness, but I cannot bear to have the walls of the house around me. I traipse through the flowering gardens, then past the new-harvested fields and the orchards and I notice that the trees are heavy again with fruit. I pick an apple but cannot bring myself to eat it; it goes in my pocket.

I think of Aoife, reading me the tale of Aislin and Connor, of the boy being sacrificed to the sea-queen in the dimly lit cave. I think of asking my grandmother whether it was true or not, of her shrugging in that way she had when she wasn't quite lying, but wasn't being entirely honest. I think of her telling me not to be such a child. I hear her saying, 'Stories are history, whether they're true or not.' I think about that book of lies and truths and tales all mixed together so no one could tell them apart.

I think how it was never a secret, what we did to our own. Or at least, never a secret amongst us, the O'Malleys. I think of all those children, sent to the sea to pay a debt incurred long ago, one to which they'd not had the chance to either agree or otherwise. I think of how no names were kept, of how they were deprived even of that; I think how only Connor was known, recorded, written, because of a misfiring of a mother's heart, a preference for one child over another, making a choice bold and shameless and defiant. I think they couldn't have gone to the sea cave because the sea-queen was kept in the cellar, so the poor boy was taken there by his sister to meet his fate. And the maid, the scullion who followed the children? What had happened to her? I can never know, only suspect: found out and fed to the thing in the well so she could not speak of what she'd seen.

I think of Isolde leaving me behind, the branded firstborn, knowing I was the only child that might be safe at Hob's Hallow because I was the last. That all hope for a future rested within me; that I was the sole thing to keep Aoife from hunting her down. Did Isolde flee so she might save any other children who came after? She sacrificed me as surely as those who'd gone before her had sacrificed their own children. And I cannot say that I don't understand, but also I cannot say that there isn't an agonising pain in the pit of me – gut, heart, soul? – that feels like the sum total of the agony of every one of those discarded children.

I think of the mer singing *When you are gone then we will be free* – waiting for the death of the last true O'Malley to release them from an ancient bargain. For as long as one remains, there is the possibility of more to fulfil that agreement and keep them bound.

And at last I'm running, trees flashing past me in the lowering afternoon light.

I'm running to try and escape that agony.

I'm running because maybe I'll outdistance it all if I'm fast enough.

I run until I come to the thin stream on the way to the village, and that's where I trip and fall, almost in. That's where I weep and my tears join the liquid in the rill itself, and I cry until I believe there's nothing more in me. When at last my eyes clear, when I think I will simply stay there, crouched over the current and wait for the darkness to draw in and swallow me, to properly be as lost as I feel, in the dying light I see a shimmer beneath the surface. That reminds me of the first day I rode out with Edward Elliott, a silver flicker in the water catching my eye then.

I reach into the cool flow, to pluck out the shining thing and cup it in my palm.

It's a scale.

It's silver, properly metal, not some fishy membrane.

It's the size of two of my thumbs sat side by side and feels heavier than I'd have believed possible. I touch the ship's bell pendant at my neck and think that the scale would be the perfect size to craft just such a thing.

I think of the sea-queen trapped by the woman with the bone harp, about the clever construction of the cellar trap in the gut of Hob's Hallow. I think about the locked cellar in the depths of Blackwater House. I think how the silver mine has not been producing since my mother "left". I think about a man who stumbled upon a fine kingdom, who fancied himself its new king when he saw an opportunity, but did not understand how it worked, what was required to keep the tiny world turning and healthy.

I'm sitting there when Jedadiah Gannel comes ambling past on his long legs, a lantern in one hand to light his way. I'm so still he almost doesn't see me. In fact he doesn't see me until I speak, and the effect of my voice is to make him jump. I laugh in spite of everything. He comes over to sit beside me, places the lantern between us. The circle of light seems to grow warmer against the night.

'What are you doing here, Miren?' He touches my face and I lean into his palm like a cat, and don't answer. 'Are you well? Are you safe in that house?'

'I think so,' I say, but I don't know if I am. I hold up the scale so it glimmers. 'Have you ever seen anything like this?'

He takes it from me, turns it over in his fingers, and nods slowly. 'Sometimes we find these in the mine; not in a seam, not embedded in the rock, but scattered in spots where water trickles out.'

I take it back from him, examine it a moment longer, then slip it into my pocket. I wonder what might be done with such a thing, if it might be used as a seed of some sort. 'My uncle knows nothing about mining, you could tell him anything. *Are* the seams running out? Truly?'

He snorts. 'Truly, Miren.'

'You all live here in secrecy.'

He looks away. 'It was the condition of the life she offered us. We did not ask questions, Miren. Blackwater… many of us lived in terrible places, scraping by an existence, then your parents – your mother – came and she promised a better life if we'd work for her. Apart from the flood, we have had far better lives. There was no reason to break our oath to her, to leave.'

I touch the scale in my pocket. Somehow Isolde found a way to *make* a fortune. I think of her fertility magic with the crops and stock. I can think of no good reason she couldn't apply herself to *this*. I remember Malachi's words, about Isolde and her talent for making things big or small. I think about the red price that would have had to be paid to turn barren earth into a rich silver mine. *Oh, Mother, what did you do?*

'Why are you here?' I ask. 'Wandering in the dark?'

'Going to see my father. He reckons something's been trying to come over the hedge the last two nights.' He shakes his head, grins. 'Maybe the old man's hearing things.'

'Who wouldn't, here?' And the air around us is not as silent as before. There are chirrups and shrieks and squeaks, snuffles and snorts and barks: the animals have returned to Blackwater, as the place has grown to giving again. 'It's out of your way, but will you walk me to the house?'

'Of course.' He smiles and rises, then helps me up, pulling me into his arms. We kiss, but I nudge him away before it goes too far; I need a clear head, no matter how pleasant his attentions might be. I hold his hand as we walk so the rejection doesn't sting too much. He's a smart man and doesn't push his luck. I kiss him goodbye when we reach the last of the trees before the house lawn, then send him off into the darkness. I watch as the fiery pinpoint of the lantern grows smaller and smaller and finally disappears. Then I face the place I'd hoped to make my home.

* * *

I stand at the threshold of the room containing the burnt cradle and hold my carefully crafted silver lantern high, then take a deep breath before pushing myself into the space. Last time I approached ignorance sheltered me. Though I have no proof, only suspicions, now I feel as if my skin has been peeled off, that I've no protection left. The tall window by the baby's bed, its panes cracked from the heat of the fire; only blackness is outside, and my own reflection on the inside. I barely recognise myself.

Ena, when not teething, is such a happy child. Nelly was frustrated by her but as far as I could tell not to the point of losing her temper and offering harm. But what if Ena is not Ena? What if it's Nelly's own child, her own Meraud? What if Ena, the true Ena, with her tantrums and crying, drove Nelly to distraction? Nelly whose patience is a thing in short supply? Nelly who, I am willing to bet, was not a highly paid nurse in St Sinwin's or anywhere else, despite her boasts to Miriam.

I cover my face. Did my little sister burn alive? What could she have done to incur that kind of fate? Or was it something else, something gentler but no less lethal a loss of temper on Nelly's part? A pillow pressed over an ever-open, ever-screaming mouth, in hope of a few seconds of silence… and suddenly those seconds dragged into minutes and Ena, true Ena, lay still and pale and blue at the lips? Was the fire a clumsy means of covering up?

But my parents…

Would they have believed it?

I can't know my father, but my mother… she was a witch. She was Aoife's daughter and no fool. When she saw her child's body… I do not think she'd have believed in any accident, not for one second. And so there was no way she and Liam could have been allowed to live. Nelly and Edward, plotting and scheming to cover up, stripping the house of other servants, pretending to be my parents leaving in the dark hours, telling tales until they seemed to be true, and replacing Ena with Meraud, a happy little girl who knew no better. Edward Elliott, protecting Nelly because he cared for her or because the chance to be lord of the manor was too enticing and he simply believed he could get away with it.

And then the estate began to fail.

And then I arrived and it began to flourish once again.

I might have been killed so very soon, but that I quickly proved useful on the estate; and for his prurient interest in me, his boredom with Nelly (for what kind of a man would tell the woman he loves she is to be a drudge in a grand house while he enjoys himself?). No wonder she hates me so. She hates him too, I think, but isn't brave enough or angry enough to show it in full yet. How long until that is displayed in all its glory, an inferno such as the one that engulfed my little sister, and how will Edward Elliott hide that?

I reach down to touch the partially burned baby blanket; it feels oily. Fat. Burned fat and that smell I could identify the first time I was here: cooked meat. My sister.

'Miren!'

A shout from the doorway, fear and rage making it so very loud. Yet I don't startle or spin around. I finish the action, rub the blanket with my fingers, feel the greasiness of it, the melted fat of once-Ena, and I clench my fist. Then I straighten and turn at my leisure.

Edward Elliott hangs in the doorway like one of those gallowscrows, as if afraid to enter, and that fear weighs more than his anger. His face is red and I think, if he could bring himself to cross the threshold, he would do me harm no matter what else he feels for me. He locked this room; didn't get rid of the cradle, just locked the room and assumed no one would ask questions. Over-confident. Edward Elliott couldn't have known I would arrive.

'Miren. Miren, come out at once. It's not safe,' he says, trying for a semblance of control in his tone.

I don't answer, I just stare at him, daring him. At last he knows he must enter or lose all authority (for he still seems to think he has some), and he comes, his gait strange, like a high-stepping, uncertain horse. Until he is in front of me and he grabs my shoulders and shakes me.

'Miren!' He shouts as if my name is a command that will make me *heel*. 'What are you doing here? Didn't I tell you? Didn't I tell you not to come here, that it was dangerous?'

'You tell a lot of stories, *Uncle*. You know how I love them. Won't you tell me another?' I smile. 'What happened? What happened to my sister?'

35

Edward Elliot draws back his hand to slap me.

'That might work on Nelly, but I'm a different kind of creature altogether,' I say softly. I lift my chin, keep my eyes on his and slowly the hand is lowered. He's shuddering now, sweat breaking out all over his face, and I wonder what he saw in here. Then he rallies and pulls me along behind him towards the door of the nursery, so fast it's hard to keep my footing, as if dragging me out of the room will change everything, as if we will go back in time and the new knowledge of *this* place will be forgotten, sins fading into a fog. That we will be able to revert to the way we were.

I dig my heels in before we get to the doorway, shake off his hand. He looks at me in surprise. He's forgotten I'm almost as tall as him, that I'm not some tiny girl…

'Shall I begin, Uncle? You're not usually so reticent about your tales.' My tone is encouraging. 'Shall I tell you about changelings? One child swapped for another by the fairies or the trolls or stolen away by those of the sea? Kept as servants beneath the earth, or fattened up as tasty treats, or fed to the waters in the hope of prosperity? There's always a bargain, Uncle, always a swap: my mother left me behind in order to gain a life of her own, that is my story. One thing for another: I will have this one in return.'

And Edward Elliott seems to deflate as if someone let the air out of him. He's a big man, suddenly small. He sits on the floor, a sort of collapse, but slow, and I back away, the light in my hand retreating from him until I'm at the rocking chair once more. I put the lantern down, and then I sit in the chair, staring at him.

'Come along, Uncle, do it properly. Once upon a time...'

He blinks and swallows. 'Once upon a time...' he clears his throat. 'Once upon a time there was a woman with a babe of her own, a babe as sunny as could be, whose laugh lifted the heart. And this woman took a position looking after another infant as well, how hard could it be? But the new child was monstrous unhappy, crying and screaming, never joyful, always hungry. She fed both children, but her own babe never seemed to get enough milk, and the other took the lion's share yet still demanded more. The woman knew all of the tales and superstitions; she wasn't educated, but told herself not to be silly, there was no reason to think the true baby had been stolen away by those who hide in the green or under the mountains or beneath the waters. The child's own mother managed to love it, after all, did not see anything unnatural in her offspring, though she *was* impatient. So, the nurse tried to love it too, just as she did her own; she thought that if she loved it enough, it would be enough.' It seems as if the further he gets into his story, the more comfortable he is, but he's still not telling me everything; my listener's ear can detect the off-note, the places where he is keeping something back and trying to cover the lack.

'But…' I prompt.

'But she came to regard the baby as a changeling. In her mind, that's what she called it, and in doing so she was able perhaps to distance herself from it, so that when she at last lost her temper with the little thing's rages and rants, it was not so very hard to do… what she did.'

'And what did she do, Uncle?'

'She put a pillow over that squalling little mouth and held it down until it was no more,' he says quite viciously.

He says "it", not "the girl" or "the daughter". He does not give either child a name. 'And then?'

'Then she set a fire, thinking to hide what she'd done.' He wipes a hand across his brow.

'And did that work?'

His eyes are very dark blue when they meet mine. 'Even fire cannot cover all sins.'

'And the mother?'

'What mother doesn't mourn her own child, no matter that it's a little monster?'

'And the father?'

'Fathers, as you may be aware, often care for nothing but the gaze of their wives; and this wife's heart was broken, so he sought to avenge that.'

I hear again the off-note in his recounting, and I realise at last that it wasn't a matter of what he *saw* in the nursery but rather what he *did* there.

As much as I dislike Nelly, she has cared well for Ena, and when Ena was teething she was a monster. Yet Nelly never lost her temper with her – with me, yes, with the child, no. Of course,

I might be wrong; there's no guarantee that a woman won't kill a child. Even though Nelly is the sort who, like so many others, loves in the wrong place, who stays with a man she ought not to, I do not believe she killed the real Ena. Not after hearing my not-uncle's rendition.

And I realise, if I did not before, just how very dangerous Edward Elliott is. He smothered my little sister because she cried too much and tells himself she was a monster the world is best rid of. He killed my parents, who had been his friends, to cover up his crime and he took their home. He has happily blamed Nelly, the mother of his child, for his own sin. He eradicated an entire family all for *this*.

'Where is my mother buried?' I ask, and the way he smiles says he'll never reveal that. Why would he? If he notices that I don't ask about my father I cannot tell.

'Who are you?' I say before I think better of it; a kind of wonderment and despair push the words out of me.

I see his expression change: he'd thought himself clever, thought he'd told such a tale as to cover himself, render himself free of all blame. But just as I heard the lies in his story, so he hears the disbelief in my voice. He looks like one of those ghostly robber bridegrooms who found themselves hung on a gibbet. He lives his life the same way as they did, doing as he will and fie for all consequences, figuring he can always outrun them or blame someone else.

He smiles, wolfish. 'Only your dear Uncle Edward, my darling girl. Who else might I be?'

'I think... I think you are a man who drifts and takes what he wants.'

'Do you think so?' He rises, steps towards me, more confident now. 'And do you know what I want?'

'I've an inkling.'

He's smart enough to stay a few steps away. 'Miren, there is everything in Blackwater for *us*. With your presence, what had stultified is once again blossoming. We can rule here.' He kneels as if proposing. 'And I will let you take your revenge on Nelly for what she did to your poor innocent sister.'

I drop my gaze to the floor. He cannot know that I don't believe Nelly did *that*. He knows I don't believe in his identity, but he doesn't know that I have divined the lie in everything else. All I can think of is the sister I never knew, monster or not, burning in her cradle. I want to believe she was not alive, that she'd already been smothered before the flames, but in my mind she is screaming. She's screaming and I'm not sure she'll ever stop.

I stand, and I smile, I give him my full face and he makes a mistake: he takes my expression for acceptance, for *yes*. As he approaches, I pick up the lantern and I throw it at him as hard as I can. The glass fuel reservoir breaks and the flame devouring the wick turns its attention to the man who claims to be my uncle. He screams, and his screams mingle with the imagined echoes of my sister, so high and loud that my head aches, that I fear my ears will bleed.

Edward Elliott, or whoever he is, spins like a dancer, trying to beat out the flames on his stolen finery for I've no doubt these things were taken from my father after his death. Edward spins and whirls, a rapidly flaring column of fire, beautiful and awful, and loud and foul-smelling as he begins to cook. He dances and dances, round and round, until he comes to the tall window by the cindered cradle, the window with its cracked panes, and he dances right into it. The glass shatters, he is unbalanced, and he tips over the sill into the void of the night.

Abruptly, his screaming stops, and so does the sound of my sister.

I'm grateful for that at least.

My knees are shaking and I have to sit down for several long minutes before they are solid enough to stand upon. My steps are still tentative as I make my way back towards the other part of the house. To find Nelly; to ask her questions, to get the answers Edward Elliott can no longer give me.

36

But Nelly will answer no questions ever again.

Nelly is too busy lying on the floor of the entry hall of Blackwater, bleeding crimson onto the black and white marble tiles. I run to her, kneel, reach out, but realise that the blood has long since stopped flowing from the cut in her throat. Was this Edward Elliott's act? Was this how he rewarded her for her loyalty? Or did she finally put her foot down? Was she sick of the glances he gave me even as he pretended to be my uncle? When I tormented her about how he would look favourably upon my requests, was that the last straw for poor Nelly? Turned into a drudge then set aside for younger meat? Nelly, with blue eyes staring and her expression one of surprise and terror: what was the last thing she saw?

'Oh, Nelly. I'm sorry.' I touch her face: her skin is still warm, her death quite fresh. Nelly gone and all her secrets with her. My lavender skirts are soaking up the rapidly congealing blood. I think... I think she would be colder if Edward had killed her before he came to me, the blood on the floor spread further. I stand, unsure what to do; tears, unreckoned for, trickle down my cheeks, onto my lips, tasting like salt. *Salt daughter*. Then I hear Ena – *no, Meraud* – crying.

Not from upstairs but from the library. The library Edward had made his own; and I cannot recall that he ever had her in there. She was his, I believe, but I did not see him hold her or tend to her; he spoke of her fondly to me, but that was only how he created his camouflage. Truly she was of no interest to him. I wonder how long she might have survived if she'd started to make too much noise or lost her sunny nature; if I'd not cured her teething pain when I did so she stopped her weeping and wailing. How long before he snapped and sent his own baby the way of Ena?

I move towards the library, anxious to get the child away from a house where both her parents lie dead. She's not my sister but I too am a girl in a place where both of my parents have lain dead. I would spare her that, though I know she's too small to understand. Just outside the library door, I pause.

I pause because I hear a voice I'd hoped never to hear again.

'Miren, join us please.'

I hesitate only a fraction, but it's long enough for him to raise his volume and say, 'Miren, if you do not get in here, I will wring this brat's neck.'

I step through the doorway.

Aidan Fitzpatrick has lost a lot of weight, presumably from the vicissitudes of the road. He looks harder and his gaze is unfriendly, like I'm a recalcitrant child who's caused him considerable inconvenience. His trousers and shirt and jacket are travel-stained, and his overcoat's been discarded on another chair; I can see dust and mud patterning it. Ena is sitting in his lap, tears streaking her face.

'Hello, Aidan.'

'Throw me that wicked little pocketknife I know you carry, then take *this*' – he jiggles Ena as though she's some sort of rubbish to be removed – 'and sit down.'

I do as told, watching sadly as the mother-of-pearl handled knife flies to Aidan's hand. Then I take Ena – *Meraud*. No. She's always been Ena to me and Ena she shall remain. She clings and I kiss the top of her head, shushing her gently. I sit in the chair Aidan indicated; it's across from him in front of the unlit hearth. He steeples his fingers beneath his chin and contemplates me as if ordering his thoughts, marshalling his arguments to best make me understand all the ways I've disappointed him.

'How did you find me?' I ask, thinking to distract him.

'Well, I imagine that you are quite aware I sent a man to look for you.'

'The man you paid to murder Aoife,' I state, and he startles.

'Who told you that?'

'The man you sent to find me, Aidan.'

'Is he here? What deal did you do with him to make him quit my employ?' His colour is high and I can see him imagining all the womanly ways I might have drawn a man from his side.

'Do you really think, Aidan, that I would have any sort of truck with the man who murdered Aoife?' I suspect he misses the double meaning in that. He doesn't need to know about *before* the green-eyed man murdered Aoife.

'Then where is he? He came highly recommended,' Aidan demands in the same way as a man complaining his sheepdog has failed to fulfil its duties.

335

'He's dead, Aidan. Oh, he was determined to bring me back to you, but I was equally determined not to go, so one of us had to be removed from the equation.'

'You?' He looks at me as if he simply cannot believe it. 'But you've always been so quiet. So obedient, Aoife swore. Yet you've proved anything but.'

'Nonetheless, cousin, I'm Aoife O'Malley's granddaughter – a fact both of you seemed to have forgotten – and there was very little Aoife did that she did not wish to.' Ena has quietened in my arms and I'm glad, for these men who think children can be shut up with violence make me most uncomfortable. 'And so I ask you again, Aidan: how did you find me?'

He sits back in his chair and crosses his fingers over a belly that's a good deal smaller than it used to be. 'When my man failed to return, I decided not to bother sending anyone else. He'd sent me a missive from Bellsholm, that he'd found your trail there, so I took myself that way.'

The green-eyed man hadn't told him who helped me, but he had told Aidan where I'd been. Easy enough to find the troupe. 'It seems rather a lot of effort to go to for a runaway bride, Aidan, surely there are plenty willing in Breakwater.'

'But none with Hob's Hallow to their name. None with the old O'Malley blood, Miren. None like you.' He leans forward, elbows on knees. 'None with the power you've got.'

'I've got no power, Aidan, I just want to be left alone.'

'No power? Yet you gleefully murdered a man, didn't you? There's power in that, there's will and determination, Miren. There's your blood and your belly and the children I'll plant there. We need offspring from you, we need to reconsecrate the covenant with the sea. Only you can do that, you and I.'

'I will not see those old ways come again. There is no *we*, Aidan. I will not feed my babies to the waters because of your greed.' He reaches for Ena and I pull away, thinking quickly, thinking that he might not hurt her if he thinks she's one of us. 'This is my sister. This is Isolde's child.'

The surprise on his face is clear. He sits back. 'Ha. Isolde, always doing what wasn't expected of her. Well, the brat might prove useful, after all. Perhaps I can replace you with her.'

'Do you have the time to wait for her to grow?' I ask lightly, thinking of the assassin's words, that Aidan had made a deal with someone whose demands might outstrip what he could deliver. 'Would Bethany Lawrence be pleased to wait another couple of decades?'

He slits his eyes. 'Little gatherer of information, aren't you? I shall have to watch you more carefully, Miren, you're more than you appear.'

'Really I'm not. I just want to be left alone.'

'Alas, that is not to be, for others have needs to supersede yours.'

'Again, how did you find me?'

'In Bellsholm. Imagine my surprise to learn of my friend Ellingham's presence there. Imagine my greater surprise to go to the theatre one evening as they performed, and sit in the audience only to hear the automaton do something new. Its lovely songs, and then a tale, oh such a tale, a tale no one else but an O'Malley would know, and told in an O'Malley's voice.'

'I'm an Elliott,' I say, but he ignores me.

'And if that wasn't enough, there was the small matter of the earring you left with that woman. Ellingham wouldn't sell it so she'd turned it into a rather fetching pendant. It didn't take long to extract the information I needed from him.'

'What did you do to him?' My voice rises higher.

He lifts an eyebrow. 'Nothing. Not to him anyway – he cares more for others than himself – so I threatened that woman, the one with red hair. And he told me of this place, this Blackwater, drew me a tidy map.'

He doesn't mention Brigid so I can only hope he doesn't know about her and Ellingham. Aidan plucks at his clothing, and I ask, 'Where are your men? Where is the carriage? Where are all the folk you pay to do your dirty work?'

He does not answer, so I poke a little more. 'Where is your *fine* carriage?' I think of Jedadiah saying his father had said something had been trying to surmount the hedge. I look anew at the tears in his trousers and jacket, the spots where blood has seeped through. 'Where are your men, your clean clothes? You've been sleeping rough, travelling hard. What has happened, Aidan Fitzpatrick, to all your lordly things?'

He glares. 'You must understand, Miren, that your departure has greatly affected my life. Our marriage was part of an agreement I made – without you, that deal is void, so I will have you back whether you want to or not.' He leans forward again. 'You cannot possibly imagine that you are worth all this trouble for the sake of yourself alone?'

I think again of the green-eyed man's words about unwise bargains and deals that link to other deals, about bigger fish eating little fish. 'I have enough value to you that you traipse across the country, all unsupported, to drag me back. What,' I ask evenly, 'does Bethany Lawrence think our union can bring *her*?'

'I promised her silver,' he says, slumping in his chair. 'Silver like the O'Malleys used to produce in the old days, silver that used to come from the sea. An endless supply. And that required you, the last O'Malley, you with the most pure blood, you and your womb and the children you'd produce.' He snorts with a sort of amusement. 'But your little escapade made the Robber Queen think I couldn't deliver, that I wasn't in control of all I said I was. She has sequestered my assets until such time as I return with you. This venture, she said, would be good for me, make me use my own hands again and remember how important personal oversight is.'

'Does she know about Blackwater?' I ask as casually as I can. Gods forbid Aidan should find out about the mine – about how Isolde made it produce.

He laughs. 'I'm neither fool nor minion, no matter what she thinks; I don't provide reports on my progress. She knows nothing about where I am, only that if I want my life back I will return with you.' He grins and it's an ugly thing. 'And you will give me children, Miren, and I will feed one at least to the sea and our bargain will be reforged. Or rather, the sea-queen.'

I catch my breath. How much did Aoife tell him? How much did she share with him that she did not share with me, to get him to agree to her scheme? Before she realised too late he had plans of his own, bigger and better; bigger fish eat smaller fish. Can he know what I merely suspect? He sees the question in my face.

'Oh, Aoife told me about Isolde and her light fingers, what she stole.' He smiles. 'Quite handy, in the end, that you ran away and led me here.'

And I think about the size of the mer I've seen, and think again that the sea-queens are even bigger, so how did Isolde take such a thing? I think about Malachi saying that Isolde had a talent for making things big or small, and the silver scale in the rill. I think about Maura telling me tales of a witch who wished for immortality but forgot to ask for eternal youth, so as she aged she shrank down, down, down until she could be put into a bottle, and there she stayed making noises everyone around took for summer insects. I think about the glass boxes I've seen in Isolde's workroom, how they might be perfect for something the size of a healthy bass or cod.

'And now, I think, Miren, it's time for me to take back that stolen item.'

'You have no right to it,' I say. 'You're not an O'Malley, you're some by-blow who thinks he's better than he is. Do you think if Aoife had any other choice she'd have made a bargain with you?'

His colour heightens; he's not quite angry enough to hit me, but he's angry enough, I hope, to become careless.

'No matter what you think of me, Miren, I *will* be your master. And I like breaking spirits. The longer you resist, the happier I will be.' He rises. 'And now, it's time for me to collect my property.'

'And precisely how are you going to take her back to Hob's Hallow? Have you learned spellcraft, Aidan? Can you do what Isolde did? Shrink the thing down so you might put it in your pocket?' I laugh.

'I will make arrangements. Now, there is a cellar?'

I nod. 'But I've never been able to find a key to the locks, of which there are three.'

He snorts. 'Do you think Isolde would have wasted her
with ordinary keys?'

I think about the cellar door at Hob's Hallow with no
mechanisms at all because the latches had all been removed;
there were only the old warnings from my grandparents and
Maura not to go down there. 'I have what we need. Take the
child, she will keep your treacherous hands busy and I'm sure
I'll find another use for her.'

And I worry that I've not bought Ena any time at all.

37

Ena has fallen asleep in my arms and she is heavy as a bag of wet sand. She snuffles against my neck and all I can think of is how to keep her alive. I've killed two men without a second thought, but they earned their deaths. This child, though she is nothing to do with me, has done no wrong. I'm walking slowly as we leave the library and Aidan registers his annoyance:

'If I go any faster,' I say mildly, 'the child will wake. And if she wakes she will cry. Do you want to listen to that again?'

He harrumphs in response. 'Which way?'

'Follow me, the entrance is in the kitchen.' The corridor seems suddenly far shorter than it ever has in this enormous empty house.

'Who was the man?' asks Aidan, and for a moment I think he means Jedadiah and I'm not happy at the idea of him knowing about my lover, but then he continues, 'The man who went into the other wing of the house and did not come out. He was arguing with that slattern. More importantly, *where* is he?'

Nelly probably was a slattern, but I bristle at him calling her such. 'Dead. He fell out a window. He claimed to be my father's brother, said his name was Edward Elliott. I believe he wormed his way into my father's good graces, then murdered him and Isolde. He's been playing lord of the manor for months.'

Aidan laughs. 'Liam Elliott had no family. He was ju~
pretty boy from the Breakwater docks that Isolde fancied.'

'You knew my parents weren't dead,' I state. I don't expe~
to get much out of him.

He shrugs. 'They were beyond Aoife's grasp, so to her they
were. Mind you, if she'd found them I think she might have fed
Isolde to the waters.'

And I cannot deny that my grandmother might have done
that. 'But she didn't know where Isolde had gone.'

'That was part of my bargain with her – that I would use all
my resources to find Isolde, or at least what she had stolen.'

I laugh loudly, painfully, and Ena stirs. Yet he killed Aoife –
thought to take everything for himself.

'How did you find this place, Miren?'

'I found letters from Isolde to Óisín; there were only three,
but she said Blackwater was north of Bellsholm, so I came this
way, more or less.' No point mentioning the old silversmith and
his wandering memories. 'I think perhaps she was lonely, but not
lonely enough to tell him exactly where she was.'

'Poor Miren,' he sneers. 'So close to rescue, so many times,
so many failures.'

I don't answer that. We've reached the kitchen, so instead I
say, 'You will need a lantern before we descend.'

As I have my hands full, he takes one from the wall, and admires
the workmanship of silver, the iridescent glass; I think of throwing
one at Edward Elliott, how it made him burn and dance. Aidan lights
a taper from the flames in the great kitchen hearth, then the lantern.

I nod and lead him to the back of the cavernous space, to the
door to Isolde's workroom; I think about how it was unlocked

he took no precautions. I think about the broken glass the brown stain that may well have been dried blood. I think that perhaps Edward Elliott killed her here. At the back of the chamber with its workbenches and shelves, measuring spoons, glass bottles and tubes, mortars and pestles, is the trapdoor. Again, left unlocked, but I suppose that hardly matters when it leads down to the much bigger door with the silver locks.

Aidan gestures for me to go first – he raises the lantern high so I can see my way, but he's smart enough not to trust me behind him. I grab my skirts so I don't trip, feel them sticky and cold and remember that I have Nelly's blood on me. I hitch the sleeping Ena up higher on my shoulder and begin the descent. 'Why did you murder Nelly?'

'Who?' He barely even recalls killing her.

'The woman. The woman you left in the foyer.' *This child's mother*.

'She began to shout when I entered the house. I didn't know how few people were about.' He pauses. 'But I'd have killed her anyway. And him, but apparently you took care of that for me, didn't you, little Miss Miren? There's no escaping the O'Malley blood and its urges.'

'How is Brigid?' I can't help but ask.

'Well enough,' he says shortly. 'When we return to Breakwater, I'll marry her to a man I can trust.'

He definitely doesn't know about Ellingham then, or his friend would not still be alive.

The stairs seem to go down forever, then at last we are at the large door with the three silver locks. I've stood in front of it only once before, when I tried all the keys on the ring an none of them fit.

'What now?' I say.

He hangs the lantern on a hook on the wall and says, 'Give me your hand.'

I don't want to. Oh, how I do not want to. But I stretch forth, palm upwards. He grips my wrist, hard as he ever did, and squeezes until the bones grind beneath his strength, just to remind me of what I can expect. Then he produces my mother-of-pearl handled pocketknife and uses the tip to prick my finger. In spite of myself I cry out, less from pain and more from umbrage.

'*Vena amoris*,' he says and chuckles. *The vein to the heart*. Then he remembers that this finger once bore the massive ruby and pearl engagement ring he put there. 'Where is the ring?'

'In my room. It's safe, along with most of the jewellery Aoife bought.'

'Gods, but that old bat could spend. She'd have had me in the poorhouse before year's end,' he says, and I can't say he's wrong. 'Good to know Bethany Lawrence doesn't have control of everything.'

He pulls me closer to the door and holds my cut finger above the hole in the first silver lock, then squeezes. It hurts and a crimson drop, two, three, drips into the keyhole. For a moment, nothing.

Then a soft whir and a click; the runes carved into the metal of the lock flare, as if a brief flame has run through the thing – it falls open. Aidan looks pleased with himself. He moves my finger to the second lock and repeats the process.

'What will you do with her?' I ask.

345

w do you know about her? Aoife kept you in ignorance
ou behave like your mother, refuse to pay the tithe, respect
e pact.'

'I found… I found the tale. The first story of the O'Malleys,
how we came to be.'

He looks surprised. 'I was never allowed to read the book. No
one was who didn't have the O'Malley name.' His tone's bitter
as aloe. 'Aoife told me snatches of it, but not enough.'

'I have the pages, Aidan. You can read it.' And as strange as
this whole situation is, I cannot help but recall that we're family.
We have different parts of the tale, different gaps and lacunae
in our histories; I think how mine have injured me. Might they
not have warped him as well? All the wealth in the world cannot
make you feel accepted if you lack the one thing someone else
values above all else: a name.

'Let me leave her out here, Aidan.' I tilt my head towards
Ena, drooling on my shoulder. 'Give me your coat, I'll make a
little bed for her.'

'No,' he says, and he moves my finger down to the final lock.
Squeezes: the blood is slower, more reluctant now, so he hurts
me more.

'Aidan. We can stay here,' I say. 'This place is rich; this estate
has people who rely on me, on me keeping the land fertile. We're
far away from Bethany Lawrence and whatever she wants of
you. You don't need to go back like a hunting dog sent out by
its master. Stay here. Be safe.' I loathe him so much I can barely
believe I keep an even tone.

And he looks at me as though considering it. As though
considering the idea and whether or not he can trust me. Whether

or not it's what he wants. But in the end, I think, it's su
enough. He's been hungry all his life and this will not suf

'I want Hob's Hallow. That's what I want.'

'Then take it – leave me here but take it! Gods, Aidan, you
had it. I was gone and you had it.'

'Ah, but Madame Lawrence took it and more, all from me,
and now you are the only way back.' There's the final whir and
click, and the last lock drops open. He pushes the door wide,
then retrieves the lantern. 'Come along, Miren, this only needs
to be as unpleasant as you make it.'

38

Aidan grabs my upper arm and together we step forward into the darkness, shoes echoing on stone. The light does not go far ahead of us. He raises the lantern higher and higher, then releases me, saying, 'Wait here.'

Without the support of his hand I feel strangely untethered. I turn, trying to locate the door, but there's nothing around me except shadows, as if the egress was lost the moment we stepped through it; I'm too scared to move. The blackness feels like treacle, something I might drown in, and it smells stale, of dead things or something that should be. I watch Aidan get further away, becoming nothing more than an orange point in the darkness; it makes me think of Jedadiah and I wish he was here now.

But he is not.

Ena doesn't stir. She's damp and hot against me in the cold air of the cellar that smells of dead things. I check to make sure she's still breathing; she's alive, just sleeping deeply. The brand on my hip is itching, itching, itching as though I've brushed against scratchweed. I listen hard: Aidan's footsteps; the drops of water coming from somewhere, going somewhere else; a splashing sound, furtive as if not to draw attention to itself.

Then something changes: the darkness is retreating. Aid.
traversing the broad cavern and lighting a series of wall sconce
until the space is a combination of dancing shadows and bright
specks of flame. The ceiling is vaulted, just like the one at Hob's
Hallow, and in the centre of the room is a well, the stone wall
perhaps three feet high, perhaps four. I throw a glance over my
shoulder: still I cannot see the door. It must be fear; I'm sure it
must be there somewhere and if I could only look without this
shiver of panic in my mind, I would see it.

I wonder about the men whom Isolde hired to build
Blackwater, who made this chamber. I think about the story, the
pages she'd brought with her: whom had she hired to design
such a thing, such a trap, such a mechanism? Here at least,
unlike Hob's Hallow, she could simply have dropped the sea-
queen in from above, then cast whatever spell she needed to
restore the thing to normal size... but the means for catching
the scales as they sloughed off? She would have had to trust
someone to design it, to build it, to know its purpose. Those
men, not the men of Blackwater, for Jedadiah had said the house
was already built when Isolde began to bring people to her ...
those men ... she could not have let them live. She could not – as
Aoife's daughter, would not – have let them live and risked them
telling anyone about this strange place. I look around the walls,
trying to see if there are any bones lying about, proof of what my
mother might have done.

Nothing. I wonder if she used them in the mine? The first
blood to seed it, their bodies dropped in some deep hole. Those
who followed later – Jedadiah's wife and the others – were a
consolidation to increase what the earth would give. Perhaps the

ᴊd was simply a mistake – or perhaps not, all that salt water. ᴍe alchemy of blood and salt and dirt and the sea-queen's silver scales. Isolde and her talent for making things big or small.

A hand grabs my upper arm once more and I jump. It's just Aidan.

Just Aidan, who else?

He jerks his chin towards the well at the centre of the room.

'Did you see it?' I ask and find my breath is mostly gone. 'Did you ever see it at Hob's Hallow?'

He shakes his head. 'It wasn't spoken of; most of the extended family don't know about it. It's not something that was paraded, two gold bits for a gawk, Miren.' His tone is reproachful. Then he swallows and I can see he's as nervous, as afraid, as I am. 'Come along, Miren, time to meet your great mother.'

And I think perhaps a truer word has never come from his lips, but I still correct him: '*Our* great mother, Aidan.'

If he thinks the words a long-delayed kindness he gives no sign, but push-pulls me to the wide, wide mouth of the well. There's too much spilt blood and bitter spite between us anyway. The distance takes longer than it should, as if time is stretching, as if our path leading here has not been quite long enough, but at last we are there. We lean over, though I'm careful of my balance with Ena held to my chest with one arm, the hand of the other touching the rim of the well wall.

Aidan still has his lantern and he lifts it high so the light darts straight down to illuminate what lies perhaps twenty feet below.

There is water, dark and deep, and beneath it a sheen of silver – all those scales that haven't been washed into the mine because my mother was dead and Edward Elliott had no idea

350

about the truth of this place. And in that broad circle of .

the mer-queen, coiled in a space not quite big enough for .

and the brand on my hip burns as if the hot iron has only ju.

been applied to my skin. I think, in the old days, the shedding of

her scales would have been enough, once, twice a year, to fill a

chest with the silver for which the O'Malleys were famous. But

Isolde… my mother found a new way to *harvest*.

She doesn't look well. She looks old. I wonder how and on what my parents used to feed her – not the people of Blackwater, no, but perhaps drifters and tinkers on the road, folk tempted from St Sinwin or another distant port? But she's not had such sustenance for some months perhaps, or none supplied by Isolde. Then I think of the lack of fish in the black lake above (below? around?) – perhaps she's summoned them but the waters are fished out. Perhaps my parents were not entirely murderers, perhaps they put fish in the waters at regular intervals; only Edward knew there were no fish in there but he'd only been here six months before I arrived. Perhaps I will believe better of them in this at least. At Hob's Hallow she'd have summoned fish easily from the ocean, but here… The fish: how long between her call and their arrival? How many would come after the lake was emptied? How strong would her power be over how far a distance, at such great age, and so poorly nourished?

The sea-queen, ill though she looks, exhausted and old, is still the most terrifying thing I've ever seen. Twice the size of the mer who pulled me into Breakwater Harbour; her hair like a tangle of silver-green seaweed that moves of its own accord; her eyes so very dark, dark as a storm or the deepest sea depths; the gills in her neck cut deep, and I can see them shiver in and out breathes above the waterline; her lips wide and thick and ck as they draw back over terribly white, terribly sharp teeth; and that tail.

Oh gods, that tail.

Coiled round and round and round, a silver spiral that I almost lose myself in. I feel my balance wavering; Aidan's hand drops from my arm, grips at the rim of the well for support. I feel as if I cannot stop myself, then he has me again, his grasp so tight it's painful.

'No,' he says. 'Not yet.'

He puts the lantern on the lip of the well, and we both step back.

From below there's a disappointed hiss. I think of the story of Aislin and Connor, of the song the mer sang to lure the boy closer. But then I look more carefully, avoiding her gaze: she's got her mouth open wide, and that terrible noise is coming up to us. I realise that there's no tongue. From this angle I can see, I think, a mass of dead tissue where one should be. So, some long-ago O'Malley cut it out, which makes sense: she wouldn't have stayed captive for long if she could enchant her captors with her voice. I imagine the woman with the harp doing it, somehow. Perhaps she was even more witch than Isolde. I think of the book of tales that are lies and truth and story all mingled and mangled.

'You!' Aidan's voice booms out, echoes off the walls and ceiling like thunder. 'You!'

There's no response from below, but she's glaring at him. I take the chance to look at her face whilst her gaze is directed elsewhere. How long has she been held like this? She's eternal or as close to as can be – such things always are. There's hatred in her expression and not a small touch of madness – and locked up like this, who could blame her? Fed nameless babies to other offspring alive, to keep ships afloat and treasures com to the O'Malleys, her scales harvested against her will, all fo our prosperity.

'We are the children of the O'Malley who bound you, come to renew the covenant in blood. We're here to pay the red tithe. We will observe our obligations, and you will resume yours: a safe sea, our ships all home to harbour, riches aplenty, in return for a child of every generation.' Aidan's still gripping the rim of the well, with both hands now. He's looking into her eyes, the fool, no doubt thinking it will convince her of his sincerity.

And just as I'm busy thinking him a fool he whirls away and plucks Ena from my arms before I can stop him. My own fault. I was standing too close. I wasn't planning ahead. I'm a fool and the little girl will die because of me.

But he doesn't dash her straight down into the well as I thought he would; he holds Ena up so the sea-queen can see her, but keeps her close to his chest, and she begins to howl. His face is rich, as red as hers, wearing their expressions of irritation and outrage: hers at this waking, his at the lack of response to his proposal. I know him well enough that he will not throw the child – his lucky coin – unless he gets acknowledgement. How long before he realises there's no tongue? That she cannot speak? How long before it gets through to her animal brain, to the awareness that's still there, that's helped her survive, for any high function has surely gone, any sanity after all these years – only madness would keep her going.

I move slowly so he doesn't notice me from the corner of his eye. I stand behind him, then call his name ever so gently, as if lover, a confidant, as if I might acquiesce to all he desires. ..d despite the number of times I've lied to him, he turns as .f in hope – might the mer blood work in my veins or simply the power of the first O'Malley? – *salt daughter* – might I have some touch of the siren in my tones? Whatever it is, he turns and I punch him in the throat as hard as I can.

His hands go to his neck, Ena goes into freefall, and I grab at her with both hands, then drop my shoulder and charge him. He's too close to the low stone wall, he's already unbalanced, he cannot breathe and he's panicking. He tips over the edge like a dropped toy and, voiceless though she might be, the sea-queen produces a sound that can only be some sort of triumph, before there is the splash of Aidan hitting the water and the noises of her feeding to overwhelm his final screams.

39

When at last the queen is finished – when the noises of her meal cease – I force myself upwards from where I've huddled on the floor, hunched over Ena, rocking her until she subsides to hiccups and a troubled sleep. Then I lie the child on the ground, gently, and approach the lip of the well.

I look at the red, red water, at how it splashes over the silver tail, obscures the bed of shed scales beneath the sea-queen – how many months' accumulation? At least five. How often did my mother do this... reaping? I can never know. I walk around the well, around its great circumference, and come to a metal lever. With only the smallest hesitation, I push it, and it takes all my strength, but eventually I hear a grinding (no one's kept this oiled since Isolde went away), then a gushing. Then the lever swings itself back into position and I look into the well again. The water is refilling, but the bed of scales is gone, washed into the chutes that will take it to the mines for one last harvest. I can feel the creature watching me, but I still don't meet her eyes – once was enough.

'He,' I say, 'had O'Malley blood. I don't know what you can or cannot understand of me, but I promise you this: I will set you free. But that was the last of us you will have and in

ou will be held captive no more.' I swallow. 'I'm sorry
nat was done to you. I can never make it up, but I can
er you your freedom. I will never return to Hob's Hallow.
will not return to the sea and nor will any child of mine. I
will set you free, and you will leave the lake and swim to your
home, for all the waters in the world are joined.' I say this last
like a prayer.

I risk a glance, and see she is considering me.

'Promise me you will go, and cause no harm to anyone here.'

A beat, a long pause, then she nods. A sharp simple motion.

'I will need help to free you, but I will be back, I swear. It will
take me some time.' A feathery, finny eyebrow is lifted. A lack
of belief, certainly. I touch the bell-shaped pendant at my throat;
crafted, no doubt, from one of her scales. 'I can only promise. I
am... not like my kind.'

*Not entirely... but there are three dead men who might say
different.*

I turn around and I can see the door now, quite clearly, and
open, open wide! How could I have missed it? Fear. Fear renders
everyone blind. I gather Ena against me and she makes a kittenish
noise but does not wake; I retrieve Aidan's lantern to light our
way back up, up, up where the air does not smell so much like
the dead things of the deep.

* * *

From the bottom of the blanket box I pull out my duffel bag, and
from it I take the tattered bridle with its silver fittings. I dragged
Ena's cradle from her room and put it in mine, for the moment
at least, and she sleeps there, quiet as a mouse. I pull out the
book of tales, too, the one that Isolde started, and I look more

closely at the coat of arms on the front. I trace the bas
the embossing, of the silver foil, the cunning way the line
and flow; seeing it in a way I never could the old version with
its detail rubbed away.

It takes a while but eventually I see it: at last a new picture
emerges as if there are two layers to the art.

The uppermost, the most obvious, is the Janus-head, double-
tailed mermaid of my childhood. The other, however, is entirely
different: two figures, back to back. The one on the left, a woman
in profile, with flowing hair, draped over the shoulder of a harp,
and the upward curve of the soundboard looking like a section
of a split tail. On the right, the mer-queen, her head close to the
woman's, also in profile so they might be taken for two-faced,
her tail arching up on the same angle as the soundboard, but both
of them joined at their spines, never able to move away from
each other.

I sit on the floor and stare. I stare for a long time – so long that
perhaps I sleep – and when I finally rouse the sky is greying with
light. I leave Ena sleeping and go outside, the bridle jingling in
my fingers. I run to the edge of the lake, stop carefully, then with
only the slightest hesitation, I kneel.

I hold the bridle over the surface, watch how its reflection
becomes clearer and clearer as I lower it. My hand shakes – I
will never lose my fear of this for as long as I live – then with
a sharp intake of breath, plunge the bridle beneath the waters.
It is so cold. I feel the tremor once more, the lightning hit of
the liquid on my skin, think how salty it is, and wonder again
how Isolde made this happen. I think there will always be some
tiny mill grinding, grinding, grinding on the bottom of the lake.

shake the bridle, and speak: 'Kelpie, the salt daughter and she claims her boon.'

I sit back, hope it is enough. I cannot know how long he will take. Or even if he will honour his word. He might think carrying me here was recompense enough.

Perhaps I should go inside and check on Ena, feed her; perhaps the kelpie will knock politely on the kitchen door and ask for tea. I laugh and the sound is high and silvery, a little mad; I'm exhausted.

I wait a while longer and just as I'm beginning to doubt, the lake starts to boil up, white angry froth, and the kelpie leaps out onto the grass beside me. I manage a smile and climb to my feet, offer a curtsey. He bows in return, then asks briskly what I want, just in case I should think this a social call. I explain what I need and he looks unhappy, but I insist, saying, 'Just swim fast.'

I watch him jump back in with barely a splash, give me one last reproachful glance, then disappear beneath the surface until it appears as smooth as glass once more. I run inside and get Ena, who is well behaved and quiet in her crib. In the kitchen I fill a bottle from a crock of milk and take the child outside with me. I sit a wise distance from the lake and feed her with one hand, and myself with the other with the freshly discovered apple from my pocket.

In the cellar I could see no mechanism for opening the sea-queen's cage. I suspect Isolde had it built without such a thing; after all, she did not have to lure the creature into the trap (unlike that long-ago O'Malley), all she needed to do was drop it into the water then cast whatever spell was needed to make it large again. She had no intention of ever freeing the mer-queen.

Once the silver scales had been removed, I thought I cc_
markings on the bars of the grille in the water below, c
see them flash like flames because blood had been spilt. T_
magic of Isolde's, of the O'Malleys', was forged to keep the
sea-queen in her place. Attuned to her and her kind. But what
might another magical creature be able to do? Something not
as terrible as her, but almost. Something strong and strange like
the kelpie? A monster that owed a boon to another, with all the
power that entailed.

Either it will work or it won't. If not, then I will need to find
other means of keeping my word. What I would prefer is for
both sea-queen and kelpie to be gone before anyone from the
village should think to come and visit. I would prefer to keep
to myself most of what has occurred here, for the daughter of a
witch, even a beloved witch, will at some point make someone
uncomfortable – and there's a big difference between a girl who
can bring fruit from the trees and one who can keep a sea-queen
captive and command a water-horse.

I'm almost finished with my apple when the lake boils and
froths once more, one spot close to the shore, the other further
out. The kelpie's handsome head emerges from the former: he
glares at me, nods. The message is clear: his debt is paid. I nod
in reply, then toss the bridle to him. He catches it and dives away.
I doubt I'll see him again.

In the other spot: the sea-queen. She's staring and I can feel
the pull of her will. She'd like to have me walk into the water;
she'd like to tear me limb from limb, swallow me then shit me
out, wipe the last O'Malley from the face of the earth. But I can
also tell she's not really trying. I suspect if she were I *would*

...to the lake. I might even bring Ena with me as a snack. ...she's a creature who understands a bargain; she will abide it.

I nod to her. She nods back. And then she is gone, and I *know*, though I cannot, that I will never see her again. But then there is another disturbance in the water and something flies towards me. It flashes silver and iridescent white and lands on the ground in front of me. Ena laughs. I reach for it.

It's Óisín's pearl-handled pocketknife, last in Aidan's possession when he cut my finger, when he tumbled into the well.

40

We found my mother, at last, buried in the kitchen garden. Why Edward and Nelly put her there and not down the mine with my father, I'll never know – perhaps soon after true Ena's death he took Liam walking on the pretence of a friendly chat to separate him from Isolde. Then Edward returned to the house and dealt with my mother. I hope she did not know anything about it; I tell myself she could not have or she'd have touched him and made him care enough to not hurt her – although Malachi said that she could charm *almost* everyone, so perhaps Edward Elliott for whatever reason was one of the rare exceptions. I recalled how closest to the house had been the only place where the plants had kept blossoming when everywhere else was stagnating. Isolde the witch, the magic in her kept everything growing in that tiny corner of Blackwater. I wonder too if, even in death, she kept a grip on the villagers even though it would have made sense for them to move on when the land stopped giving them a living. They'd talked about it, but hadn't quite managed to actually do it.

In her arms was a blackened little figure, my sister, the true Ena, whose crime was no greater than to cry too much; placed there, I think, by Nelly. And I think of the storm the night my mother died, and think how perhaps it was even more violent cause my sister died then too, in the burning cauldron of her cradle. All three rest now in the cemetery that serves the village. It took me a long while to realise that Blackwater is without a church, and the big house itself without a chapel. I can only assume that hidden out here Isolde saw no need to pay lip service to a god not her own, nor her people's. The more I hear them speak of her, the more I think she was as close as they got to a deity. But there is so much I will never know.

There are only tales of things that might once have been, and I write them in the book of stories Isolde had begun. I write the old from memory and the new when I can bear the pain of them.

I'm considerably rounder and slower than I was five months ago, so it's a relief there's been no sign of anyone else coming to find me. I remind Lazarus every day to remain alert at the hedge gate, and another gatehouse is being built at the now carefully concealed other entrance. One of the Cornish brothers will take up residence there.

Bethany Lawrence has Aidan's fortune, she has Hob's Hallow; she has no need to seek me out. I doubt she'll bother to hunt after Aidan. In a few more months, I'll send someone to Breakwater to see how the land lies, to see how Brigid fares. I'll dispatch a letter and suggest she come for a visit or to stay for good.

The Woodfox boys returned from Bellsholm just this morning. Jago and Treeve took goods to sell while they made discreet enquiries about Ellingham and his troupe. They brought news that they are well enough, although Viviane has a scar on the right side of her face courtesy of Aidan Fitzpatrick; of the wolf-boy Ben there has been no sign, although Ellingham

has said the boy is known to wander. I hope he was s̶
away, roaming the roads on four feet. But they now hav̶
permanent spot in a small theatre, for Ellingham has decide̶
to give up travelling.

The boys took a letter from me saying I was well and handed
over a purse of the silver scales, which Ellingham accepted with
no complaints; yet he wrote no reply. One day, perhaps, I will
visit. Perhaps Brigid will too. Or they will come here. One day,
when the baby is born and she can travel, for I will not leave
my own behind, not for any reason at all. It's a girl, I know it, a
daughter I hope I can do better by than was done for me.

One day I will have the blacksmith here make delicate things:
ship's bells from the scales I have kept, bells for all my children to
protect them should they ever take to the sea – though I promised
the sea-queen they would not, what mother can guarantee her
children's actions? For Ena, too – I believed she was my little
sister for too long to cast her aside. She cannot bear the burden
of her parents' sins, and I will never tell her or anyone else that
she is not an Elliott. But I will never tell her she's an O'Malley,
either, for I think that has done generations more harm than
good. Best to let the old name die, living nowhere but between
the pages of dusty books, whispered in legend and rumour. I'm
Miren Elliott now, for it's what I can bear – you claim what you
can endure from your once-life and burn the rest.

I miss Maura and Malachi and think of them often. I miss
Óisín and I even miss Aoife some of the time. I cannot say I truly
miss my parents for I never knew them, but I miss the opportunity
to have found out who they were; I think some days that I would
not have liked them very much. But I can never really know. The

think of most, however, is the sea-queen. Daily, I wonder
w she fares and touch the ship's bell necklace, made from her
scales – this was why the mer could not hurt me. Some nights
I dream I am beneath the sea, that I swim beside her, that she
is hale and hearty once again, that she's found her people and
reclaimed her place. She'll never leave me, shadowing my life
forever, it seems.

I do not think of the men I have killed.

We don't live in the big house. It's falling into disrepair,
some of the fine furniture taken by the people of the estate, some
used for Jedadiah's cottage which I now share, and Lazarus's
gatehouse, too. I don't miss the mansion: it was only ever a
waystation for me, and Ena and I would rattle around inside it
on our own to what end? We're happy enough here and she treats
Jed as if he is her father, and he behaves that way. I'll tell her
about her – our – parents when she's old enough to understand.
I imagine he will be the same with the new one.

He says he loves me.

But I am wary of love.

Says he needs me.

And I am weary of need.

He is hurt when I don't reply in kind; I've been finding he's
easily hurt. But he is gentle so I say to him something I hope he
will one day understand.

'I don't need you,' I say, 'I want you. That should be enough.
That should be better because it means I've made a choice.'

Perhaps one day he will understand.

AUTHOR'S NOTE AND ACKNOWLEDGEMENTS

You might recognise some of the tales Miren tells herself in this novel. That's because some of them are versions of stories from my Tartarus Press collections/mosaic novels *Sourdough and Other Stories* and *The Bitterwood Bible and Other Recountings*. I wanted to have a world where the tales I've told readers in the past are ones that these characters also grew up with.

Thanks to Mike Mignola for letting me tweak his version of the Brothers Grimm's "Three Wishes" from the Hellboy graphic novel *Strange Places*.

My deepest gratitude to the Australia Council for the Arts as their support made the writing of *All the Murmuring Bones* possible.

Thanks to Meg Davis, agent extraordinaire, Queen of the Silver Ideas.

Thanks to Cath Trechman for her wonderful and intuitive editing, and to Hayley Shepherd for a superb copy-edit.

Thanks to Ron and Stephen for the sanctuary.

Thanks to J.S. Breukelaar, Angie Rega and Suzanne Willis, Neil Snowdon, Maria Haskins and Lisa L. Hannett for comments and support.

To note: Delphine the automaton is a nod to both Nike Sulway's *Rupetta* and to the dolls made with slivers of souls that

...r in "A Porcelain Soul", one of the tales in *Sourdough and ...er Stories*.

The title *All the Murmuring Bones* is adapted from a line in Faulkner's *The Sound and the Fury*.

"Skin" originally published in *The Lifted Brow*, #3, February 2008.

ABOUT THE AUTHOR

Angela Slatter is the author of the supernatural crime novels *Vigil*, *Corpselight* and *Restoration* (Jo Fletcher Books), the novellas *Of Sorrow and Such* and *Ripper*, as well as ten short-story collections, including *The Girl with No Hands and Other Tales*, *Sourdough and Other Stories*, *The Bitterwood Bible and Other Recountings* and *A Feast of Sorrows: Stories*. *Vigil* was nominated for the Dublin Literary Award in 2018. She has won a World Fantasy Award, a British Fantasy Award, a Ditmar, an Australian Shadows Award and six Aurealis Awards. Her short stories have appeared regularly in Australian, UK and US *Best Of* anthologies.

Her work has been translated into Bulgarian, Chinese, Russian, Italian, Spanish, Japanese, Polish, French and Romanian. She has an MA and a PhD in Creative Writing, is a graduate of Clarion South 2009 and the Tin House Summer Workshop 2006, and in 2013 she was awarded one of the inaugural Queensland Writers Fellowships.

All the Murmuring Bones is her first book for Titan and will be followed in 2022 by *Morwood*. Both are gothic fantasies set in the world of the *Sourdough* and *Bitterwood* collections. Follow her on Twitter @AngelaSlatter.

For more fantastic fiction, author events,
exclusive excerpts, competitions, limited editions and more

VISIT OUR WEBSITE
titanbooks.com

LIKE US ON FACEBOOK
facebook.com/titanbooks

FOLLOW US ON TWITTER AND INSTAGRAM
@TitanBooks

EMAIL US
readerfeedback@titanemail.com